Demon (

Book 1 of the Nexu

By
Robert Da

Published by Robert Day

Copyright 2010 Robert Day

Other titles by Robert Day

The Nexus Wars Saga

Book 2: Ashar'an Rising

Cover Art by:

Dale Ziemanski

For everybody who believed in me.
Without their love and support, this book would have remained just a dream.

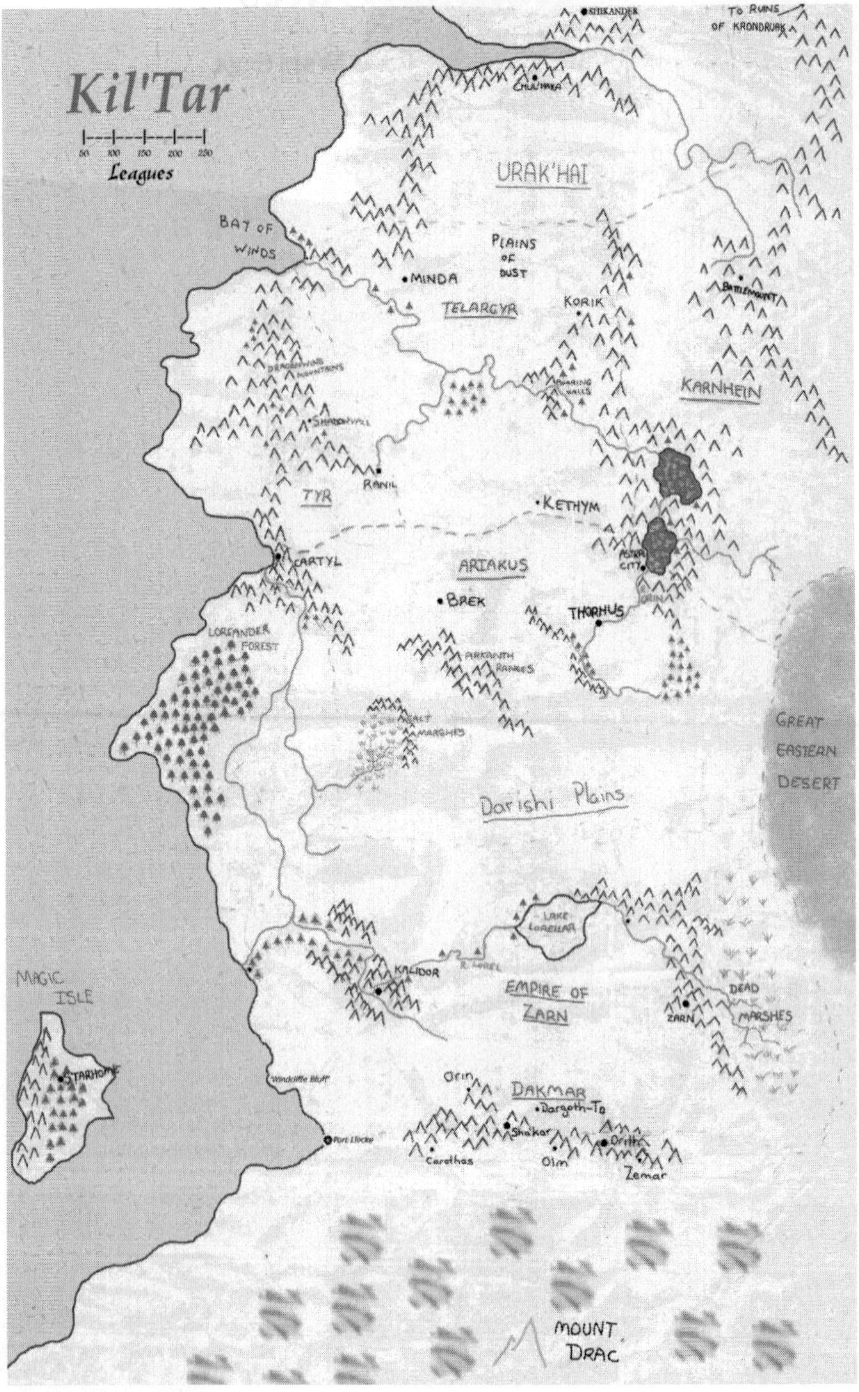
Kil'Tar
50 100 150 200 250
Leagues
SHIKANDER
TO RUINS OF KRONDRUAK
URAK'HAI
BAY OF WINDS
PLAINS OF DUST
MINDA
TELARGYR
KORIK
BATTLEMOUNT
KARNHEIN
TYR
RANIL
KETHYM
CARTYL
ARTAKUS
BREK
THORHUS
ASTRA CITY
LOREANDER FOREST
ARKANTH RANGES
SALT MARSHES
GREAT EASTERN DESERT
Dorishi Plains
KALIDOR
EMPIRE OF ZARN
ZARN
DEAD MARSHES
MAGIC ISLE
STARHOME
Windcliffe Bluff
Orin
DAKMAR
Dargeth-To
Shakar
Orith
Carethas
Olm
Zemar
MOUNT DRAC

'When in the city of the ancient ones, those from the endless darkness shall step through the flaming gate, HE shall come, from the shadows of the Dragons Wing, bearing the Eye and Horn of the Dragon. The land will sing with his passing and they will know fear who oppose him, for he is the Lord of the skies and protector of the Realm.'
:*The Child's Prophecy. T.E. 2147*

Prologue

Faradhar slumped over the aged stone table, yearning for sleep. Wan, slender fingers clenched a sheet of pale parchment, tightening to tear the fragile sheet as his blood-shot eyes scanned the flowing script.

With a rueful sigh, he tossed the letter aside. Sifting through the clutter on the desktop, he found a clean sheet and pondered a response. Dark ink gleamed like fresh blood in the dancing light from the cave's sole lantern as he began to write.

Master Zaleef,
Although much about the portal remains a mystery to me, my request for reinforcements still stands. I believe the cracking of the Seal indicates the magic used to create it is fading. I implore you to take my request before the Council. Better to err on the side of caution now, than rue a bad decision later.

Faradhar

He blew gently on the ink to dry it and wiped the quill-tip on the sleeve of his gray robes. Rolling the parchment, he secured it with a length of cord. Though it further drained his weary body, he cast a warding spell so only his Master, to whom it was intended, could open it without being consumed by the harnessed energies. Incanting another spell, he sent the letter to his Master's office over two thousand miles away.

As the spell took effect and the parchment faded from sight, his skin tingled for several moments. Concerned something had gone wrong, as he had never encountered such a reaction, he passed it off as a result of the exhaustion that plagued him, as otherwise the spell seemed to have worked.

Just too damn tired!

He rose and collected his staff, blinking several times to force moisture to sleep-deprived eyes. Total darkness engulfed the chamber as he extinguished the lantern. Chanting softly, his eyes adjusted as the tip of his staff began to glow, building to a soft illumination.

Weary legs carried him down a short, roughly hewn passage linking his makeshift study with a vast, alien cavern. Two hundred feet high at its domed peak and twice that in diameter, its smooth stone walls were etched with carvings and symbols, the like of which he had never seen before.

Set against the sloping stone wall on his right was a raised dais. At its center was a mound of what appeared to be melted stone. Perhaps it had once been a statue or chair, now worn away by time. Perhaps. Like many other things in this enigmatic place, it was best not to speculate too much.

Questioning looks greeted him as he entered their fire-lit camp in the center of the chamber. He sat on his bedroll with his staff across his knees and let his gaze flicker about the camp. As had become his custom, he checked every detail, while striving to appear calm.

Against the stone wall to one side was a mountainous pile of firewood and beside it were stacked crates of provisions. Bedrolls encircled the fire, more for comfort than warmth. Those who were not on watch rested fitfully, as if plagued by nightmares. Weapons and shields lay within easy reach. Faradhar shuddered at the memories of his own dreams of late.

Smoke permeating from the fire did little to help his already stinging eyes. Whispering a curse, he peered up at the shadowed ceiling high above. A lattice of fissures helped collect the smoke and carry it from the chamber, although sometimes it didn't seem to help very much.

Not even the smoke can escape this wretched place!

With a sigh he turned to look at the one thing that haunted both his waking and sleeping hours.

The dark Portal, striking from the smooth stone wall behind the dais, rose to the height of three men. Etched into its arched frame were silver runes and sigils. It was made of a material Faradhar had never seen before, a metallic substance which when touched, exuded a cold, which was in no way natural. Even now, it seemed to swallow up the light from the fire and his staff, lending the chamber an eerie cast.

"Any luck?" came a voice at his side.

Faradhar jumped, and then gave a nervous chuckle to hide the reaction as a young man sat down beside him.

"None," whispered Faradhar. There was no need to let the others know just yet.

Drav was the military leader of the squad. The charismatic young warrior had a rapport with the others that Faradhar could never attain. It was he who kept their spirits up and made sure the warriors looked after their gear and trained regularly. While not clad in full battle attire, he still wore a heavy chain cuirass over a light leather suit.

"They didn't train us to handle anything like this, did they?" said Drav with a wry chuckle.

Faradhar grinned in spite of his weariness. Drav defied the stereotype of a warrior, being both intelligent and articulate. He would have made an excellent addition to the ranks of Lorewielders had fate not led him down another path, though either way he served the Astral city.

"What are we really doing here?"

It wasn't the first time the question had been asked of Faradhar. As a student of the Lore and wielder of magic, everyone assumed he knew most things, especially that which bordered on the arcane and mystical. In truth he knew little more than the rest of them in regards to the Portal.

"I don't know, Drav. I might have said to appease an eon-old tradition, but you are right. Something is happening here beyond our wildest imaginations."

Drav was thoughtful for a time, yet Faradhar knew he had not finished. "Do you really think these Portals are gates to the Voids? I know our history, as do you. I know of the 'War of Storms' and the struggle between the Lorewielders and the Demon hosts. That was centuries ago. Surely Demons no longer exist."

Faradhar shrugged. "I can only go on what the High Master said. You heard him yourself: the Seal keeps the Portal closed, and we are here to make sure it remains that way."

"But now the Seal is breaking, isn't it?" It came out as an accusation more than a question.

With a sigh, Faradhar rubbed his face to fight the clutches of sleep. Drav was correct. Two days ago, they had discovered hairline fractures in the Seal.

"It may not be bad. Zaleef says the Seal may have no magical properties. We just have to wait and see."

Drav ran a hand through his hair and stretched. "Doesn't make the wait any easier."

Faradhar silently agreed. He hated to admit it, but he was scared. When the council had offered him the assignment of leading the squad, he had considered quitting to find service as an adviser or personal envoy to someone in the nobility. The Masters had stipulated however, that after one year he would be free from the assignment and could return to his studies, or train further to become a teacher at the academy. With less than a year remaining on his studies, he had reluctantly agreed.

Ten squads had been picked. Faradhar's had been sent south into the wastelands of Dak'mar. The maps referred to it as Mount Drac, a volcanic protrusion that dominated the blighted lands it towered over. Its exterior was forbidding enough, but once inside the weight of the dark mountain pressed down on them.

Seeing the Portal for the first time had been an awesome and fascinating moment for Faradhar. He did not have any talent as a Traveler, but the idea of a gate that crossed planes was a wondrous thing.

"Faradhar!"

Drav clutched at his arm, drawing him from his thoughts. He became aware of the crackling of power and knew immediately what it signified. His blood ran cold.

Waves of pulsating light coruscated through the Portal, turning the stygian gate into a candescent pool of electrical energy. It blazed and dimmed like a beating heart, rhythmic... Hypnotic...

Slowly it gained intensity, stronger than a lantern, then brighter than the glow from Faradhar's staff. It blazed like the Sun and became unbearable to look at.

Suddenly the Portal erupted with a deafening roar that shook the chamber. Faradhar found himself on his knees. He groaned as his body tingled and drained of energy. A painful high-pitched keening sliced through his mind, shattering his thoughts. Though his vision was blurred, he could see the others rising around him. Some rocked unsteadily, and most sported minor cuts and grazes.

Vision and awareness returned to him slowly. He turned to find the Portal was now azure in color, still and reflective. Drav was at his side, barking orders for the warriors to form a defensive line.

Shakily, Faradhar stood, using his staff for support. Around them, small fires shot up where the glowing embers from the scattered fire caught on bedrolls and clothing. That was the least of his worries at the moment.

The Portal was active. Now he had to figure out what to do about it.

As his reeling mind tried to formulate a plan, two clawed hands pressed through the Portal, which rippled like the surface of a pool. Defined, powerful arms followed, then a leg. Wickedly curved claws clicked on the hard stone dais. Pale flame flickered off dark lava-like skin. Shoulders appeared, followed by a muscular torso.

Amid horrified silence, the Demon stepped free of the Portal. Around it, tiny appendages reached into the chamber as if smaller Demons sought to pull their way through.

It towered twice as tall as the warriors from the Astral City. Its appearance was warped by the fiery aura, though it was obviously humanoid with a muscular body and an elongated ursine head. It carried in its clawed right hand a huge sword, single edged and curved. The blade also flickered with its own darker flaming aura.

Intelligent black eyes regarded the armed men. A deep growl rumbled in its throat, menacing... Deadly... Suddenly its tooth-lined maw parted and it bellowed a deafening roar, which echoed like thunder through the chamber.

It was all Faradhar could do to not turn and flee.

"Defensive line!" barked Drav as the warriors visibly faltered. "Hold ground!"

Drawing courage from Drav's sudden calm, Faradhar gathered himself. He raised his staff and chanted the arcane words of his most powerful destructive spell. Energy coursed through him. He became a conduit for the magic, at one with the life force around him.

A glittering ball of silver formed at the tip of his staff, like a globe of tiny stars. More and more sparks accumulated, and then shot away, targeting the Demon. Less than a heartbeat passed in flight, but in that instant the ball elongated into a bolt of lightning, which struck the Demon with a concussive blast. Sparks erupted as the Demon writhed in agony and clawed at the air.

With its pained cry still echoing through the chamber, the Demon leveled its dark eyes on them and raised its sword. A ball of fire ten feet wide shot from the outstretched tip. Faradhar and his men had no time to react as it blasted into them. Bodies were tossed aside like dolls amid agonized cries and screams.

The heat launched Faradhar backwards as his skin seared, and pain clawed at him. Landing hard, the wind blasted from his lungs. He coughed and gasped for air and almost retched as the stench of burning hair and flesh assailed him. He barely had the strength to push himself to a sitting position as every muscle and nerve protested the effort.

A quick look confirmed two of his men would not rise again. Both were mercifully unrecognizable masses of charred flesh, having caught the full force of the fireball. The others warriors doggedly rose to re-form before Faradhar. Oozing flesh and scorched skin showed beneath burned clothing and armor. A hand clutched Faradhar's arm as Drav helped him rise. The fear in the young warrior's dark eyes was unmistakable.

With the words of another powerful spell all but spoken, Faradhar faltered as the Demon moved. With a single leap it spanned the twenty-foot gap to land before them, its clawed feet gouging deep furrows in the stone floor. Another spell replaced the one Faradhar had been about to cast as he desperately formed a protective ring against the heat emanating from the Demon's body. Shielded, the men were able to stand against the looming creature without shying away.

Led by Drav, the warriors surrounded the Demon. Swords and axes lashed out against it in concerted attacks, only to recoil as if they were striking stone. Enchantments cast upon each blade ensured they were sharp enough to cut through most material.

Stunned horror gripped Faradhar as the towering creature exploded into motion. The fiery sword blurred as it sliced one warrior in half, the cauterized body segments toppling before the warrior could even scream.

In the face of death, the men fought with all the skill and courage of heroes. Many were descendants of proud warriors and kings, and they did them no dishonor in the face of impending doom.

Yet one by one they fell, victim to the fiery blade.

Faradhar unleashed his arsenal of offensive spells against the Demon. Drained both physically and emotionally, only through sheer determination and will to survive did he keep going, far beyond the normally safe limit.

His attacks seemed only to infuriate the creature from the Void.

Drav was the last warrior to fall, pierced through the chest by the Demon's blade as he swung in a vain attempt to wound the fiend. In a rage, Faradhar threw the last vestiges of his energy into another bolt of lightning. It struck the Demon as it turned towards him. Sparks showered the corpses at its feet and the Demon howled in pain.

To Faradhar's horror, the howls turned to laughter as the demon's infernal gaze descended upon him. With a whimper, he crumpled to his knees. His staff clattered to the stone as it slipped from powerless fingers.

"You have no power to fight me," mocked the Demon in a voice both powerful and compelling. "Your powers and those of your people are weak, unchanged from an age long past."

The Demon looked around the chamber with what could only be described as rapture. Mocking laughter echoed through the cavern, assailing Faradhar. His reeling mind could not concentrate, could not focus enough to piece together what was happening and what it meant.

His thoughts turned to agony as the Demon loomed over him. Its intense heat crushed his waning magical defenses and engulfed him. He neither saw nor heard the blade's descent, but his last thought before oblivion was a silent prayer for the people of Kil'Tar.

Chapter 1

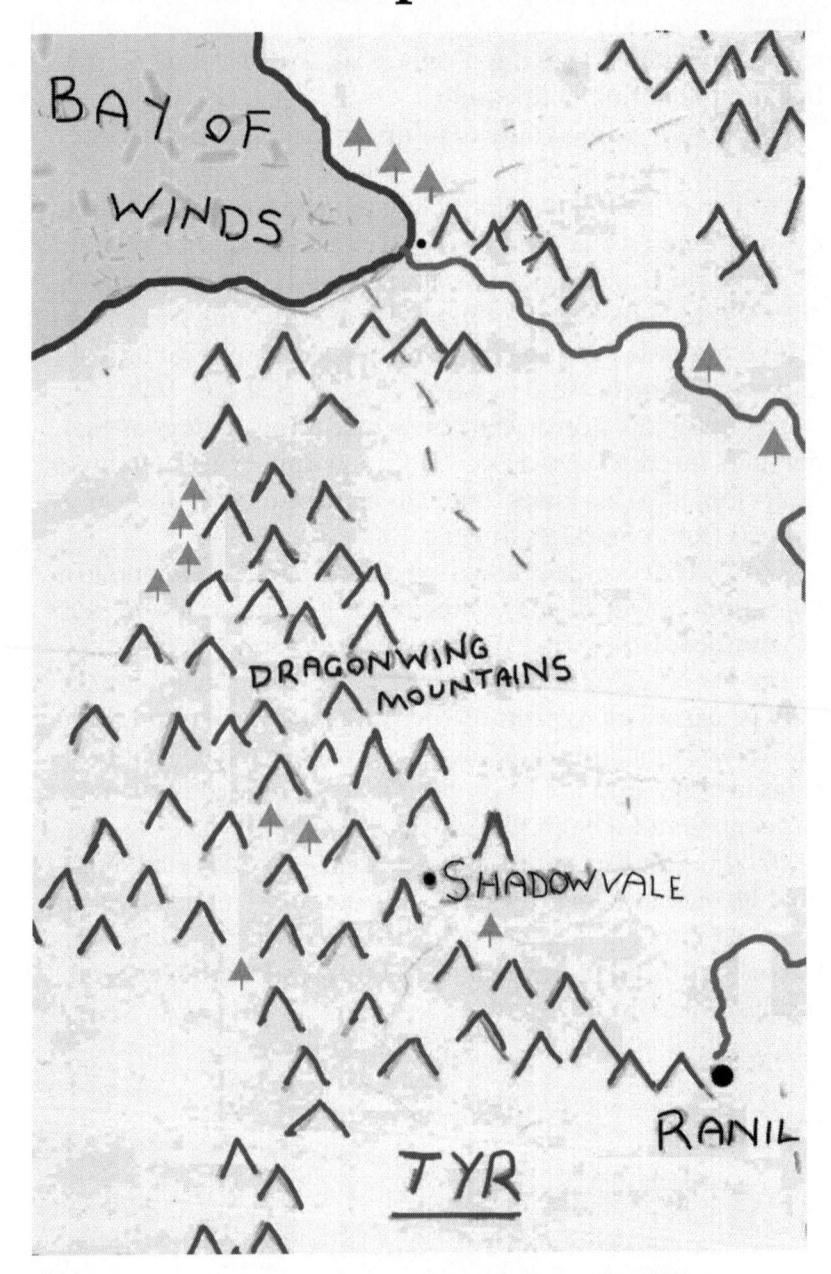

The horse-drawn wagon clattered along the dirt trail, gouged with potholes and furrows from a recent downpour.

Riding slightly ahead on his horse, Valdieron turned occasionally to warn his father of particularly uneven areas.

The twisting trip into town was about two miles, with the trail following roughly the same course as the stream that wound down from the northwestern slopes.

"Damn this road," cursed Garrik as one wheel struck a deep crevasse. "If we didn't have to pick up the colt, I would say damn the council meeting and stay home."

Valdieron agreed. Although it was good to get away from the farm, the last thing they needed was a buckled wheel or snapped axle. There was more than enough to do around the farm already. The transition from summer to autumn was always a busy time for them.

When they reached the outskirts of the village, the streets teemed with activity. Here the compact ground was more level, yet where ditches gave way, running children and dogs took over. This made progress just as slow as youngsters and animals capered around the wagon, oblivious to the danger. Amazingly there were no accidents as Garrik stopped and started the wagon when necessary. He cursed softly under his breath each time and waved the children away, though his beard could not hide his smile.

Valdieron was also forced to pull his horse to a halt each time a child passed perilously close under hoof.

"Shakk, stop that!" he scolded, as the horse resisted the restraining pull on the reins. Shakk turned a belligerent gaze to Valdieron, as if to assure him he was only playing.

The children seemed to realize this, which brought a stream of tormenting youngsters sauntering across their path, daring the big stallion, who enjoyed the game as much as any of them.

"Simple things...." mumbled Valdieron, laughing at his immature mount.

They followed the road as it circled the center of the village, eventually drawing to a halt behind the Inn. The large building was built from chiseled gray rock and dark mortar. Its thatched roof was worn and faded in more places than not. A weathered barn lay in its shadow. The huge building sat at the edge of what the villagers called the Oval, an open grassy field by the stream. A large wooden bridge spanned the stream, allowing access from one side to the other.

Garrik pulled the wagon to a halt and tied off the reins. He stepped down as two men emerged from the Inn.

The two could not have been more different in appearance. William Otterman, the owner of the Inn, was balding with a few wisps of grayish hair. The aging Innkeeper wore a stained white apron stretched across his ample girth.

Roland, the local animal healer, was a wiry man of average height. His pale skin was pockmarked and his rusty hair tangled down past his shoulders. He walked with the wilted step of a man who carried the burdens of many on his shoulders.

"Ah, there you are Garrik," greeted Will as he waddled down the stairs with considerable spring for a man his size. "I was beginning to think you were never going to come again. Good afternoon, Valdieron. How are you lad?"

"Fine, thank you sir," replied Valdieron, dropping lightly from Shakk.

"Though truth be told, you've not missed a lot since you were here last," confessed Will as he turned to Garrik. "The only real news is the wolf pack sighted in the lower flats."

Garrik raised his brow at this. "Wolves? We have seen scant few for many years. Who reported it?"

"Col Lambert. Said he spotted about a dozen of the beasts just east of his farm. Black as night they were. He fetched his dogs onto 'em, but they bolted up into the mountains. Hasn't seen 'em since, but keeps some of his dogs out at night now."

Garrik frowned. "Col isn't the sort to be throwing around stories if they weren't true. Any sign of them hanging around?"

"None. No dead sheep or chickens, nor any other tracks. It may have just been a new pack wandering down from the mountains for a look."

"Let's hope so," grunted Garrik. "But right now I'm for a pipe and a mug of ale and a seat before the fire if it isn't already taken. Roland," the silent young man lifted his sullen gaze, "did you bring the colt to the barn?"

"Yes, Garrik. He will be fine now, though a little weak for some time."

"Good! Lad, make sure the wagon is cleaned out and throw a bit of hay down for the horses. We'll be leaving as soon as the meeting's finished. You can do what you will 'til then."

"Yes, Father," said Valdieron, leading Shakk to the barn. The huge doors were already swung open and latched to the walls.

Stalls were set along either side, each large enough for a horse to move around freely.

He found the frail looking colt curled up asleep in the first stall. Strands of hay flecked its dark coat. Guiding Shakk into the stall next to the colt, he removed his bridle and saddle then wiped him down. He was glad to find the stalls were stocked with fresh hay, so he did not have to climb up to the loft and fork more down.

Shadows were lengthening across the Oval when he finished and rounded the front of the Inn. A few people were still out, finishing their business for the day. Across the stream, Old Mister Wilcott the Furrier shifted his drying boards inside for the night. The general store next door was closed as the owners lived a small distance from the village.

The Smithy was situated beside the Inn. Its familiar sounds did not greet him as he approached, and its gate was closed. Inside, he could see the dark enclosure that housed the forge. The forge itself was made from a dark, smooth stone that defied the incessant heat. A rectangular cutting in its side allowed access to the searing red embers contained within. Two leather bellows sat on hinged metal pipes, ready to be swung around to pump air to heat the embers when needed. Before the forge was a large, worn anvil, and beside it ran a row of slender wooden troughs.

A young man, maybe a year older than Valdieron's sixteen years, moved around the smithy tidying and storing equipment. His wide shoulders and thick arms gave him the appearance of an apprentice, honed from long hours laboring with heavy tools and metal. His sandy brown hair was cut short at the back and swept over at the top so that an occasional lock would slip down over his brow to be brushed aside absently. He wore a scarred and stained leather apron over a pair of brown trousers, and a dark blue sleeveless shirt.

"Ho, Kyle," called Valdieron as he vaulted the gate into the yard. The apprentice turned, surprised for a moment before he realized who had called his name. A smile crossed his dirty face as his imposing figure stepped from the gloom.

"Val! What are you doing here?"

"My pa is at the meeting. Said I could hang out 'til they're done."

Kylaran nodded and gave a wry smile. "Yeah, my pa went

also, though probably earlier than needed. So guess who gets to clean up?" He motioned towards the smithy with his head. "I won't be long if ya want to wait."

"Sure," said Valdieron, following his friend.

From what he could see, there was little left to do save cover the forge and sweep the floor. As Kyle took up the broom, Val turned to survey some of the items displayed around the smithy. They had all been fashioned by the smith and his son, and consisted mainly of farming implements, such as shovels, plough blades, gate hinges and horseshoes. In their youth, Val and Kyle had imagined the smith as a place of great mystery and wonder, filled with magical items and artifacts. More often than not it had been the starting point for some make-believe adventure.

"Here, gimme a hand with this, will you?"

Val turned to find his friend reaching for the large plated forge cover. He moved to help and grunted at its weight. He wondered how Kyle would have managed by himself, not that it looked like his friend was bothered much by the weight. Slowly they eased it into the brackets to secure it, and Valdieron let out a relieved sigh.

"Thanks Val. That thing's a pain to get in by myself."

Kyle quickly scanned the smithy, satisfied that his work was done. "That should do it. Want something to eat? Pa won't be there, and Ma is visiting her sister down at Marsh Point." Marsh Point was another small village several leagues to the southeast. The stream that ran through Shadowvale broke into several tributaries further down the mountains, forming a large mire. A small colony of people, whose houses were predominantly built in trees or upon stilts, fished the marsh and grew rice among the sodden terrain.

Valdieron accepted and the two left through the side gate. The house was located directly behind the smith. It was small and squat, of dull gray stone with a flat slate roof. Beside it rested a run-down wooden shed, where finished works and scrap metal from the smithy were stored.

Above the jagged horizon, the western sky was dark gray, making the rear of the dwelling blanketed in near darkness. The back door was closed but unlocked, as were most in the close-knit village. Kylaran braved the interior darkness in search of a lantern while Val waited at the door. After a brief silence, Kyle returned with a sputtering lantern and Valdieron entered the kitchen. He seated himself at the table while Kyle washed up then went in search of food.

"Catch!" came a call from the pantry, as Kyle threw him a small block of cheese, then returned with a bowl of nuts and a plate of dried vegetables. Already on the table was a wooden bowl filled with assorted fruits, and a breadbox from which Kyle removed half a loaf, slightly stale but edible.

"I don't know how my Pa and I will survive for the next month while Ma is away," joked Kyle as they picked at the food. "Most times we just grab something easy, and the idea of cooking a meal seems far too strenuous after a day at the forge. I guess we'll eat at the Inn a lot."

Valdieron smiled, though it was tinged with sorrow. He knew his father had endured such a dilemma after the death of his wife, Val's mother.

"Hey, let's go outside for a while." Kyle cut off any chance of him dropping into melancholy and he nodded. Grabbing a couple of shiny red apples from the fruit bowl, he waited at the door while Kyle tidied up and extinguished the lantern.

The Oval was dark and deserted. Wind-driven clouds raced across the sky. Qantari, the greater of the two moons was waxing, appearing occasionally amid clusters of dull stars. Santari, its smaller twin, would be at its fullest later that night. The gurgling of the stream filled the air, joined by the cry of nearby birds and the humming chorus of crickets.

They moved out onto the bridge. It was a popular gathering point for local children, though they were the only ones there this late. Caged lanterns burned at both ends of the bridge. The light, along with that from the nearby Inn, was enough to faintly illuminate most of the Oval.

Kyle climbed atop the flat railing on one side of the bridge. Valdieron joined him after a wary glance into the water below. Although a strong swimmer, the swollen stream brought back bitter memories of his drowned brother, Marcus. It had been six years since the accident, but it felt like just last week that he had been playing with his brother on the bank of the swollen stream near their house.

"Winter may be here sooner than expected," mused Kyle as a chill breeze swept over them.

"Yeah," agreed Valdieron, biting into his juicy apple. "Pa

reckons we'll have snow within the next cycle of Qantari. Says it will be the earliest since the cold snap eleven years ago when we were snowed in 'til summer."

Kyle sighed. "If anyone knows, its your Pa. Nobody can predict the weather as well as Garrik, and when he says there's rain, you'd better stay indoors and light the fire, or you're gonna get drenched. Still, it will be a welcome change after the scorching summer, and it means we can go hunting snow hares again."

Valdieron emulated his friend's broad grin. "I can't wait. I've spotted a few in the northern pasture of late, getting fat and waiting for us." Mr Wilcott the furrier paid a silver piece for a good quality pelt. Though it wasn't a large amount, it let them save up some spending money for when merchants came to the village. It was also fun hunting together, trying to catch the crafty animals without damaging their hides. It had taught them both a great deal about tracking and setting snares.

The clatter of approaching horses interrupted them and they turned to the northern edge of the Oval. Two riders emerged from the darkness, and both boys groaned.

Bregan Peterson was two years older than Valdieron. He was tall and muscular, with sandy white hair, cut to shoulder length. Handsome and vain, the young man sat astride his horse like a Lord surveying his lands.

Valdieron's attention, however, was drawn to the horse. The jet-black stallion danced gracefully across the ground. Born and bred a racehorse, the mayor's stallion was worth more than many villagers would see in a lifetime.

Bregan's sister rode behind on a bay mare, not that many would be looking as low as the horse, unless it was to admire the young girl's legs. Natasha was one of the prettiest girls in the village. At seventeen, she was definitely of marrying age, with more than a few of the local young men vying for her attention. Tall and slender with hair like strands of platinum, she rode with a grace gained through years of practice. Tonight she wore a white sleeping gown, split high to expose her pale thighs. A gray woolen coat covered her torso.

The horses clattered onto the bridge and drew up before the two boys. Bregan wore a condescending smile, which turned to a scowl as he realized the two were not watching him but his sister. Val endeavored to look elsewhere and hide his nervousness. The flirtatious and calculating girl had goaded him more than once into awkward conversations. Many were deceived into thinking she was naive because of her age and beauty, but both of the boys knew her to be very cunning. Val could feel her eyes on him, and wished he were elsewhere.

"So, Ketherson! Are you and that pony of yours ready for a race yet?" Shakk was one of only a handful of horses in the area that could match the speed of the Mayor's horse. Though it was his father's horse, Bregan rode it often to show off. Whenever Valdieron had been challenged in the past, he usually made up some excuse to put it off, knowing that Shakk was no match for the dark stallion in a flat run.

"Sure," he answered, surprising himself with his sudden bravado. Usually the older boy intimidated him, but tonight he was not in the best of moods. Maybe it was because Natasha was there, or perhaps it was the young man's tone of voice. "Where do we race? Fletcher's Lookout?"

Bregan's scowl returned. Shakk was a mountain horse. His legs were stronger and more sure-footed, making him far quicker than the thoroughbred in the uphill race to Fletcher's lookout.

Kyle's laugher drew the ire of Bregan, whose scowl deepened, though he said nothing. Kyle was one of few boys in the village taller and stronger than the Mayor's son. After being thrashed by the apprentice smith several months before, Bregan was not ready for a repeat performance and steered clear of Kyle. He knew, however, that wherever Valdieron was in the village, Kyle was rarely far away.

"I was thinking maybe the South fork, if it's not too far for your horse, that is?" Bregan's cocky smile returned as he wheeled his mount. "Think about it, and check up on me next time your Pa lets you out of the house." He spurred the dark stallion past Natasha as the young girl pressed forward. He threw her an angry frown, which she pretended not to notice, and then continued towards the edge of the Oval.

"For a moment I thought you were going to accept, Val," she purred, her dark eyes sparkling in the lamplight. "Pity!" She breathed a sigh. "I was going to come up with a good prize for the winner, as long as the winner was you." She gave a seductive pout that almost made Valdieron fall from his seat, and he found himself struggling for breath and for something to say.

"Nat, let's go!" Bregan's impatient call came from the darkness where he waited for her. She flashed an irritated glance his way then turned back to give Valdieron a smile full of promise.

"See you around, Val. Kyle." She nodded both greeting and farewell to Kyle as she wheeled her horse and rejoined her brother.

Valdieron gave a wistful sigh. "I wish I knew if Shakk could match it with that darned racehorse. I couldn't think of a better way of crushing Bregan's ego than beating him in a race."

Kyle chuckled. "And the attention of Nat has nothing to do with it?"

"Perhaps," shrugged Val. "She may be pretty, but she makes me feel like I've just drunk curdled milk. I don't know if it's my defenses telling me to stay away or just a fear that I'll look like a fool in front of her."

"Probably both!"

The cracked voice from out of the darkness startled them. Bart Letterman stepped from the shadows onto the bridge. The old scholar, once tall and broad-shouldered, still carried himself with a regal air. Ghostly white hair, though thinned with age, trailed down to his shoulders. His deep gray eyes were piercing beneath a stern, weathered brow.

"Master Letterman, we did not see you," apologized Kyle, dropping from the rail to stand. "Off to bed are we?"

He said it with such innocence and a straight face that Valdieron could not help but laugh, albeit softly and hidden by a feigned coughing attack. The Librarian was often in the company of the healer, Miss Wendle, though nobody begrudged the old couple their happiness. Both had lost their loved ones a long time ago. Still, the two tried to keep the affair a secret, which was an impossible hope in a small community.

"Mock if you will young muscle-head. Not that it's any business of yours, but love calls, and I am but a man who has little to say in the matter." He nodded to Valdieron, who had managed to compose himself. "Your young friend may well find out what I'm talking about in the not too distant future if he is lucky, or unlucky, whichever way you want to look at it. Mark my words; the Mayor's daughter has her eyes set on you, young Valdieron. She has the look of a wolf on the prowl, and you are the intended prey."

"I doubt her brother would be too happy about that, Master Letterman," assured Valdieron. The old man's observation made him suddenly uncomfortable, for it struck close to his own thoughts on the matter. "He and I are far from seeing eye to eye, if you know what I mean."

Old Bart cackled. "You see, it may just be that the Mayor's son will have no say in the matter. After all, what he doesn't know won't hurt him."

"Or me!" threw in Valdieron.

"There's that," mused Bart dryly, "but he will not always be bigger than you and therefore less inclined to abuse you. Especially if you adopt young Master Kylaran's method and give him a thumping he won't want to have repeated. But enough said. I have a woman waiting, and a somewhat exhausting evening ahead of me. I bid thee farewell, and advise thee that the paths of the future are never what they seem."

Cackling softly, Bart continued on his way. His long strides carried him across the lawn until he came to Miss Wendle's house. They heard him knock lightly and whistle a short tune before the door opened and he stepped into the dark house.

"A strange old man," mused Kyle, though he wore an amused smile. "What say you we head over to the Inn and see if the meeting is finished?"

Valdieron nodded and dropped from the rail. He followed Kyle in silence. His thoughts were on Bregan and his challenge, but also on Natasha's undisguised and bemusing interest in him.

The wagon rattled through the darkness at a snail's pace. A lantern, with its shutter thrown wide, swung from a pole rising behind Garrik, but did little more than illuminate a pale arc beyond the two horses.

Riding alongside the wagon, Valdieron was lost in thought. He was brought from it with a start when the horses drew up short and stamped nervously, as if shying from something in the darkness ahead. Instinctively he reached for his bow, and quickly had an arrow set.

"Whoa!" commanded Garrik, drawing back on the reins as the horses threatened to drag the wagon from the path. After several seconds they settled, and Garrik guided them back onto the road. Their eyes were still wide as they glared warily into the darkness. Shakk, on the other hand, remained calm though alert.

"Maybe that wolf story has some truth to it after all," conceded Garrik, glancing around. Valdieron could only nod as he tried to peer into the darkness while Garrik set the wagon back in motion. He caught movement and possibly the gleam of metal out of the corner of his eye, but when he turned there was only darkness.

Realizing the wagon and the light had moved away, he nudged Shakk to catch up.

For the remainder of the journey, Valdieron was tense and quiet, straining to catch any movement or sounds in the darkness. Whatever it had been was left far behind.

Chapter 2

The first light snowfalls came even earlier than Garrik predicted, though they thawed quickly with the dissipating heat of autumn. Subsequent steady falls soon layered the land in a thick blanket of white.

Valdieron emerged from between snow-lined buildings onto the Oval and found it markedly different with a covering of snow. Like the roads, the bridge was swept clear, a stark contrast to the white pall which enveloped the village.

Shakk fidgeted in the snow. "Don't be a baby," chided Valdieron. He laughed as the stallion threw him a look that said 'shut up or you can walk in it'.

With a gentle nudge, he turned Shakk towards the Smithy. Behind them trailed a young mare, just to her full growth. She tentatively pulled against the tether which bound her to Shakk's saddle, but the stronger stallion pulled her forward, as if to say if he had to walk in it, so did she.

A swath of clear ground lay before the opened gates of the Smithy. Kyle and his father were at work before the forge. Jacob was a heavy-set man with worn, weathered features. He wielded a huge hammer, flattening a strip of metal held by Kyle over the forge with a large pincer-like set of pliers. Long gloves and a leather mask with a glass cover for the eyes, protected Kyle from flying sparks with each blow of metal on metal.

"He looks healthy enough to me, Ketherson," snarled a voice, making Valdieron jump.

He was so entranced by the rhythmic ring of the hammer that he failed to hear the Mayor's son ride up behind him. With a silent curse he turned to confront Bregan, not surprised to find him atop the dark stallion. Shakk snorted wildly and curled up his lips, but Valdieron slapped him softly with the reins and he quieted.

"Look Bregan, forget it. I don't want to race you. Get it into your head and don't forget it." Valdieron was surprised at his vehemence. Usually he would hear out the young man's challenge and insults before making up some excuse.

"Then race me, and you'll never have to hear it from me again!"

"Ugh, just hear me out, Ketherson," he hurried on as Valdieron began to protest. "Then you can ride away and hide. One race: to the South Fork and back. Your horse may not be bred for racing, but mine isn't used to carrying me that distance. The thirty pounds difference should even things up. Surely you have some faith in your animal, if not a little pride."

Valdieron began to argue, but Bregan's last words had stung him.

"What time?" he ceded with a sigh.

Bregan blinked, momentarily stunned. "One hour, at the old stump. Be there!" He wheeled his horse around and charged across the Oval, heading for the south road. Valdieron watched him leave, and wondered if he had just done something he was going to regret.

"Ho, Val! What was that all about?" Kyle walked from the Smithy to where Valdieron waited at the gates. "That's the first time I've seen Bregan part company with you with a smile on his face."

Valdieron shrugged. "Maybe he has had a change of heart and intends to be more civil."

Kyle laughed. "Bregan? Yeah sure." Then the realization dawned on him. "You're going to race him!"

"It's the only way I can get him off my back," confessed Valdieron with a resigned nod.

"Hah! You know Bregan as well as I do. If he wins, he will remind you of it every time he sees you."

"And if he loses?"

"No offence, Val, but as fast as Shakk is, he's no racehorse. I think he could beat Bregan's stallion to Fletcher's lookout, but in a flat run, he doesn't really stand a chance."

"Yeah, well, I guess we'll find out soon enough." He gave a wry smile, unhooked the mare and handed the reins to Kyle. "I'll be back for her soon."

He began to turn Shakk away, but Kyle grabbed his arm and stopped him. "When's the race?"

"One hour." He would have lied, but he knew that work would keep Kyle at the Smithy all afternoon.

"Good luck, and watch out. If Bregan thinks he'll lose, he is likely to try something foolish or dangerous, or both!"

"I'll keep an eye out." Valdieron winked at his friend and urged Shakk away.

Kyle watched his friend cross the Oval and follow the same road Bregan had just taken. He held no real fear for his friend during the ride -- Val was a very talented rider. He just knew Bregan wasn't the sort to take defeat lightly.

With a sigh, he turned and led the mare into the yard.

The old stump was all that remained of a once huge oak tree. It sat at the edge of the South road, not far from the outskirts of the village. It was charred and frayed as the result of a lightning strike. The upper part of the tree had been cut up and dragged from the road to be burned. The stump remained as a reminder of the fierce storm which marked its felling.

Valdieron was in no hurry to get there. Once outside the village he stopped and let Shakk rest and eat a little to regain his strength after the trip from the farm. When he eventually came into view of the Stump, Bregan was sitting on his horse with one leg crossed before him over the saddle. He was surprised the Mayor's son had not invited some of his friends to watch the race. He guessed Bregan would brag as much as he wanted if he won, but if he lost in front of the others, all would know of his shame.

"So, you turned up after all Ketherson. That's two surprises I've had from you today. There won't be a third, I promise."

Valdieron did not bother to respond. He wanted to get the race over with. The less time he spent listening to Bregan's boasting, the sooner he could return home. Shakk was still warm from the walk, while Bregan's horse looked as if it were cold and was still picking at the sparse grass while they waited.

Bregan shrugged indifferently. He was certain of victory, and knew bragging after the race would be just as satisfying as before. He flicked the reins and lined up beside Valdieron on the road.

"The road is clear of snow and ice. I asked one of the farmers from down south and he said it was fine between here and the fork. It hasn't snowed for three days, and the road is thawed. Remember, first back to this spot is the winner. Ready?"

Shakk broke away to an early lead with Valdieron bent low

over the flying stallion's neck. The wind whistled past, streaming his long hair behind as the dark soil rushed past below. He glanced back and saw Bregan several horse-lengths back but holding steady. Val knew that if they could limit the racehorse's lead for as long as possible, they might be able to make one last surge close to the end of the race given Shakk's greater stamina.

Surprisingly the distance separating them remained constant as the race continued. The south fork was about half a league from the old stump, where one path continued to the southeast while the other turned towards the east and led down out of the highlands to Marsh Point.

Adrenalin and excitement coursed through Valdieron as he rode. Never before had he ridden at such a speed for any length of time. His breath frosted with the cold and steamed back into his face as they sped along. The sound of Shakk's hoofs beating against the ground was like thunder ringing in his ears, as was the pounding of his heart.

Half way to the fork, Shakk began to tire. Valdieron chanced another glance back at Bregan and found the dark stallion had similarly slowed with the distance between them still the same. He assumed Bregan was holding the dark stallion back to leave enough energy for the final run home. Either that or the stallion was having trouble making up ground on the flying chestnut ahead. He could not read Bregan's face with the constant jostling, though he appeared to be calm in the saddle.

Ahead, the overhanging branches of a large Maple tree growing just off the road obscured a sharp turn to the right. Valdieron ducked low to take the bend and felt the leaves scrape his back as he hurtled past.

When he looked up, a blanket of white covered the road several feet ahead. He jerked upright with a frantic curse and pulled back hard on the reins, urging Shakk to a halt, but their speed was too great and the road too slick.

Valdieron was thrown to the side as Shakk skidded onto the snow and lost balance. Desperately he disengaged his feet from the stirrups and dived away as far as he could. Pain lanced his shoulder as he hit the ground hard and rolled to a stop, covered in snow. His shoulder was numb, and a trickle of blood ran down his face.

His first thoughts were for Shakk as he pushed himself to his feet. The chestnut stood skittishly off the road several feet away. His right flank was covered with snow.

Bregan galloped past, slowly and surely through the churned up snow. "Watch those snow drops, Val. They can be very dangerous." He waved, then spurred his horse down the road and disappeared from view.

"Easy, Shakk." He ran his hand along the neck of the frightened stallion.

"Damn him!" He discovered a few abrasions to Shakk's hindquarters. His rear right fetlock was bruised, though thankfully not broken.

"That cheating son of a..." He could not think of an obscenity bad enough for the Mayor's son. Valdieron knew without looking that the snow had not fallen from the maple. The heat of the last few days would have easily melted any snow lodged in the tree's branches from the last fall. Also, the patch of snow, albeit churned up now, had appeared too smooth for a splattering descent from above. A discarded wooden bucket, lying hidden in some bushes not far away from a freshly dug patch of snow, confirmed his suspicions. Poorly concealed footprints ran from it to the road. Bregan wasn't as efficient as he was cunning.

Val wiped the drying blood from his grazed forehead. Taking a handful of snow he pressed it to the cut and turned back to Shakk. He wiped the Stallion down with an extra shirt from his saddlebag. Then he lined the shirt with snow and wrapped it around the strained fetlock in the hope that it would keep down any major swelling.

He was leading Shakk back to the village when the sound of Bregan's return brought him to a halt. Momentarily he wished he had his bow with him, but instead picked up a stone and readied it to throw. The mayor's son was wise to the possible threat, however, and gave the road a wide berth. Valdieron's throw, guided by anger and pain, sailed past Bregan's head, barely missing him. The mayor's son waved a fist at him, but was laughing coldly as he raced off, rejoining the road further on.

Bregan held the reins of his horse as Valdieron came back into sight of the old stump. The stallion breathed heavily, a sign that the race had not been at all easy.

Bregan dropped the reins and stomped forward, his face twisted in a sneer. "What was the meaning of that rock, you s-"

Valdieron hit him. As powerful a blow as he could manage with his injured shoulder. He was not a fighter like Kyle or some of the other kids. His punch was well placed however, and knocked the surprised Bregan to the seat of his pants and blood started to flow from his nose. Though stunned, the Mayor's son rose quickly, smiling arrogantly, though he made no move against Valdieron (for which Valdieron was thankful afterwards).

"Can't stand to lose, huh Ketherson?" He bent and picked up a handful of snow and pressed it against his nose to stem the flow of blood.

"It should be me asking you that, Bregan, but right now I don't really care. You go back to the village and parade around like you're important, and maybe somebody will even listen to you and believe your lies."

Bregan sneered and pulled the crimson-stained snow away briefly to check on the bleeding. "You can't do anything, Ketherson. Even if you told everybody in the village you won, nobody would believe you."

"Possibly, but as soon as you start telling people you won, at least half of them will doubt you, and the rest will hardly care. Then you will know how shallow your 'victory' was." He pushed past Bregan and continued on towards the village. He half expected the youth to come after him and fight, but nothing further happened.

Kyle met him as he entered the yard. His face darkened at the sight of his beat-up friend. He took one look at him and Shakk, and then pushed past without word.

Valdieron knew his friend well enough to know that Bregan would be getting an unwelcome visitor very soon. Hurrying, he caught Kyle by the shoulder, stopping him.

"Kyle, don't. It happened in a fall."

"I don't doubt that, Val, but I know you too well to accept you fell without some assistance, and that would have had to come from Bregan."

"Listen, Kyle. Pummeling Bregan won't make any difference. He is what he is, and nothing you do will change that." Kyle calmed. "Besides, he does have a bloody nose for his deceit, and I daresay it'll smart for at least a few days."

Kyle turned to him incredulously. "You didn't?"

"I sure did. Dropped him on his butt. I think I almost busted my hand doing it, but by the Moons, it was worth it."

"That's my boy." Kyle laughed and clapped him on the back as they turned back towards the smithy. "I wouldn't try it again soon, though, if I were you. I bet he's chafing at the bit to get you back."

"I don't know," Valdieron mused. "I think Bregan's bark is a lot worse than his bite. Like old Bart said, you just have to stand up to him and show him you won't be pushed around."

"We'll no doubt find out soon enough, though I hope you're right. It will make teasing him a lot more fun. Come on, we'd better take Shakk to Roland and get him looked at. The mare is shod and ready to ride if you have to stay off him."

Roland gave Shakk a clean bill of health, though he confirmed the bruising to the horse's fetlock, and recommended not riding him for at least two days. He also applied a pungent antiseptic salve to the deeper grazes to ward off infection.

Valdieron picked up the mare from the Smithy and swapped his saddle over to the young horse. He mounted and took Shakk's reins from Kyle.

"Return soon, so we can start teasing Bregan."

"I wouldn't miss it for the world," Valdieron said with a smile.

Afternoon was fading quickly when Valdieron reached the farm. He unsaddled the mare and set her off into the paddock then led Shakk to the barn and placed him in a stall, where he was not likely to aggravate his fetlock. He rubbed him down, apologizing softly for making him race. He rued now that he had not just returned home, leaving Bregan alone at the stump.

His father was out when he entered the house. He shuffled to the fireplace carrying an armload of chopped wood and dumped it in the wood-box. Setting some dried leaves, twigs and oil-soaked rags onto the grill, he used a taper to light it. It burned slowly as he added larger pieces until a sufficient layer of coals was able to accommodate a few thicker pieces that would last for some time. Then he repeated the process for the stove and the heating tub in the bathroom.

When he returned to the living room to light the lanterns, he found a folded piece of parchment lying on the floor just inside the door. He had not seen it when he entered earlier, though he had been distracted. He glanced around warily and unfolded it, surprised to find a short note written for him. It simply read:

Valdieron,
Loft. Midnight Tonight. Come alone.

It was unsigned and he did not recognize the writing, though it smelled faintly of roses and was far too neat to be Kyle's. Perhaps it was Bregan's doing, a plot to exact revenge? He opened the door and glanced outside but saw nobody. The dogs were silent in their run. Bemused, he returned inside.

His bedroom in the attic was accessed via a set of pull-down stairs in the roof at the far end of the hallway. Carrying a lantern, he climbed up stiffly and pulled the stairs up behind him.

The room was long and narrow, with the walls slanted inwards on huge beams up to their apex, a height well above his head. At the far end, a tall window admitted the dying light of the afternoon, bathing his bed with a golden blanket.

Valdieron set the lantern on the table and undressed. He winced as the blood-matted shirt ripped at the graze on his shoulder, but it bled only slightly. He tossed the soiled clothes into the corner, as a reminder to clean them in the morning and mend the shirt so that his father did not ask any questions. He gathered up some clean clothes and returned downstairs to bathe.

The water was warming rapidly so he poured a bath. He winced again when the hot water covered his shoulder as he slipped into the tub. With a washcloth he gently wiped the wound free of blood and dirt. He heard his father come in through the front door, and his heavy footfalls crossed the living room towards the hall. He held his breath, expecting Garrik to rush in and demand an explanation as to Shakk's condition, but he continued past the doorway towards his bedroom with only a quick glance in and a 'Hello son.'

Valdieron breathed a sigh of relief and slid back under the water.

It was around midnight when Valdieron softly pushed open the shutters of his window. The chill air caressed his exposed skin and he suppressed a gasp. He wore heavy bedclothes, though his unprotected hands, feet and face bore the brunt of the evening chill. Reaching out and up, he unlatched a long coil of rope hidden in a niche under the eave. It was securely attached to a crossbeam inside the roof, and was knotted at regular intervals. He had often climbed up and down the rope, though for no better reason than the fun of it. This time however, he had to descend quietly. The strain to his sore shoulder made him wince. A hooded lantern dangled from his left foot as he lowered himself, pausing momentarily to press closed the shutters. A thin leather cord nailed to the inside and set under the shutters would allow him to pull them back open when he returned.

The evening was not totally dark as the full moon Santari climbed the starry heavens. Qantari would not be seen for a few more hours, rising slower than its smaller brother this night. There were few clouds, a sign that it might be a very cold morning. A distant flash of lightning showed a storm brewing in the south.

Cursing every slight sound, he finally reached the ground. A lone dog in the run barked once sleepily then went quiet. He remained still for several long seconds, then picked up the lantern and sneaked across to the barn. He wished he had worn boots now as the cold grass numbed his toes.

Opening the barn doors was out of the question, but he had another plan. Tied to the front wall of the barn was a rope lowered from an access pulley above the doors, used for lifting bails of hay up to the loft. Shutters closed the loft off from the wind and weather, but they were more easily (and quietly) opened than the heavy doors below. Once again hanging the lantern over his foot, he grasped the rope and began to climb.

He used the narrow ledge to lever into a position to pry open the shutters with one hand, though his shoulder ached from the effort. Using a needle-thin sheet of metal hidden in a crack in the wall, he slipped the catch and pulled the shutters open. He lifted his leg and grabbed the lantern, setting it inside before swinging in. He quietly pulled the doors closed before opening the shutter of the lantern. An arc of pale light sprang forth as he peered into the dull gloom of the loft.

"About time!" came a whispered voice off to his right and he spun. He almost dropped the lantern when a figure appeared, lying propped on an elbow on the hay.

"Natasha. What in blazes are you doing here?" His face clouded with anger as he glanced around in suspicion. He cursed as another dog barked.

"Relax, Val," crooned Natasha, stretching like a waking cat. "Bregan doesn't know I'm here. Nobody does."

He did relax, but only slightly. In the dim light, he could see she was wearing heavy pants and jacket. She held a pair of thick gloves, and her feet were clad in soft riding boots. "So why the note? And the secrecy?" This time his voice was barely a whisper.

Her face softened, and with it some of his anger. "I saw what Bregan did to you today. I was hidden nearby and saw everything. I came to apologize. It was a terrible and cruel thing for him to do, and I am sorry I did not forewarn you of his trickery."

"Since when were you sorry for Bregan's actions? You seem to delight in his arrogance and bullying. To all appearances you and he are very much alike."

"To outward appearances so it may seem, but to be truthful I think he is an arrogant fool. I fear one day he will do something which will shame not just him, but the whole family."

Valdieron admitted that although she had always seemed crafty and devious in their previous encounters, she had never made fun of him or acted superior -- unlike her brother.

Images of her brother remained, but given her words it was hard for him to think of her as ever being a willing participant in Bregan's plans, even if he did seem to keep a tight rein on her.

Sensing his hesitancy, she rose to leave.

"No, wait!" Valdieron reached out and caught her shoulder, which felt soft and warm. She turned to look at his hand, then up into his eyes. He quickly removed his hand and spoke softly, "I do believe you. I just wasn't expecting this." He gave an apologetic smile. "When I read the note earlier, I thought Bregan was planning his revenge for what happened today. I... I am glad you came."

Natasha smiled and wiped her eyes. Suddenly he found her

pressed against him, her arms wrapped about his neck and her face pressed against his shoulder. Her body shook from tears, but he realized they were tears of relief. After several seconds, she pulled away, embarrassment showing on her face as she wiped at the tears once more.

"But why tell me this, Nat? You weren't responsible for what Bregan did. If you had foiled his plans today, he would only try again some other time. He was intent on getting at me, and there was little you could do to stop him."

She turned her wet eyes to regard him intently. Deeply. "No. There was something I could have done which would have prevented this from happening, and that was to pay no attention to you. Then Bregan wouldn't have been jealous of you."

"Jealous!" he blurted. "Of me?"

"Yes. Bregan hates it when I pay any attention to somebody else. My brother knows he has few friends, and he foolishly thinks I am his only real friend. I think he is a buffoon, and he treats me like a serving wench. It is just that when I see you, it drives me mad to keep from touching you or speaking with you the way I want to. It drives him crazy, but I never meant for it to hurt you."

Valdieron's mind and heart raced. Did she mean that she had feelings for him -- feelings suppressed by the presence of her jealous brother? "I don't know what to say, Nat".

"I only need to know if you forgive me. If you cannot, then I understand. I hope one day you will see me for the person I really am, not for how others brand me."

Valdieron closed his eyes against her gaze. He knew what she spoke was the truth; maybe by the sincerity of her words and the pain he saw in her eyes, which did not seem feigned. He also admitted the presence of personal feelings of desire and compassion he felt for her; feelings he had paid little heed to in the past, when he thought her attentions were little more than a cruel game of her brother's creation.

"I forgive you."

His words made her cry again, and once more he found her in his arms. It was not an altogether uncomfortable position, he noted. He put an arm around her tightly, wondering if he should say something to soothe her, but he could think of nothing. She raised her head after a time, and her lips brushed his lightly, then with more intensity as he mutely returned her kiss. He could taste the saltiness of her tears on her soft tender lips, and the tension drained from her body as they shared that special moment.

When she finally drew away, he sighed. "Natasha, I don't think this is right."

He knew he would kick himself afterwards, but dimly he knew this was neither the time nor place for what he believed was going to happen. He did not know if he could resist if it went any further, even if his life hung on the line -- as it would should either of their father's found out.

"Then hold me, Val. Keep me company and wrap your arms around me." There was sadness in her words, but also relief.

Quietly he retrieved a clean horse blanket from below and returned to lay it over the soft hay. Awkwardly they lay, facing each other. Valdieron stared into her eyes, trying to sort through the emotions he felt, and what her feelings might be for him.

Hesitantly he touched her hand. She smiled, and her beauty struck him. Her platinum hair shone in the lamplight, framing her slender face. Dark green eyes held him, soft and inviting. He took in her every detail, from the curve of her full mouth to the shape of her ears. Though he longed to lean forward and kiss her again, he somehow resisted the urge.

They talked softly, eventually shifting to lie side by side with her head resting on his shoulder. Not once did their hands lose contact, even after Valdieron doused the lantern and they drifted off to sleep.

Chapter 3

Valdieron woke some time before dawn, feeling cold and uncomfortable.

And alone.

He felt around until he found the cold lantern, and crawled to the access door to peer out. When he pushed the shutters open, the chill morning air assailed him. It was still dark; about three hours till the first rays of dawn would begin to illuminate the horizon. Santari had fallen over the western hills and the waxing Qantari on its own gave off little light. The storm front he noticed earlier had faded or shifted course.

He leaned back against the wall and sighed. He remembered the heat of Natasha's body, and her soft lips caressing his when they kissed. He wondered what would happen between them now. He was not stupid, but when it came to girls, he knew very little in terms of what he should or should not do. Maybe he could ask Kyle, who was more comfortable around girls and always said the right things.

A commotion broke out from the horse run, startling him from his thoughts. He leaned out the doorway, ruing the poor timing. The pounding of hooves beat the still night air as the horses galloped toward the far end of the huge pasture, as if fleeing something. This preceded a chorus of terrified bleating from the sheep as the dogs went wild in their kennels.

He grabbed for the dark rope and slid down, cursing as the coarse rope burnt his hands. He ran toward the dark house, locating the rope that led back to his bedroom. After tying the lantern quickly to the bottom, he clambered up as fast as he could.

He reached the safety of his window and pulled up the rope just as his father opened the front door. Garrik held a lantern high in one hand, his bow in the other.

Making a show of just having woken, Valdieron leaned out the window looking for the source of the commotion. His father glanced up at him but quickly turned his attention back to the spooked animals. The sheep circled riotously, bleating pitifully in the dark as they crammed together in their pen. The horses were still snorting threateningly and racing around in the darkness farther down the pasture. He quickly threw on a heavy coat and pulled on his boots. He belted his quiver and hunting dagger to his waist and took up his bow where it lay under his bed.

"Probably wolves!" guessed Garrik as Valdieron joined him, though his face showed concern. Valdieron nocked an arrow and waited for his father. Both knew that wolves did not attack noisy farms, usually preying on sick or injured animals.

The sheep were still milling in their pen, growing more agitated by the second.

"There!" yelled Valdieron, spotting a dark shape moving beyond the sheep's pen. His father nodded. Slowly he set the lantern down and raised his bow. In all of Shadowvale, few were as good as Garrik Ketherson with a longbow. He won most of the archery contests at festivals, or at least those he attended.

The arrow sped through the darkness.

The dark shape was no more than a shadowed outline. It may have been a bear, if not the largest Valdieron had ever seen, though he had never seen one walk on its hind legs as surely as this.

He could not see if his father's arrow struck true, but a deafening roar filled the night. The growl sounded ursine, though far deeper and louder. Drawing on his own bow, he fired an arrow and nocked again but his father's hand stopped him from loosing another. If he struck, he could not tell, though the creature continued to howl furiously.

"Quickly, back in the house," ordered Garrik.

Confused, Val followed his father inside, fleeing the cacophony. The sheep continued to scream in terror, while the dogs barked and growled from their confines. The horses in the paddock continued to stampede wildly. Even Shakk in the barn could be heard pounding away at his stall trying to escape. Val's heart pounded equally as hard in his chest.

"Hurry! Light the fire and get it blazing." Garrik locked the door behind them and moved to light the lanterns. He then disappeared into his bedroom and returned with more lanterns and oil, which he lit and placed around the room, most notably near the door and windows.

Valdieron unearthed a few small embers still glowing from

last evening's fire. He set dry bark and leaves onto them and blew gently. Tiny flames consumed the tinder and took hold. Carefully he added more fuel until it blazed.

"What was that, father?" he asked breathlessly. He marveled that he had been able to light the fire. His hands were trembling visibly. Garrik stood in the center of the room with his bow half drawn. His face was stony -- no, grim, and his gaze flickered around the radiant room as if to ensure everything was in order. His head was cocked slightly, listening.

"A Hill Troll, Son. My Pa showed me one once, dead in the mountains up north. Said they were a race of cannibals, larger than a man but with little intelligence. They are excellent trackers with sharp eyes and a keen sense of smell, though their hearing is not good."

"Hill Troll!" gasped Valdieron. "I thought it was a bear." He had heard and read stories of Trolls, but always discounted their existence as nothing more than figments of overly excited imaginations.

"Half our luck if it was, son. Bears rarely attack farms, and are easily driven off. Let's just hope it's alone and too scared to come near the light. They hate bright light and fire, so they hunt at night. Maybe he'll take a sheep or two and leave."

"Can't we drive it away?" Valdieron was afraid. His father was not a person who was easily scared. He had once seen his father put four arrows into the chest of a charging bear; the latter shot felling the beast less than ten feet away and still his father had not retreated.

"With what, son? That thing is bigger than a bear and just as stupid. If he wants to do something, I don't think he's going to be swayed. Besides, we don't know if he's alone or part of a pack." Garrik hastily made a sign against bad luck.

A nervous wait ensued as they listened for signs of the creature's presence. They heard it growl several times over the bleating of the sheep and the howling of the dogs. Valdieron held his breath, anxiously releasing it when he realized what he was doing. He didn't know if he was afraid or excited, or both.

Suddenly, a window to his right shattered inwards with a great crash. Shards of glass and splinters of wood flew across the room, propelled by a dark object, which hit the floor in a spray of dark liquid and glass. With revulsion, Valdieron saw it was a headless sheep. Glass stuck from gashes in its skin as blood seeped into a pool beneath it.

A bellowing roar ensued as something moved in the firelight outside. He caught a glimpse of gray skin covered with wisps of thick hair. He loosed his arrow through the gaping window and recoiled in fear, not knowing if it struck.

Moments later, heavy thuds shook the stout door. The latch shuddered with the force of each blow, and the wood buckled inwards. Straining hinges splintered from the wooden doorframe.

"There is more than one!" shouted Garrik above the noise, pointing to the broken window. A wooden club, rough and notched, smashed away at the glassy frame, trying to clear the remaining shards. Obviously, the Trolls were not entirely stupid.

The door shuddered once again from a powerful blow, and the topmost hinge broke free with a sharp crack.

The next blow blasted it inwards where it crashed to the floor.

A creature of nightmarish stature, bathed in the flickering firelight, stooped to glare through the splintered doorway. It must have been at least nine feet tall, with a body covered with plated gray skin overgrown with thick hair. Its ape-like face was brutishly malformed, with deep eye sockets, protruding jawbone and forehead, and a broad flat nose. Its feet and hands were disproportionately large, with thick stubbed nails at the end of gnarled fingers. In one hand it held a huge club as it leered into the room, baring dull and discolored ursine teeth.

Valdieron retreated towards the rear of the room. His head shook in denial of what was happening. Trolls were not supposed to exist, especially not in Shadowvale. Vaguely he heard the crash of glass coming from the rear of the house. His body was frozen in terror.

The Troll at the door reared as an arrow from Garrik's bow caught it in the shoulder. It roared with pain and its hate-filled eyes came back to bear on Garrik. A trail of dark blood flowed from the wound. It tore the arrow free with a growl and started to push through the doorway.

Valdieron choked on a cry as another bestial face loomed through the broken window. He was less than ten feet from the creature as it tried to squeeze through the opening, unconcerned by the remnants of glass that tore at its skin.

Suddenly released from the paralysis that gripped him, Valdieron raised his bow and fired. The steel-tipped arrow sliced across the Troll's forehead, opening a wide gash revealing the white of bone, before a torrent of blood washed down over its face. It howled in pain but continued to struggle through the window.

He drew with shaky hands and fired again. This time his arrow thumped into the top of the Troll's shoulder near the fleshy part of the lower neck. At such close range, it bit deep.

The Troll withdrew, leaving lines of blood dripping from the splintered glass. It disappeared from sight before Valdieron could get off another shot.

He turned to find the other Troll almost through the doorway. Garrik had put two more arrows in its thigh and chest, but it did not seem to be slowing down. Garrik retreated slowly as he fired.

"Run, Son. Get out of here and run to the village if you can." His next shot went wide as his heel caught on the bloodied carcass of the sheep and he went down. His back was smeared with the dark blood as he rose. He wiped his hand free of sheep's blood and nocked another arrow.

"Not without you, Father!" cried Valdieron. He launched another arrow out the window at the shadowy outline of a passing Troll. He could not tell if it hit as he turned back to his father, who fired again. There came a 'thunk' as the steel tip bit into the creature's wooden club as the Troll rose inside the room. Its shaggy head brushed the beams of the ten-foot ceiling.

"Go, Son. I'll be right behind you. Keep out of sight and stay clear of them. Go!"

Valdieron hesitated. He did not want to leave his father, but he knew they could not hold out here in the house. There were few exits he could choose from, and he had little idea how many trolls were outside, so it was possible that all windows were watched or being broken into. Even as he paused, a heavy crash down the hallway made him turn to see a huge foot smashing through the door of his father's bedroom.

He tossed his bow out the window and shouted, "Hurry Father," before he dived out after it. Half expecting the heavy crash of a club on the back of his unprotected neck, he hit the soft dirt and came to his feet without incident. Hastily he gathered up his bow and nocked an arrow. Crouching, he looked around for Trolls, but the only indication of their presence was a guttural yelling from the rear of the house.

Then he was up and racing for a small gully that lay twenty paces from the house. Sliding into it feet-first, he was aware of his heart pounding in his chest as he turned to look back at the house. Setting his bow parallel to the ground, he half drew and waited.

No Trolls appeared and he breathed a sigh of relief. Moments passed and his father still did not appear. With each second he became wore worried.

"Hurry, Father!" he whispered desperately.

Biting off a curse he started to rise when movement at the front of the house caught his attention. Dropping back out of sight, he peered out and saw several shapes moving off into the darkness. His heart jumped as he noticed the gates of the barn torn from their supports. The Trolls continued, though not towards the hills as he had expected, but towards the south-east.

The Village! His thoughts were of Natasha and Kyle as he turned his gaze southward.

What he saw made his heart sink. The attack on their farm had not been an isolated incident. The gray horizon was bathed in an orange glow that could only mean one thing.

Shadowvale was burning.

Conflicting emotions gripped him as he turned back to the house. His father still had not appeared, while his best friend and the girl he thought he loved were in the village, maybe even now in danger or hurt. He cursed, and then dashed for the house, hoping his father had left by some other way and was waiting for the Trolls to depart. Cautiously he crept to the window and peered inside.

He gave a cry at the sight of his father lying sprawled on the floor. One of his legs lay twisted and mangled beneath him, and his shirt was torn away, revealing a jagged gash in his side. His breath came in shallow rasps with every rise and fall of his chest. Near him lay the still corpse of the Troll that had broken through the door.

Valdieron clambered through the window, vaguely aware of the pain as glass cut into his forearm. "Please, no!" he cried as he reached his father, dropping to his knees. Gently he lifted his father's head and cradled it on his lap. The movement brought a ragged groan of pain from Garrik.

The leg was plainly broken: the knee was shattered and bleeding, with shards of bone poking from the wound. Val guessed from his father's blood-flecked lips that his lungs were slowly filling with blood, probably punctured by broken ribs. He was no healer, but he had seen a similar occurrence years ago when a local youth had been thrown from his horse and hit a tree stump.

His father was dying, holding on by mere strength of will.

"No! Please don't die, Father," he cried softly. His body shook violently as he rocked back and forth. "I won't let you die. You have to live, for me and for mother and for Marcus. You are all I have, Father. Don't do this to me."

Caught up in his grief, he almost did not hear the groaning of timber to his left. A moment of hope filled him as he expected to see somebody from the village come to see if they were all right.

Through teary eyes he turned to find the hulking form of a Troll. The cut along its forehead and the broken arrow sticking from its shoulder marked it as the one he had shot earlier as it climbed through the window. It filled the hallway, slavering as it looked down at him.

Anger coursed through Valdieron. Gently he lowered his father's head to the floor. His eyes flashed to his bow, but it was out of reach, and he would be lucky to get one shot off before the Troll reached him. Rising, he backed towards the hearth. He fumbled for the fire poker hanging from the mantle.

With an almost lascivious grin the Troll stepped forward. "No fight, boy," it commanded in a guttural voice, startling him with its knowledge of the common tongue. "Hroth crush you like other for bleed him with sticks."

Knowing this Troll killed his father filled Valdieron with rage.

Rushing the Troll would be suicide. Even in the confined room, the troll had enough room to swing his heavy club effectively. Then he remembered the fire. Blazing in the red embers was a half-consumed log. In desperation he grabbed for it, gritting his teeth against the searing heat. With a cry that was half pain and half anger, he hurled it at the troll.

It struck the beast in the chest, with unexpected but

fortuitous effect.

The thick straw-like hair of the Troll caught alight and spread quickly. Alarmed, the Troll slapped desperately at the flames, its efforts only spreading them quicker onto its hands and arms -- diverting its attention from Valdieron's advance.

Fuelled with rage, Val swung the poker with all the strength he could muster.

The hooked tip dug into the side of the Troll's face, just above his eye. Propelled by the force of the blow, it continued along the troll's forehead, scraping across bone before ripping through its right eye in a spray of blood.

Howling, the troll recoiled and raised a hand to its rent face. Blood poured from its now useless eye, seeping between its fingers and down onto its chest and stomach.

Valdieron did not falter. With a bellow he thrust the poker at the Troll's stomach.

Whether through instinct or anger, the Troll raised its heavy club as Valdieron struck. The poker tore through tough, plated skin, and warm blood oozed down its shaft, staining Valdieron's hands as he leant all of his weight to it. The Troll's club, swung with faded strength, caught him on the left shoulder. He was thrown sideways from the force, his shoulder numbed with pain. He hit the floor hard and scrambled desperately away from the Troll.

The amazed Troll stared down at the poker sticking from its stomach. Slowly, with bloodied hands, it grasped the poker and tore it free, ignoring the extra damage the barbed tip caused. Tossing the poker aside, it turned back to Valdieron and grinned, its evil countenance accentuated by the jagged cut to its blood-lined face and its mutilated eye. It took a step forward as Valdieron retreated again, but froze in mid-stride and pitched sideways to crash against the wall. It writhed in agonized denial for a few moments, and then it was still.

Stunned and shocked by the brief melee, Valdieron stared down at his bloodstained hands. His thoughts suddenly returned to his father. Ignoring the pain in his shoulder he scrambled back to Garrik's side.

Amazingly, his father was conscious. Dull eyes tried to focus on Valdieron, and he slowly raised a bloodied, trembling hand. Valdieron caught it, but wished he had not as he felt the weakness of his father's grip.

"Father, we must get you out of here," he said, but Garrik stopped him with a shake of the head.

"There is no time." His whispered words were laced with pain, but he gritted his teeth and continued. "Listen to me, son. Beneath my bed is a box. Get it!"

Valdieron rose and ran to the bedroom, pausing briefly to grab a lantern.

The bedroom was a mess, with overturned furniture and shards of glass scattered everywhere. After a brief search under the bed he located the box. He pulled it free and hurried back to his father. He had never seen the box before, and wondered with renewed hope if it contained some magical potion that might heal his father.

"I have it, Father." He knelt again and cradled his father's head in his lap.

"A key.... around my neck." Garrik coughed, spitting blood. Valdieron wiped it away as tears rolled down his cheeks. Around his father's neck was a thin gold chain, and from it hung a small silver key. He unclasped the chain and moved to unlock the box, but his father stopped him. "Not now. You must go now, away from here. There is danger..."

Valdieron shook his head and began to sob. "I won't leave without you."

With surprising strength, Garrik gripped his hands and regarded his son with a fond smile. "I'm not long for this world, son, we both know it." His smiled faded with the onset of painful spasms. They passed, but his face was deathly pale and his eyes vapid. "Gather your things quickly and leave, son. Those trolls may be back soon if they think we are still alive... or if they get hungry."

"I think the village was attacked too, father."

"The Trolls will stay... Run. Hide in the mountains... You will know what to do."

Valdieron screwed his eyes shut and rested his face on his father's chest.

Although he felt like a coward for forsaking the village and those in it, he decided to hide in the mountains for a few days until he was sure the danger of the Trolls had passed.

"I will, Father," he assured with a forced smile. He looped the gold chain around his neck. "I will return soon and finish what you started many years ago." His father smiled as his eyes closed slowly. He began to whisper, and Valdieron realized it was not to him as he bent closer to hear. "I'm coming, Li. I'm coming." Valdieron swallowed hard. To sit there watching his father die in his arms was unbearable. A feeling of insignificance washed over him, and he wished he were the one dying, not his father.

"Pa," he said, and his father shifted slightly, as if faintly hearing his voice. "Say Hello to Ma and Marcus for me. Tell them I'm all right. I will think of you all every day."

His father's smile remained even after he breathed his last, ragged breath.

Chapter 4

Valdieron cried for what seemed like hours. Sobs racked his body as he knelt over his father. He didn't care that there was still the threat of danger. His father was dead; the only relative he had in the world. It was hard to just turn his back and run.

Tears streaked down his face as he rose.

His first stop was his room. His pack already held many of the things he might need, as he took it with him whenever he went out. Inside were clothes, cooking items, his fletching kit, extra bowstrings, a tinderbox with flint and a little food. For safekeeping, he tucked the small metal box inside.

Throwing his heavy ulster over his shoulder, he returned downstairs.

From his father's bedroom he retrieved a purse of money from the overturned dresser. He also found a small lantern, unbroken and filled. It went into his pack along with two ceramic flasks of oil, tucked protectively inside his spare clothing.

Returning to the living room and trying not to glance at his father's body, he gathered some more food from the pantry and crammed it into the pack until it could hold no more. He filled a canteen with water and secured it to his belt. He had to struggle with his pack to get it on. The pain of his injured shoulders made wearing it uncomfortable but bearable. Luckily the blow had not broken anything.

Taking up his discarded bow, he held it for a time then tossed it aside. Instead he picked up his father's bow and slung it over his shoulder.

He returned and knelt beside his father, one last time. Softly he kissed his still warm brow and lifted his lifeless hands to place them across his chest.

"Goodbye, Father. I love you, always."

Choking back tears, he grabbed a handful of arrows from his father's quiver to replenish his depleted supply, and then rose. He did not look around again as he walked out the door.

It was still dark outside, and he realized that less than half an hour ago he had been in the barn, asleep.

Cautiously he glanced around. There were no sounds, not even of the dogs or sheep. In the gloom, he saw a couple of dead sheep littering the yard. He had assumed the Trolls had killed for food, but this senseless massacre made it seem they were doing it for pleasure also.

Unless they were coming back for it?

In the distance he could still see the orange glow of the burning village. It made him pause. Returning quickly inside, he gathered the still-burning lanterns and smashed them against the walls. Oil splashed and caught alight, igniting the wooden walls and floor. Soon, the room was burning intensely and he fled. He would not leave his father's body as food for any returning Trolls, nor did he wish to return to the house again.

The Trolls had ransacked the barn. He found Shakk's stall empty, the gate having been torn from its hinges. He hoped his horse had survived, but didn't think it very likely. There was only one way out of the barn, the way the Trolls had got in. The dogs run lay in ruin, and he was glad the darkness hid the bodies of the dogs he knew would be there.

Reluctantly, he condemned the barn to the same fate as the house. Igniting the lantern near the door, he threw it into the loft where earlier he had lain with Natasha. It took only moments for the hay to catch as flames licked the darkness above.

The sound of the razing house and barn taunted him as he walked away to the north, using the light of the conflagration to guide him. No doubt any nearby Trolls would be able to see the fire, so he had to get away as quickly as possible. He did not use his own lantern, knowing it would be like a beacon in the darkness.

With his bow in hand and an arrow at the ready, he made it to the stream and followed it northwards. The stream wound languidly down from the highlands, and was easy to follow for the most part. Sometimes the darkness and occasional rough terrain made it difficult, especially with the heavy pack burdening him. Only when the first light of dawn peaked over the mountains did he realize he had covered a considerable distance.

He remembered his father saying that Trolls were not fond of light, so if they were around, they were probably hidden among the many crags and caves the mountains afforded. That meant he had a whole day to get clear of the valley and put some distance between himself and the Trolls. As return to the village was fraught with danger still, he continued into the mountains.

Lack of sleep, coupled with the incessant ache of his shoulders and the pain and anguish of the morning's tragedy soon left him stumbling. Doggedly he put one foot in front of the other and pushed on, gritting his teeth against the agony. He tripped and fell a few times, but each time he willed himself to rise and continue.

Rise and leave the pain behind.

The day grew older. A light rain threatened but held off. He fell one last time, asleep before he hit the hard ground.

The sun was well on its way towards the horizon when he woke. His shoulder was aching and stiff from the blood that dried it against his shirt, while his legs felt leaden. Memories flooded back to him and he cried.

Berating himself to be strong, he glanced around for signs of danger. There were none. With luck the Trolls would not return to the mountains for a couple of days until their new food supply ran out. That was possible, especially if the villagers had not chased them off.

Pushing the worrying thoughts aside, he set off again. After a time he mounted a low crest, unmindful of the excellent target he showed against the sky. Turning, he saw that the hills fell away, and in the distance lay the valley. A thick plume of smoke rose into the gray sky.

'They are probably still putting out the flames' he told himself, wanting so much to believe it. The alternatives were not very pleasant. His thoughts were of Kyle and Natasha, and he prayed that somehow they had escaped unharmed. He had to believe that. It made him nauseous to think what the Trolls may have done at the Village. Dropping to his knees, he loosed the contents of his stomach. He cried again while softly cursing the gods who had let such a thing happen to these goodly people. They had not deserved such a fate.

Though satisfying, his condemnation of the gods was pointless. He wiped his mouth and rose. Nausea still clung to him, but he had nothing more to bring up. For the first time he noted the lands looked dead, devoid of life. Even the call of birds was distant and sporadic, as if they were frightened to voice their whereabouts.

Resolutely he drew a deep, steadying breath. Glancing up at the sky, he saw it was past midday; he had slept for too long. The Trolls were at home in the hills, which made his very presence there a danger. His father had said their vision was keen, and they could follow a scent, so it would be best if he were as far away as he could get. He set off again, leaving the burning village behind, out of sight though not out of mind.

After an hour or so, hunger and weariness tugged at him so he halted. Though he still felt sick, he forced himself to eat and drink a little to keep his strength up. He also washed and dressed the wound to his shoulder. The club had torn and badly bruised his flesh. It had stopped bleeding, and would hopefully heal quickly.

As a child, he had ventured rarely into the hills, even with Marcus or his father. When he was given the responsibility of minding the sheep, sometimes he would have to retrieve runaways, but those would seldom take him into the mountains, and even then only one or two miles beyond the valley. Where he was now, perhaps three or four miles from the valley's edge, was further than a lot of locals would have ventured, with the exception of the trappers and hunters.

He pressed on for the remainder of the afternoon, though exhaustion and pain slowed him to barely a shuffle before too long. His legs ached and sent jarring spasms up his back with each staggered step. His shoulders felt like they were being branded with hot irons, making the weight of the pack seem like that of a mountain. Each time he stumbled (which was often), he cursed and willed himself to rise. Defy the hurt. Defy the pain. Defy the cruel fate that had put him there. As if he could somehow outrun each of these, he pushed harder, despite the sting of old and new blisters. He promised himself that at the end of the day he would remove his boots and soak his feet in the icy water of the stream.

At the end of the day.

Darkness came quickly in the mountains. One moment it was light and he was making slow progress over the rugged terrain, then the star-specked blanket of night covered the land. Even so he pushed onward, using what little light there was to guide him. Finally, he crumpled in an exhausted heap onto the cold ground. It was too risky to travel further in the dark, he told himself, relieved at the opportunity to rest.

Crawling to a nearby outcrop of rock, which offered suitable shelter, he stretched out to rest. He barely managed to relieve himself of his pack before sleep consumed him, too tired to care about Trolls or food or his aching feet.

He woke with a stifled cry, immersed in darkness. He scrambled to a sitting position, breathing heavily. Fighting disorientation, he waited while his eyes slowly focused in the dim moonlight.

Calming himself, he focused on the canopy of night, which was littered with stars. He could make out the constellations. There was the Huntsman with his faithful hound and spear. Near him was the Owl, watcher of the lands. The Great Wheel dominating the north. The Dragon's Claw. Local favorites, the Milk Pale and the Old Woman's Broom -- also known as the Dread Lord's Trident. There was also the Hourglass, through which all time runs its course before starting anew, and the lonely South Star, the brightest body in the southern sky save the moons.

High above the eastern horizon hovered Qantari, shining orange against the dark backdrop, bathing the land in gentle luminescence. It was probably a few hours past midnight. The big moon was rising late in this cycle. It would still be seen in the western sky as a pale gray form well into the morning. That would make it, what, almost the third month of autumn?

With a groan he stretched, feeling the aches and pains from the previous day's march and the tightness of his bruised shoulder. Rubbing his weary eyes, he wondered what had caused him to wake. He had slept well. He was not cold, the small outcrop gave protection against the light breeze, and he doubted he would have wakened from sleeping on the hard ground -- it was mostly smooth and he was too tired to have felt any discomfort.

It could have been nightmares. A myriad of scenes and sounds had assaulted him in his dreams. None stayed too long or too vivid for him to remember any specifics other than they had definitely been nightmares.

He rose unsteadily, wincing as his shoulder protested. Bathed in moonlight, the land looked peaceful and serene. Nothing moved or made a sound.

No sound?

Instantly he froze. His ears strained to hear and his eyes scanned the darkness. Whatever had silenced the animals had probably woken him. He reasoned it might have been a wolf passing close by or some other preying creature, yet it may also have been Trolls.

For several seconds he stood unmoved, his nerves strained to breaking point as his heart pounded. Suddenly he caught a flicker of movement at the edge of a copse at the base of the small rise. He tried to zero in on the movement, but the darkness swallowed whatever he had glimpsed, though it had been man-like in appearance.

A guttural bark pierced the silence. His heart rose in his throat. The unmistakable call of the Troll emanated from the copse.

Dropping to a crouch, he quietly slipped on his pack and lifted his bow. An arrow was already nocked, and he drew it half the length of the cloth-yard shaft. The outcrop was high enough to block his silhouette against the sky. He hoped the call had not signified his discovery.

He could see no further movement in the copse, and an uncomfortable silence ensued.

An echoing call from down the rise was all the confirmation he needed that there were more than one out there, and they were too close for comfort. Stooped over, he rounded the outcrop and followed the stream, away from the copse.

The sound of his footfalls seemed deafeningly loud, making him wince with every step. His father had said Trolls had poor hearing, but it didn't ease his worry. He could hear no sounds of pursuit, but he dared not linger. Every shadow caught his eye as he glanced around nervously, expecting to be set upon at any moment.

He topped a rise and was looking over a semi-circular valley set against the rocky face of a hill. Rough foliage covered the bluff, which was not as smooth as it first appeared, with many protrusions mingled with bracken and weeds. The stream he had been following wound through the center of the valley, concealed in places by thick tangles of undergrowth. It flowed out from the base of the bluff.

A barking call from behind made him drop to his stomach. He was sure the Trolls were onto him. Several more calls followed, more distant than the first, chilling him with fear. There were definitely more than just two out there, and possibly as many as a dozen going on the spread of the calls. Luckily, all had been from behind him.

Running into the hollow, he followed its edge around to where the cliff cut away, a distance of half a mile. Half way around, the calls sprang up again, this time much closer. He slowed to glance over his shoulder and caught the silhouette of what must have been a Troll topping the rise. There was no doubt it saw him as it paused and barked a long call into the night. Answering calls rang out again, this time not far away.

Fear spurred him onward as he raced for the cliff face. All thoughts of hiding had vanished. He knew his only chance of survival lay in flight. He had to keep ahead of the Trolls until daybreak.

At least two hours away.

The hill beyond the cliff rose higher into the night, and he realized he was near the base of 'The Sentinel'. Seeing the towering peak up close was awe-inspiring, and he found it markedly different than it appeared from several leagues away. It was a singular hill, surrounded to the Southeast and west by rolling tablelands, with the dominant massif stretching away to the north.

He climbed out of the hollow when he reached the cliff face and skirted around to the north, going higher as he ran. He was no longer concerned that the Trolls were behind him, just how far. He could hear their trailing howls as they labored after him. Running like his life depended on it, he focused on staying on his feet, placing each step surely in the tricky terrain.

He rounded the mountain, but by the time he reached the northern face he knew he could not outrun the Trolls. Their incessant howls were closing. Hasty glances showed that not only were they following him, they had branched out to flank him.

Desperately he began to look for a tenable area where he might be able to hold them off for a while, which was unlikely, with only his bow and a dagger as weapons. Without even a fire, his chances of surviving an encounter with the Trolls were slim at best.

Over the din of his pursuers he made out the trickling of the stream somewhere ahead. It might be of some aid, if he could just reach it.

The higher he climbed, the rockier it became. He stumbled several times or was tripped up by rocks or narrow crevasses. All the while, the Trolls' howls drew closer. Louder. With each trip or false step he expected to feel the blow from a Troll's club or their fetid breathe on the back of his neck.

He scrambled desperately up another steep rise that passed through a narrow gap between rocky hedges, and found himself on a narrow ledge. On one side rose a wall of rock, while the other side fell away sharply. The rear also dropped away into darkness. He drew to a sharp halt, almost skidding over the edge. He could barely make out the dark surface of the stream below.

Grunting howls sounded behind him, very close. Inadvertently he had stumbled upon a location from which he could hold out the Trolls if his luck held. A Troll appeared at the base of the incline. Huge and dark, its eyes gleamed like pale moons in the darkness as it struggled up the uneven slope.

Dropping to one knee behind the gap in the rocks, Valdieron drew and fired. From less than ten yards the arrow caught the Troll in the chest as it stumbled on a stone. The force of the arrow knocked it backwards. Wounded and off balance, the Troll fell flat on its back and slid roughly down the slope, grunting as the rocks tore its tough hide. It finally stopped sliding and climbed unsteadily to its feet. Blood dripped onto the rocks below. With a defiant roar it wrenched the arrow from its chest and started to climb again.

Valdieron grabbed a hand-full of his arrows and dropped them at his feet before fitting another and firing. He cursed angrily as the arrow grazed the Troll's shoulder and ricocheted into the darkness to shatter against a rock. Again he drew, this time calming to focus on the Troll. Then he loosed.

The arrow, backed by the force of Garrik's bow, tore into the Troll's right eye and dug in with a dull thud, which was drowned out by the beast's pained howl. It reared back, jerking the arrow free in a rage. It snapped the arrow in its gnarled fist and tossed it away defiantly. With a roar, it took another dogged step up the slope.

Valdieron's fourth arrow caught it in the right shoulder, biting deep. The weakened Troll spun and fell, probably already dead from the previous arrow, but not smart enough to realize it. It slid down the slope once more and came to a stop. This time it did not rise.

His satisfaction was short-lived as two more armed Trolls loomed out of the darkness. Compassion was obviously not a Trollish trait as one of them stepped on the dying form of the first. That Troll wore a small leather vest over its torso, tied at the sides with an assortment of leather straps. Obviously it was meant for somebody smaller as it barely covered its chest and sternum.

Valdieron loosed arrows frantically down upon them without taking the time to aim. He was in serious trouble, and had to hope that in his haste he got in some lucky shots.

Their tough hide proved a bane to his steel-tipped arrows, as did the second Troll's protective breastplate. Two or three arrows managed to strike and bite deep, though not causing enough damage to slow them.

He recoiled instinctively at a loud crash to his left. Shards of rock struck him as something glanced off the wall. At first he thought it was a club from a Troll sneaking up behind him. Then he realized Trolls on the other side of the stream were hurling stones across at him.

There wasn't much he could do about them, so he turned his attention back to the Trolls scaling the rise. He was surprised to find only one still climbing. The other lay in a heap down near the first Troll, also unmoving.

The second Troll was almost on him. He raised his bow to fire, but a searing pain and sudden jarring in the back of his right leg knocked him hard, and his shot flew high into the darkness.

The Troll pushed through the rocky opening before him. He tried to draw away from it, but a wave of pain from his injured leg assailed him, and he cried out. It was too close for him to nock an arrow and shoot in time. The heavy club raised as the beast roared, exposing its ursine maw.

Valdieron knew it was over for him. His father's death had merely been a prelude to his own, merely postponed by his exhausting trek through the mountains. He saw the club descend, and his mouth opened to scream, but no sound was forthcoming. In a final desperate attempt he tried to evade the blow.

The slashing club caught him on the left shoulder. Numbing pain washed over him as the force spun him off balance and knocked him across the ledge. He tried to move his feet to regain balance, but his wounded leg failed to respond. Suddenly the ground disappeared beneath him, and he flailed into darkness. An even greater numbness consumed him as he plunged into the icy stream.

The shock broke him out of his stunned daze, but forced the air from his lungs and cold water in. Heavy clothes and numbed muscles dragged him under. Fear consumed him. The strong current kept him under as he tried to orient himself. With his useless arm and heavy pack, there was no way he could swim.

The sudden scrape of rocks against his feet saved him. Desperately he kicked upwards, breaking the surface with a choking gasp for air; only to be dragged back under as the swirling current caught him. This time he remained relatively calm, and let himself be carried along, before he sank deep enough to push off the bottom again and resurface for air.

No sooner had he broken the surface for a second time, when suddenly he was falling. He wanted to draw a breath, but could not as he plummeted under the weight of falling water.

He felt as if he had fallen only a moment or two when suddenly he was underwater again. Vertigo hit him as the eddying waters spun him like a stick, and his lungs burned. He yearned to draw breath. He kicked out, trying to claw his way through the water. A stabbing pain exploded in his mind and his struggles weakened as he lost consciousness, carried away by the cold waters.

Chapter 5

Zaleef stood silhouetted against the pre-dawn light as he leaned against the frame of the large window in his office. Before him, the tip of the morning sun peered over the rough horizon, casting a blazing trail across the dark surface of the Twin Lakes. From the south, a dark cloud front approached inexorably, marring the otherwise perfect sky.

Yet it was another imminent storm that clouded his mind.

As if on cue, there came a soft yet urgent tap at his door. "Enter!" he commanded, his normally strong voice cracking slightly. He did not turn as the door opened. The swish of thick robes accompanied the novice who entered.

"Everything is in readiness Master Zaleef!"

With a pensive sigh, Zaleef turned away from the window and the beautiful sunrise. The novice stood in the doorway with his head bowed respectfully. He was young, barely past his twentieth year.

Young, for a Novice.

"The men are gathered in the hall, awaiting your arrival, Master."

Zaleef nodded. "Has Saratholeus arrived yet?"

"Yes, Master. Only moments ago."

Zaleef sighed again. At last, everything was in readiness. He reached for his thick staff where it leaned against the wall. He was not as young as he used to be. *Too old for this running around, anyway* he mused silently.

"I will be there presently, Novice Jerome. You are dismissed."

The Novice swept a low bow before departing. Not for the first time, Zaleef wondered at the future of the Novices, and for that matter, the school itself. The breakdown in communication with the patrol in Dak'mar portended bad news. If it turned out to be as bad as he expected, it was likely the schooling of the students, both of Lore and the Blade, would be discontinued indefinitely.

As his equipment was already with the men, he quickly finished his last minute tasks. He left several warded letters for the other Masters in the event of trouble. He also made sure his chest of personal items was locked and warded. With one fond (but hopefully not final) look at the office that had been his for over four decades, he quietly left.

The hall was a short walk from his office. Its huge gilded double-doors were thrown wide. Two armored warriors flanked the entry. Both held gleaming halberds with silver pennons that flitted at the caress of a faint breeze.

With a heart heavy, he entered the hall. His shuffling steps echoed through the room, breaking the silence.

Three rows of lightly armored warriors, all graduates of the Blade Academy, stood rigid before a large dais at the far end of the vaulted hall. Another line of students, in robes of various hues, marked those of the Lore academy. All students bore a heavy pack and none were unarmed, even the Lore Students who bore fine staves of dark wood.

Off to the side, looking out of place stood another figure. He wore woodland green leggings and a brown shirt with the sleeves rolled to above the elbow. Tall and lithe, he carried a long bow slung across his back. A quiver of white-fletched arrows hung at his waist beside a slender sword. At his feet rested a small pack.

Zaleef studied the lone figure as he approached. The man was an Elf, one of the 'long-lived' as they were known to many. A usual life span for an Elf was counted in centuries rather than decades and years. His features were delicate, almost feline, dominated by large slanted eyes of emerald. His hair, long and golden, was secured into a single tail by a silver ribbon.

He was a Traveler, gifted with the ability to use magic to transport himself or others over long distances. Zaleef could feel the inner power of the seemingly frail young man; young in that his features were youthful. In fact he was far older than Zaleef, who himself was nearing his eighth decade.

He was also the only Elf to have studied at the academy, learning all he could from the Masters of yore. It wasn't that the Elves were not magically gifted, far from it. Elves with the talent for magic were usually taken by the Sylvan Druids of the Elvin city and given instruction in the traditional and almost rustic magic of their race.

Yet Saratholeus' unique talent had led him to forsake his people and their magic in an effort to discover his true potential. He was destined to be one of the greatest Travelers to ever study and teach at the academy. Though he traveled far and wide using his talent for profit, occasionally he obliged and gave classes when he had the time.

The young Elf smiled as Zaleef approached. It was not often that one found the Elvenkind anything other than gay. They were optimistic as a people, finding pleasure in merely being alive. Zaleef wondered if the Elf knew the importance of their mission, or the possible danger awaiting them. Probably, he mused wryly. Of all of the races of Kil'Tar, the Elves were most knowledgeable in the lands' history. It was likely the Elf knew more about the Demon host than many of the Masters of the Academy.

"Saratholeus. It is good to see you again, my friend." Zaleef managed a smile, though just. His thoughts were more on the mission than cordiality. The Elf did not seem to notice, however, and grasped the old Master's hand warmly.

"Zaleef. It is good to meet with you again, though it would have been more pleasurable under less forbidding circumstances." The Elf's smile faded. Obviously he knew the implications of what had happened.

"Verily, Saratholeus. Still, let us not give up hope yet. It is not unlike some of the younger Students of Lore to miss a message or two."

He did not have to remind himself it was not just a matter of missed reports. The last message he had received from Faradhar requesting backup had been his last. That had been a month ago, and Zaleef had asked to be constantly updated on the Seal's condition. Faradhar was one of the more experienced and reliable students the school had sent on the patrols, so it was not likely that he had forgotten.

"True. It could be an Essence imbalance. It is not uncommon in the south. The vortex of energies it creates can prevent messages from being sent along the proper paths. Hopefully it is so with Faradhar."

The Elf seemed apprehensive, and Zaleef knew why. In times past, message links had been very unreliable. Major work over the last three or four decades had made them fail-safe under most circumstances, the exception being an Elemental Storm, and these storms were very rare. It was not likely that Faradhar's flow could have been tampered with, and if it had, the student should have known, and established another link via a different route. The flows were of the Essence of the earth, the unseen power from which the world was created, and a multitude of these flows criss-crossed the earth like a fisherman's net. It was the basis of the spells by which the Loremasters drew their magic, reshaping it for their purposes.

"There is only one way to find out, Saratholeus. How long will it take us to reach Mount Drac?"

The Elf paused for several seconds to recalculate the distances he had no-doubt already formulated. "Four days with sixty men. At five hundred miles each jump, and with time to rest between, it will put us in the wastelands, some miles to the northwest of the mountain. I will be able to carry us in small jumps after that."

Zaleef knew that to jump blindly into unknown territory was extremely dangerous, even for the most experienced traveler. Therefore, the first such pioneers had erected dozens of obsidian obelisks throughout the realms. Each was marked with unique magical runes, which allowed navigators to chart their paths, like waypoints. One only needed to find the desired obelisk to teleport safely to it. Even so, the strain of jumping with so many would be tiring and dangerous, even for Saratholeus, thus the necessity for shorter jumps.

Still, it was faster than walking.

Zaleef excused himself to address the group. There was little need for speeches now. Everybody in the room knew what the mission required, along with its inherent dangers. None were there who were forced, and all were willing to face whatever dangers lay ahead.

"Form up around us. Remember, nobody is to draw on the Essence while Master Saratholeus casts his spell."

The gathered men and women formed up around the Elf, who bade them draw in as close as they could to make the effective area smaller. Once they were all tightly pressed together, he addressed them all.

"Do not struggle or attempt to cast while we are traveling," he reiterated. "You will feel a moment's vertigo but it will pass quickly. Closing your eyes will make the experience less traumatic."

From around his neck he removed a small silver talisman and grasped it firmly in his hand as he chanted. Zaleef recognized the object as a power enhancer, a somewhat rare artifact created by the earliest Lorewielders, which multiplied one's ability to draw power from the Essence flows. Each person was born with an innate ability that could be enhanced with study and practice. Drawing on too much essence was dangerous in the extreme, but with an enhancer, one could draw more without added strain on the body. Many were the tales of Lorewielders, both Masters and Students, who had killed themselves and others trying to cast spells beyond their level of power. The power enhancers were thus a very valuable asset to those who manipulated the Essence, and came in many different forms, from weapons and armor to jewelry and ornaments.

Zaleef knew this because the academy had a chest of such objects secreted in a guarded vault deep beneath the school. He also wore one himself -- a plain gold ring, the most powerful among the collection that he could find and use effectively. Some were linked to certain talents, like the elements or illusion or nature. He would have liked to know where Saratholeus received his, for obviously it was linked with traveling, and as such very rare.

After several minutes of silence, save the soft clang of someone's armor, or the whisper of fine robes being brushed lightly, the image of the room before Zaleef blinked like a hasty shimmer, from light to dark back to light again. When the instant of darkness dissipated, they were no longer in the hall, but instead in a tree-lined glade.

Awed whispers went up among the group. Zaleef turned slowly, scanning their location. As he expected, a tall obsidian statue stood in the center of the lea. It was in the form of a well-endowed woman, rising atop a square brace of obsidian. He did not recognize the large runes carved in gold upon it.

It looked to be mid afternoon, if not later as the sun sank slowly towards the western horizon. Where it seemed to have taken barely a moment, the jump had actually entailed several hours' travel. He would have to ask Saratholeus about the anomaly, though he guessed it had to do with their number.

He was unsure of their location, but the suddenly gaunt Elf pre-empted his query.

"We are in the Arkanth Mountains of central Ariakus. We will be in the Empire of Zarn tomorrow, and after that, southern Dak'mar. The fourth jump will be made to an almost forgotten Obelisk northwest of Mount Drac."

"Make camp! First watch up, second watch at midnight."

Zaleef's command snapped the men into action. Within fifteen minutes of his order, camp was set.

Zaleef retired to his tent. It seemed even magical travel wearied his aging bones. He nodded to the two guards who stood without, and asked that warm tea be brought. Age and rank had their privileges as well, and for once he was more than happy to take advantage.

As Saratholeus had predicted, they reached Mount Drac late on the fourth day. Their first view was from a distance of fifteen leagues, but as they reoriented after the latest jump, the ominous mountain loomed over them. In the flat, barren wastelands, it appeared mysterious and unique, huge and forbidding with its rough surface and sinister appearance. It looked more like a volcano, tinged with a reddish-brown hue.

Most of the men became silent and withdrawn as they watched the mountain. Saratholeus rested briefly after the small jump. In the wastelands, calculating exact locations was difficult, and often needed a certain landmark, like an old stump or a large rock for guidance. As they waited, one of the Students of Lore, dressed in Orange, approached Zaleef, as he had each of the past four days.

"There is still no contact with Faradhar or the other men, Master. There does not seem to be any wards preventing my probes. As you asked, I have tried to determine if there has been a disruption in the Essence Flows, but I have found nothing to suggest it."

"Thank you, Treil."

Zaleef frowned as the young man departed. Treil was a Mentalist, a person capable of using the powers of the mind for certain tasks. He was particularly good at communicating with people, even over large distances. Thus, it perplexed Zaleef somewhat that he had not been able to contact Faradhar. It also added to the likelihood something had happened to the squad. There was no hint of an Elemental Storm having passed recently, or if there had, it was not easily noticeable in the scorched and bleak land.

He met Saratholeus' gaze. He knew the Elf had heard the message, despite the fact it had been meant for Zaleef only. The senses of the Elves were greater than those of humans, especially their vision and hearing.

The Elf's features seemed wan and pale, though he still wore a crooked smile. He nodded, as if agreeing with Zaleef's thoughts that things were definitely not well.

Zaleef nodded back, vowing silently that he would discover the truth behind Faradhar's mysterious disappearance. In the past few days he had recalled all he could of the Portals they guarded. For some reason, the histories of the Lorewielders were vague on the subject, with most knowledge having been passed down from generation to generation. The Portals were known as Nexus Gates, and had been used before the War of Storms by the Demon hosts to invade Kil'Tar. How they got there was more legend than history. Some said they were created and used by the Gods in the infancy of the Universe. Another myth proffered that they had been created by the early Lorewielders as a means to Travel, not only around Kil'Tar, but also between worlds. Saratholeus would probably have more idea which was the more correct version, or even if the Gates were a feasible method of Travel and if so, why the need for the obsidian obelisks.

"Can you make one more jump?" he asked the weary Elf. He wanted to be inside the Mountain as soon as possible, preferably while it was still day, though it would make little difference once they were inside. The Elf nodded, but took several more minutes of rest. When he was ready, he motioned for them to gather again and cast his spell, his gaze fixed upon the distant mountain.

They blinked into existence less than a mile from the ruddy peak. Up close, they could see its unnatural barren shape. A huge archway opened a hundred feet above the gray ground. Steps were cut in a zigzagging stairway leading to it. The opening looked to be fifty feet in height but half that in width, with a narrow ledge where the stairway alighted.

Without being ordered, two patrols hastily spread out in a wedge formation to scout ahead. Zaleef glanced eastward and estimated that about two hours of daylight remained.

What will it cost to answer the puzzle of Faradhar's disappearance? he mused, his stern gaze fixed upon the mountain.

Chapter 6

The huge archway opened into a stygian ante-chamber, dark and impenetrable to human eyes. Silent and forlorn, it had a pervasive air of decay and age. On the platform, undisturbed, lay a coating of dust and ash. This was both a good sign and a bad sign, though if there had been any strong wind of late, all tracks or signs on the ground could have been eradicated.

Though worn and tired, Saratholeus moved ahead of the group, motioning for them to remain where they were. Zaleef joined him, though he felt just as weary as the Elf, ruing not having stayed back at the Astral City and sending one of the younger Masters.

"Let us see what lurks in the cold, dark depths of the underworld," chanted Saratholeus softly, though whether it was said in jest or not, Zaleef could not tell. He did catch the reference to the domain of the Sable Elves, those who dwelled deep below the land of light, and the hated enemy of surface-dwelling Elves. His icy hands clutched his staff as he ran through the words of several spells in his mind, ready to utter them in an instant.

The passage from the light into the darkness seemed more profound than any of the magical jumps they had done in the past four days. Zaleef blinked as they paused in the darkness, though he could pick up nothing in the veil of darkness around him. Hastily he whispered a minor spell of perception, which turned the darkness to a blurred gray ambience.

At his side, he sensed rather than saw Saratholeus peering around, and knew the Elf needed no such spell for himself, having the innate Elvin trait of Night Vision. As well as being far-sighted in the light, they were able to shift their perceptive vision. This allowed them to view everything in terms of heat, with cold things being dark and gray, and warmer things, like fire and people, in red or orange. Zaleef's spell employed the same method, though it lasted a limited time and would have to be renewed periodically.

The cavern was shaped like a bell cut down the center. The ceiling towered about seventy-five feet at the archway, sloping down the further it pervaded the darkness. Its walls were smooth and plain, yet at intervals, pillars rose from the floor and ceiling, thinning to points at their end. They ran all around the chamber, except at the rear, where large double-doors were set into the wall.

"Looks safe enough," whispered Zaleef, moving off to the left. Set in all of the teeth-like pillars were arched niches. Most were empty, though some contained what appeared to be old lanterns. Zaleef moved to the nearest one, and found it rusted and useless. It was the same with each as he moved around the room.

"Let's bring the men inside and make camp," suggested Saratholeus. "We could all use the rest."

Zaleef nodded. In short order, the men were gathered inside and nervously set up camp. Several of their own lanterns were placed in the niches, bathing the cavern in a dull light that grew brighter as the outside light dimmed. It might have been a trick of the light, but it seemed as if the strange white pillars glowed, as if soaking in the warmth of the lanterns.

"It appears to be palite," mused Saratholeus, lightly running a hand over one of the pillars. "I have never seen so much in one place before. Palite was among the most rare minerals on Kil'Tar, and a thousand times more valuable than common steel. It was a mixture of Adamantium -- a steel and titanium alloy, and Platinum. Only Mithril, fabled metal spoken more of in Dwarven legends, was more rare and valuable.

"It is strange that our records do not tell of its presence," said Zaleef. "It is not something that is usually overlooked. The Mountain is officially owned by the Astral City, purchased from the Dak'mar when we began our vigil over the Nexus Gates. Still, that does not explain why brigands and thieves have not come to partake in the bounty it offers."

Saratholeus seemed equally perplexed. "The Dak'mar are a warlike people with little knowledge of mining. Also, it is over two hundred leagues to the nearest large village or city. A long way to come through harsh terrain, but I agree. The potential wealth would far outweigh any difficulty in access and cartage. There are other means to transport hundreds of pounds of equipment and people, for the right price."

Zaleef smiled, for he knew the Elf was not suggesting taking part in such a scheme. As such a thing would entail theft from the Astral City; it went against his every ideal. Saratholeus had always been aloof, but never a maverick.

"Perhaps they view it as a sacred site, the Dak'mar? It is rumored they have a close affinity with the ancestors of the land, and this may have been a place of great power once."

He mentally made a note to have wards cast on the metal, as it would be a shame to have this historical location defiled.

The large double doors at the far end of the cavern were similarly worth a small fortune. They were single slabs of polished obsidian twenty foot high by ten foot wide. Dark as the night and smooth as silk, they were reinforced with gold and inlaid with jewels and gems of varying hue. There appeared to be no lock, and from each hung a simple ring of gold. Both doors were unmarked, and perfectly inset in the rock foundations.

Mystical and perfect, they were a reminder of the might of an era long past.

"Seems safe enough," confessed Saratholeus.

Zaleef nodded. Although dark and ominous, he did not feel the room held any dangers for him and his men.

"Let's get some food and some rest."

The night passed slowly for the company. Despite the constant glow of the lanterns, an unseen darkness seemed to choke at them, trying to break through the barrier of light and engulf them. It was also deathly silent, especially outside, where one usually expected to hear the whispered conversation of animals that did not exist here in the wastelands. Few slept for the several hours they camped, and those who did battled nightmares, dreaded and elusive on waking.

When Zaleef ordered the breaking of camp the following morning, the mood was one of nervous anticipation. He ordered packs to be lightened with only the essentials for the journey. The path to the inner caverns of the mountain was long and winding, but would not warrant tents and cooking utensils. Weapons were cleaned and sharpened while the students of Lore ran through their array of spells and calming exercises to prepare the mind. When the barren landscape outside began to be sheathed in the pre-dawn grayness, Zaleef ordered the doors to be opened.

Though they appeared unused for some time, the doors swung inward without so much as a protesting squeal of hinges. Seven Blade Students stood arced before the doorway, prepared for the worst. Nothing but absolute darkness waited in the corridor beyond.

Lanterns were thrown open, while the Lore Students illumined the tips of their staves with magical light brighter than the lanterns. Zaleef, standing at the center of the company with Saratholeus, removed a small glass globe from his pack. It was as large as his fist, and contained within a swirling mist. With a stifled command, he tossed it into the air above him. Several murmurs of wonder came from the Bladesmen when it did not fall, but hovered and started to glow, first with a warm glow, but soon grew like a tiny sun blazing in the underground passage. Those who held lanterns extinguished and stored them, preserving oil and freeing hands in favor of weapons.

The arched hallway before them was large, easily twenty feet in height, with curved walls and a domed ceiling. It seemed to slope away before them, drawing deeper into the blackness beyond their light.

Zaleef ordered the company into three columns, Lore Students flanked by Blade Students. He and Saratholeus moved to the fore. He gripped his staff anxiously, while the now solemn Elf had drawn his long sword.

A thin layer of dust swirled about them as they moved down the passage. It passed around them like a haze, mingling with the many lights to form a shimmering mist. Zaleef pressed into it like he was facing a raging storm.

After about half an hour of anxious descent, they came to a new section of passage, leveled out and narrowing. Zaleef conferred with Saratholeus briefly, and they concurred that they had probably covered two miles, and were maybe as much as a furlong beneath the surface.

After about a hundred paces, Zaleef drew the company to a halt, motioning for silence. Before them, on the edge of their light, the passageway opened up into darkness. They had come to the first cavern. Zaleef remembered them from reports. Faradhar had referred to them as 'Conjoining Halls'. There were several such caverns of varying size along the main passageway, where smaller passages joined from different areas of the 'Undercity'.

"Lights out! Darkvision spells activated." Each student of Lore was knowledgeable in the spells necessary for the mission, while each student of the blade possessed a bracelet temporarily empowered with night vision. Zaleef signaled for a scouting party to go forward, and two Lore Students, one in black robes and the other in dark blue, moved towards the Cavern, followed by six Blade Students. Zaleef momentarily wondered if he should have brought along a few other Masters from both schools, but knew there were simply not enough to take them away from the academy, despite the urgency of the mission. As he watched the students' heat patterns merge with the darkness, Zaleef tensed with a mixture of worry and excitement.

Seconds passed, which lengthened to minutes. Finally, the group returned, silent and cautious. They approached the spot where Saratholeus and Zaleef crouched. One stepped forward: a Lore Student whom Zaleef recognized as Hashik, a short, muscular young man who may have served just as well in the Blade Academy.

"It appears as if nothing has passed for many years, Master. There are no tracks, and the dust remains settled." Hashik grimaced, as if perplexed by some puzzle, though he said nothing. Zaleef noticed this and pressed him to speak.

"Its huge, that's for sure, with eleven passages leading from it at almost even intervals. One, the largest, lies directly across from this one. I cannot say for sure, Master, but the chamber gave me a strange feeling. It felt dead, although that is no different from the rest of the passages, but it felt cold and clammy, and more than once my skin crawled. It was like we were being watched, but there was nothing in the cavern." The others nodded, backing up Hashik's claims.

Zaleef bade them return to the line and drew Saratholeus aside. "What are your thoughts, Saratholeus? I have yet to hear them. Of all of us, you probably have the greatest knowledge of what we may be facing."

The Elf frowned, fondling the hilt of his longsword. "We cannot forget the reason the Seals were created. At the very worst, we may once again be facing a resurgence of the Desolate Wars, though this time, there are few Loremasters left. Alternately, Faradhar and his squad may have fallen victim to sickness, or an ambush by brigands after metals, or even a raid by dark elves." This last was said with a contemptuous sneer, and momentarily the Elf's gleaming eyes pulsed with fiery warmth. "Still, this is only the first chamber, and will probably be of no danger, despite Hashik's premonitions."

Zaleef sighed. He was definitely getting too old for this sort of work. "Gray and Blue teams, flanking formation inside hall," he commanded. "Yellow team point position, Brown team last!" He moved with Saratholeus to the front of the formation ahead of the Yellow team. Saratholeus drew his sword from its sheath with a steely hiss.

Zaleef motioned forward, and instantly the Gray and Blue teams ran quietly ahead, weapons drawn. As soon as they disappeared into the dark hall, Zaleef started forward with the rest following warily behind.

It was difficult to tell the hall's dimensions at first glance. The Dark-vision made the dull gray walls appear blurred and indistinct, though the darker sections at intervals were obviously the passageways leading from it.

Slowed to a walk, Zaleef moved towards the center of the hall. He could feel the soft reverberations of their footsteps echoing off the smooth walls. The damp chill Hashik had spoken off clung to him. The hair on the back of his neck rose in nervous anticipation of the danger he expected.

All was quiet as the group came to a halt. His heart pounded like a drum and he breathed a ragged sigh of relief. "Lanterns lit! Make camp and prepare for meal. We rest here for three hours. Gray and Blue teams on patrol; set wards at fifty feet. Get to-"

The shriek of pain and terror pierced the gloom, cutting Zaleef's words in his throat as his blood ran cold. Other cries followed from behind him, amid shouts of anger and panic. It was from the area of the Blue team, back towards the entrance.

Instinctively, Zaleef tossed his Glow-Globe into the air, commanding it to light. Like the sudden unveiling of daybreak, the hall illuminated with eerie orange light. With light came vision, momentarily blinding Zaleef, whose eyes were still searching for heat patterns. Slowly the spots of searing white faded from his eyes and he blinked at the pandemonium reigning around him.

Hybrid creatures, part human part animal, swarmed amongst the ranks of his men. They had black exoskeletons made of a bony material. Their elongated heads had flared inlets for nostrils and two smaller vents on either side for ears, dominated by deep-set eyes of pure white. Gaping maws showed rows of razor-sharp teeth. Arms ended in clawed hands and flat webbed feet were tipped with hooked claws. Like fish in a feeding frenzy, they swarmed amongst the colored robes of the men from the Astral City.

As if caught in a horrible nightmare, Zaleef could feel the action around him with unbearable clarity. He could hear every scream, every cry, and every metallic scrape of steel across bone. At his side, Saratholeus moved, his slender sword arcing down to slice through an arm as a Demon reared. The creature recoiled in shock and pain, its maw thrown wide to emit a piercing shriek. A vicious lunge from the slender Elf ended the Demon's life, impaled through the chest. Saratholeus jerked his sword free, yet as the Demon slipped to the bloodied ground, more dark forms swarmed in around them.

Zaleef broke from his stupor. He had been momentarily stunned by the appearance of these creatures. His voice cracked as he recited a mystical spell of lightning and raised his staff. The tip of the dark stave blazed then burst into a dazzling bolt of intense light. Jagged like an outburst from the stormy heavens, it lashed out like a snake at one of the closest Demons. It struck with a flash of heat and a scintillating shower of sparks. The scorching blast knocked the Demon back several feet through the air, where it rolled limply to a stop, weeping dark blood onto the cold stone floor. It did not rise.

At Zaleef's side, Saratholeus barely noticed the explosion caused by the old man's spell as he took stock of the battle. Magical energies raged all around as Lore Students battled the dark forms, given what protection they could by the Bladesmen, whose weapons were hard pressed to pierce the bony armor of the Demons. His skin tingled with an energy he knew was not excitement but the effects of a protective spell he had cast upon himself. An invisible layer of energy encompassed his slender body, and would help to repel physical attacks against him.

A dark, agile form flitted in the corner of his vision and he spun. He barely avoided a lightning-fast attack from the Demon. Without his protective shield, he would have felt the breath of its passing. The Demon hissed and spun back for another attack, but Saratholeus' sword was quicker as he slashed at the Demon, cutting into its right shoulder at the base of the neck. As sharp as it was, his sword barely penetrated more than a few inches through the exoskeleton, but it was enough to send the beast tumbling away, screaming. Blood spurted from the wound as the slender blade tore free.

Keeping step with the Demon as it reared back, he thrust into its chest. It desperately tried to fend off the attack with a clawed hand, its other arm hanging limply at its side. With a steely hiss, the Adamantium blade pierced bone, followed by the agonized scream made suddenly mute as green ichor sprayed from the beast's maw.

Only his quickness and alertness saved him as another creature fell at him from above. He dived to the side and felt a stinging sensation on his left forearm. The Demon launched itself at him again, before he had time to rise. Instinctively he rolled to the side, knowing that he wouldn't be able to raise his weapon in time. His left shoulder snapped back as it was struck, and he was thankful for the magical protection that kept the powerful claws from his flesh.

Fortunately for Saratholeus, the Demon's claws slipped on the stone floor as it tried to turn, giving him the chance to rise and thrust, catching it in the chest as it lunged back towards him. His blade hissed in steely protest as it pierced the bony shell. The Demon reeled back catching Saratholeus off guard, and his sword was torn from his grasp. He reached desperately for it, but was knocked sideways when a second Demon ploughed into him, carrying him beyond the first Demon and his weapon.

Like a cat, the Demon used its razor-like claws to rend the flesh of his chest and back as they fell, and Saratholeus struggled desperately to raise an arm to fend off a bite. As they struck the ground, its fetid breath assailed him and he heard the snap of jaws near his ear as the Demon was jarred free. The sting of claw wounds made him wince as he rolled to rise.

The Demon turned and launched itself for another attack without seeming to touch the ground. Weaponless but not defenseless, Saratholeus shouted the words of a spell and raised his bloodied hand. It looked for a moment as if he was too slow, but suddenly his fingertips pulsed with light as two bolts of lightning streaked towards the Demon and caught it in mid-leap.

The Demon was propelled back several feet as if an invisible hand had swatted it. Two cauterized holes the size of fists bored through its chest.

He became aware of a cold breeze as he spun in a crouch, ready for further attacks, but the tide of battle left him unopposed for the moment. Using the reprieve, he searched for the familiar pommel of his weapon until he spotted it, protruding from the body of the Demon he ran through, lying several feet away. He darted for it and gripped the cold hilt. It hissed with pleasure as he jerked it free of the corpse.

Surprised to find himself still free of the melee, he was drawn to the soft breeze spreading through the cavern, growing stronger with each passing moment. It carried the hint of magic, vaguely familiar yet for the moment unrecognizable. Then he realized that the combat around him was slowing as one by one Demons collapsed, though not from wounds inflicted from any weapon. Astonished students watched as their opponents dropped lifeless to the stone floor.

As recognition dawned on Saratholeus, he turned to look for Zaleef. The old Master stood untouched amid a pile of Demon bodies. His arms were upraised and his pale face clenched in concentration. Then, as if drained, the old Mage faltered and toppled. In that instant the cold breeze stilled.

No Demon remained standing, though Bladesmen continued to hack at their still forms, as if suspecting a trick.

"Form up! Form up!"

Saratholeus leapt over Demonic corpses and raced to Zaleef's side. Around him, the squad re-formed in a circle. He reached Zaleef's side and crouched. The old Mage's seemingly frail face was deathly pale, and dark rings had formed under his eyes. Saratholeus knew Zaleef had overexerted himself with the draining spell, and was on the brink of death.

Saratholeus did not know the spell but realized that casting it on so many had taxed the old master's energies to their limit.

One of the students came forward, a young woman wearing the Brown robes of a healer. She dropped and studied Zaleef, and her frown only confirmed Saratholeus' fears.

"I can do little for him here, Master Saratholeus. I can give him what aid I can, but even then he will be incapacitated for several days."

"Do what you can," ordered the Elf. He rose and regarded the others around him, taking stock.

More than half their number had been killed, while many carried deep wounds that needed medical attention.

"We must away," he shouted over the agitated clamor of the students.

"What do we do, Master?" pleaded one student, a Mage of the Yellow robes with a wound along his side spreading a slow stain of dark crimson over his robe.

"We must press on, find the source of this evil and destroy it," spoke up a young bull-necked bladesman hefting a bloodied Battle-Axe and sporting more than a few cuts. There was little support for his idea, several even cast him incredulous glares and insults. The youth continued, defiant. "We have traveled too far now to return with so many losses. At least we may be able to determine the magnitude of this threat and the possible course of action for us to take."

Saratholeus was not keen to continue further into the dark depths of this underground city, but there was some truth to the young man's words. It was still possible to salvage something worthwhile from the mission. They knew already that the Nexus Gate must be functioning and Faradhar's patrol were likely dead. He realized all eyes were upon him, awaiting his order.

Curse you Zaleef, what am I to do?

"We go on! But you two," he pointed out two Bladesmen, "will carry Zaleef to safety. Return to the first chamber and re-seal the doors by whatever means possible. There is enough food and provision there to last you for many days, by which time Zaleef should have recovered sufficiently to carry you to safety." The two young men, both of whom looked to be carrying non life-threatening wounds, nodded hesitantly and moved to lift the unconscious Master between them. The healing had restored a little color to his skin, but he still looked very frail.

"Let us be gone," ordered Saratholeus. He took up Zaleef's Glow-Globe and cast it into the air, lighting the chamber again with its intensity.

With a deep breath and a quick prayer, he led them into the large passageway that would take them deeper inside the mountain.

Chapter 7

A foreboding silence clung to the group as they marched cautiously down the passage, away from the dreaded chamber. Saratholeus, who was at the rear, warily glanced back over his shoulder every few seconds. At the fore of the party, the young axe-wielding youth, Darrik, kept them on the move. All eyes were focused anxiously on the shimmering edge of light thrown up by the Glow-Globe, searching for movement from the darkness that would herald a new attack.

Only Saratholeus, whose Elvin hearing was keenest, could hear the clicking of many clawed feet on the rocky ground behind them, still some distance away, and not seeming to be getting closer, as if the pursuing Demons were driving them onward.

Herding them like sheep.

After they had gone perhaps a mile, the passage widened and the walls became smoother. Etched into the stone on either side were a myriad of drawings, carvings and writings. Caked in a layer of dust and grime, the images were difficult to see. Those that were clear portrayed numerous intricate scenarios of war and battle between many unknown races. Two which were always present were huge beings enshrouded in fire, opposed by armor-clad figures of noble bearing. In some loomed the recognizable form of a Dragon, creature of legend and myth.

Saratholeus slowed unconsciously and admired the carvings, for their beauty and delicacy was evident. The artwork was akin to that of his brethren, who were amongst the most gifted artists in the realms. Almost magical in their intricacy, detail and color, the images shed some insight into the history of ages past for the Elf. The battles shown had not taken place on Kil'Tar, at least not the Kil'Tar he or his people knew. There were volcanic landscapes and lakes of lava set beside burning deserts and jagged heights. He wondered at these armored figures, and whether they were once of Kil'Tar.

A raised hand from Darrik brought the company to an anxious halt. Jolted from his thoughts, Saratholeus nearly stumbled over the youth in front of him. Shaking off distant memories of ancient tales, he joined Darrik up front and found they had come upon another conjoining chamber.

Saratholeus motioned for complete silence. Followed by Darrik, he crept forward to peer into the hall though it was not likely that anything in the chamber would have failed to observe their intense light. Still, fear enforced unnecessary caution, and there was no telling what was in that dark room.

The cavern was not totally dark due to several long veins of Palite running along the walls and ceiling. The walls were flat and smooth, and it appeared that the unmined metal was as much a part of the walls as the stone itself. Like the white alloy columns in the first cavern, the precious metal seemed to draw in and accentuate their own light.

The chamber was only half the size of the previous one but still had several passages connecting with it.

Saratholeus motioned the group forward and they entered with caution. He noted the absence of dust on the walls and floor, as if it had been recently cleaned.

As with the last chamber, there was one larger archway leading off in the opposite wall, which seemed to indicate the continuation of the major pathway. Eyes scanned the dark recesses of the other passageways as they crossed the cavern, but this time there was no ambush as they moved into the new passage.

The Gigantor stood in the darkness.

Towering at nearly twenty feet in height, the bulky Demon barely cleared the domed ceiling of the corridor as he waited, silent as death. To those that saw him in light he appeared as a statue with the chiseled muscular features of an athletic humanoid, with a large bulging head and protruding jaw. In one six-clawed hand it grasped a long ebonite lance, while at its waist hung a wickedly curved saber proportionate to its huge bulk.

Silence filled the musty corridor, broken only by an occasional drop of moisture from the ceiling. The Demon waited, neither moving nor breathing -- a living statue.

A soft glow appeared down the length of the corridor, the radiation of a light source still some distance away around the bend. The Demon's eyes, like burnished coal, shifted imperceptibly, not for the light but what it brought.

The glow intensified until its source entered the passage. The Demon could see two Humans assisting a third, making slow progress. They appeared frightened and anxious, and more often than not swept glances over their shoulders.

The middle figure caught the attention of the Demon. It could feel the power of the human, a tangible aura that set its dark blood racing.

The trio came closer. Fifty feet. Forty-five feet. Like the rising sun, the Demon could feel the warmth of the approaching light. Forty feet. Pale light washed over it, but it blended with the stone. It moved only slightly to shift weight onto its front leg. Almost thirty feet, and still it remained unseen.

At thirty feet it sprang into motion, sweeping its arm forward to launch the dark lance in the same instant the left figure caught its silhouette in the outer glow of the light. What was going to be a cry of alarm turned into a gurgle of pain as the lance tore through his chest, exploding in a burst of light as it ripped through him.

The second figure staggered with the weight of the unconscious man and almost fell, but was able to lower his burden to the ground and spring forward with surprising quickness. He stood between the Demon and the prone figure, fear and disbelief evident on his face.

The Demon began to laugh, a booming, mocking laughter that reverberated down the corridor. The overwhelming power of it made the Bladesman's answering attack heroic. With a shout of defiance he leapt at the Demon, sword raised above him to strike.

Casually, the Demon caught the warrior in mid-air by the arms, freezing the sword's descent. Like swatting a fly, it tore the arms from the screaming man's torso and watched him fall to the ground in a fountain of blood. Death was not long in claiming him.

The Demon grinned. Indifferently, it tossed the human's arms aside and almost crooned at the fresh tang of warm blood in the air. Its gaze returned to the slumped third figure.

Taking a step forward, the Demon extended its clawed right hand, as if grasping for something. A tearing of rock down the corridor forewarned the return of his lance from where it had pierced the stony wall, as it returned to the Demon, who caught it with the ringing clang of stone against metal.

Almost sensually, the Demon knelt and lifted the human, exposing the smooth flesh of his neck. The impending rush of pleasure was overpowering as the Demon lowered its maw around the cold flesh and bit down, its razor-sharp teeth puncturing the skin and sinking into warm flesh.

Like a mountain spring, blood pumped from the wound, warm and invigorating as it coursed down the Demon's throat. It drank slowly, drawing in the lifeblood of the human, feeling its force empower him. It felt the human's small heart beat faster to accommodate the loss, but it became too much and fluttered to a stop. Like a small oasis in the desert, so too did the blood dry up, barely sating his thirst. The human was now nothing more than a wrinkled gray husk. With a muffled cry, the Demon tore the throat out of the corpse and stood, with eyes closed as it basked in the afterglow of the kill.

Euphoric energies pulsed within it, making it tremble with a hunger for more. And there was more, waiting for him. It sent out a mental command, and seconds later several Demons appeared down the corridor and silently approached.

"I have a mission for you to fulfill," it told them.

There were four Hunters -- eight-foot tall humanoids with metallic skin and feline heads. With them were two Shadows -- slender assassins wearing cloaks of darkness obscuring their real form. Leading them was a pale-faced Soul Seeker, also in a black cloak. The Soul Seeker had the ability to take the form of almost any figure. At present it was featureless, a blank opal face beneath the deep cowl. "Go forth and bring me news of the Dragon People. I do not feel their presence, but it may be that they are far from here, or concealing their whereabouts. Once you have word, contact me, not your Master. It will be I, Hammagor, who will sit at the right hand of Sett."

The Soul Seeker nodded. With a mental command it ordered the others to follow and led them towards the surface. Their orders were clear, and they would stop at nothing to please both Hammagor and the Dark Lord, Sett.

Hammagor, meanwhile, strode deeper into the caves. There were still others in his new dwelling, ones which he was eager to slay himself, especially the Elf, whose presence angered him to the point of madness.

Saratholeus was dying.

Propped up against the warm corpse of a young Bladesman, his head drooped against his rent chest. His eyes were screwed shut against the pain. His magical reserves were exhausted, preventing him from sending a warning message to the other Masters back in the Astral City. One of his legs was broken from the crushing force of a charging Demon, and blood blanketed his body from a lattice of wounds. His left arm was limp, with his shoulder torn open to reveal bone.

He was not alarmed by his forthcoming demise, just angry for making the stupid mistake of walking into the second ambush. As he had expected, they had been herded through the extensive passages to another huge chamber, much similar to the first. They had entered cautiously, of course, but had no option but to proceed. At the heart of the dark chamber, scores of Demons flooded from the joining passages and fell upon them. This time, there were other Demons, hairless ones with muscular bodies and skeletal faces; others hulked over the rest, huge and muscular with an array of weapons wielded in one or two hands with great skill and ferocity.

His men didn't stand a chance. Overpowered as they were, their numbers dwindled rapidly. Magic streaked around dangerously and recklessly in desperate attacks, while near berserk swordsmen were as much a danger to their companions as to the opposing Demons. Finally, only Saratholeus had remained standing, while the Demons milled around, seeking to overwhelm him with numbers. Eventually they succeeded, and it was only a matter of time before they finished him. For some reason, they remained in a circle around him, waiting for him to die.

He was vaguely aware of something looming over him, and looked up at the towering form of a stone-skinned Demon. He was reminded of the illustrations etched in the passage earlier.

A cold hand, powerful and huge engulfed his neck, lifting him bodily from the ground. His body was struck by paroxysms of agony, and he could feel the oncoming darkness of unconsciousness. He tried to resist, but could not fight the grip that death held him in. As he succumbed to the relieving embrace, his last thoughts were of his Sylvan homeland far, far away.

Chapter 8

Valdieron started awake in a world of darkness and cold. An instant of panic was replaced by a frantic anxiety as he realized he was no longer caught in the dark swirling waters. He looked around, but could perceive nothing in the impenetrable darkness. He knew where he was, or at least he remembered how he got there -- the battle with the Trolls, which had resulted in his fall into the chilled mountain stream.

He could only guess that he was in an underground cave. The air was damp, while he was lying on rocky ground. The powerful crash of the waterfall echoed through the cave. From what he could remember of his descent, there was little chance he would be able to climb back out that way, but the stream must have an outlet, and therefore a possible exit for him.

Pushing to a sitting position, he winced as his shivering body protested. His muscles felt leaden from his fight for survival under the chill torrent. His right hamstring was also bruised and lacerated from being struck by the rock thrown by a Troll, while his left shoulder was feeling more than a little abused -- bruised, cut and caked in a mixture of blood, mud and grit.

He still wore his pack, though his father's bow was gone, probably miles downstream by now. Four arrows remained in his quiver, left over from the battle and the unexpected dunking. Anxiously, he felt over his pack, seeing if anything had been lost, but the straps were still secured. He pried at the straps with cold fingers. Searching for the lantern and his tinderbox, he gasped when his fingers brushed something warm. Tentatively he felt around again, and realized that the warmth was coming from the metal box given to him by his father.

Bemused, he drew it out. He remembered from having touched it previously that it had not been warm then. It had been wrapped in wet clothing for some time, so if anything it should have been cold to the touch.

Intrigued, he removed the chain from around his neck and grasped the slender key. Feeling for the tiny keyhole, he managed after a few attempts and muffled curses, to fit the key into the lock. With a twist, it unlocked.

A thin thread of light sprang free of the open lid, and he gasped with wonder. Looping the chain back around his neck, he grasped the lid and tilted it open a little more.

A warm glow radiated from the opening, almost blinding Valdieron, whose eyes had known absolute darkness for some time. He turned away and blinked to soothe his eyes until they became accustomed to the faint light. Then he turned to look into the box.

The source of the light was a faceted crystal, shaped like a raindrop. It was secured to a thin golden chain with no apparent link, as if interwoven. It rested atop a dark cushion. Folded beside the crystal was a small piece of parchment.

Though stunned by the light-emitting jewel, he picked out the note. Was it meant for him to read, or an explanation of the mysterious pendant? For his father to remember to tell him, it must have been important.

But how?

On it was a note written in a flowing script. Slowly he read;

My Son,
This Dragon's Tear is your birthright, secured for the day when you are ready to accept it. I give it to you, along with my everlasting love. Do not be afraid of its power, and remember that your heart can often make wiser decisions than your mind. This may seem enigmatic now, but some day I hope you will realize its meaning.

With Love eternal,
Your Mother

His Mother? The note was both mysterious and seemingly misdirected if he was the intended reader. Why was this strange jewel his birthright? Was it a family heirloom? How did his parents come to possess it in the first place? Going from the note, it had power, which was obvious by its ability to create light, for which he was grateful given his current predicament. Yet what other power did it have?

With a confused sigh, he rolled onto his back and screwed his eyes shut. Tears flooded down his face as he thought on what had happened to him over the last few days. Now there was this strange jewel and note that seemed to belong to him, but he was just the son of a horse breeder. He was lost in a world of pain and confusion.

Finally, the wellspring of tears dried up and his sobs turned to a dry cough. He had many unanswered questions, but he knew they would remain unanswered if he did not get out of this cave. Then, should he make it that far, he would get to the bottom of the mystery of the glowing gem and the note addressed to 'my son'.

He vowed to take revenge for the death of his father and the possible deaths of the people of Shadowvale -- those of his friends and others whom he had held dear. This he vowed as he gripped the warm jewel in his fist and raised it to his forehead in a solemn gesture he had once read about once.

His first goal was to see to his physical needs. With the glowing jewel hanging from his neck, he saw to his wounded shoulder. It was still very tender and stained a dark purple from bruising. Scabs had formed over the lesions, crusted yet soft from the damp bandages. He was glad for this, as the old bandage peeled away from the wound much easier, and did not tear away the scabs and bleed. With new strips of cloth, he rewrapped the shoulder.

His hamstring was also tender, yet the bruising was not bad. He flexed his leg and found the muscle was tight and ached a little, but at least he was able to stand and walk on it.

Next, he saw to his groaning stomach. His pack was soaked, along with all of the rations, making the bread soggy. Not wanting to waste it, he set the two crumbling loafs onto a flat rock to dry out. Wax coating had saved the blocks of cheese, while the round of ham was folded in an oiled cloth that had repelled most of the water. He sliced off a piece and re-wrapped it. It was heavily salted but delicious nonetheless. He then set his other belongings out before him and took stock of what he had.

He still had his lantern, along with oil and tinder, though the Jewel was more than adequate for the provision of light, so he made sure they were still useable before putting them aside.

His spare clothes were soaked, so he wrung them out and set them to dry also. His fletching kit and extra bowstrings were still there, along with the old frying pan he had thrown in. Lastly, the small pouch of money he opened into his palm, surprised to find two gold, seven silver and nine copper pieces, the extent of his wealth. This pouch he secured in the metal box and returned to the bottom of his pack, not trusting it at his waist, for he may need to return to the water to make good his escape from the cavern.

Sitting back, slowly chewing on the ham and some cheese, he went through his pockets. His front shirt pocket held the pulped mass of the letter Natasha had left for him. How long ago had that been? Two days, maybe three. It felt like years, yet he could still picture her beautiful face, slender and delicate.

In the back pocket of his pants he found a damp silken kerchief, lavender in color and smelling faintly of roses. He knew instantly that it was Natasha's, for he had seen her with it several times, and the scent was definitely hers, yet he did not know how he had come to be with it. He could only assume that she had placed it in his pocket the night they had slept in the barn.

So as to remind him of the importance of his survival, he secured the kerchief to his upper left arm, where every movement brought the faint scent of roses to his nostrils and the image of her face to his mind.

After some time, during which his thoughts wandered, he repacked his belongings and stood, shouldering the weighty pack and his near empty quiver. The Tear rested against his shirtfront, glowing a milky white, which did not penetrate the darkness as well as his lantern, but he might need his oil in the advent of an emergency at a later date.

The section of gravel he had come to rest on was like a small beach, an angled area less than several feet across from the water to the barren rock wall of the chamber. It was shaped like a crescent moon, extending forty feet along the arcing wall.

At the far end of the chamber, he could not find the exit point for the water within the radius of the jewel. It occurred to him that maybe the exit was beneath the level of the water, and if it was, he could not see himself leaving via that route unless it was his only choice.

The crushing waterfall sent out a little spray, causing him to curse the wetness as he approached it. Twenty feet above, the silvery arch of water sprang from what appeared to be a narrow ledge. Its edge extended into the darkness on the other side of the pool, and Valdieron wondered how far the cavern might extend and if there might be another exit from the chamber.

It took him only a short search to find a narrow walkway, less than a foot wide, rising from the waterline several feet from the shore. It extended behind the fall and beyond the limit of his light, but he hoped it would give him access to the ledge.

The pool was shallow at the edge, and only rose to his knees before he reached the walkway. He was surprised to find that the walkway extended beneath the water and ended at a platform of rock. Using this, he stepped up onto the slippery surface and waited several minutes for some of the water to drain from his boots.

The narrow ledge forced him to face the cold rocky wall and edge up the difficult slope. There were scant handholds on the slippery face, so he relied on shuffled sidesteps for safety.

Cold droplets struck his neck and soon soaked his shirt as he edged past the fall. He was glad that there was some power in the fall, for he would not have had much success trying to maneuver the ledge if the water merely fell down the wall face.

Beyond the waterfall, there became a slight ridge pattern to the walkway, almost like small steps, probably for the safety of those who chiseled it, for the narrow pathway was likely man-made. This may have extended all the way along the walkway once, but the constant wear of water over the decades would likely have erased it long ago.

Finally, he was able to grasp the ledge above his head and guide himself along until he could pull himself up onto it. Kneeling, he slowly scanned the landing.

It was crescent shaped, like the little rocky beach on the other side, and was about fifty feet wide as it followed the wall around the chamber. The floor was of smooth flat stone, free from mould and moss. Where the stream entered through the northern wall, the ledge continued around, something he had not noticed from below.

Following the wall, he spotted a dark entry about half way around. It was an archway, twelve feet high and several wide, reinforced with a brown-hued rock finely crafted and set with strange symbols.

Removing his knife from its sheath at his waist, Valdieron edged towards the doorway. Carefully he peered around and glanced into the darkness, but seeing nothing, he crept through.

The jewel lit the darkened entrance to show nothing but a smoothly crafted passageway leading into darkness.

Following the passage, he left the echoing chamber behind. It turned sharply to the right and then left after several hundred feet before snaking to the right again. As he walked, he kept his eyes roaming the darkness in front and behind, fearing danger at every step.

The passage opened into an immense circular chamber, easily three hundred feet in diameter. The light from the jewel, as if reflected and magnified by the smooth walls, allowed him to see most of the room, including archways opposite, left and right.

Pausing, he pondered his options. He had no real idea where he was, though after some thought he surmised the far arch must lead deeper into the mountain. Although on any other occasion he would have welcomed such an opportunity to explore, he was more eager to leave this place and return to the outside world.

He chose the right passage and followed it around in a semi-circular direction before it straightened and then turned right and opened into another huge chamber, this one twice the size of the previous. As before, his light was able to filter through the chamber with a soft ambience, so he could see an exit in the far wall. A stream, which must have come from the waterfall cavern, divided the chamber in two. There was no means for him to cross the twenty-foot gap, and the short drop to the stream did not look inviting, for it disappeared into a fissure in the left wall and continued further into the mountain.

Turning, he retraced his steps to the first chamber where he chose the opposite passage, still not wishing to venture deeper into the mountain.

This passage grew slightly larger as he followed it, while it also felt as if it were rising slightly. This spurred Valdieron on, for he guessed it might have been an access tunnel to the surface. He noticed there was little dust around, making him wonder if the passage had been used recently.

The corridor twisted back and forth before straightening again, still rising slightly. Ahead, another archway appeared, so he approached cautiously, knowing his light was giving him away, but there was no other option.

The chamber beyond was quiet and still. Valdieron paused at

the entry and stared. Beneath him, a short flight of steps led down into the square room. Against the far wall, five hundred feet across, was a raised stage.

Alighting the stairs, he glanced around, noticing an open area cut away in the wall above the entry, like a cave. It seemed immense, and as he crossed the floor and backed up the stairs of the dais, he could see it extended many hundreds of feet back into the darkness.

His legs brushed against something and he spun, dagger at the ready, but it was only what appeared to be an old throne. Its surface was covered with a caking layer of what appeared to be dust, yet it was hard and crusted, like mud. It stood several feet in height, although its details were obscured. Set in the wall behind it was what looked to be a hingeless door of dark stone, arched at its height of twenty feet and inset with etched runes and sigils. Set in the stone above it was a flat disk of silvery material.

Resting across the two armrests of the aged throne was a long, slender object. It, too was caked with crust, yet it was unmistakably sword-like in appearance. Carefully he pried it away from the throne, using his dagger to break through the crust binding it. Grasping it by the encrusted blade, he gently rapped his dagger against the hilt.

The first blow broke off a sizeable portion, revealing a golden surface underneath. Excitedly tapping and chipping away, he slowly freed the pommel from its shell.

It was a golden ball, smaller than fist size yet unmarred and even. It was connected to a wooden grip, smooth and etched with a silver Dragon figure. The guard was a simple golden crossover, tapering inwards.

The blade began to appear as he continued to chip away. First a few inches, a silvery white in color and not burnished by misuse and grime. Indecipherable spidery runes began to appear, running along both edges and on either side almost right up to the tip.

Grasping the sword by the hilt, Valdieron chipped away the last of the crust, and as it fell away he sheathed his dagger and held the sword up before him, and it was like a crystal bell sounding in his mind as clear words rang out from behind him.

"Welcome Valdieron. I have been expecting you!"

Chapter 9

Valdieron spun quickly, bringing the sword up protectively. He gasped as he beheld the figure before him, lowering his new weapon in wonder.

The man was tall and imposing, wearing a simple white robe with a thin gem-encrusted silver circlet upon his brow and twin gold-studded bracers covering his forearms. He appeared youthful, yet there was about him an aura of age and wisdom. White locks marred his long, raven-dark hair, which was held back in a ponytail by a silver ribbon. He had no visible weapons.

His eyes, however, intrigued Valdieron as he was drawn into their crimson depth. Set deep and unblinking, they held Valdieron like a vice, and he shuddered as he tore his gaze away. The man, as if sensing his struggle, merely smiled.

"Who...who are you?" stammered Valdieron warily. "What are you doing here?" He sensed no danger from the man, but after everything he had been through, he was not about to take any chances.

"My name would mean little to you, yet I will tell it. I am Astan-Valar, and I have been awaiting you for some time, Valdieron." He gesticulated slightly as he talked, his hands appearing slender yet strong, and he glanced around occasionally, smiling at nothing.

Valdieron frowned. "How do you know my name?" The man did not seem to hear as he glanced up to the high room set above the entrance. "And what do you mean you have been waiting a long time for me? How long?"

The man turned his gaze back to Valdieron, his features taking on a sad expression, while his eyes seemed to blaze with color.

"Time has little meaning for me, yet the span would run into many lifetimes. As for knowing your name, I cannot explain, other than I know it as I know water is water, or rock is rock."

The man called Astan-Valar took a step towards the dais, slowly and without threat. "Stay, stranger," warned Valdieron, setting himself for action should the need arise.

Astan-Valar glanced up at Valdieron as he mounted the steps, locking gazes with him. "I mean you no harm, Valdieron. Please take a seat, for I have some things to tell you which you must hear, as much as you might wish not to when I am done."

Valdieron began to speak, but an overwhelming desire to do as he was told came over him. The stranger's eyes seemed to grow, encompassing him within their cool embrace. He shrugged it off uneasily. "All right, but I'll be watching you." Cautiously he stepped back to the throne and seated himself upon its edge, resting the sword across his knees. Astan-Valar reached the top of the stairs and took three steps forward before kneeling on the hard floor with barely a whisper of noise.

"Ah, how the times change," he muttered, watching Valdieron seated on the throne. "Has it come so fast?"

Valdieron frowned at his mutterings, wondering just how the madman had survived in these caverns, for by his appearance he must have been here for a time at least. Madman? He searched the figure carefully, wondering if the old man was as senile as he appeared. His appearance was definitely puzzling, for Valdieron had not seen his like before.

Finally, Astan-Valar looked up, and his face was set in a grim visage, as if he had bad tidings to tell.

"This World of Kil'Tar is one of the oldest in the universe. It has a unique history of war and tradition. This story I will impart to you, and you will be one of a chosen few who hold its deepest secrets."

"Why me?" asked Valdieron incredulously, realizing the stranger must be mad. Who but a madman would talk world history to a complete stranger in a cavern beneath a snow-capped mountain? What he was doing here and how he had survived for any length of time was still a mystery. Yet how did he know Valdieron's name?

"Why not you?" Astan-Valar returned with a challenging smile. "Worry not, Valdieron. It will all become obvious to you one day. For now, listen and do not interrupt."

"There were, after the time of the creation of the universe, beings of great power, not unlike the one power, or god, or creator, however you wish to see him. These figures were the

Kay'taari. They had the ability to manipulate the Essence, the lifeblood of the Universe. These beings traversed the Universe as it grew, not seeking dominion or power, but to learn more of this universe and those minor races who were springing into existence.

Kara'Tar was one of the first planets they encountered, a planet so pure and rich in Essence they decided to make it their own, for it was as yet unoccupied by race or creature.

Being numbered in the hundreds, there became several factions amongst these Essence Lords and their Families, each co-existing with the others for the greater benefit of their society. There was one family, however, ambitious and greedy for knowledge, the Ji'Ta'Har family. This faction was made up of non-related members who were innately more powerful than most, hence their thirst for power and knowledge was greater. This thirst was enhanced with the study of arcane and dangerous magic. Their plans for rulership and power were not discovered for many centuries, until it was too late, and war resulted.

In a final, desperate effort, Silmarel, greatest of the Essence Lords, unleashed a fiery retribution upon Kara'Tar, slaying many of her kind and those of the outcast Ji'Ta'Har. She and her family fled to the planet Kil'Tar, and those left of the Ji'Ta'Har fled to the voids.

As the time passed, Silmarel and her people came to notice an evil growing in the universe. First there were reports of strange creatures, as yet unseen in the worlds they had traveled. Then there came meetings and battles with these Demons. It was found through study that these creatures were born of the negative energy of the Universe, and though bound to the voids, the decline of the Essence throughout the universe saw the breaking of their barriers, and thus some were able to slip through the Astral Portals that Vighor and his people linked to Kil'Tar.

Silmarel knew her time to strike was near, for should Vighor and his people continue on their hazardous path, they would doom the Universe to damned eternity with the Unlife. Knowing also that their numbers were too few, they enlisted the aid of the Dragons, magical and powerful creatures whose very existence was the anti-thesis of the Demons."
Valdieron shifted excitedly on his throne. Astan-Valar's

enchanting and emotive voice had drawn him into the story, so much so that he could picture the events taking place as he listened.

"The Dragons were willing to assist, for they knew the danger of the Unlife. Bloody and mighty was the battle; the Dragons and their new allies against the Ji'Ta'Har dynasty and the Unlife. Thus was it remembered as the BloodKin war.

The Dragon People prevailed, slaying the Ji'Ta'Har and driving the Unlife back to the voids. Then they combined their diminished powers to create Seals with which to lock these Demons in their Voids. Realizing the error of their past, they destroyed most of their works and those of Vighor's people, knowing the dangers inherent in their powers."

Astan-Valar paused, and Valdieron found himself drawing in a breath as he shook his head, brushing away the trance-like ambience that surrounded him. He was engrossed by the old man's story, as unreal as it seemed.

"Those Portals I spoke of, there is one behind you."

Turning warily, Valdieron glanced at the dark surface of the doorway he had noticed earlier but forgotten.

"But I stray. There is still much to tell. Let me proceed."

Valdieron sat back on the throne, waiting to see what else the strange old man could come up with.

"With the creation of the Seals to bar the Portals, the Dragon People fled Kil'Tar, returning to roam amongst the heavens. Throughout the Universe, new worlds were springing up while others, crushed by the War between the two powers, faded away and were lost. Thus ended the First Era.

Races sprang to existence on Kil'Tar: the Elves, beautiful and long-lived, linked closely to nature; the Dwarves, rugged and stocky with the desire to build and create; Humans, with desires for wealth and power to offset their short life spans. Trolls there were also, creations mutated by the remnants of the Unlife, powerful yet bestial, and also the Barbarians, cousins to the Humans yet larger, reclusive and bound by their customs and honor.

At first, these races knew little of each other, for they were diverse and uncivilized. After many eons, however, the Loremasters appeared. They were sent by the Dragon People, come to warn the Races of the existence of the Unlife and of its dangers."

Valdieron's eyes widened. He had read about Loremasters, practitioners of magic. Astan-Valar, however, sighed softly and Valdieron thought he heard him whisper, "Our greatest mistake."

"The Loremasters, however true their intent, ended up settling and forming their own order, so those of the other races could come and learn the Lore. The Dwarves learned to manipulate the Earth and its Ores, while the Elves, more graceful and aesthetic, discovered paths which allowed them to more easily interact with nature. The Barbarians and Trolls shunned the arcane and mysterious practice, while the Humans were the most willing to learn.

It was during this Era that the Unlife returned, due to the enormous amount of magic being drawn upon. Their return was discovered, and the Loremasters set about thwarting them, realizing their error. War raged for many decades, bloody and ever shifting from one side to another. Finally, the Demons were returned to the Voids and the Seals were restored. Thus ended the second Era.

The Third Era is the one in which we live. Up until now, the year Five One One Eight, has seen the rebuilding of the Academy of the Loremasters, though they have more strict entry requirements as well as bans on many forms of Art. They have also kept a constant guard over the Seals."

Astan-Valar paused again, and his eyes grew hard as they stared deeply into Valdieron's. "Know, Valdieron, that the third return of the Unlife is near at hand, for the Loremasters had not their Master's powers and their Seals are breaking. The Demonic hosts of the Voids are returning!"

A long silence ensued while Valdieron stared at the stranger. Finally, Astan-Valar rose and moved backwards from the stage. Valdieron rose also.

"Heed my words, Valdieron. You have been chosen to bear the weight of these admissions, and will be called upon to act upon our needs. Be ready when the time comes. You have with you the Dragon's Tear. It can give you aid when you least expect it, even while asleep. The Blade you bear is of more importance than you yet realize. Guard them both with the utmost care."

He smiled ruefully when he reached the base of the stairs. "You have many questions, many of which I cannot answer, Valdieron. Just remember that all will be revealed in time. I will speak with you again. Farewell, Valdieron!"

With a shout, Valdieron dashed forward. "Wait!" Instead of turning and fleeing, however, Astan-Valar became enshrouded in a glowing aura, which grew in intensity until Valdieron could no longer bear to watch. Shielding his eyes, he could feel the heat of its radiation, building to a near inferno before ceasing abruptly. He glanced back, but Astan-Valar was gone.

He was alone again.

His first thought was to run after the old man. It had to have been some trick, to make him look away while he made good his escape. Whatever he had done, it had worked and worked well, for Valdieron hadn't seen or heard him depart.

Returning to the stage, Valdieron approached the strange doorway Astan-Valar had called a 'Portal to the Voids'. He caressed its cold ebony surface. The contact created sparks across his fingertips. He pulled back in surprise then tried again with the same result. He studied the strange Seal, which was crafted in the image of a dragon with its wings spread as if preparing for flight.

Returning to the throne, he seated himself and contemplated the strange meeting. As unusual as his past few days had been, he realized Astan-Valar's story was not as unbelievable as it seemed. If somebody had told him that Trolls existed more than a week ago, he would have thought they had been too long at the ale barrel.

As he sat, he ran a hand over his new sword. It in itself was an enigma. The old man had said it was important, probably worth a lot as well, by the look of it. Somehow its blade remained untarnished, despite the fact he had only just freed it from what looked to be several centuries of dust and grime. It was also surprisingly sharp, drawing a line of blood on his fingertip.

Stifling a yawn, he rose. He was tired and hungry again, and wondered if it would be a safe place to rest, with the mad old storyteller Astan-Valar running around. The old man had not tried to harm him, but there was no telling what he might do if he found Valdieron asleep. He had been holding a sword, after all, and the old man had not been armed, but he may have had weapons nearby.

Eyeing the elevated room above the entryway once more, he wished he had some way of getting up there. He had no rope, however, and the walls were silky smooth, so there was no way of climbing. Removing his pack, he rested it against the front of the throne and lay down with his back against it. His newfound sword he placed at his side, his hand not leaving its smooth hilt. The light of the jewel still posed a problem, and he wondered if he could make a little pouch for it. For now he tucked it beneath his shirt so it rested against his chest. It was warm and did not emit much light, so he leant back to relax. Before long, his head lolled to the side and he was asleep.

A milky white globe surrounded him. The fog-like shroud was dense yet had no moisture to it, for he was sweating more than a little.

There was no noise but for his breathing, yet he sensed something approaching in the gloom. He did not know how he felt this, but he turned to find a spectral figure floating silently towards him. Not floating, he noticed, but his dark voluminous cloak billowed around him as he walked, creating the illusion. Valdieron only guessed he was male, as the dark gray cloak masked his every feature besides his height, which was impressive, easily half a head taller than Valdieron.

The figure stopped three paces away from Valdieron.

"Welcome, Valdieron!"

Valdieron drew back defensively, reaching for the dagger at his belt, only to find that it was not there: neither his weapon nor his belt. He was also wearing white trousers and shirt, loose and light and secured with a thin cord. His feet were bare.

"Who are you? Where in the abyss am I? How do you know my name?"

The questions tumbled out as he struggled to comprehend what was happening. He had to be dreaming; yet it felt so realistic, down to the feeling of the fog's caress on his skin.

"I know all who enter my domain, Valdieron, for none but of my choosing can enter here." The figure's voice was soft yet powerful, almost guarded, and he paused slightly. "As to where here is and who I am, there lies an explanation yet beyond your grasp or understanding. Suffice to say that here I am teacher of the Ways, and you are a student."

"The Ways? The only way I want to know is the way out of this stupid dream!"

If the figure was in any way perturbed by Valdieron's comment, he did not show it. "The Ways are the cornerstones of life. Discipline! Knowledge! Honor! Empathy! Awareness! These are the Ways, and only through understanding and devoting one's time and commitment to them can greatness be attained."

"Greatness? Yeah, sure." He chuckled softly and turned to walk away. "Get away so I can have a decent dream." As he had many times before, especially in the months after the death of his brother when nightmares had been common, he began to will himself to wake.

His eyes blinked open sleepily and he was back in the cavern, resting against the throne. It was dark around him, yet not so much that he could not make out a small area around him, illuminated by the faint light escaping from beneath his tunic. Removing the pendant, he shielded his eyes quickly from its brilliance, marveling at its heated red depth. It was warmer to the touch than before.

Vaguely he recalled some of Astan-Valar's last words regarding the Dragon's Tear. *"It can give you aid when you least expect it, even while asleep"*. Maybe the pendant was responsible for the memorable dream, for never had he had one of such clarity. Shrugging sleepily, he tucked the pendant back under his tunic and nestled back to sleep, thinking of home and memories once bitter, but now bearable.

The fog surrounded him like a prison cell and he groaned with despair. What were the chances of having the same dream again? He could remember having some dreams two or three times as a child, but those were usually of more memorable events, unlike this one. He was almost willing himself awake again when the figure appeared from out of the fog.

"You have returned, Valdieron. What is your desire?"

"My desire? What am I doing back here?"

"You are here to learn, Valdieron. That is the power of the Dragon's Tear."

At mention of this, Valdieron ceased his curses and glared at the figure. "What do you know of the Tear?" How did this figure know of the pendant that had belonged to his mother, and was now out of sight beneath his shirt, warm against his chest? Strange, that he would still have it, when again his weapons were gone and he was dressed in the white trousers and shirt. He lifted his hand and pressed it against his chest, feeling the warmth of the pendant against his skin. So real! With a sense of foreboding, he began to realize that this was no dream he was caught up in. By some magic, he was transported here in his sleep, but where here was he had no idea.

"The Tear is your birthright, Valdieron, given to you so that you may discover your heritage. The learning begins here, in Kel'Valor, the first steps, but definitely not the last. Here you will learn the Ways of the Kay'taari."

"There you go again about these Ways. What use are these Ways when I will forget them upon waking from this sleep, which I am about to do to dream of Nat or revenge on Trolls." He spoke this last quietly, but with more venom than he had intended. His vow to avenge his father still played heavily upon his mind.

"A dream this is not, Valdieron, and if it is revenge you are after, do not lament the past. What has occurred is now etched in the histories of this world, and nothing you do can change that. Revenge can easily consume you quicker than a conflagration, and with far more pain."

"Yeah, well I am already in pain, stranger, what's the difference. I shall have my revenge!" His voice was lowered to scarcely a whisper through clenched teeth.

The figure was silent for several moments, and Valdieron thought maybe the conversation was at an end. He snickered and turned away, only to hear a soft exhalation of breath from the figure, like a sigh of regret.

"That is not as it should be, Valdieron. In doing so, you dishonor not only yourself but your father, and all he has given you. What good would it do to fall to a Troll's sword or victim of a trap? For all eternity your soul will cry out in anguish at never fulfilling your desires. Is that what you want?"

Valdieron faltered. His head was lowered and his eyes were clenched shut as he listened to the figure's words. This was no dream: maybe his worst nightmare come to life, but no dream, of that he was sure. Desperately he wanted to repay the Trolls for their attack, yet the figure's words had reminded him of something his father used to say, something about water under the bridge, and he knew it applied to his current predicament. Still, he was finding it hard to come to terms with what was happening to him. In only a handful of days his life had been torn apart, first with the death of his father and his deadly flight into the mountains. Now, in this mysterious cavern complex, he was meeting with strange figures who told mystic stories, and 'dreaming' of being in some place of learning that to the best of his knowledge was no dream at all. At least in all of it he could now say that magic did indeed exist, and strange creatures did walk the lands, if that was any consolation.

"I have given my word that those responsible for my father's death will pay, and I intend to carry out my oath. Therefore, I will be your student. Teach me the Ways and I shall learn as best I can."

The figure nodded slowly. "That is all anybody ever expects, as long as it is you who is your harshest critic, Valdieron. Come with me. We have a lot to do."

Turning noiselessly, the figure retreated into the fog, making Valdieron scamper after him. As hesitant as he was, he stayed as close as he could. The ground beneath them felt hard, like stone, but any noise his footfalls might have made was strangely muffled. The fog seemed to cling to him, constricting his movements, forcing him to strain slightly against its bond.

They walked for some time, seemingly in a straight line with no indication of progress as Valdieron matched strides with the strange figure before him. "Where are we headed, Master?" He adopted the honorific more because he knew not the figure's name or identity.

"To yonder halls, named the Halls of Combat. There you will learn the Way of the Warrior." The figure nodded ahead into the fog, though Valdieron could see nothing.

"What is this shroud which surrounds us? I can barely see more than a foot in front of me."

The Master slowed, as if expecting the question. "It is no more than the limit of your vision, Valdieron. You possess the innate ability to see beyond this fog, but it will not come without practice and a belief in your ability."

They walked on for a little more before the figure halted once again. This time, Valdieron could barely make out a looming wall before him, carved with bas-relief figures and surmounted by statues of figures without facial feature. A large arch was set in its center, lined with torches emitting a ghostly radiance.

"We are here." The Master turned to face Valdieron, his arms crossed at the chest. "From here on, you will watch, listen and learn. Question me at will. Ready?"

Valdieron nodded, and the figure took a sweeping step forward with his right leg, which ended with his foot a shoulder width from his left foot. He shifted his weight slightly to his right leg and bent his knee, turning his toes inwards. He did not turn to Valdieron as he spoke. "A warrior's biggest concern is balance. Without balance, there is no coordination. Learn the stances, make them flow from one to the other as you must in combat."

He repeated the stance again, this time with the left foot forward, showing the transition from foot to foot, sliding gracefully forward. He repeated them several times, turning in the gloom and returning to Valdieron. Valdieron watched for a time before trying it himself, matching himself with the Master as he moved forward into the fog. They turned and performed several more lines with the Master giving him instruction when necessary to correct form or posture before they moved to another stance. Valdieron found himself transfixed by the lesson, amazed at his desire to learn what the Master was teaching.

Backwards and forwards they went for what seemed like hours, yet not once did Valdieron feel tired or hungry. His concentration was challenged as he performed line after line of forms, blending one stance with another and then reversing them. It was only when the Master ceased his movements that Valdieron knew the lesson was at an end.

"The time is upon you to leave, Valdieron. Farewell. I will be expecting you soon."

With that, he turned and strode towards the archway to the Hall. Light engulfed him, leaving only a silhouette that faded like one of the smoke rings his father would blow beside the fire at night. Overcome by the sudden emotion of the memory, Valdieron willed himself to wake once more as darkness rushed to engulf him.

Chapter 10

Valdieron woke once more to the claustrophobic darkness of the cave. He stretched against the hard floor, groaning at his many aches and pains. For all his reservations, there was no possibility what had happened to him in his sleep had been a dream.

Pulling the Tear from beneath his shirt, he averted his eyes as its radiance encompassed the room. For some reason, the light comforted him.

His growling stomach reminded him of its emptiness. Famished, he devoured half his meager rations then washed it down with a little water. He took a quick re-stock of himself then rose, more refreshed than he expected, but still feeling more than a little abused.

With the Tear resting against his shirtfront and his newfound sword in hand, he exited the chamber.

He made good time as he found his way back to the first large chamber. He was not as intimidated by the oppressive darkness beyond his light nor the weight of the immense rock above and around him. He chose the passage to the left of the one he had just exited.

This new passage sloped slightly away as he walked cautiously forward. He constantly checked behind and above for unseen and unheard dangers. It turned gently to the right. A broadening of the light's radius before him indicated the tunnel was either widening or entering another chamber. It proved to be the latter, though to a smaller scale than the others.

Wide panels of bas-relief carvings were set into the wall at waist level, seemingly of worn brass or copper. In each of the scenes, there was at least one figure, some garbed in chain mail or plate armor, others like the robed Astan-Valar. The memory of the mysterious figure made him clasp his sword tighter and glance around. He wondered who had carved them, not the Elves or Dwarves, for it was unlikely they would show homage to human-like people in such a symbolic way. Maybe it was the Loremasters or Essence Lords that Astan-Valar had spoken of, though he still doubted the authenticity of the man's crazy story.

Not wanting to waste time or dwell too deeply on that which he didn't understand, he pressed onwards, crossing to the exit. The dark passage swept away, this time to the left. Some distance further on it turned back to the right, and after a while he realized he had traversed a semi-circle since leaving the inscribed chamber.

He was beginning to wonder if maybe the passageway was a loop leading back to the first main chamber when it forked before him. He listened for several moments and tried to picture in his mind the layout of the caves. The passage to the right was silent and still, while the left passage carried the distant sound of running water.

He turned down the left passage, which snaked along for a few hundred paces. He halted to weigh up his situation and rest, sating his thirst and hunger with bread and water. He guessed that maybe two hours had passed since he awoke, and over a mile of passage lay behind him.

He set off again, and the sound of flowing water drew closer. The passage widened and its right edge dropped away to where the steadily flowing water ran from a rusted metal grate in the wall. Following it for some distance, he found it disappeared through a similar grate while the passage swept around to the left. Squatting, he refilled his water bottle from the chill waters and drank some more.

The path of the passage and the stream diverged. He desperately wanted to keep following the stream, knowing at some point that it had to escape the cave system. He followed the passage, hoping it would meet back with the stream further on. He came across an intersection, though down the passage to the right he heard the distant rippling of the stream and followed it.

The passage twisted again before widening into another chamber, this one by far the biggest he had encountered so far. His light, as if challenged by the darkness, seemed to pulse brighter, yet even it could not catch the distant walls. The ceiling rose over a hundred feet above.

He made his way hesitantly into the cavern. It was like a vast amphitheatre, with ledges dropping away every few feet to a new tier. He counted fifty such ledges as he hopped down them onto a flat floor. Across the way he could just see the edge of the tiers beginning to rise on the other side, about a hundred paces away.

An exhaustive climb up the other side revealed the stream running along the upper tier. It created a gap between the seating and a raised dais, this one set with a semi-circular staircase leading up to its elevated platform. Four marble balusters were set around the foremost edge, several feet in height and topped by crystalline globes, dark and lifeless, which may once have been lighting devices. Atop the platform, a row of marble-lined apses were set in the semi-circular wall, flanked by twin globes of smaller design than the others, held in upturned talons emerging from the marble.

Inside each of the five apses were circular blocks on the floor and ceiling, inscribed with silver runes and symbols, though each was different.

Three marble bridges spanned the narrow stream, lined with balustrades. The drop was not great, nor was the span wide, making it appear that the structures were more for show. A long stride would suffice to traverse from one side to the other.

The stream disappeared into a wall, but instead of a grotto, the water flow had long since eroded the rock forming a narrow walkway to either side of the waterway. It was barely high enough to crouch in. What drew him was the faint touch of a cool breeze, fused with the glorious aroma of fresh air, driving away all curiosity at the wondrous chamber. He had to wrap his sword in his spare shirt and strap it to his back to free his hands as he sidled into the opening.

The path continued for some distance, but thankfully did not grow narrower. His hopes of freedom were rising along with the strength of the cold breeze.

After an agonizingly long time, he came to the end of the path and gave a despairing groan, as his fear became reality: the passage ended.

A closer inspection revealed the wall was rough stone interlaced and held together by foliage, with narrow gaps where slender beams of light filtered through. The stream disappeared into the base of the wall, which appeared more solid. With renewed hope he pressed against the wall of debris and felt it shift a little. He drew his knife and hit the rough stone with the hilt, pulling away decayed vines reinforcing the mud and stone. A shaft of light blinded him as he reefed aside a grasping vine but he had never seen such a welcome sight as the snow-capped land beyond. Using his knife to pry at the more stubborn areas, he soon cleared a fissure as wide as his fist. Once more he glanced out, this time more carefully as he remembered the threat of the Trolls. Gloomy clouds marred the sky and he guessed it was late afternoon.

Soon he was able to squeeze through the narrow opening. Before him lay the semi-circular valley at the southern base of the mountain he had skirted during his flight from the Trolls. It felt like it had happened an eternity ago, but was no more than a few days. The very thought of the Trolls was enough to make him hesitate and glance around. Although he doubted the danger had fully passed, the many hours under the oppressive rock had him yearning for open spaces, though he stayed with his back to the mountain.

Like waking from a nightmare he took in his surroundings with relief. The smell of the trees, crisp and fresh; The cold caress of the gentle southerly breeze, carrying with it the touch of snow, which might come before the night's end; The open sky, like a mirage in the desert, surreal in its beauty. He couldn't remember feeling so relieved to be outside.

Time was inconsequential as he rested there, his eyes open to drive away all thought of the clinging darkness of the caverns. A drop of moisture, as gentle as a feather on water, broke him from his trance, and he knew the weather was turning foul. He considered returning to the protective shelter of the cave, but decided to chance his luck with the Trolls and weather. He knew the cave was there if he needed it.

He was glad the snow wasn't deep as he crested the eastern rise of the small valley. Nearby trees showed the remnants of a recent heavy downfall. He scanned the horizon in search of smoke, which would mark the smoldering village, but he could see nothing against the gray cloud.

His number one priority was to find shelter. Being unfamiliar with the surroundings, he knew of only one reasonably safe position besides the caves. The rocky outcrop where he had fought the Trolls just days earlier was out of sight and difficult to approach without detection, and was accessible from only one direction.

He turned to the north and followed much the same route he

had when fleeing the Trolls. It was almost two miles to the spot. It had seemed much shorter at the time of his flight.

The location appeared more serene to him in the light of day. However the still forms of two dead Trolls lying in a heap at the base of the rocky incline broke the tranquility. They were bloodied and mutilated, most likely from scavengers who were drawn to the freshly killed meat like moths to a flame.

It was Valdieron's first lingering look at one of the creatures up close, albeit not too close as they were beginning to grow a little stale. While marveling at the close resemblance they bore to humans, he noted their obvious differences. Their faces were brutish and pronounced, with prominent jaws and foreheads with wide noses, almost snouts. Their bodies were muscular, legs stout and arms longer in comparison to humans.

He found one of his misfired arrows embedded in the packed snow thirty feet from the slope. He gathered it up and wiped it clean before adding it to his depleted quiver, making the total five. His next surprise came when he mounted the incline. Lying near the far edge of the ovular clearing was his father's bow. He had presumed it lost when he plunged into the icy water of the stream. Picking it up, he checked it for any signs of damage. The string would need replacing after being subject to the elements, but it was otherwise undamaged.

He did not want to risk a fire, though he did gather enough wood and dried leafage to prepared a small fireplace in a ring of rocks in case any more Trolls showed up. He also gathered several yard-long sticks and bound the ends with dry bark held with vine to use as brands if needed.

It was getting dark by the time he had everything to his liking. Several spears crafted with his knife were set against the rock wall, along with his bow and quiver. He sat beside his pack, slowly chewing on pieces of dried ham from his almost depleted rations, his sword resting across his knees.

The rain threatened as the sky darkened further as he rose uncomfortably. Grasping his sword, he slowly worked through the movements he had learned the previous night. The lessons had to have been real; else all but the most memorable parts would have quickly been erased from his waking consciousness.

He couldn't deny the enjoyment he felt while he worked through the movements. Many times he had dreamed of being a warrior, play-acting scenes of derring-do with Kyle or on his own. The forms offered him an escape from bitter memories as he focused on the movements, not just performing them for the sake of practice, but breaking down each movement in terms of weight distributions, flexion, facing directions and opposites. He also grouped together the stances that naturally blended with each other, both offensively, defensively, and a mixture of both.

The sun sank behind the horizon, replaced by the pale twin moons. Even when it became quite late and difficult to see, he continued, though somewhat hesitantly, careful not to take another plunge into the icy stream.

When he was nearly exhausted he halted, feeling his way back to the wall to rest. Above, only a vague outline of thunderous clouds was visible, blocking Santari's full brilliance and Qantari's waxing radiance. There was still no rain, yet its presence was tangible in the chill air. Rolling up in his cloak, he lay for a while in silence, alone with his thoughts.

The first drops of moisture hit him as he was half dozing. He was sleepily thankful for the rain, hoping it would keep the Trolls indoors, not in the least bit caring that by morning he would probably be soaked, or worse, snowed under. He drifted off to sleep, conscious of the darkness around him taking on a foggy atmosphere, and he knew in an instant where he was.

* * *

Faint movement came from within the dark confine of the cave. Its entrance, a worn vertical gash in the cliff face, was almost unnoticeable in the afternoon gloom, but Valdieron had been watching the cave for more than a day now, so he knew where to look.

He lay horizontally on a large tree branch overhanging the cave entrance, less than thirty feet away. The lower branches and leafage of the rounded Holm concealed his position.

He stretched to ease his cramped muscles. He took a little extra time to stretch his right leg, the gash created by the rock's impact almost healed over, yet the bruising and soreness were gone. His left shoulder was still a little tender and stiff, but it too was healing fast.

He had found the cave late the previous afternoon. His

search for the Trolls had followed the stream north towards the more rocky terrain of higher country where he guessed they dwelled in their caves and burrows out of the sun. His decision had proven fortuitous, for a chance glimpse of a lone Troll late in the day had allowed him to follow it undetected, which led him straight to where he was now. In his rage he had nearly attacked the Troll on sight. He checked himself with the grim reality that this Troll would die eventually, along with any others it may lead him to.

This thought stuck with him now as he sat his silent vigil, cursing softly once as his stomach rumbled. He took out a block of cheese and the remainder of his bread, regretting not having taken the time to hunt for more tasty fare that morning.

It was an hour after sunset, with fading pink clouds lying over the jagged western horizon. More movement drew his attention back to the cave's opening. He made out four figures, obviously Trolls by their size, gathered outside the cave waiting for the deeper darkness of twilight before moving noisily off to the east.

Pondering this small group, Valdieron slipped down from his perch as silently as possible and set off after them, using the sound of their movement to guide him in the gloom. With an arrow nocked in his bow, he used trees and foliage to mask his movements as he moved parallel with them.

They walked for some time, thankfully not too fast so Valdieron didn't have to scamper to keep up. Still, the darkness hampered him and he cursed silently every now and then when his footfalls broke the silence. The Trolls seemed to be more determined to reach their destination.

After traveling for what Valdieron guessed to be two or three miles, the Trolls slowed, their movements more cautious and silent. They made not a sound between themselves other than loud sniffing and an occasional guttural grunt. Each carried a stout cudgel as thick as a man's leg, and each wore what appeared to be vests of thick hide.

A faint glow from up ahead caught Valdieron's attention and he slowed, skirting away from the Trolls as he scanned the area. The glow was coming from a large copse of trees, flickering with what he guessed to be firelight.

The Trolls had slowed to barely a crawl, creeping closer to the light with remarkable stealth and intelligence, for they approached from downwind. They were obviously scouts, sent to investigate a trespassing into the area.

A large clearing opened up as Valdieron edged closer. A rough uprising of snow-topped rock sprang from the center, several feet in height and twice as many across. Visible beneath the dark boles of small trees were several figures, camped around the rock. Three large tents and several smaller ones were erected off to the left. A long line of horses was tethered to a rail opposite the tents. There were easily forty horses, outnumbering the men at least two to one. From where he crouched behind an old stump, Valdieron could not see any sentries. As a result of the thick canopy above, the ground supported only a sparse scattering of snow.

Movement brought his attention back to the Trolls, and he found they were retreating away from the light. Once they were far enough from the faint glow, they rose and began to retrace their steps, probably back to the lair.

Valdieron hesitated. Were the Trolls returning to report the presence of the men? It was likely, as the presence of few men and great number of horses presented the Trolls with a rare opportunity to feast.

Valdieron considered following the Trolls to discover their plan, but decided against it. The men at the camp appeared to be armed and could probably handle themselves. He thought about warning the men, though something about them held him back. Armed men so far up in the mountains was very odd. He wondered if they were poachers, which would account for so many horses. He decided to sit back and see what eventuated, hoping the men would give a good account for themselves. If however, he saw the men might be something other than poachers, he could still alert them later.

He shifted to make himself more comfortable when he was grabbed him from behind and a gloved hand was pressed against his mouth. He struggled as best he could; yet the person was strong and knew how to keep him at bay. Finally Valdieron ceased his attempts to break free.

"Drop the bow," came a whispered command, and when Valdieron hesitated the hand holding his mouth tightened, twisting his head painfully. He relinquished the hold on his weapon, albeit slowly.

"Now, what have we here?" The question was rhetorical,

whispered in a calculating tone. "A boy? No, a young man by his look. A spy? I think not. Yet he has weapons. Bow, strong yet not particularly well crafted. Knife, old and worn, but not on men's hides, I'll wager. And a sword? Gold pommel, archaic design, looks authentic... Who are you boy? Where are you from?"

Valdieron's mind raced as the grip on his mouth was relinquished slightly. He could tell by the man's attitude that he should not speak in more than a whisper.

"Valdieron, Sir. I am from the village of Shadowvale, not far from here to the south." He saw no point in lying to the man, as it would serve no purpose later if he were made to repeat it.

"A village, you say. And how came you upon that sword you wear? That is no farmer's weapon, though your bow may be."

He hesitated, and something pressed against his back, digging in enough to make a point. "I chanced upon it in a cave not far from here, Sir. That is truth, I swear it."

"Hmmm. Look at me, boy!" Valdieron was spun sharply, finding himself level with the man, who stooped slightly to stare at him. He was lean and angular, wearing dark leathers for concealment and his face was marred with a dark smear of dirt or mud. He appeared youthful yet stern, with unblinking dark eyes that held Valdieron in their depths.

"I believe you are what you say you are. Take up your bow and leave. Return to your village. This is not a good time or place for you to be here, understand!" Valdieron nodded grimly, wondering at the man's actions. Did he know of the imminent danger of the Trolls, or was he referring to something Valdieron did not know about?

"But, Sir -"

"Not now, Kid. Look, it's-. Damn!" The man cursed as he cocked an ear, as if hearing something which Valdieron failed to catch. Suddenly, from out of the darkness, another figure appeared, like a specter, silent and invisible.

"What have you there, Cash?" asked the new man, who appeared short and bulky beneath his dark apparel. His voice was low yet harsh, and Valdieron could tell that the two men were not particularly fond of one another.

"A boy, Telor, armed but apparently not dangerous." His tone sounded slightly condescending to Valdieron, yet if the man Telor noticed, he did not show it.

"A spy, you mean. Bring him along. Hakkel will want to interrogate him." Seeing Valdieron's bow, he picked it up and turned to lead them back towards the camp.

The man who caught Valdieron hesitated, as if weighing up the wisdom of some other action, yet finally he clasped Valdieron by the arms and deftly secured his wrists together behind his back.

"Sorry about this, kid," he apologized. They followed Telor towards the glow of the clearing.

The clearing was in fact egg-shaped, fifty paces across at its widest with the rocky outcrop in the midst of the wider end, while the horses were lined up at the narrower end. Muffled shouts of warning rose as the three passed from the veil of wooded darkness into the light. Men were standing with weapons drawn. Valdieron surreptitiously counted twelve men, making the total fourteen with the two scouts, Cash and Telor. Half a dozen possible sentries made the number a score of men, give or take a few.

The group dispersed when they realized there was no threat, back to the blazing campfire to the left of the rocky outcrop, others to their tents. One man stepped from a dimly lit tent, disheveled and wobbly, the cause of which probably being the tankard he carelessly waved around in his hand. He seemed to half-turn to address someone back inside the tent, and made some ribald quip that seemed somewhat out of place until a long-haired but equally disheveled woman peered outside the flap to make an equally ribald remark back at the man.

He was large of build and slightly more than average in height with black skin, though tanned more than naturally colored. He was also the hairiest man Valdieron had ever seen, with a full, tangled beard and a matt of hair where his chest should have been, visible beneath his unbuttoned shirt. A long, pointed weapon which Valdieron thought was a rapier hung at his waist, opposite a long-bladed knife.

"Well, Cash, what have you found? A spy, perhaps?" The man Valdieron assumed was Hakkel stepped before the three and gripped Valdieron by the hair, forcing him to lock eyes. His blood-shot eyes gave him a menacing appearance as he glared at Valdieron, who held his gaze even as the stench of ale on the man's breath and clothes threatened to make him gag.

"I'll warrant he's a spy, sir," interceded Telor, drawing a dagger for emphasis, which he pointed at Valdieron. From the corner of his eye, Val noticed the man, Cash, tense slightly. "He may look like a boy, but they're not gonna send a man with 'Spy' written on him, are they?"

"And what do you suggest we do with him?" sneered Hakkel.

"Torture, to be sure, Captain." Telor's eyes widened with pleasure as he twisted the knife around before him and leered wickedly. "Force him to talk, or we cut out his heart and torch it on the fire before his dying eyes." It appeared to Valdieron that Telor was not one to think out a situation before he spoke. By the defiant look he shared with Cash, also, it was obvious he was trying more than a little to gain the favor of Hakkel.

"If I may, Sir," interceded Cash, speaking for the first time. "If this boy," he emphasized the word 'boy', "is in fact a spy, he will likely tell you nothing, even at the point of a dagger or with his heart grasped in front of his eyes. I suggest," once again he emphasized this last word with a quick glance as Telor who scowled, "that we keep him tied up in plain sight. That way, if any others come after him, they will think less of approaching, especially with me standing beside him with a dagger at his side."

Hakkel stood unmoved for several moments then laughed coldly. "Why the hell not. I'm too busy right now anyway. Search his pack, and bring his sword to me when you're done." He let Valdieron's head drop as he released his hair, but not before growling angrily. He nodded for Telor to return to his duties then disappeared back inside the tent, which erupted with a bellowing growl and playful female laughter. Telor cast one last defiant glance at Cash then disappeared silently into the darkness of the woods.

"Come, boy," growled Cash, grasping Valdieron by the arm and propelling him towards the rocky outcrop, not roughly, but seemingly forceful should anybody notice.

He was forced to sit at the base of the rock while Cash removed another piece of cord from a pouch at his waist and secured his feet. As he worked, Cash glanced from Valdieron to Hakkel and back. "I'm sorry for this, kid, but it was the best I could come up with given the circumstances. You're lucky the Captain is tired or he may have just strung you up, just for the pleasure of it. Spies aren't that welcome around here, if you get my meaning."

"I'm not-" began Valdieron, reiterating his claim, but Cash threw up a cautioning hand, glancing quickly at Hakkel. "Not so loud, boy. Hakkel may have been lenient this time, but if he thinks you're trying to give warning to any in earshot, he'll be quick to change his mind. Understood?" Valdieron nodded with a grimace as the cord tightened around his ankles.

"I'll take these," he quipped, untying Valdieron's sword from his back and removing his knife from its sheath. "Captains orders, you know," he added softly. Valdieron nodded, as Cash tossed his sword to one side. Maybe as some sign of remorse, the man gave his pack only a cursory check, as if to satisfy anybody watching.

"You're making a big mistake," he whispered, not threateningly, but with a quiet surety. "I did not happen upon your camp by chance. I was following a scouting group of Trolls who crept up on you. They've probably returned to the others right now, a cave less than an hour away, and will be returning soon."

"Trolls, you say?" asked Cash indifferently, moving a short way to the side with his back to the rock, holding Valdieron's sword. "Saw some signs of them back in the lower country, tracks and dung. How many did you say there were?"

Valdieron sniffed defiantly and turned his gaze to the front, staring at the darkness beyond the tree line. "You'll find out soon enough," he promised.

"Right," returned Cash softly, glancing between Valdieron and the sword a few times, lost in thought.

After his initial anger had passed, Valdieron scanned the clearing, this time with more care. He couldn't see the tents as they were situated behind him and the rock, yet he used his other senses to gather information. He barely heard the hint of a whispered conversation and the rustling of what he assumed were blankets, and then a low, drawn out moaning, first as if it were the wind in the distance, and then louder, as if someone were in pain. This led Valdieron to some interesting conclusions as he turned his attention to the men around the fire.

A more ragged and different group of men Valdieron could not imagine. Tall, short, dark-skinned, light-skinned, lean, muscular, these men had the look of a pack of mongrel dogs. They wore patched clothing with odd pieces of armor ranging from greaves to breastplates and helms; with no one man wearing what was close to a complete suit. Their weapons were just as numerous, from swords and daggers to spears and bows. Each was armed like they were ready for war. He guessed most were mercenaries, sturdy looking men with military background, though some looked as if they were street thugs turned bandits, for every distant noise in the night caused heads to turn in nervous fear.

Finally he came back to the man, Cash. In the light he was tall; close to six feet in height, with a lean physique which spoke of speed, though from experience Valdieron knew he was not weak. His hands, which gently turned the sword before him, were slender, as if designed for artistry, not brigandry. Even his face, which was handsome and defined beneath the grime of camouflage, was one Valdieron did not expect to see on a man whose life revolved around stealing horses.

His attention turned to the horses. Even at the distance, Valdieron could see they were dirty and worn out, some thin and shaky where they stood, probably the first ones the poachers had captured. Amid the mass of their own urine and excrement, their bridles were secured to long logs dragged into the clearing. There was scant grass available, just out of reach of the animals, and there were no signs of there being any grain to supplement their meals. Such treatment was inexcusable for even the lowliest of creatures.

He seethed with anger when he spotted the faint black outline of a newly pressed brand on the closest animal, a bay mare. The icon was indistinguishable, yet it was obviously new. Amid the cluster, many a tail flicked at annoying insects seeking scalded flesh.

His eyes passed over the last of the horses along the line, probably the most recently 'acquired'. His breath caught in his throat as he noticed the dark main of a sorrel beast. Shakk! He squinted to get a better glimpse of the creature, yet lowered his gaze as he felt Cash's eyes upon him. Was it possible that they had captured Shakk? It was not unreasonable, as many of the local animals would have been scared off in all directions, even herded by the Trolls towards their homes.

"Seems a real shame, hey lad," said Cash, as if he shared Valdieron's thoughts. "They deserve better." Valdieron half turned to speak, to see whether or not Cash was mocking him in some way but sighed instead. As it was, he barely heard the man's whispered words. "Better than this scum give them!"

Valdieron shifted restlessly against the rocks, trying to get comfortable. He could not sleep, knowing he could not afford the comfort even if he so desired it. The Trolls would return, of that he had no doubt. It was just a matter of when. Cash brought over a couple of sawn logs to sit on, a welcome respite from the cold snow.

A faint noise away to the left caused him to stir from his thoughtful silence. Beside him Cash stirred also, gripping Valdieron's sword. He glanced around studiously before zeroing in on the direction of the noise, which sounded like faint footsteps and muffled conversation. *Not the Trolls*, mused Valdieron, though he doubted if sentries would make such a stir.

Three men entered the clearing. Two wore the dark clothing of sentries and carried short bows. Between them they shouldered the half-limp form of another man, his brown leather clothes torn and ragged, stained with both dirt and blood. His tangled hair was also matted with blood, hiding a downcast face, as if he were too tired to lift it, though he still mumbled to the sentries. They bore him straight to Hakkel, who approached and ordered them to lower the man to the ground. Water was brought, and bandages, as Hakkel leaned close to converse with him. He appeared dazed as his head lolled around loosely as he spoke, but Valdieron was too far away to hear what was being said. He did make out one word, the name of the man, Cash. Hakkel swiveled towards them, eyes narrowed with anger as he reached for his weapon. His face registered surprise, and Valdieron realized Cash had disappeared, where he had been seated within touching distance a moment ago.

"Catch that Traitor! I want him alive so I can rip out his heart," boomed Hakkel. "And the other spy," his eyes leveled on Valdieron coldly "he is of no further use to us. Probably one of Cash's men, though the coward has left him to his fate." A cold dread hit Valdieron as the men began to spread out around the clearing, drawing weapons and whistling loudly to signal the sentries. The signals were not returned, which added to the confusion, yet Hakkel only cursed Cash louder and warned the others of trickery. One man, grinning maliciously, approached Valdieron carrying a wickedly curved scimitar, its trailing edge serrated to half way up the blade. He was middle-aged, and appeared manic in appearance, as if his nerves were on edge. He approached on steady feet with murder in his eyes.

Chapter 11

The sudden screaming of shocked men filled the air amid a cacophony of roaring. Trolls clambered into the clearing bearing weapons and barking their inhuman cries. Valdieron spun to check the approach of the man sent to finish him, and found him lying prone with the hilt of a dagger protruding from his chest. Glancing around, he cried out as a figure dropped beside him from above and he tried to roll away defensively, but his bonds held him as surely as a fish in a net.

"Easy, Lad!" He recognized the voice of the man, Cash, who loomed over him, a dagger held in each hand. "Let's get you free of these bonds." He began to slice through the ropes, glancing around for nearby attackers.

"Who are you?" asked Valdieron, bemused by the man's actions.

"I'm a spy!" conceded Cash with an indifferent shrug. He tore through the last of the bonds holding Valdieron's hands then handed him the dagger. "Here. Loose yourself, quickly."

Valdieron took the dagger and sawed at the bonds securing his feet while Cash watched for any attack. The melee continued around them. One brigand fired an arrow towards them moments before being downed by a Troll's club. The arrow flew wide.

"We must free the horses," shouted Valdieron over the din of combat and the macabre cries of the Trolls. The horses pulled frantically at their tethers as Trolls closed in around them.

"They must free themselves, lad. We must flee. There are more Trolls beyond the tree line. It won't take them long to defeat these men, and we shall not remain unseen for long."

As if to prove his point a nearby Troll turned towards them and roared, brandishing a long club driven through with long metal spikes. With surprising speed it lumbered towards them as Cash turned to meet it. "Hurry lad!"

Valdieron cursed as the stubborn rope refused to yield to the keen edge of the dagger. He could hear the desperate cries of the horses as the Trolls closed in on them. Acting on an impulse, he raised one hand to his mouth and whistled a long, piercing note he had used many times. Though it caught the unwanted attention of two more Trolls, he heard an answering snorting from the midst of the horses as Shakk responded to his Master's call.

With an angry grunt he hacked through the remaining rope and sprang to his feet, wobbling momentarily as his tired legs gained strength. The two Trolls were closing rapidly on him. Realizing he had only the dagger, he scanned quickly and spotted his bow and quiver nearby. Thrusting the dagger into his belt he scrambled for the bow and dumped some arrows.

Drawing with the practice of a thousand pulls he turned and lowered to one knee, bringing the Trolls into sight and letting loose at the one on the left. The arrows whistling flight ended with a thud as it sank deep into the Troll's shoulder. It reeled with a howl of pain, which turned to one of anger as it continued its charge, gaining speed.

Valdieron drew again and fired, this time piercing the Troll's unprotected chest. It snapped the shaft with a flailing arm but collapsed slowly with an anguished cry, defiantly squirming on the ground, refusing to die.

The second Troll bore down on him at a frantic lope, maw twisted in a baleful visage, club raised in both hands. Being too close for a bowshot, Valdieron cursed as he remembered his sword was being wielded by Cash who was engaged with two brigands nearby.

He tossed the bow at the Troll hoping to distract it as he scrambled to the side and scooped up the dropped scimitar and the dagger Cash had used on the man. He tucked it into his belt with the one Cash had given him.

Rising to his feet, he held the heavy weapon in his hand. His own sword, easily a foot longer than this one, was much lighter and he could hold it effortlessly in one hand. The scimitar felt unbalanced, forcing him to grasp its short pommel with both hands.

The Troll towered above him, its club in descent. Val brought his scimitar over in an arcing parry while sidestepping to the left. The simple movement and the force from his block threw the club harmlessly to the side. Still, his arms jarred at the power of the diverted attack, and he winced as the club thudded into the ground. He imagined what sort of damage it would have done to him had it connected.

Not dwelling on such thoughts, his riposte came in the form of a thrust, hasty yet effective. The scimitar's narrow tip gouged the Troll in the throat as it recovered from its missed attack. Metal scraped bone as he twisted the weapon savagely. The Troll grabbed at its torn throat. His roar came out as a gurgle as bubbled blood oozed between its fingers.

Valdieron scowled angrily as the Troll took a halting step towards him. He felt a cruel satisfaction as the Troll stumbled to its knees and toppled forward with a long rasping sound.

Another dark form loomed to his right. He spun with his weapon raised, his heart caught in his chest. His snarl turned to a cry of joy as the sorrel form of Shakk drew to a halt before him. Surprisingly, the Stallion looked healthy and showed few ill effects of captivity. He seemed as yet unbranded. A broken bridle dangled down from where he had broken free from his tether.

"Hey, boy. I didn't think I'd see you again," he whispered, taking hold of the bridle as Shakk tossed his head as if in agreement. Valdieron glanced around to find Cash had dispatched the two men and was further across the glade being pressed by Hakkel. The dead forms of Trolls and brigands littered the glade. The remaining Trolls seemed intent on rounding up the horses. Distant noises carried from beyond the trees to the south, but whether that was from more Trolls or brigands he could not tell.

Though he rued the fate of the horses, to engage the Trolls single-handedly was suicide. He retrieved his pack and bow then leapt astride Shakk, still clutching the bloodied scimitar. With the added height he could see the tents had been trampled and ravaged, their contents scattered. As he watched, several horses broke free of their bonds to dart through the closing ranks of Trolls. One took a vicious blow to the head from a club and skidded for a short distance then came to a stop, twitching in its death throes.

Valdieron wheeled Shakk from the sickening scene to find Cash leaning heavily on his sword. The battered form of Hakkel lay motionless at his feet. Even at this distance he could see the many bloodied wounds Hakkel bore. Urging the nervous Shakk forward, Valdieron drew up beside Cash just as the spy turned to him.

The wound in his side appeared small, yet a dark stain of

blood spread rapidly. The self-proclaimed spy grimaced as Valdieron dropped from Shakk to support him.

"I'll be fine," breathed Cash. "We have to get out of here, though."

Not needing to be told twice, Valdieron remounted Shakk then lent a hand to the wounded spy who grunted with pain as he was pulled up.

"There are some things at the tents which I must retrieve first," pleaded Cash, so Valdieron wheeled Shakk back to where the tents lay trampled into the snow. They skirted the rock away from the Trolls who were herding the horses. The plaintive cries of the animals were being cut off and turned into painful neighing as the Trolls went to work. Valdieron tried to cut the noises from his mind.

"Here!" urged Cash as they drew up to the tents. He returned Valdieron's sword then dropped awkwardly to the ground, gasping sharply at the pain. Hurriedly he sifted through the belongings, digging up items that must have been of importance, and stuffed them into a small pack found nearby. Valdieron tossed aside the bloodied scimitar in favor of his own sword and also dropped from Shakk, noticing a dark leather saddle amidst the mess. He hastily set it atop Shakk and secured it, then tied the ends of the reins together and looped them over Shakk's neck. He was no sooner back in the saddle when Cash returned and passed him the full pack before being pulled back up.

Angry growls from behind caused them to turn as more dark Trolls entered the glade. They saw the two riders and gave chase with long, loping strides.

"Time to get out of here," agreed Valdieron, looping the cut string of his bow around the pommel of the saddle to hold it in place. Grasping the reins in one hand he turned Shakk and urged him towards the trees. The frightened yet brave stallion was more than eager to comply.

The darkness beyond the fire-lit glade forced Valdieron to rein in the eager stallion, letting Shakk's eyes adjust, but urgency and the approaching barks and growls of the pursuing Trolls kept them moving. Valdieron contemplated removing the Dragon's tear from beneath his shirt to give himself and Cash some light to see, but knew Shakk could navigate without trouble in the darkness. Cash remained silent behind him.

Every few minutes, Valdieron reined in Shakk and listened for signs of pursuit. At first he could hear the cries of the horses being slaughtered and the bestial howling of the Trolls. These sounds grew distant at each pause until there was nothing but an eerie silence, broken only by Shakk's labored breathing and the beating of his heart.

The trees thinned after a time, while the ground sloped slowly away and became rockier as they approached the eastern escarpment of the range, where it met the plains. Overhead, the twin moons offered a gloomy luminescence through the broken canopy. Valdieron urged Shakk into a slow canter. With one hand he grasped Cash's hands at his waist, realizing the man had lapsed into unconsciousness.

Knowing he had to stop to attend to Cash's wounds, he searched for a safe area to do so. Few presented themselves as he began to get desperate.

Winding Shakk carefully down a small coulee, a rocky alcove opened up to the right, sheltered by foliage and covered overhead by a stone outcrop. The opposite wall of the ravine widened a little to about fifteen feet.

Satisfied the spot was as defendable as any, and masked their presence from prying eyes, he drew the tired Stallion to a halt, amazed at the horse's stamina. It was unlikely he would have eaten much in the last day or two, yet he had carried both men and their loads with hardly a misstep.

Looping one leg over Shakk's neck, Valdieron dropped to the ground and turned quickly to prevent Cash from falling. He clutched him under the arms and lowered him as softly as he could, then dragged him into the alcove.

He pulled clothing and bandages from his pack. There was nothing of use in Cash's pack, which was filled with documents and scrolls, and a tiny silver box which he did not bother with.

Blood had congealed around the narrow wound in Cash's side. Valdieron drew out the Tear, which was dull and emitted a faint light. He saw no other wounds save a bruised left shoulder and a narrow gash to his right forearm, neither of which he gave a second glance.

The stomach wound made Val grimace. He slowly poured water over it to loosen the blood's caked grip on the wound so he could peel the shirt away.

He held no illusion of being a healer. Although he had a

passing knowledge of animal healing methods, he had no idea how to dress such a serious wound on a human. The wound had to be cleaned and the blood-flow stopped with what little he had to aid him.

Gathering dry leaves and twigs, he set flint to tinder and got a small fire going. He added larger sticks until a good base of embers were set. Into the cooking pot he dropped wax stripped from his cheese and ham, and placed it onto the fire. He cut the sleeves from his spare shirt and tore them into strips, rewrapping the food in what was left of the shirt.

Once the wax melted, he removed the pot from the fire and added the shirt strips, soaking them briefly before pulling them free. The wax dried quickly, making waterproof (and hopefully blood proof) presses. He poured half of his water into the pot and set it atop the flames to warm.

Carefully he peeled Cash's shirt away from the wound, using some water to soak the wound. The cloth tore at the wound, revealing the oozing pink lesion. Cash groaned in sleepy unconsciousness but did not stir.

With the blood-soaked shirt removed, he wiped away most of the remaining mixture of blood and water with his own shirt, shivering slightly as the cold night air caressed his skin. Testing the water with his finger, he dipped his shirt and wiped softly at the wound, once again bringing movement from Cash who did not wake but murmured something through clenched teeth. He was sweating heavily despite the chilly air.

After the wound was clean, Valdieron used the waxed presses to cover it and then wound a bandage around Cash's waist to hold it in place. Fearing fever or hypothermia, he removed the Dragon's tear from around his neck and placed it on Cash's chest, willing it to warmth. He then covered the injured man with his ulster.

While Cash slept, Valdieron retired to the rear of the alcove and restrung his bow using a new string from his fletching kit. Taking up his sword, he moved out to where Shakk grazed silently on the sparse grass of the rocky ravine.

"Rest, boy," he murmured, stroking Shakk's muscled neck. Over the past few days, he had thought he had lost all remnants of his former life: his family, his friends, even his horse. Now there was renewed hope. If Shakk could survive, maybe some in the village could have. Once again he turned his gaze to the south, where he knew somewhere in the distant lowlands lay Shadowvale, where maybe hope of life remained.

Shakk shifted beneath him, as Val's cold-filled sleep was overtaken by the pre-dawn. He rose to a crouch as Shakk stood, snorting through flared nostrils at the darkness. Overhead, only Santari remained, meaning dawn was about two or three hours off.

He glanced at the still form of Cash, relieved to find him sleeping peacefully. He placed a steadying hand on Shakk's flank, quieting him.

He grasped his sword, feeling its assuring hardness in his chilled hands. He guessed the Trolls would be relying on their sense of smell to find them. He took mark of the wind's direction and followed it downwind, leading him down the shallow ravine. A command to Shakk stopped the nervous horse from following.

Inching along the high side of the ravine, he had gone less than a hundred feet before it sloped down sharply, falling away to merge with the surrounding land. Several Trolls milled in the open space, their hulking forms easily recognizable in the dim light.

Cursing silently, Valdieron retraced his steps to the makeshift camp. He assumed the Trolls would not take long to catch a decent scent and bring them storming up the ravine, so time was definitely precious.

He retrieved the Tear, which now glowed a somber orange. Waking Cash proved difficult given his state. At first he shifted only slightly as if resisting the urge to wake, then his eyes snapped open, a startled cry muffled barely in time by Valdieron.

Cash groaned, his hand going instantly to the wound at his side. "What the hell is going on?" he moaned through parched lips. He glanced around the small camp, as Valdieron passed him his water bottle.

"Trolls!" whispered Valdieron as he shouldered his pack. A sudden clicking of stone from above caught his attention. He cursed, realizing there were more Trolls than the ones down the ravine. They were probably being surrounded at that very moment.

Desperately he came up with a plan. Cash could not walk, let alone run, and Shakk would struggle carrying the double burden again for long. He removed what food he had from his pack and passed it to Cash, who regarded it curiously.

"There is no way both of us can escape together. Take Shakk and ride. Even now, Trolls are surrounding us." Of this he was almost certain. "I will try to slip through them in the other direction. Head straight South from here and you will find a burnt-out village, about five leagues from here in a large valley. I will meet you there when I can. Do not tarry past the night, however, if I do not arrive, understood?"

Cash nodded, realizing the truth of the young man's plan. He clasped Valdieron's hand warmly. "I have much to thank you for, lad. Should we not meet again at this village and you find yourself in Thorhus, ask at the court for Kalamar, and I will return to you your horse and whatever you ask."

He rose unsteadily and Valdieron helped him onto Shakk, then passed him his pack.

Valdieron turned to Shakk, taking the beast's head in his hands, a sudden grief once again taking hold of him. "You must run fast Shakk. Do as this man says. He will take good care of you until I find you again."

Shakk's fear-filled eyes softened momentarily and he pressed against Valdieron. "I will take good care of him, Valdieron," assured Cash. "You just get out of here alive, ok?"

Cash spun Shakk and urged him over the shallow wall of the ravine. Quickly the two disappeared down the steep embankment. Shakk's hooves clicked on the stony ground as howling cries rose from all around.

Setting his bow over his shoulder and grasping his sword, Valdieron set off up the ravine. All around he could hear the sounds of the Trolls' howls and their noisy chase after the fleeing stallion.

Rounding the narrow bend of the ravine, a dark shape loomed up before him. The Trolls' attention was focused on the fleeing stallion but he spun at the last moment as Valdieron stepped around the rock wall. Val was faster. Razor-sharp steel pierced thick hide and scraped rib-bone. The Troll collapsed in agony and Valdieron nearly lost his grip on the sword so surprised was he at the effectiveness of the thrust. The blade pulled free with a hiss of displeasure.

More dark shapes appeared higher up the ravine, coming toward him in a wild charge. Valdieron scrambled up the steep bank to his left, using the foliage to help pull himself over the rise. Incensed by his flight, the Trolls scrambled after him, too stupid to retrace their steps back up the ravine.

Using the light of Santari, Valdieron turned to the north. There was movement off to his left as a dark shape crashed through the trees in his direction. With its long strides it would only be a matter of time before the Troll caught him. He began a long, sweeping arc to his right, one that would bring him around to the south.

The Troll closed the gap quickly. Valdieron could hear its heavy steps close behind and the exhalation of its strained breathing. Back in the distance echoed the howls of the other Trolls.

Valdieron veered towards a small wooded area, the trees sparse yet young with strong, low branches that hindered the Troll's movement. He turned with his back to one of the trees and threw his pack off to the side. The Troll battered its way through the overhanging branches as if to crush him.

The size of the Troll stunned Valdieron as it loomed over him through the branches. Easily twice his height, its massive frame was covered with dark brown stringy hide, while a single strip of gray hair grew from its gnarled scalp. In one large hand it carried a wooden hammer, easily six feet in length with the head resembling the anvil on which Kyle and his father used to pound metal.

The Troll snarled as it snapped branches from the trees. It held the hammer wide, ready to be brought down quickly to strike. Valdieron contemplated taking his chance in flight, but the beast was too close. Raising his sword, he dropped into a stance he had learned from his 'dream' training, ready to attack.

Unlike the other Trolls who had rushed blindly into melee, this one held back, as if waiting for Valdieron to attack. It smiled coldly, almost condescendingly at Valdieron, the club bobbing hypnotically at its right shoulder.

Valdieron did attack first. With a feinted thrust he swayed back a step as the Troll's hammer whistled past his chest, missing by scant inches, crushing branches and blasting through one not so slender tree. So relieved was he that the blow missed, Val almost lost his chance to counter. He thrust forward with a quick sliding step. His ill timed strike gouged a vicious slash along the Troll's right thigh bringing a howl of outrage more than pain. It tore the hammer free of the branches and swept it back in a sweeping motion. Valdieron rolled away backwards to avoid it.

Coming to his feet in a defensive crouch, he found the Troll looming over him, the hammer already descending in an overhead chop.

Desperately, Valdieron rolled again, though not away from the Troll but forwards, inside the dangerous arc of the weapon. He felt more than heard it thud into the stony ground he had just vacated. He came up from the roll, sword thrusting upwards as he rose.

With the momentum of the roll and his upward force, the sword pierced the Troll's leathery hide with little resistance. Warm blood spattered his face and arms as something struck him in the side. He lost his grip on his sword and was thrown from his feet. He landed with a painful jolt. His head struck something as it lashed sideways. His senses reeled. In the background the cries of the tormented Troll grew distant as the world faded to darkness.

Chapter 12

Overhead, the afternoon sun descended inexorably towards the pale red clouds blanketing the horizon. The morning would dawn warm and clear as autumn drew forth the last of the heat, defying the cold snaps of the past few weeks.

Valdieron crouched beneath a harsh rocky defile, his sword resting on his knees. Tears came unbidden to his eyes as his somber gaze drifted over the familiar circular vale below. Where once he would have seen the almost perfectly split green of the Oval surrounded by houses and buildings, a dark blight now infected the place once called Shadowvale.

Charred foundations of stone and rock sprang from the chalky gray terrain, the only remnants of some buildings. Carrion skipped among ashen skeletons in search of flesh untouched by the fire.

Valdieron wiped away the tears as he mentally pictured where buildings had once been. The central core of the forge remained intact beneath a sea of ash. The house and walls were but a memory, their disappearance mocking him, questioning his memories as if they had never existed. Nearby, the lower rock walls were all that remained of the Inn. The rear wall had collapsed inwards, probably from the pressure of the upper level as it was consumed. As he had expected, the hay-filled barn was totally destroyed, leaving no remnants but ash. Even the library, which he had once thought to be fire resistant, was now merely a foot-high frame of charred rock, its burned contents no doubt spread by the wind.

How long will it be before a fresh snowfall covers up the remnants of my home?

He watched and waited as twilight descended like a pall over the vale. He had waited several hours for signs of Cash or Shakk, but as yet there were none. He pondered going down to the ruins of the village, but could not. The pain of the discovery was nearly all he could bear from the distance. He was not certain what the effect may be if he walked the village's desolate paths.

He turned his attention off to the left, where earlier he had spotted the unmistakable forms of Trolls. Their presence during the brightness of the afternoon had come as a surprise. They were of the same kind Valdieron had slain in the small copse the previous night, larger and lighter skinned, with the streak of gray down the center of their large heads.

He unconsciously rubbed his forehead above the left eye. When he had awoken that morning, the stiff form of the dead Troll lay not far from where he had stabbed it, his sword still embedded in its stomach.

Nervously he checked the wind, which swirled from the south, a chilly tempest that would carry his scent back up into the mountains.

With the evening came the eventual rise of the brother moons, shedding their mystical luminescence over the land, turning the lifeless scene below into one of eeriness as the orange glow bathed the ruins. Valdieron dozed restlessly, waking as the waning moons were almost touching the gray outline of the dawn-filled horizon. He could not remember how long he waited and watched; only that neither sight nor sound had he seen of Cash or Trolls. Ruing the missed rendezvous, he shouldered his pack and rose, stretching against the light of the new day. Turning his gaze again to the south, he pictured in his mind what roads lay beyond the horizon. Cash had spoken of Thorhus, greatest city in the realm of Ariakus and Tyr's distant neighbor to the southeast. To make such a journey would take him many days, perhaps even months, some three hundred leagues lying between here and there. He thought of Ranil, ruling city of Tyr, some ninety leagues away also to the southeast.

Conflicting emotions held him as he pondered the road to another land, while behind him lay the legacy of his oath to his dead father. He now knew about the masses of Trolls inhabiting the mountains, yet he could not shirk his responsibility, nor go back on his word. He would prevail, he vowed, as he sheathed his sword in the makeshift scabbard on his back, secured with leather straps from an old bridle he had found in the yard of a burnt farm. With eyes downcast, he did not look back as he strode up the mountain, towards whatever fate lay in store for him.

The overwhelming stench of the waste and offal assaulted him as he sidled around the narrow rocky ledge, his nose and mouth covered by Nat's rose-scented kerchief. Below, the pinnacle of the surrounding trees rose up from the base of the scree slope, a reminder of the great height of the ledge on which he perched.

To his right a dark stain trailed down the gray stone wall, like a river on a barren landscape. Carcasses, large and small, glued together in a mass of hide and excrement, were lumped at the base of the cliff. Not all were horse or sheep.

The opening from which the Trolls dumped their remains was less than three feet wide, and not much higher. Valdieron awkwardly lowered himself onto his haunches on the ledge, using the rising sun over the trees to illuminate the dark opening. He had hoped that whatever may be beyond would not be there with the morning sun directly outside, and from what little he could see, there was no indication of a presence inside the room.

He took a deep breath of fresh air and held it as he shuffled through the opening, pausing only briefly to re-check the interior. The room, domed and rough, was ten feet across and fifteen feet high at the center. An arched opening lay almost directly across from the hole, showing a rough twelve-foot high corridor receding into the darkness.

Disgusted, he picked his way through the piled waste, and came to rest against the wall beside the passageway. He freed his sword from its makeshift sheath, and listened intently for any noise. Distantly he could hear what sounded like the guttural barking of the Troll's speech, but could pick up nothing close by.

Removing the kerchief from his face, he retied it to his upper left arm and checked his belongings. His pack was left hidden back at the small cave he was using as his campsite, as it would only burden him in the cave's confines. At his waist he had both of his daggers. In his pouch he had his tinderbox and two flasks of oil. He was ready for a fast, desperate fight, hoping that hit and run tactics would serve him better than standing ground like a berserker until he was the last standing or not standing at all, although a tiny part of him wanted it to be like that, like the heroic stories of ages past.

Stepping into the dim tunnel caused him to look back longingly at the narrow opening. The lack of visibility in the cave put him at a perilous disadvantage. He had the Tear ready beneath his shirt to bring out at sign of danger. Its brightness would aid him while hopefully hindering the light-sensitive Trolls, though he could not risk having it out while he searched the caves. His plan was to strike first, surreptitiously, in a place where he had many escape routes and an advantage of height.

Hit and run. Hit and run. He repeated this silently to himself as he inched down the passage, though silently adding the words 'very fast' at the end.

What little light there was faded quickly as the passage curved sharply to the left. A dim luminescence remained, almost like the pre-dawn glow where all appeared gray and undefined. He was glad for even this small amount of vision as he sidled along the wall.

The first intersection came after about thirty shuffled paces. A tunnel angled away to the right, while the one he was in continued around to the left. Knowing it would be easier to find his way out again if he followed the left wall, he gave the right entry a cautious scan as he crept past it, amazed at the lack of activity. He wondered with a wry grin if somehow the Trolls had disappeared on him.

The passage ran for another twenty paces before a greater darkness appeared, marking a chamber or a widening of the passage. He inched towards the archway, his eyes unblinking and his ears cocked for the slightest sound.

The labored sounds of heavy breathing emanated from the dark chamber. He paused momentarily, studying the sounds. He glanced inside the room. Along the walls to the right and left were rough sleeping pallets, their long wooden frames covered with the thick hide of animals. Of the cots he could see, most bore the prone forms of Trolls. Sleeping? It surprised him that the creatures were akin to humans in such ways, yet the more he thought on it, the more natural it seemed. A dark corridor ran from the right wall. The pallets were situated in a circular pattern around the chamber, about twenty in all, with junk and garbage littered throughout.

Drawing back from the chamber a little, he began to formulate a plan. He considered backtracking to another passage, but knew that an opportunity such as this may never eventuate. He considered an attack against sleeping Trolls as cowardly, but a vision of his father lying dead in a pool of his own blood quelled any notion of honor.

He drew both flasks of oil from his pack. He soaked two thin strips of cloth torn from his shirt and tied one around each of the ceramic containers. Using his flint, he set flame to both strands of cloth, which took hold quickly.

Stepping to the entry, he tossed the first flask towards the pallets closest to the side passage. It smashed open, spreading its contents over a wide area. Flames flared quickly.

Angry and confused roars filled the room as first one then the other Trolls roused. Their fear was evident as they scrambled away from the flames, which were as yet small. The fire grew as it took hold of the oil-doused wood and hide. Two Trolls who had been spattered with the oil became lined with flame. Their desperate cries mingled with the din of roaring and howling as they thrashed around. This only served to spread the fire, however, as they smashed furnishings and careened into the other Trolls who frantically sought safety from the flames.

With a victorious cry, Valdieron tossed the second flask as he backed out of the room. Angry Trolls spotted him and realized the cause of the fire. The second flask struck the pallets closest to the entry and exploded, slowing the Trolls as they shied away from the sudden flame.

Valdieron drew his sword and stepped away from the entry, waiting for any Trolls to emerge. The chamber filled quickly with smoke. The rancid smell of burning skin and hair began to permeate the air. He gagged as he fumbled for his kerchief and wrapped it over his mouth and nose again. Luckily, the heavy smoke followed the contour of the ceiling, four feet overhead.

A Troll stumbled through the flickering fire and cloud of smoke, reeling off the corner of the entry. Its dark eyes settled on him and it charged forward groggily, without weapons or clothing.

Luckily for Valdieron, the Troll was hindered by the intoxicating fumes and smoke and he leapt back easily from its clutches. He followed with a thrust that caught the creature's right thigh, biting deep. Once again oblivious to the pain or shock, the Troll stepped forward and swung a languorous backhand at him, which he ducked easily. Rising, he swept a horizontal cut across the creature's abdomen, feeling the sword scrape bone as it nicked the Troll's spine on its way through.

This time the Troll roared with agony, reeling back and clutching at its spilling internal organs. It staggered forward a step, and then tried for another, when suddenly a sharp cracking sound split the corridor and the Troll toppled forward limply, causing Valdieron to dance back hurriedly. A dark stain spread over the stones beneath its head, which looked as though it had been bludgeoned.

A bellowing roar brought Valdieron's attention back to the smoky passage as a second Troll stepped onto the dead form of the first. A huge club seemed light in its hand, smeared with the blood of the dead Troll, which it regarded with a sneer. Valdieron realized this Troll was similar to the one he had encountered alone in the small copse a few nights before. It was larger and more deadly than the others, but hampered more by the small corridor as it stooped.

Its first erratic swing sailed harmlessly over Valdieron's head as he ducked backwards out of harms way, though he winced as the weapon struck the stone wall, showering rock fragments into the air. The second attack was much the same, a diagonal slash which Valdieron barely stepped to the side of, feeling the rush of wind at its passing. He began to lunge forward for a thrust into the creature's side, expecting the club to crash into the floor, yet with surprising agility the Troll reversed the slash and Valdieron found it sweeping at him at chest level, too fast and too close to dodge.

The club brushed his parrying blade aside as easily as the wind tossing a leaf. His breath exploded out of him as the weapon caught him squarely in the chest. He was already moving with the blow, trying to weaken its impact. Fortunately the swing had not been at full force, but still enough to throw him against the wall. The impact jolted him again and his legs fell from under him.

Shaking off a sudden wave of dizziness, he focused in time to see the club descending with the full force of the Troll's strength, its roar of triumph and pleasure drowning out the pitiful wailing of those still caught in the burning chamber behind.

With speed born of desperation, Valdieron rolled away. He felt the club strike the ground where his head had been, showering him with more stone fragments. Rising in a crouch and wincing at the pain in his ribs, he expected to see the Troll looming over him again, ready to strike. Instead the Troll was tossing aside the splintered haft of the club, the other shattered end lying smashed on the floor at its feet.

With a furious roar that reverberated through the passage like a shaking peal of thunder, the Troll lunged forward to grab at Valdieron. He stepped quickly inside, raising his sword up in a vertical slash, which caught the beast in the face as it shifted forwards. The weapon's metal tip scraped across the bone of the Troll's skull, preceding a spray of ichorous blood which splashed across Valdieron's face and arms. It was warm to the point of almost burning.

In his defensive position he half expected the Troll to grasp him or pummel him, but the towering creature toppled back, twitching violently with post-death spasms. It came to rest over the corpse of the first Troll.

Valdieron paused with sword raised. His heart pounded furiously. Every nerve was strained to breaking point. From the smoke-filled chamber echoed the shouts and howls of the trapped Trolls as they crashed about blindly. Over the chaotic din, he could hear the bellows and grunts of Trolls back down the passage, cutting off his escape route. He cursed vehemently. Should they mill and press him, he would have no choice but to re-enter the blazing room.

Rather than risking a fighting retreat into the room, he vaulted the twin corpses and landed at the chamber's entry, crouching low to be clear of most of the dangerous fumes and smoke. He could make out dark forms silhouetted against the flickering flames, crashing about in what resembled a macabre dance. Remembering that the second passage leading from the room lay to the right, he backed against the right wall and sidled towards the other exit.

From the choking mist a Troll loomed over him menacingly, yet it did not register his presence as it ran headlong into the wall directly to his left. It reeled away even more dazed and disoriented. Valdieron swung blindly at it as he pressed his kerchief over his mouth and nose. The weapon bit deep before he pulled it free, his tear-filled eyes too blurred to see the result. The Troll's cry of pain mixed with the collective roars nearby.

He found the exit closer than he had expected as he suddenly tumbled backwards, losing the support of the wall behind him. He half crawled, half scrambled from the chaotic chamber, feeling his lungs clogged with ingested smoke as he coughed desperately for clear air. He drew back suddenly as the charred corpse of a Troll appeared before him. His smile of pleasure was quickly replaced by a grimacing scowl as the nausea kicked in.

A second body, not as badly charred as the first, but still smoldering, appeared not too far on as the passage wound to the left. The air above grew even heavier with acrid smoke, which made the surroundings barely discernable. He fumbled with his shirt chord and brought forth the Tear, which blazed furiously with a deep red core, but did little to penetrate the pall.

Stepping over the prone body of the Troll, he thought he could make out a widening of the passageway into a chamber ahead. He strained to see or hear any movement from within, but could perceive nothing over the echoing cries of the dying.

He took a tentative step towards the chamber and an enormous hand clasped his lower leg in a vice-like grip. His heart leapt to his throat as he realized the charred Troll he was stepping over was not dead.

But it was close. One look at the burnt pink skin of its face and chest triggered an onslaught of nausea. Its heavy-set features were slack. Deep burns over its entire upper chest and face oozed. Its throat was half melted away with a cauterized wound, which produced rasped breathing.

With a cry of surprise and fear he chopped at the Troll's arm, slicing through its wrist and into the rocky floor. Blood seeped from the severed limb as the Troll cried out mutely, an action bringing a moment of sympathy in Val.

Then he ended his and its torment with a thrust to its chest, where he assumed its huge heart was.

A sudden desire to be free of the cloying cave had him leaping for the next chamber. He knew dimly that if he followed the right wall, he would end up at the small chamber he had entered. There had to be another larger exit used by the Trolls.

The air was gloomy and thick with smoke as he battled a sudden wave of vertigo. A glow in the left wall caught his attention like a beacon and he staggered towards it, finding an arched recess in the wall with a raised walkway of roughly hewn rocks, leading upwards. Wisps of sunlight filtered through a thick veil of foliage. With a cry of relief he pulled himself towards the freedom of the outside world. Behind him he could hear the renewed roaring of several Trolls, their heavy steps echoing in the chamber as they rushed towards him. He slashed angrily at the leafy door, each stroke bringing a near blinding beam of light from the outside. His strokes became frenzied as the Trolls drew back a little from the hurtful light, though they howled with despair.

Valdieron lowered his shoulder and crashed through the remains of the door. He ran, the direction and speed of little consequence. He ran from the roars and the smoke and the death. Finally, as the surging emotions faded, he stumbled to a halt and dropped to his knees, his sword falling from his grasp. Tears streaked his face as he raised his head to the sky. Choking from the smoke in his lungs and overcome by anguish, he threw shouts of rage and hatred to the heavens, hearing them echo mockingly off the valleys and peaks around him, returning without the answers he so desperately craved.

After a time uncounted he rose and retrieved his sword almost tentatively. He was reassured by its solidity and cold reality. He turned back to where a plume of smoke rose over the rocky rise. For the first time realized the extent of his vow, which he knew with a surety he could not fulfill. With the weight of this revelation dragging at him he turned, winding his way to his cave to the south, seeking the sanctuary of sleep.

* * *

Many leagues from where Valdieron slept, a lone figure rested in the hollow of a small ravine. Kalamar clutched his cloak around him for warmth as he sifted through the documents contained within his pack. Already he had found many pages of information concerning the locations, names and activities of the major horse thieves of the central realms of Kil'Tar. It would be worth much to him when he returned to Thorhus and reported to the King.

Yet he would gladly have traded it for knowledge of the whereabouts and safety of the lad, Valdieron. He knew there was now a bond between him and the youth who had saved his life and risked his own in doing so. Such courageous and unselfish actions were more important to the honorable Spy than the money he would get for his endeavors. Thinking back, he remembered the pride with which he had watched the youth battle the Trolls in the lea. Like a wolf cub, innocent yet inherently dangerous, he had stood, defiant, even under the weight of the odds against them.

Raising his eyes to the clouded heavens he silently prayed that Valdieron was still alive, though he knew such a possibility was slight. Still he prayed, hoping to one-day repay the great debt he owed to the mysterious lad.

Chapter 13

The Great Merchant Highway was a flat, brown track as wide as two wagons, raised so it was two feet higher than the land flanking it. Parched and cracked, as if it defied the recent downfall which had briefly transformed its surface to mud, it seemed to draw in the sun's meager warmth, while the nearby rolling hills were scattered with patches of snow.

Valdieron stretched on the cold grass in the shade of several trees, a stone's throw from the road. For two weeks he had followed the highway as it snaked its way South. Several times he had passed travelers, in convoys of loaded wagons or groups of riders. Most were headed south, their destination likely to be the capital, Ranil. The land to the north was mostly farmland until it reached the northern coastline.

A young man traveling alone, armed with sword and bow raised suspicion, so he wasn't surprised that most people passed him with caution and offered little in terms of conversation. This suited him, as he usually gave the passers-by a wide berth, yet smiled and nodded greeting if any were to acknowledge him.

His destination was Ranil, to at least let it be known that the Trolls had destroyed Shadowvale and posed a threat to the lands and farms nearby. The presence of Trolls in the mountains was unlikely to be isolated to near Shadowvale, so chances were the authorities knew already. This irked him, as he bitterly wondered how anybody could let this happen to the people of his village.

Twelve days of slow travel ate up about half of the eighty-league trip with most of his time spent sleeping, hunting and practicing his martial skills. He found a tranquil release every time he visited the shroud-filled domain in his sleep. Only there could he forget the harsh reality which awaited him upon waking.

Yet the allure of company grew the closer he got to Ranil. It was a place beyond his imagination having seen only one small town beyond his village. He had some knowledge of it from old Mister Letterman and the Mayor, both of whom had been to

Ranil at least once, and it was rumored Mister Letterman had once lived there.

The distant rattle of hoof-beats caught his attention. It sounded like a group of riders approaching fast from the north, something he had not encountered before. That morning he had been passed by a large caravan of a dozen wagons, with as many guards on horses, which he had also steered clear of. Perhaps these riders were members of the caravan, or simply in a hurry to reach Ranil.

The first rider to come into view rounded a bend at a speed that would quickly tire his horse, which Valdieron noted was not particularly built for either speed or endurance. The rider wore heavy hide armor and carried a short, curved bow over his shoulder. Hanging from the saddle pommel was a quiver of green-fletched arrows and a curved Saber.

The rider, trailed by nine others of identical appearance, covered the short stretch quickly and disappeared around the next bend. His interest piqued, Valdieron waited briefly to see if others followed close behind, then sprang up and dashed after them.

He did not expect to keep pace with the horses, though he did know that at the speed they were traveling, they would not last long. He had a feeling the riders were not traveling all that far, probably meeting with someone or stopping further down the road.

The road arced over a low hill. He slowed cautiously as he topped the rise. Beyond, the road dipped again into a shallow valley, flanked by copses of thick trees to either side and leading into a narrow rocky pass at the far end. Drawing to a halt, he saw the riders disappear into the pass, followed by a trailing cloud of dust as the rock walls engulfed them.

He was half way down the slope when the distant neighing of a pained horse echoed from the rocky pass. Simultaneously, surprised shouts and the din of metal on metal warned him that a conflict had erupted beyond the pass, and thoughts of the riders being ambushed flashed in his mind. Without pause he sprang towards the pass. His long strides carried him quickly over the rough ground. The echoing sound of battle was lost in the pounding of his heart and heavy breathing.

Rather than follow the course of the riders he bounded up the shallow slope to the right of the road, finding a flat, wide platform set in layers of rising elevation, like an elongated stairway. Mindful of the loose surface, he flanked the pass, which angled to the left. The ground dropped away before him, which he almost failed to spot as his eyes flicked to the scene of mayhem below. Skidding to a halt, he took stock of the battle.

The dozen wagons of the large caravan that had passed the previous day were spread out in a line beneath him. The foremost two were aflame, though the fire burned without ferocity, as if seeking purchase on the wood. Each of the wagon's horses was dead, riddled with arrows.

Wagoners clambered around the wagons, armed and seeking cover as arrows arced through the air towards them. As he watched, one man caught in the open toppled with a green arrow embedded in his back, sending him sprawling facedown onto the road.

Green-fletched shaft!

His gaze flashed around the rocky pass where dark-clad figures shifted among the rocks. Some raised bows and fired down at the caravan while others sought a better position. The ten riders he had followed had drawn their sabers and were slowly walking their horses through the pass towards the caravan. Armed guards emerged from the caravans, clad in similar leather jerkins. They numbered only half that of the riders, while even more brigands scaled down the rock walls to the road and closed on the caravans.

Valdieron stood in horrid fascination of the carnage. Dimly he was aware of the wagoners, most of them men, probably drivers. He could not see any children, though at the center of the column, a tall old man clutching a staff shielded a young female.

As near as he could tell, thirty or more brigands surrounded the caravan, who numbered no more than twenty counting the remaining drivers and the old man. Dropping to one knee and unhitching his bow, Valdieron drew and fired at the group of riders passing almost directly beneath him.

His first arrow streaked past the face of one rider and struck a neighboring horse in the side. The horse reared with a scream and toppled. The rider was thrown against the wall of the pass before the weight of his steed crushed his lower body against the stones. His agonized cries echoed through the pass as he tried in vain to move the prone beast.

Valdieron faltered. Previously he had only slain a handful of Trolls, their deaths easily justified by the memory of his dead father and the razed village. These were living, breathing men, probably with families. He did not even know the full reason for the attack. Perhaps they too had been forced from home by Trolls and were trying to make a living.

Yet that was no excuse for the ambuscade that had claimed the life of innocent wagoners.

His second arrow caught the next rider in the shoulder and pierced the thick leather of his jerkin. The force threw him from the saddle. His feet, however, became caught in the stirrups and he was dragged screaming back down the pass as his horse took fright and bolted.

The wagon guards took advantage of the fortuitous break and charged the riders, who were caught off guard by the surprised loss of two of their number.

The whizzing of an arrow dropped Valdieron to his stomach as a flight of shafts passed overhead. Bow-wielding brigands further down the pass had spotted him taking out their comrades and turned their fire to the new threat. He rolled, but found the ground no longer supported him until a jarring impact took his breath away. He had no time to recover as he slid on his back over rough stone. Disoriented but aware enough to know his plight, he twisted to slow his descent as the ground fell away again. He rolled onto the floor of the pass and came to a crouch amid a rain of dust and shale.

Wincing against the sting of grazes along his shoulders and back, he pulled his sword free as the guards collided with the rallying riders with a crash of steel on steel and cries of the injured.

While they may not have been well armed, the guards seemed organized as they speared into the riders. Their leader was a burly man of aging years carrying the facial scars of a man familiar with battle. His thick double-edged sword swept horizontally before him in great sweeps. To Valdieron's horror he aimed not at the riders, but at the defenseless horses. One mount fell to the weapon, rearing with its chest split open as it flailed futilely. Its rider rolled from the saddle, only to be skewered by another guard's slender rapier.

Valdieron almost leapt into the melee, remembering at the last moment the other wagoners who were hiding from the brigands above. Several brigands dropped from the walls and charged towards the unprotected wagons. The old man bearing the staff still guarded the young girl. Several wagoners milled around them, forming a protective circle, watching apprehensively for more arrows, though it seemed the brigands were going to finish them off with the blade.

With no time to ponder why fate had suddenly thrown him into this, Val sprinted towards the closing brigands as conflicting emotions rose inside him. He tried to force them out: to clear his mind and focus as he had been taught by his dream Master. Two brigands closest to him noticed his charge and turned to meet him, one wielding a slender rapier and the other a single-edged axe.

As he slowed, the closest brigand foolishly closed without waiting for his companion, sensing an easy victim in a lone youth with a sword. The brigand feigned a charge then planted his feet at the last moment and thrust. Valdieron desperately twisted with a parry, which deflected the lighter weapon but not before its sharp tip tore a gash in his shirt below the arm.

Continuing with the spin, Valdieron raised his weapon in a vertical block, stopping a second chopping attack by the brigand, a move that seemed to surprise his foe.

Pushing the blade away, Valdieron chopped diagonally at the brigand, hoping his heavier weapon would break his defenses. The brigand was forced to parry several quick cuts to the left and right, with only one chance to riposte with a thrust, which Valdieron easily defeated.

As the brigand retreated defensively, Valdieron's blade struck aside a desperate parry and sliced into his side, the leather providing little protection. Val did not have time to press the advantage against the wounded man as he found an axe blade arcing towards his face.

Rolling away from the blade, he came up in a crouch, only to find the axe reversing in an overhead chop. The brigand had surprising control over the weapon, though one look at his huge frame and muscled torso showed that he did not lack strength.

Valdieron's sword met the descending axe in a double-handed parry, the dull metal of the axe sliding down the silvery blade as the force of the blow pushed at his arms. Rather than fight the movement, Valdieron shifted his weight and let the axe continue its descent, twisting his sword when the axe was too low to do any harm and reversed it in a slash at the brigand's exposed stomach.

The blade sliced through soft leather armor with a steely hiss, splaying an arc of blood. The brigand's enraged face drained of color as he stumbled back. He staggered to a sitting position and slumped forward, unmoving, his axe still in hand and his head hanging slack against his chest.

Valdieron spun frantically, searching for more brigands. They seemed more concerned with the wagoners, having met their slack ring and cut through their defenses like a scythe through wheat. The shouts and joyful cheers of the brigands drowned out the dying cries of the pressed wagoners. Over the clamor, the wailing of the young girl carried to Valdieron, like a beacon. Desperately, he leapt towards the nearest brigand, and was caught within the mayhem of the melee. Cutting and thrusting, parrying and twisting, he became lost within the vortex of images and sounds, finding it hard to distinguish brigand from wagoner.

A lull came in the battle and he found himself caught in a trance-like state, where every detail seemed more focused. Brigands and wagoners lay slashed and torn, looking more asleep than dead against the bloodstained ground. Combat still raged around him, the sounds of their struggles warped so that the clanging of steel rang like the tolling of distant bells.

Then came the realization that the crying of the girl had ceased. He turned to find three brigands surrounding the girl and her aging protector. He took a struggled step forward, as if wading through waist-deep water. One brigand staggered back from a strike from the old man's staff, but another stepped forward to strike him in the side with a short sword. At this, the girl loomed up; a dagger clutched in her small hands, and lunged at the brigand. The dagger bit deep as the girl twisted it viciously.

Taking another faltering step, Val watched in horror as another of the brigands raised his sword and chopped at the girl's back. The cry of warning from his lips came out in an incomprehensible gurgle.

The girl fell slowly, like a feather, her face set like marble in a soundless open-mouthed scream, her large eyes open and flashing like jewels catching the rays of the sun. She toppled to the ground, her dirtied white dress now stained crimson.

Suddenly the trance that seemed to hold him back was gone, and Valdieron moved with a speed born of rage. Leaping at the two brigands, he met them without concern for his well-being.

He parried the slash of the brigand to the right and punched at his face, feeling his fist connect with the man's nose with a crunch of breaking cartilage. With his weight moving forward, he twisted around the thrust of the second brigand's rapier, and using a move he had learned only a few nights earlier, spun a kick at the man's chest, catching the brigand squarely and knocking him backwards. The man flailed and fell to the ground, rolling awkwardly to his feet, lost for breath.

Valdieron danced in quicker than the brigand expected, slashing viciously downwards. The brigand managed to raise his weapon to parry, but the ferocity of Valdieron's blow shattered the thin blade into tiny shards of flying metal. Then followed a muffled cry from the brigand, as Valdieron's sword sliced into his right collar and continued into his chest, and through his heart.

Valdieron lost grip of his sword as the brigand toppled backwards, his fingers suddenly numb. He was unaware of the trickle of blood running down his face from a gash in his forehead, or the cries of the dying around him. He was even oblivious to the approach of the few remaining guards who had driven off the last of the brigands. His gaze locked onto the dead man before him, though his mind pictured the body of the girl close by.

Anger. Regret. Sadness. Powerful and conflicting emotions assailed him in a matter of moments, before the release of darkness crashed about him as something thumped into the back of his head, and he knew no more.

* * *

The six Masters of the two Academies were seated around the large ebony table. They were dressed casually, though their demeanor and expressions showed their consternation. More than a few eyes flashed to the unoccupied seat at the head of the table, that which would normally have seated the High Master.

One man paced slowly around the large fire-lit room, his

hands clasped behind his back, his eyes downcast. Tall and powerfully built, Nortas, Master of the Blade Academy, dominated the room with his imposing presence. Three inches over six feet in height and thickly muscled in the chest, arms and thighs, he had a fierce reputation as a ruthless warrior and a master tactician. Many feared not just his magical accoutrements, but also the man himself, as capable in battle with or without weapons. A native of the southern Realm of Dak'mar, this enigmatic man had proven a great boon for the city, though his beliefs were too radical for many to credit, let alone give credence to.

Turning with the slightest creaking of leather and the clink of chain mail, Nortas leaned over the empty seat which had been Zaleef's and pressed his palms onto the table, letting his dark eyes drift over the other Masters, trying to gauge their expressions and thoughts.

There was Kezella, the raven-haired Mistress of Varella, Goddess of the Healing Arts. Her normally beautiful and serene face was twisted in a grim frown as she stared at her slender hands clasped before her, as if she were praying.

Yellow robes hid the skeletal figure of Jazachi the Conjuror, a bald-headed man of aging years with leathery skin, once dark ebony like a starless night. His face was expressionless, yet his piercing hazel eyes darted from master to master, as if waiting for somebody else to speak.

The next two figures could have been brothers, and in many cases were mistaken as such by those who did not know them. Both were tall and slender, with cat-like eyes and lobe-less pointed ears. Yeremis, clad in the dark robes of a Magician, was a Noble Elf from the Magic Isle, with flowing silver hair down past his shoulders and pale green eyes. Calanaar, wearing the woodland green robes of a Druid, had shorter platinum hair, while his eyes were of the darkest gray. His tanned skin marked him as a Woodland Elf. He was like the earth in many ways, beautiful yet strong, silent yet menacing, made more so by the pale Yew wood bow across his back and the quiver of gold-fletched arrows at his side.

The last figure drew Nortas' attention and held it longer than the others. A woman of mystical beauty, not just of face and body, but also of temperament and demeanor was the Horse-Maiden of the Fire Stallion Clan. Valkyra the Darishi captivated the proud warrior as no other could. Tall and athletic, she moved, fought and spoke with skill and grace, and her indomitable will and pride only elevated her in the opinion of the honorable Dak'marian. So even now he was angry that he could do little to wipe the frown and the worry from her flawless face as she cradled her chin in her hands leaning forward over the table, her curled auburn hair unable to fully hide her expression.

"I cannot see that we have any other option! It has gone beyond the point of waiting and hoping. The failure of our seers to locate Zaleef and the others must lead us to prepare for the worst. We can only assume the Seal at Mount Drac has failed and a Portal has opened." Tired and hoarse, Nortas worked moisture into his throat as he turned to Jazachi and regarded him with raised brow. "You of all here have greater knowledge of denizens from the other dimensions. Going on the reports of the past and your knowledge of the present, what can we expect from this, assuming we are correct in our supposition?"

The grim-faced old man smiled, though more in denial of his own knowledge than of mirth as he silently deliberated for several moments, though these thoughts were nothing new to him.

"The best case scenario would be that this Portal is, and will be, the only one to open, whether from luck or merely a fault in the Seal. Therefore, we could probably repel any attacks from this point of origin, considering the knowledge we have of the area, and the time we have on our side. The Demon Lords are not of this Plane, and their very existence depends on one thing, Unlife, the antithesis of existence. Therefore, they will send forth their minions, not to kill and spread mayhem through the realms, but to garner knowledge of our strengths and weaknesses. They will prepare for the arrival of their Masters who will be severely weakened the further they are away from the Unlife that is the Voids. Thus, depending on the size of the force they send through, we could not expect the more powerful Demons for several years, maybe a decade."

Whispers of surprise and fear echoed through the chamber as all hung on Nortas' next question. "And the worst case scenario?"

Jazachi coughed pointedly, screwing his nose as he paused.

"In the worst case, to the peril of mankind, the eight Portals we know of are open or opening, and all the hordes of Demon kind from every level of the Voids are coming through. As such, we could be facing a war the likes of which the legends only hint at, in less than a year, maybe two if we can somehow temporarily close a few of the Portals or quell the numbers coming through."

A stunned silence descended upon the room as all eyes turned to Nortas, whose head slumped against his chest as he muttered curses under his breath.

"Then this is what we must do. We need all the help we can get from the Kings and Queens of the realms. Have our best advisers and emissaries briefed on the possibilities of this war and have them sent to every ruler in the land. Many have followed us in the past, or have needed our help, and now we must seek to have those favors returned.

Also, we need reports and updates from the other Patrols. We must be forewarned about any indication of the breaking or failing of the Seals. This includes clarifying the situation in Mount Drac. Covert is the order of the day, so I propose that we enlist the aid of the Navigators.

Finally, we need every piece of information about these Portals and Demons in order to help us fight them. We also need to come up with a way of sealing these Portals, so I'll leave that to you, Jazachi. Also, any weapon, spell, device or item which may aid us, we must find, even if we have to buy, beg or steal them, understand?"

He once again let his gaze wander over the others, though they remained thoughtfully silent and dour as a whole. They offered little else save acquiescing nods or sighs. "Then let us begin. Grim times approach, and we must be prepared for them lest they overwhelm us. We have much work to do."

Chapter 14

Valdieron became groggily aware of the shrouded ambience of the place he had come to know as the 'Dream Plane'. He peered around, his senses and emotions still reeling from the ambush. He wondered if he were unconscious, asleep, or even dead, and assumed that a brigand's blow had felled him. He dismissed the last notion, fearing he would be in a far different place if he were dead.

Around him lay the bare plaza he had arrived at every night for the past several weeks. To his left lay the Hall of Combat, and to the right the Hall of Magic. Straight ahead loomed immense double doors which led to another part of the mystical city unfamiliar to him, for the Master had told him he would come to know it in time, but not now.

He turned and strode towards the large archway of the Hall of Combat, which emitted an arcane light, more orange like firelight when viewed from without, but crystal-clear within. He did not feel like training at the moment, but when he tried to will himself back to wakefulness, he was unable to find the release he craved. Dimly aware that the usual fog-like haze was not as thick or clinging, he stepped into the Hall.

The Master was present as always, standing in the very center of the hall, clad in his familiar gray robes and carrying no weapon as he slowly ran through patterns of varying difficulty, amazingly graceful yet subtly dangerous. Valdieron had recently begun to learn some easier offensive and defensive patterns, concentrating on stances, balance and techniques of strike and parry. He hoped one day to work up to what the Master was doing now.

Yet now he did not feel the usual excitement and anticipation at this prospect, only anger at not having knowledge of these moves so that he may have saved the life of the young girl and her older protector. Never had he felt so worthless, even when Marcus had disappeared, or when the Trolls had attacked and killed his father. This came as a surprise, though he surmised it was because now he felt he should have been able to do more with his newly learned skills, when before he had been powerless.

"Self flagellation can be both an obstacle and a driving force, Valdieron." He gave a start at the dulcet words of the Master. With a silent curse he raised his head to see the Master approaching on silent feet. He was definitely not in the mood for another of his puzzling speeches or lessons. Realizing he was weeping, he let his head drop again.

"You have learned an important lesson today, Valdieron. Now you know what it is to be helpless in the face of danger, to have no control over a situation no matter how much you would have it otherwise. And perhaps most importantly, you know what it is to face defeat."

Valdieron shook his head and cursed again, then raised his head with a bemused frown. "But why her, Master? She was only a child. Defenseless, yet still they cut her down like she was their most bitter enemy, without hesitation or remorse."

"It was as it was destined to be, Valdieron. You cannot change that."

Valdieron shook his head in denial. "She should not have died. She did not deserve to die! I could have changed that."

"Yet you did all you could to aid her. Her death was inevitable. Only she could have changed her destiny, Valdieron."

"Did I? I think there was more I could have done for her." He nodded his head, convinced of this, for deep inside his heart he knew it was true. "And I swear it will not happen again, and never will I be out of control."

He turned and left the hall, wanting to be alone.

The figure of the Master chuckled softly and turned away, hands clasped behind his back. "So ends tonight's lesson, Valdieron, a more important one you may not learn. Learn it well."

Outside, Valdieron strolled aimlessly, painstakingly trying to block out the pictures and images that assaulted him. He came to the double-doors and rested with his back against them, feeling the strange warmth of the metallic surface at his back.

After a time that seemed both ageless and instant, he looked up, as it compelled by some force. He thought the figure of the Master approached through the fog. Although much akin to the Master, there were subtle differences that became apparent as he came closer, and Astan-Valar drew up in front of Valdieron, exactly as he had last seen him.

"What... what are you doing here?" He had last seen the figure of Astan-Valar in the underground caverns beneath the Sentinel after falling into the stream while fighting Trolls. He had figured him mad then, being told tales of Dragons, Demons and wars long forgotten. He also had a seemingly excellent knowledge of Valdieron and his possessions, especially the Tear which had been passed to him by his mother, saying it had magical properties that could aid him.

And now he stood before Valdieron, as darkly mystical as before, if not more so, and Valdieron had to blink several times before believing he really was there.

"There is more that I must impart unto you, Valdieron. Be seated and hearken unto my words."

Valdieron began to tell the strange man he was not in the least bit interested in what he had to say, but realized he was indeed curious about this mysterious man and his mystical tales. He sat back down with a wry smile, admitting defeat as Astan-Valar watched him intently.

"You have learnt many lessons since we last met, Valdieron, and that is for the best. You know what it is to hate and what it means to fail. More importantly, you have taken heed of your emotions and in doing so you will be a better person. So many men, warriors in particular, do not let their emotions bother them, for they fear what their emotions tell them, yet you are one with yours. This will make your learning far easier and quicker.

"Do you remember the tale I first told you back in the Sable Realm of Dragonwing Mountain?" Valdieron nodded, for surprisingly he had taken great care in listening to the strange man's words on their first encounter. He was surprised at what Astan-Valar called the caverns in which they had met, as if they had once been a place of dwelling.

"Excellent. There is something I need you to do. Call it a quest, if you like, for it will involve a great deal of commitment on your behalf. There is a relic from the first age, a Disk, which was used to create the Seals blocking the Portals to the Voids. After the creation of the Seals, the Disk was broken into six pieces, for the Dragon Lords believed it to be of no further use and scattered them over the lands. Only the Disk can restore the Seals which even now are failing."

Valdieron frowned. Why was this man asking him to undertake the journey? From what he had seen, though apparently mad, Astan-Valar had to have some sort of power at his disposal, or how else could he have entered the Dream Plane? He voiced this question, to which Astan-Valar smiled as if expecting it.

"I cannot explain, Valdieron, for reasons you will soon realize, but you must believe me when I say that it is of extreme importance you find these pieces."

"But why me? Surely there are people far more capable than I. Could you not have the whole of Kil'Tar searching for them? Surely their locations are known to many."

"There is much danger in that, Valdieron. The existence and function of the six pieces of the Disk are in fact known by only a few. There are also those who would seek to prevent the Disk from being recovered, and although the Disk cannot be destroyed, it is possible that some will be very difficult to recover."

"How would I find these six pieces?"

"You will know it when you are near them, Valdieron. The Dragon's tear will be your guide in finding them. I can tell you, however, that your first piece can be found in the city of Thorhus."

Chuckling incredulously, Valdieron rose. "At least this must mean I'm not dead," he muttered. "So, you want me to find and recover six pieces of a Disk, the locations of which you know of only one. Their owners are probably powerful and not keen on giving up the pieces, while others may find out and try to recover them before me?"

Astan-Valar smiled ruefully, as if in apology. "That is true. Even now there are those who sense your growing power and would have you destroyed for your potential threat. Yet they also fear you, which may work in your favor."

Valdieron turned and pressed his forehead against the metallic doors, for the first time seeing its finely crafted surface. It showed the picture of a lightning-struck battlefield, over which countless figures stood, all still and staring upwards over the distant mountains.

"Somehow I do not think that you are asking me to do this," he sighed.

"We all have our choices, Valdieron. Most of us make the

wrong decisions, though I hope you do not."

"But how will I find-" he broke off, as the figure of Astan-Valar was gone, swallowed by the swirling mist.

Valdieron shouted curses after Astan-Valar, but the man did not return. Suddenly struck by the dull throbbing of a headache, he lowered himself back onto his haunches to fight off the swirling tide of thoughts and emotions. His fingers sought the lavender kerchief on his arm, conjuring the image of one dark-haired girl in his mind and he smiled slightly for the first time in many days as he remembered Natasha before their parting, crying in his arms yet happy.

The distant, haunting melody of a single harp slowly brought Valdieron from a deep sleep. He could clearly remember his conversation with Astan-Valar, yet felt somehow as if it had transpired some time ago. Maybe he could sleep as well as visit the Dream Plane, shifting between the two? He instinctively felt for the Tear, and found it rested against his chest beneath a thin blanket.

He knew he was inside a caravan, whether it was one from the caravanserai or not, he was unsure. The interior was cluttered with furniture and equipment, with the bed he occupied pressed against one wall beneath a small, curtained window. A narrow wooden door was situated in the wall at the foot of the bed, flanked by a small wardrobe and a table cluttered with odds and ends. A small ceramic burner atop the table created the not unpleasant aroma of rose and garlic.

His belongings lay in a pile in the corner, his pack resting beside his weapons.

'Which means I have not been captured by the brigands, at least', he mused. There was also a platter of food on a small stool beside the bed, a mixture of soup, bread, cheese and water. The soup was heavily flavored with garlic, mint and basil, but his sudden hunger forced him to taste it, and its surprisingly pleasant flavor had him spooning it out quicker than he could consume it. Its warmth revealed that it had not been sitting for long. He finished with the bread and cheese together, finding both freshly made. Even the water tasted like chilled spring water fresh from a mountain brook, and he drank thirstily.

With his hunger sated for the moment, his focus switched to

the strange music which emanated from somewhere outside the caravan. Its tune was by no means rousing, rather a slow lamentation. Pushing aside the blanket, he found that he wore a pair of loose blue trousers and a thin white cotton shirt.

Feeling the back of his bandaged head, he winced as he gently probed the tender wound. *'What struck me?'* The bruised lump suggested something blunt.

Swinging his legs over the side of the bed and onto the carpeted floor, he pulled on his boots and rose unsteadily. He reached for his pack and weapons, but hefted his sword only, slinging the makeshift baldric over his shoulder. Moving to the door, he gently pulled it open and stepped out into the gloom.

Broiling clouds masked the waxing brightness of the Twin Moons, signaling an impending storm forming in the east. It was perhaps two or three hours until midnight, with a deep chill permeating the air. *'Probably snowing back home.'* Here, however, in the lowlands, come the morning there would probably only be a covering of frost.

What few caravans that remained of the original dozen were clustered beneath the bowers of several holms not far from the trade route. To the north loomed the barren passes where the ambush had taken place, a not too distant reminder.

To the west beyond the sparse glade, a flickering fire created dancing silhouettes of several figures around it. He could hear a harp's moody consonance from among the small group. Curious, he slowly made his way towards the fire, careful of his step as he folded his arms across his chest for warmth.

He was shocked to find that the large fire was in fact a funeral pyre, slowly growing to its fullness, engulfing the wrapped bodies laid out formally within. The harp echoed into the night, a wordless farewell as those who survived the ambush watched on, silently fare-welling their friends and family.

Valdieron pressed up against the bole of a large tree and watched the ceremony. His gaze shifted from person to person. One of the first he recognized was the aged man who had been protecting the girl during the fight. He now leaned on a large staff for support, with his left arm cradled in a sling. Relieved to find him alive, Valdieron knew he could not hope for the same for the girl, who had been struck down during the melee. Silently he empathized with the old man, sharing his torment and once again the terrible feeling of powerlessness.

Nearby stood the scar-faced old warrior who had led the guards against the brigands. His shoulders slumped as if carrying a great burden, yet his head remained high with dignity. Beside him stood four other guards, dressed in their best clothes and wearing dark bands on their upper left arms, probably a symbol of sorrow or farewell for the fallen.

Further around the circle stood a line of men, women and children who must have been hidden inside the caravans. There were fourteen in total, probably family of the caravan owner and of the drivers.

As the harp continued its wordless dirge, the conflagration built on the pyre until its great heat turned on itself and it began to fade away, soon to drop to a ring of embers and then to scaled ash, to be scattered by the winds. At one point, the old man with the staff turned to see Valdieron, as if he had felt his presence, and he gave him a brief nod, his eyes red and blurred from tears. The action, whether from greeting or acknowledgment, struck Valdieron as uncommonly courteous under the circumstances.

With the ceremony ended, the people began to drift back to the caravans, many passing Valdieron and flashing him a wan smile or a word of greeting or thanks before passing. One who did not register his presence was the scar-faced guard, who departed quickly.

The injured old man appeared before him and stopped. A woman of the same age followed him. Her eyes, though red and moist, regarded him with concern, and Valdieron guessed her to be his wife. She smiled weakly at him then continued past, leaving her husband with Valdieron.

The old man stood regarding Valdieron for some time, as if contemplating what to say, or struggling with the awkwardness of the situation. Finally he sighed deeply and turned away to face the dying ring of fire.

"To the dead, with heavy hearts, we say our soft farewells." He spoke in a whisper, but loud enough for Valdieron to hear his sorrowful litany. "You risked much to aid us, young man."

Was that a question or a statement? Valdieron wondered whether or not he was expected to give an account of his reason, but the old man denied him the chance.

"Who knows how many more would be among the pyre,

had you not." He brought the gnarled staff sharply back to butt his forehead painfully against it. "Yet how many could have been saved had I not been foolish and trusted those miscreants."

Valdieron wondered if the old man was not perhaps a little mad, as he turned to face him again.

"Again I lose myself in thought. You must be wondering at the reason for the assault on our caravan. Nothing more than the honorless act of ignoble men, for those who led the attack were men of my employ, or at least up until seven days ago, when they disappeared. I had assumed them gone back to their homes or to the nearest Inn. Now I know of their plan since the day I signed them on as guards. I wish I had questioned them more thoroughly, though I was short of time and they seemed decent enough for my purposes and claimed to have reputable references, which I unfortunately had not the time to question."

A fresh trail of tears ran down his pale leathery cheeks. "And now my idiocy has cost the lives of my friends and family."

Valdieron had no reply to sympathize with the old man, knowing anything he said would probably come across as mocking. "I am sorry for your loss Sir, and wish to thank you for your hospitality and caring. I regret arriving too late to have been of more assistance."

"I am sorry, my young friend. My mind grows fickle with remorse and guilt. Let not what happened here be a burden to you, as it was neither your battle nor your fault. I am grateful your path crossed ours or I fear the outcome would have been far worse. I assume you are one of the many young warriors heading for Thorhus this time of year for the Trial?"

"Trial, Sir?"

The old man collected himself and shuffled past Valdieron, motioning for him to follow.

"You haven't heard of the Trial of Combat which is held each year in Thorhus?"

Valdieron shook his head in reply.

"The annual Trial of Combat brings many of the lands greatest warriors to do battle for both money and prestige. This year, Hagar, a Dak'marian warrior, vies for his fifth successive victory, one that will grant him a boon from the King. It is rumored that he will ask for the hand of Princess Kitara, a young woman of great beauty."

Though intrigued, Valdieron knew he had other matters to deal with in Thorhus. "No, Sir. I am visiting my sister who moved there recently. I hope to be there in time to see this Trial, however. When does it commence?"

"On the first day of every year, New Years Festival. That is not for some time, however, as winter is not yet upon us. In the meantime, you may journey with us, if you like. We will terminate our travels in Ranil three days from now, after which you may be able to get a job as a guard on a caravan bound for Thorhus. The pay will not be good, but you will get there eventually, and I can pull a few strings to get you a good Master. Besides, to be honest, we could use your presence for the next few days until we reach Ranil."

Valdieron hesitated, though the old man was too preoccupied by his thoughts to take much notice. "That would be much appreciated, Sir. I thank you for the invitation."

The old man halted at a caravan, this one larger than most and seemingly unscathed from the battle. He pulled open the thin door and stepped up inside before turning. "There is no need for thanks, young man. I will see you on the morrow. Rest where you will and make yourself at home. The caravan in which you woke is there for your use, and food will be provided. Sleep well and good night."

The door closed softly before Valdieron could give more thanks, so he turned with a sigh and made his way back to his caravan.

Several of the wagoners and guards had built a small fire in the center of the cluster of caravans and were eating and chatting softly. Rather than confront them so early, Valdieron gathered up his gear and some blankets and moved into the secluded wood a little, where the whispers of the wagoners and the crackling of the fire were barely perceptible. Overhead, the clouds rolled in fast, and a few drops fell, though nothing heavy ensued. He drifted into a troubled sleep, willing himself to a normal night's sleep rather than visiting the 'Dream Plane'. For the first time in a while he dreamed, and although they were tormenting, it was as if they were penitence as his sleepy tears mixed with the falling drizzle.

Chapter 15

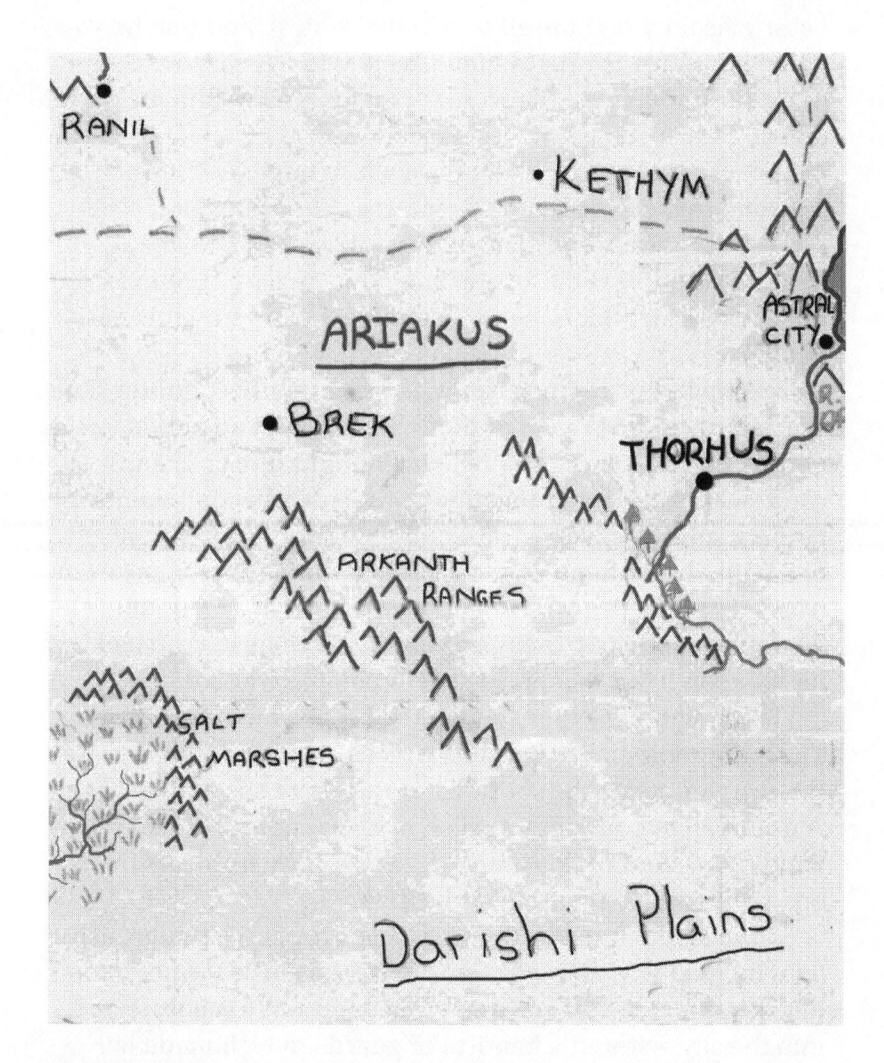

Princess Kitara leaned forward with her slender hands pressed against the smooth stone sill of her window, overlooking the gardens between the southern wall of the keep and the thirty-foot high fortifications that surrounded it. It was a scene she always enjoyed watching, though the skeletal trees and sparse bushes showed the menace of winter, despite the day being warmer than usual with only sparse clouds in the sky.

Yet she had little to be light-hearted about. Rumors were spreading that Hagar of Orin, a warrior from the Realm of Dak'mar, was already in town, preparing for the Trial of Combat held on the first day of summer. He was believed to be betting heavily on himself to win the contest, and that he was going to ask for her hand in marriage when he did win. As a five-time winner, people were saying he was within his right to do so.

She rose and kicked away the chair in anger, sending it crashing to the floor several feet away. She had some unpleasant ideas about the young warrior, but she knew nothing could be done, other than hope he would be defeated in the Combat, which seemed unlikely, considering his past efforts.

Despite her grudging acknowledgment of his fighting skills, she had never been fond of him. Though tall and athletic, with no lack of charisma or beauty, she thought him cold and condescending. Even in battles he regarded his opponents as pathetic and worthless. The Combat was full contact, one on one with armor and weapon, yet his brutality had often seemed over the top. Several of his opponents had died from the wounds he inflicted, including last years finalist, who had had his weapon hand then head severed by the warrior.

With a sigh Kit turned and made her way to her bedroom. The main room of her quarters was hexagonal in shape, with the entry opposite the south window where she had just been. A doorway led out onto a railed balcony there, but the cold winds prevalent of this time of year kept her from leaving it open or venturing out there too often.

Kitara skipped down the steps and dropped languorously onto the bed with another sigh. There was little for her to do this day. Her father had commanded her not to venture out into the city without a handful of guards, which made her angry, though she did admit it made sense considering the many strangers who were coming into the city for the Combat.

But that did not mean she had not been out. She rolled over and glanced at the large oak wardrobe built into the right wall of the room. Inside she had hidden a magical item she had acquired at great cost. It was a facemask, like one worn to a masquerade. Although plain looking, it had the ability to change one's appearance. She used it to alter her appearance and venture into the city alone. She used it often, especially when she wanted to practice her barding at the local Inns. It was also useful for mingling with others and finding out news first hand.

A large mirror set into the door of her wardrobe returned her reflection, and she cast a wry smile at herself. At seventeen years of age, she was tall with coppery skin, a trait of her half Dak'marian heritage. She had always felt mature for her age, and had often been mistaken for much older. Her hair was raven-dark and hung loosely about her shoulders. Her large eyes were pale blue, like a clear sky, yet they could shift hues, and darken when she was angry.

A soft knocking on the outer chamber door brought her upright with a groan of frustration. She was not in the mood for visitors, and had left instructions for her maid, Meka, to politely ask visitors to come back later.

She rose and returned to the main chamber, seating herself on the large cushioned divan near the doorway.

"Enter!" she said firmly, setting her hair around her in a semblance of order.

Her brother Andrak entered the room quickly. Only a year older than Kitara, he had the same litheness as her, but his skin was paler and his hair a light brown, almost sandy. He was handsome, with angular features and flashing brown eyes that matched his smile when he showed it. This day, however, his face was grim as he strode over to Kitara, who rose to embrace him.

"Kit, the rumors in the city are not good. They say that Hagar has arrived already, and some are saying that when he wins the combat, he will ask for your hand in marriage."

"I know, Andy." Kitara sighed as she released the hug. She flopped back onto the divan.

"You haven't been going out again by yourself, have you?" Andrak frowned. He was the only person who knew about her disguised sojourns into the city, though she suspected her father's Spy, Kalamar, also knew.

"I'm sorry, Andy, but you have been so busy with this merchant evaluation that I couldn't ask you. Besides, nothing ever happens, and I can take care of myself, despite father's doubts."

"I know you can, Kit, but that doesn't mean that I'm not

going to worry. The streets grow rougher every day. With Kalamar gone, father is slowly losing control of the guilds, especially the thieves guild."

Kitara had noticed this shift during her last few visits, and had even been forced to shake off a thief who had stalked her for several blocks

"Is there any word from Kalamar?"

Andrak shook his head with a frown and sat beside her. As he wiped his gaunt face, she saw how tired he looked.

"No. Father does not say it, but I think he is troubled. There has been no word for several weeks, and no sign of him. I think father blames himself for sending him on such a perilous journey."

Shaken by the news, Kitara shook her head and smiled wistfully. "Kalamar was the only one who could get to the bottom of the Horse-thieving racket. He is most likely playing it safe."

"Probably. Anyhow, back to Hagar. What do you think Father will do about it?"

Kitara grimaced. "I do not know, though I hope he is not forced to abide by the law of the Combat." She motioned to her study, where on the table lay a tear-streaked parchment that covered the rules of the combat and the rights of the victors. There was a list of things which could not be asked by the victor on his fifth consecutive win, such as an amount of gold over ten thousand, or the crown of the King. "There is nothing that says the winner cannot ask for a son or daughter's hand in marriage. Such an oversight will put father into a difficult situation should Hagar win, given that the general population seem to welcome such a thing."

Andrak nodded. He had heard that many people were all for such a marriage: the half-blooded daughter of the King to an invincible warrior from the South.

"I'm sorry, Kit. I'm sure Father will come up with something. I don't think he's about to give you away to some warrior, no matter how good he is. If need be, I'll enter the combat and defeat him myself." He flashed her his charming smile, which warmed her, and she pressed against him thankfully.

"Andy, you can't do that for me. I won't have you risk your life. You have seen the tournaments, and you know how brutal they can be. I would never forgive myself if something happened to you."

He nodded and turned away. He would readily enter the tournament for her, though he wondered if he had the skill to defeat the young warrior, Hagar. He had been trained with the sword as soon as he could hold one, but Hagar was strong, fast and unmerciful, and had killed before.

Kitara gripped his arm softly in appreciation and pressed her head against his shoulder.

"Don't worry, Kit. If Father cannot come up with something, I'm sure Kalamar will when he returns."

Andrak rose and gently freed himself from her grasp. "I must go. There is a dinner tonight to celebrate the birthday of the leader of the Merchants Guild, and I must attend. Do not fret, little sister. Everything will work out in the end. Hey, trust me!" Giving her a wink, he pulled open the door and exited.

Kitara sighed again and stretched out on the divan, eyes closed in thought. Her life had abruptly reached a crisis. She had not thought much on her direction in life before, but she knew marriage had not been a priority. She had always dreamed of travel, to learn the art of Barding and exercising her skills in exotic places like the Magic Isle or Lloreander, the Elf-City, whose Bards were reputed to be the greatest on Kil'Tar. With her mind suddenly turned to the Elves and their city, she did not know when sleep overtook her, yet she slept long into the evening, as Meka dutifully kept others away.

* * *

Valdieron felt more like an outcast than a guest traveling with the merchants. Their solemn demeanor made him feel a little depressed, more than he had been, anyhow. He sat beside a middle-aged driver at the rear of the caravanserai, so he was able to watch those before him. He still felt guilt over not having been able to do something more in the battle which claimed the lives of the seventeen men, women and children. The scar-faced veteran who was the captain of the guards did not seem to like him very much, and every so often turned to Valdieron and gazed unblinkingly at him for several seconds. His face remained impassive, and he said nothing.

The white-haired driver at his side shifted with a grumble to refill his pipe, skillfully juggling the reins of the two horses and his tobacco pouch. This seemed to content him as he leaned back and sighed. Suddenly feeling himself being watched, Valdieron turned to find the Captain regarding him again, but he turned away slowly when Valdieron locked gazes with him.

"He doesn't like me very much, does he?" Valdieron softly asked the driver, not expecting a reply. They had hardly spoken over the course of the previous day and this morning, apart from introductions and occasional comments about the weather. That his name was Hubert, Valdieron did know, and he had been driving for the old merchant, Nagus, for eighteen seasons.

"Nuh!" Hubert's voice was raspy, from many years of facing the harshness of the trails and too much tobacco as company. Though surprised, Valdieron nodded as if he had known the answer.

"But why? I cannot see that I have done him any offence, have I?"

Hubert drew another long puff on his pipe.

"Now that depends. Old Dane is a little on the stubborn side, and everybody knows how he likes to get his own way. Well, the other night, after the ambush, it was he who knocked you out near the end, thinking you to be another of the brigands. Nagus reprimanded his for his actions, and pointed out the six Brigands you had slain. Dane did not like that, which is why you aren't one of his favorite people at the moment. You won't have to worry about it after we get to Ranil."

Valdieron sighed ruefully. He could hardly wait to reach Ranil, probably the following afternoon if they continued at this steady pace. They were not expecting trouble this close to the city, though the five remaining guards kept their hands close to their weapons.

"What is Ranil like?" asked Valdieron hesitantly after a long silence.

Hubert regarded him askance before reaching for his pipe and tobacco again. After he has taken his first draw he began to speak.

"Ranil is more a large market than a city, being situated on the Highway. They get all of the wagons heading north and south, so you usually encounter a variety of people and product. The Duke supplements the town's wealth by taxing merchants who must use Ranil as the focal point of the northern trading route. Also, all merchants must join the Union and pay their dues, thus raising the prices merchants charge for their goods."

Valdieron frowned. "Why not just detour Ranil?"

"Many do!" Hubert took another long draw on his pipe. "However, many merchants operate from Ranil, despite the costs, so freight is often taken there from the north, and picked up by buyers to be taken south."

Val pondered this. "So many merchants reduce their travel time and return with their goods, allowing them to make faster and more trips."

Hubert nodded. "Exactly. It works both ways. The northerners, who are predominantly fishermen, foresters, miners and craftsmen, are able to get things like clothing and exotic goods from the south."

"But don't the higher prices affect the Duke in the end?" asked Valdieron. "His people must also purchase these goods, and although he gets the taxes from them, sooner or later they won't be able to afford to purchase them. Then they buy less, and he gets less taxes from the Merchants."

"Yes and no," agreed Hubert with an approving nod, finishing his pipe before continuing. "Sooner or later, he will have to come to a compromise with the merchants, or he is not going to be very popular with his people, or even less so than he already is."

Valdieron was trying to sort through the confusing information. "Then why don't they get rid of him and elect somebody else?"

Hubert laughed, a dry cackle that lifted the tips of his graying moustache. "This man is nobility, lad, probably with some ties even to the King in Thorhus. You don't just elect somebody else. There are those under his command who advise him concerning matters of the people. If the people are not happy, they let him know, and he does what he can to fix whatever problems arise, but never at a cost to himself. That is the way of nobility, lad."

"There is nothing to stop him from doing as he pleases, apart from common sense. You said before that the people would not buy if the prices were too high. He is not going to threaten his well-being by disregarding the people. There must be demand to meet supply, in all things, but especially in trade. If the people did not buy, or the merchants did not trade out of Ranil, the Duke would indeed lose out."

"But that doesn't tell you much about Ranil. All in all it is a decent sort of place, though there are more unsavory characters about than most places, due to all the money which is passed around."

His desire for conversation apparently sated for the time being, Hubert lapsed into silence and Valdieron did not press him, lost in his own thoughts. Nagus had told him that he would link him up with another caravan heading to Thorhus, which was what he needed if he was to find the first piece of the Disk.

"The mare is favoring her left foreleg," he said suddenly, noticing for the first time the animal's discomfort. Hubert strained to see, cursing under his breath as he saw the sorrel mare was pulling up on her paces.

"Should have seen that myself!" Drawing the wagon to a slow halt, he waved for the others before him to continue as they slowed, wondering at his stopping. Two of the guards on horseback slowed to wait as the wagons continued down the trail.

"I'll have a look," offered Valdieron as the wagon rattled to a halt. He dropped lightly off the side, glad for the chance to stretch, his behind having grown numb from the hardness of the wooden seat. He approached the mare slowly, knowing that if it were hurt, it might be irritable or apprehensive. The horse flicked its tail nervously, but allowed him to slowly run a hand over its neck. Speaking softly to the animal, an aging mare probably getting too old for this kind of harsh work, he was able to softly run a hand over its foreleg and fetlock. Raising its hoof, he turned so that its foreleg rested on his upper leg as he knelt and spotted a small stone caught beneath its hard metal shoe. Drawing out his knife, he carefully pried the stone loose, drawing a nicker of discomfort from the animal, though she did not pull away. Checking to see the stone had not caused too much damage, Valdieron lowered the foreleg slowly to the ground and patted the animal softly before leaping back onto the wagon.

"Just a stone," he stated, taking his seat.

Hubert regarded him for several moments before nodding and taking up the reins again. "Won't be long before we stop for the evening. I'll swap her for one of the guard's horses tomorrow." With a whistle and a flick of the reins he set them into motion again.

"Where did you learn horses, lad? I know men who have driven for twenty years who wouldn't have known the horse had a problem."

"I was raised around horses. My father bred them."

"Near here?"

Valdieron winced at the question, for it brought back some bitter memories. "To the northwest, Sir. In the mountains."

"A village?"

"Yes."

"Why are you going to Thorhus?"

Although he felt like telling Hubert to mind his own business, the desire to tell of the recent events rose in him. "They were all killed, Sir. Trolls…" The short answer seemed to satisfy Hubert as he nodded and grumbled his condolences.

"Always a threat, Trolls. Seen a few, even had one attack our caravan once. Killed four guards and took off with one of the horses. Big bastard he was too, maybe ten feet tall. A War Troll, in broad daylight. Those others, they're hurt by the light, but not these ones. See any like him?"

"A couple."

"From a distance, I hope?" joked Hubert, his worn face split with a wide grin.

"Not far enough!" Valdieron smiled as he patted the sheath of his sword over his right shoulder, indicating the dried hide which wound around the leather and metal frame. This brought another smile from Hubert. With a sudden conspiratorial look, he reached into his cloak and drew out a small ceramic flask with a leather handle. Undoing the stopper, he took a large swig and screwed his face up like a dried apple before he lowered it, cursing happily. He wiped his mouth with the back of his hand and passed the flask to Valdieron.

"Have a swig. I usually keep it for when it gets cold, but it seems you have a story to tell lad, and like my Pa was fond of saying, 'If you're gonna tell a story, wait until you're drunk, then it'll sound twice as good." This made him break out into another soft chuckle, struck by his own humor.

Valdieron tried not to laugh as he raised the flask to his mouth. The liquid inside had a heavy apple scent. He had only drunk a little wine at home, or some ale he and Kylaran had smuggled from Mister Otterman's cellar. Not wanting to offend Hubert, he took a small mouth-full, tasting the apple flavor, but swallowed quickly as Hubert had.

Whatever the liquid was, it burnt his throat fiercely on the way down, and he could feel his nostrils flare as he gasped for air. He coughed sharply and his eyes watered. He was vaguely aware of Hubert cackling beside him, and took several huge gasps of air. He was smiling, though, caught up in Hubert's mirth and the unexpected friendly turn of events.

"What is that?" he gasped, taking another mouthful. This time he was prepared for the wave that hit him, though his eyes watered again and he thought his breath must be ablaze as he exhaled sharply.

"Jahad's fire, lad. The best companion a man can have in the dead of winter, let me tell you!" He took the flask from Valdieron and shook it, testing its volume. "You talk, I'll drink."

Laughing at Hubert's suddenly funny comment, Valdieron began to relate the events of the past few weeks, beginning with the attack by the Trolls, and ending with him coming across the ambush not far down the road. As he spoke, he occasionally took a drink from the flask. He was careful not to speak of the Dragon's Tear around his neck or his mysterious visits from Astan-Valar. Hubert seemed enchanted by his tale, his face set in awe, though broken by bursts of spontaneous laughter or gulps from the flask. When Valdieron spoke of his brush with the horse thieves, Hubert showed his distaste by spitting over the side of the wagon, though he did not interrupt.

When it was over, Valdieron felt relieved, as if an unseen weight had been lifted from him.

Hubert complimented him on his great tale and once again offered his sympathies. He then began to relate some wild tales of his own journeys, though they seemed more story than truth to Valdieron. He listened as Hubert chatted on into the afternoon, and was dozing before they stopped for the evening, somehow getting down from the wagon and crawling beneath it to sleep. Not surprisingly, he did not visit the Dream Plane that night, though if he had, he did not know if he would have remembered it, anyway.

Chapter 16

Hammagor rested impatiently on his new throne before the ebony Portal leading to the Voids. At his right, within easy reach, was his fifteen-foot long Ebonite Lance, a dark as the Portal behind him. Forged in the fire pits on the highest plane of the Voids, the weapon was as deadly as it was evil, having its own thirst for blood and death, like its wielder and master. Its twin, a Saber, hung at Hammagor's waist, silently impelling the Demon to take action and sate its own thirst for blood. The Gigantor repulsed these thoughts, knowing the time for killing would come.

He roared angrily as the inactivity pressed at him. Lesser Demons throughout the chamber and outside cowered with fear at the sound, for more often than not it was a precursor to one of the Demon's rages, where he would kill anything he laid eyes on. This time, however, there was no explosion from the Demon Lord.

Hammagor had never been one for watching and waiting, and normally he would have taken his force of Demons and started a bloody rampage across the realms, but he was acting on a higher authority, the Mighty Demon Lord Sett.

The small reconnaissance group he had dispatched had reported no signs of Loremasters, only several small colonies of humans, which they had steered clear of on Hammagor's command. They were only just past the border where the northlands met the wastelands of the South, so the possibility of finding something increased the further north they went.

Hammagor grinned in silent anticipation. There would be no mistakes this time. In their last encounter with the Loremasters and their armies, five thousand years earlier, greater numbers and sheer desperation of the Loremaster armies had defeated them. This time, with the Demon Hordes multiplied tenfold, and no Dragon Lords remaining to battle, he was confident of an easy victory over this Plane. He cursed that the armies would take some time come through the portal, but knew it would not be long before they were numerous enough to take action. With the information the Soul Seeker was sending, he would have a plan of conquest organized before long.

With another silent command, twenty Hunters and ten Shadows stood before him, led by two Soul Seekers.

"It is time to gather supplies. Scour the land to the north and bring to me some humans. Keep to the small villages, those who will not be missed. We do not need many, only enough to build our strength until the time comes to relocate." With no further instruction necessary, the two Soul Seekers led the group of Demonic killers from the chamber.

With his spirits raised, he rose quickly and strode from the room, his lance appearing in his clawed hand as he silently commanded its presence. He smacked aside several smaller Demons, which were not smart or quick enough to get out of his reach, killing only three of them. He was in a good mood and knew every one would count in the upcoming war. In the meantime, however, he had an underground city to explore and plans to formulate.

* * *

As the merchant column topped a small rise, Valdieron was afforded his first view of Ranil. At a distance it appeared crude, a misshapen conglomeration of wooden and stone buildings interwoven by winding, dusty streets. Its outer area was a mass of tents, wagons and shelters, housing those who were just passing through, with no intention of staying longer than a night or two.

The Keep was easily discernable over the undulating sea of buildings. It was a large high-walled building, much like a fortified palace, with rooftop walkways and crenellated towers at each corner.

As they closed upon the outer limit of the city, they passed more wagons, riders and caravans heading north. Many yelled greetings to Nagus, who rode at the fore of the column. Some noticed his dark armband, which they recognized as a symbol of mourning and simply gave him a curt nod or a sympathetic tip of a hat.

Riding beside Hubert, and nursing a tender head from the previous afternoon, Valdieron was eager to be inside the city, though he was glad he was in the company of the merchants and drivers. As they passed through the tent city along the outskirts, he noted there were more people in one group than there had been in the whole of Shadowvale, and there were dozens of such groups.

A small outpost signaled the entrance to the city. The change from tents to houses was the only other indicator of the start of the city proper. Hundreds of people wandered seemingly without purpose along the wide street. Voices mingled and carried through the air.

Valdieron watched it all in a state of shock, studying many of those who passed him, noting likeness and differences between them. There was a definite mix, from the scantily, shabbily dressed to the pompous-looking in laced finery and bright colors. Others wore armor, while most carried a weapon of some sort.

"Where are we going?" shouted Valdieron over the bustling noise of the crowded street. "Shouldn't we have stopped outside?"

Hubert shook his head in answer, though not vigorously, as he was also feeling the effects of his heavy drinking the evening before. "Nagus has his own compound further inside the city, near the markets. We'll stop there, and his people will get us unloaded."

Valdieron guessed that Nagus must be a fairly high-ranking Merchant.

The road continued more or less straight, passing numerous cross-streets and lanes lost between the dilapidated buildings. Warehouses were dotted throughout the city, some with their own guards, even in the day, though it was approaching evening with the sun sinking slowly over the western horizon.

The market was a huge area situated in the middle of the city. A misshapen collection of tents, stands, wagons and benches constructed in no apparent order, and with people passing between each with practiced ease, it merged with the line of large wood and stone buildings which marked its edge. Nagus guided them around the market's edge. Half way around, he steered them onto a side street, away from the teeming market.

A large wooden fence enclosed Nagus' compound with a single sliding gate at its entrance, and a small wooden barbican beside it, upon which a single guard stood. As the wagons approached, his command carried down to somebody below as he recognized Nagus' caravan. The gate swung open. Guards flanked the entry so that nobody else entered the compound.

A large courtyard opened beyond the gate before a large building, long and flat with many doorways and a long rail skirting a flat patio. The guards all rode to this and dismounted, looping their reins over the rail and entering the building as several servants appeared to tend the horses. Nagus turned the team to the right of the building and entered into a long barn-like building, which easily accommodated the dozen wagons. More workers arrived to begin unloading and storing the goods.

Nagus disappeared at this point, heading across the yard to the house. Valdieron watched him go, then turned and leapt onto the back with Hubert who was uncovering their load, a pile of small sacks filled with grain and flour.

Although Nagus had invited him to accompany them to Ranil, he did not want to be considered a freeloader, so he helped Hubert unhitch the wagon. Nobody said anything to him about it, nor did he feel uncomfortable doing it.

He and Hubert slowly tossed down the small bags to the others who waited in a line to stack them on large wooden pallets against the nearby wall. Once they had finished, Hubert shouldered a worn duffel bag from under the wagon seat and gave Valdieron a thankful smile. Val wondered if Hubert would have been forced to unload the wagon by himself if he had not been there to help him.

"Let's go and get some food and rest, lad. Nagus wants you to go with him in the morning when he looks for buyers and more tenders. He will hook you up with a caravan heading to Thorhus if he can, or at least point you in the right direction."

A separate building for the live-in drivers and wagoners was situated across the yard from the warehouse. It was a single-roomed wooden building of solid construction. Two rows of bunked beds ran along either wall, room enough for a hundred people, with small chests for personal belongings and a few wardrobes scattered about for larger items. Hubert tossed his small bag onto the lower bed nearest the door.

"Close to the outside air as I can be!" he said with a smile. Valdieron dropped his heavy pack onto the floor against the wall but kept his sword on his back. He loosened his belt and tossed it onto the upper bunk.

The aroma of spiced meats and vegetables wafted from a petitioned area at the rear of the room as several cooks prepared food for the people who slowly began to filter in.

"What about the families of the dead?" asked Valdieron softly.

"We have no family, lad, at least none who would mourn our passing. Some of us are, or were married, but only to others in Nagus' caravan. We lead solitary lives, with no commitments other than our jobs and responsibilities to Nagus and one another. There is no room for personal lives for us. There is simply not enough time for settling down between trips. We will probably be leaving again tomorrow; day after at the latest, and that is how it is every time. Anybody who desires something else quits. Only Nagus has family who do not travel with us, and I'm sure they are learning of the loss at this moment, if they do not know already."

Valdieron nodded. Silently he wondered what sort of a life these people led, with no family and few friends. With a wry smile he realized he was much the same in his present situation.

The evening meal was tasty and filling, which Valdieron savored as he sat silently beside Hubert at the large table. Conversation at the table was hushed and sporadic, and Valdieron said little unless directly spoken to. He was glad for that, still not comfortable around so many strangers.

When the meal was finished and cleared away, most went to their beds to catch up on lost sleep. Hubert and some others remained at the table, talking softly about many things. A deck of cards was brought out and a game that Valdieron soon learned was called 'Royalty' was started. Small toothpicks were evenly distributed between each player as stakes. Valdieron moved his chair to the side of Hubert's.

As the game commenced, he realized it was a game he and his father had played occasionally, but they called it 'Crowns'. Each player was dealt a hand of five cards. They were then allowed to give up some or all of their cards for others from the pack in an effort to improve their hands. The better hands included four of a kind, with Crowns (thus the name) being the highest-ranking suit, followed by Suns, Moons and Stars. The best hand consisted of the top five cards of the Crowns suit, and a bad hand was made up of no pairs or a low pair, though the number one, called the Scepter, was the highest in each suit. It was an easy game to play once you got to know it.

When a flask of Jahad's Fire appeared, the game took on a competitive yet jovial air. After watching the first few hands being dealt, and passing on a drink of Jahad's Fire, Valdieron rose and decided to take a walk outside.

Here in the lowlands there would be no snow unless the weather turned really cold. The night was cool and the sky overhead was free of cloud. With stars dim on their celestial perch. The city was hauntingly quiet. He did not wander far from the house, seeing several guards patrolling the grounds. He sat on the ground with his back to the front of the building. The chatter and laughter of the men carried dimly from inside, and he took time to reflect on his current situation.

Despite his better judgment, he felt that Astan-Valar's quest for him was legitimate. He realized there were things in this world beyond his imagining, like the learning of Martial Skills in his dreams. His battle against the Trolls and the Brigands showed that he was indeed learning something. Then there was the Dragon's tear, the gem that glowed on command and enabled him to enter the Dream Plane at will. Not so long ago had he been told that these things were possible, he would have laughed uncontrollably, but not now.

Drawing out the Tear from beneath his shirt, Valdieron found it to be as it usually was, glowing a faintly pale orange color, shifting almost imperceptibly as if there was a mist contained within the gem. Astan-Valar had said it could be used to guide him to the pieces of the Disk of Akashel. Grunting with disbelief, he quickly returned the Tear back to its place against his chest and closed his eyes. Not for the first time in the last few days, his thoughts were of Kyle and Natasha. Had any of them escaped the fiery encounter with the Trolls? His heart hoped they had, but his own confrontations with the Trolls told him that such hopes were slim.

He thought of his father, and unbidden tears came to his eyes. He drew his knees up his chest for comfort. He knew his father would tell him not to mourn his passing, but to remember him as he had been, and for what he was, and for what he had believed in. *'Live for yourself son, but do not forget that I will be watching always'*. The thoughts were similar to the words Garrik had used at Marcus' funeral those many years earlier, yet he felt his father had actually spoken them to him just now, and he smiled, knowing in his heart his father still lived and was watching over him.

Rising, he went to his bed. The game of Royalty was still in full swing, though a little quieter in consideration of those who slept. Valdieron removed his boots and sword. He held the sword close to his side as he crawled beneath the heavy blanket, its cold presence reassuring and protective. He was determined to see his quest to the end, both for the memory of his father, and for himself. He needed a goal, and to have that feeling of fulfillment upon its completion. Drifting slowly to sleep, he was more than ready when the dark of the Dream Plane came into focus around him.

Turning towards the Hall of Combat, he pulled up sharply in wonder. Usually, he would have to peer carefully through the fog-like shroud of the Plane to catch the faint glimmer of light from within, but this time the fog had lifted considerably and he could easily make out the archway of the huge building. With his first glimpse of the structure, he found to his surprise that it was actually an enormous dome, with arcing crystalline windows running the length of the huge roof. At its apex, a thin spire stretched towards the starless heavens overhead, a silver needle shifting with rainbow hues, its size difficult to discern at such a distance.

Perched atop the strange shaft was the enormous statue of a Dragon. Valdieron blinked several times and wiped his eyes to be sure it was not real. Its long, sinuous tail, barbed at the end, was wrapped around the shaft, while its taloned hind legs clung to the tip of the spire. Its wings were half spread, as if it were ready to leap into flight at that moment, its long neck arcing down and around so that its horned head faced the courtyard. He could almost feel its dark eyes on him. Like the shaft, he was unable to determine its size, but it must have had a wingspan of over a hundred feet, even at half sweep.

"*Valdieron!*"

As tall and imposing as ever in his mysterious hooded cloak, the Master motioned to him, and with one last look at the Dragon he hurried over.

"How is it that this fog has lifted, Master?"

"Do you not remember the first time you were here, Valdieron?" It was not a question. "I told you then that the fog was merely a blindfold for you, one which you could overcome with practice and time. As you can see now, your vision is improving, though there is still some way to go."

Valdieron raised his brows. "But I have not noticed my vision becoming keener of late, Master." In truth, he had thought he had been able to see distant things with greater clarity than he should, but it had not improved to such a point that he could make out things he might previously not have been able to.

"It does not necessarily mean that your physical vision is increasing, Valdieron. It is more an awareness. Greater awareness is a talent that marks a great warrior from a good warrior. Being aware of your surroundings is of the utmost importance, especially in battle. Not just your vision, but also your every sense, can be used to aid you. It can be called situation awareness, and it is both the easiest and hardest thing to learn. Those who have the innate ability often reach greater heights than those who must work at it, though some who have struggled with it at first have gone on to great things."

"And how do I learn this situation awareness, Master, if I do not have the innate talent?"

"Fear not, Valdieron. You have that talent, but only need the practice, which the Combat Ambit will give you. Follow me!"

Instead of turning and entering the Combat Hall, The Master led Valdieron across the courtyard, to the closed double-doors. This building was a circular tower, with a spire at its peak, no higher than three levels high. The crimson wall appeared to be polished marble.

As they approached, the doors began to swing slowly inwards, without a sound or a touch from the Master. Though surprised, Valdieron did not hesitate to follow the Master into the darkened interior, yet he did glance sideways at the doors as they passed.

The inside of the tower was huge, much larger than it appeared from the outside. The floor was of flat stone, and the walls the same crimson marble as the outside. There was no light other than that of a large glowing sphere in the center of the room. It was soft silver in color, and every now and then it would spark brilliantly sending an incandescent shower of silver stars across the entire surface before returning to normal. It was about fifteen feet in diameter, and appeared as if it had sunk a little into stone floor, so that it looked more like a dome than a sphere.

"Behold, the Combat Ambit." The Master approached the sphere on silent feet and turned to Valdieron. "Here you will encounter every conceivable type of combat. Enter and learn, Valdieron, and know that to you it will be as real as any Combat, yet you may end it at any time. If you get hit, it will end. It will start off slowly but quicken as you advance, adapting to your level of skill. Afterwards, you may ask me anything concerning it, and I will tell you what you need to improve for the next time."

Eager yet tentative, Valdieron turned to the sphere. He took a step towards it, and near its top a spark went off, raining down a shower of star-like particles, and he almost cried out in shock. He laughed as he realized how nervous he was. With one last look at the Master, who stood impassively, he reached out and touched the sphere.

He expected a jolting shock but received instead a slight tingling on his skin where it broke the silvery surface. Like stepping into a fire-lit room, he entered the Combat Ambit.

Almost instantly, the sphere pulsed around him and he braced himself. The silvery dome began to change hues, swirling and blurred at first, but hastily becoming sharper and clearer, until a ruined landscape surrounded him. The ground felt like dry, parched dirt, and the landscape was of twisted, skeletal trees, free of leaf and stunted of growth. In the distance lay a wall of mountains, while in the other direction a layer of warped heat shimmered over the land.

High above, almost directly overhead, a large orange sun flared with all the heat of a real sun, and he began to sweat. His sword was in his hand, though he had not reached for it, nor thought about it.

A sudden piercing cry, like that of an eagle, caught him by surprise and he spun, seeking its source. A small group of figures approached him at a run. As they closed, he scanned them intently as he dropped into a defensive crouch. Taller than he by maybe a hand, they were lean and angular, human in form, but moving with a fluidity that defied human grace. He could not make out their faces, as they wore dark veils and robes of pale gray. In their hands they held long, arcing sabers, and had small buckler shields of plain wood strapped to their left arms.

They approached quickly, spreading out to surround him. The figures did not attack instantly, giving Valdieron a further chance to study them. Their weapons were slightly shorter than his sword, and seemed capable of both thrusting and slashing. They were definitely light on their feet, their steps long and excellently balanced. They did not appear to have any obvious vulnerability.

The first attack came from the rear, and he was almost defeated by it as two figures before him feigned attacks. A shuffling of light feet from behind alerted him of movement. He spun quickly and found a figure with raised sword descending in a slow diagonal slash. Had it been any quicker, he knew he would be dead already. He raised his sword in a vertical parry with both hands clasping the long hilt of his weapon.

Surprised at the realness of the figure, Valdieron pushed him back and stepped away to give himself room, throwing his head to the side as the stranger thrust at him.

The next figure danced in quickly with short, shuffling steps, leading with a snaking snap-thrust at Valdieron's face. This one he flicked aside with the tip of his sword, held low in both hands. The figure returned with a backhand slash which would have left Valdieron a foot shorter had he not swayed back, then stepped forward with a thrust at the figure's thigh. The attack caught the slowed figure cleanly, entering below the hip and nicking a bone before he pulled free. Blood coated the tip of his sword and a heavy trickle flowed down the figure's leg, staining his robe a dark crimson. Drops of blood struck the parched ground and gave a boiling hiss.

The figure withdrew and was replaced by another, who forced Valdieron into a parrying retreat, blocking high and low thrusts at increasing speed. He knew he was backing straight into the circle of figures, but could do nothing about it as his attacker moved left and right to counter his efforts to turn. Desperately he tried a diagonal cut at the figure, who parried it easily and returned with a low thrust, from which Valdieron had to arch away to avoid. As he did, a sharp pain exploded along his back and he knew that a figure had struck him from behind. The figures and harsh landscape began to fade and the Master stepped inside the globe.

"Tell me what went wrong, Valdieron."

Valdieron mused silently for several moments, running a hand over the place on his back where he had felt the weapon strike. There was no wound, nor any signs that he had been struck. "I was too defensive, Master. I could not break free of the attacker's advance."

"Why?"

"He countered every move I made or tried to make. I couldn't shift my retreat."

The Master paused, as if in thought. "Counter the counters, Valdieron. Instead of fighting against your opponent, use your opponent's force to your benefit. If he counters, you counter again, always trying to break his rhythm. Feign if you wish to break free. Use your head, your weapon, your body, and your feet. Speed is the key, speed and rhythm. Remember your forms, one movement following another.

Valdieron nodded and grasped his sword eagerly. The Master turned and silently left the globe, which instantly shifted to another image: Rocky ruins of what was once a city. Caked with dust and silt, it seemed to have lain in this state for many hundreds of years. There were no visible remains of any structure beyond a small wall or a doorway. Valdieron stepped onto a wide dusty road nearby, cobbled with flat gray stones.

A cracking of rubble nearby alerted him of a presence. He turned his head to the right to find a short, stocky figure picking its way through the ruins towards him. Its body was humanoid, yet its face resembled that of a Troll, ape-like and brutish. It wore a thick leather vest and a pointed metal skullcap, and it bore two curved swords, much like scimitars.

Behind the creature others appeared, more than a dozen, hopping skillfully through the rubble as they sought to surround him. With a cry he turned to meet them. Their resemblance to Trolls made his mind cry out for revenge but he pushed such thoughts to the back of his mind and stayed on the road where his footing was sure.

He waited only long enough for them to form a loose circle around him before attacking. The first creature, though small, blocked his overhand chop with ease and swung under his parry. Valdieron quickly stepped back to avoid being sliced in half. Rocking forward again, he feigned a thrust at the creature's head, but reversed the swing as the creature threw up a double sweeping parry, and stepped in to chop at its leather-clad side. His weapon bit deep with the familiar steely hiss and the creature screamed in pain. Blood erupted from the wound when Valdieron jerked his sword free.

Kicking the dying figure in the chest, Valdieron watched him from the corner of his eye. Another of the creatures stepped forward and attacked. He parried an overhead slash and stepped to the side of the follow-up thrust, then swept another parry down and away as the creature thrust again with his first weapon. Sweeping the scimitar across in front, Valdieron had the creature exposed and lashed out with his foot. Instead of striking him, however, he tripped the creature's lead foot out from under him with a sweeping kick, and as the figure struggled to regain his balance, he recovered to thrust into its chest, breaking past a desperate parry and through the leather armor with ease.

With two down, Valdieron turned to find not one, but two of the creatures approaching him on either side. Cursing, he tried to get on their outside, so that they couldn't flank him, but they shifted so that he was forced to fight them both at the same time. He cut through the defenses of one, but another quickly replaced it.

He found himself back within the silvery Ambit, wondering what the wound in his side would have felt like had the scimitar been real. Silently the Master entered again, and Valdieron moved to meet him.

It was going to be a long night.

Chapter 17

The chill late-autumn wind battered the city with relentless fury. Overhead, sparse clouds raced past, driven by the raging front. In the streets, masses of people went about their business, fighting the chill and the force of the gusts. The low sun, when it got a rare peek through the clouds, could do little to counter the wind's bite, which seemed to squeeze through even the tightest of cloaks.

Walking behind Nagus, surrounded by several bodyguards, Valdieron pulled his ulster tightly around him, though more to stop its incessant flapping than to keep out the cold. Born and raised in the snowy mountains, he found this wind more an irritation than anything.

Nagus guided the group through the press of people, navigating them through the crowd with ease. They were bound for the *Wheel-less Wagon*, an Inn on the other side of the city where he hoped to get Valdieron onto a caravan heading to Thorhus.

The *Wheel-less Wagon* proved to be a large stone Inn situated in the center of one of the more affluent areas of the city, not far from the keep. Large stone steps led to double doors closed against the wind. Overhead, thin chimney smoke was caught quickly by the wind and scattered, and the aroma of wood fire was heavy in the air. Even over the whistling of the heavy gusts, the noise inside the Inn could be clearly heard.

Dane, the scar-faced old guard moved forward to open one of the doors, casting a quick glance into the dim interior before leading them in. Valdieron blinked as his eyes focused on the fire-lit interior. He stared around him in wonder at the first Inn he had ever seen beyond the small one in Shadowvale.

The room was enormous. A wood-paneled wall encircled it, dotted occasionally by mantled hearths, grilled to stop errant sparks. Against the far wall was a long wooden bar, four feet in height and topped by a flat sandstone bench. Behind the bar, several men and women wearing stained white aprons shouted and conversed loudly with the patrons. A row of tables ran along either side of the room and every available seat was occupied. In the center of the room a huge circular stairwell led to the upper level.

A few people noted their arrival and drew back to allow them easier passage through the throng, though the sour-faced presence of Dane may have prompted that. Some nodded to Nagus as he passed, and he returned a few pleasantries with those he recognized, though he didn't pause as he pressed through the crowd.

They finally came to a halt before the bar. Several black-clad guards moved forward protectively as Nagus' guards approached, surrounding two men. One of the men barked a command when he recognized Nagus, and the guards stepped back. Motioning for all others to remain, Nagus urged Valdieron forward.

"Fender."

"Nagus. It's good to see you again. You have my commiserations for your recent loss: such a tragic occurrence. Please, take a seat. Are you thirsty?"

"No, thank you," said Nagus, pulling up one of the high stools and taking a seat before the two men. "Kelgar." He nodded a greeting to the second man, young and thin, with long dark hair tied back. His face was rat-like, his dark eyes quick and alert. Valdieron guessed him for a broker, and probably the brother of Fender.

"I hear you are going to Thorhus." Nagus directed his statement to Fender, but Kelgar cut in before his brother could answer.

"That's no concern of -" Fender's restraining hand on his arm silenced the young man, and he glared at his brother momentarily, but sighed and turned back to stare at Nagus. It was obvious to Valdieron that Nagus was no friend of these two merchants.

"That's right," confirmed Fender. "Twenty hundredweight of grain, flour and wood." At this, Kelgar turned sharply and whispered something to his brother, causing Fender to smile coldly.

"What do you want?" asked Fender.

"My friend, Valdieron here," he motioned to Val with his hand, "needs to get to Thorhus for the Trial. I need you to take him on as a guard when you leave."

First Kelgar, then Fender began to laugh, either at the request

170

or at the idea of Valdieron being a guard. A low snicker went through the bodyguards behind the brothers.

"This boy!" Fender rose and stepped towards Valdieron, who backed up cautiously. "He wears a sword, but that doesn't make him a warrior. Besides, I have all the guards I need."

"Surely you can take on one extra. He can also drive and tend horses, if that makes any difference."

Kelgar snorted with amusement. "And I'm sure he cooks and cleans, but that doesn't make him a warrior. I know fighters when I see them, Nagus, and this boy aint' even close to being one. Pakash here, however," he indicated a tall, solidly built guard at his right shoulder, who was fingering the hilt of a long saber at his waist, "will be more than happy to show you what a warrior is, if you don't stop bothering us. Now, leave us!"

Kelgar thrust his head forward to emphasize his statement though he made no move towards Nagus, his eyes flicking to the ever-present Dane behind him.

Nagus rose slowly, his eyes on Kelgar as he addressed Fender.

"You should keep your brother on a tighter leash, Fender. One day his ratty face is going to get the both of you into trouble."

Kelgar bristled at this, and despite a warning bark from Fender, reached for the dagger at his waist. Dane moved quickly, reaching for his weapon and for Nagus at the same time.

Valdieron had half been expecting something like this from the volatile young man and lashed out with his left foot, catching Kelgar's wrist as he pulled the dagger free. The blow jarred the weapon from his hand and he pulled away, clutching his wrist and turning on Valdieron. Val straightened his leg and pressed his foot against Kelgar's scrawny throat, the slight bend in his leg showing that he could have continued for another few inches had he wanted to. Shaking his head, he watched as Kelgar stumbled backwards.

The guard, Pakash, stepped in front of a startled Kelgar, while Dane simultaneously stepped before Nagus, hand on the hilt of his sword, a foot of the thick silver blade showing.

Fender pushed past his own bodyguard to step between Dane and Pakash. He glared at his brother before turning to Nagus.

"I am glad my brother's eye for business is better than his eye for warriors." Both Kelgar and Pakash scowled. "I will take him to Thorhus with me."

Kelgar began to argue, but was halted by Fender, whose unblinking gaze showed the decision was final. Kelgar grunted indignantly before motioning to his guards and leaving the Inn, a lingering look at Valdieron showing his dislike for the young man, and hinted at future trouble.

"And I have your word there will be no 'unpleasantness' in store for him along the way?" inquired Nagus with a raised brow.

"Aye, you have my word, Nagus. One Silver Crown per week."

"Six!"

Fender feigned surprised. "Three. The boy is untested."

"Five. You saw what the boy can do, Fender. He's worth it, believe me!"

"Four, Nagus. That's more than I should, but it was worth it seeing what he did to Kelgar." He lowered his voice conspiratorially and leaned towards Nagus. "Watch out he doesn't have somebody make trouble for you while we're away."

"I can handle myself, Fender".

"That's what I'm afraid of," barked Fender with a grin. "Kelgar is too impulsive at times. I want something to come back to after this trip." He turned from Nagus to Valdieron. "Get your gear together. We have rooms here tonight and leave in the morning." He nodded off to the side where some hired guards were seated at a few tables. "Those men over there are part of our team. Do your job, and you'll stay on my good side."

"This is the time for our parting, Valdieron," said Nagus. "I hope that one day we will meet again, perhaps under more cheerful circumstances. Here!" He pressed a small pouch into Valdieron's hand.

"Ah, I cannot take-" began Valdieron, but Nagus cut him off. "You will have to eat when you get to Thorhus, Valdieron, and there is no guarantee Fender will even pay you when you arrive. You saved me a lot more than that with the Brigands, so it is only fair that you take it."

Valdieron accepted the purse with a nod of thanks and

tucked it into his shirt. "I too hope that we meet again some day, Master Nagus. Thank you for all your help."

Nagus grasped him softly by the shoulder before turning away, stepping past the silent figure of Dane and pushing through the crowd. Dane regarded Valdieron for a moment before nodding once to him, then turned after Nagus and the others. They were soon out of sight, swallowed up by the spectral crowd and smoky haze. Valdieron was once again in the company of strangers.

Valdieron moved to join the hired guards at the nearest table. They stared openly as he approached, and seemed disinclined to afford him room. He walked past them to the last table, where only three figures sat watching him curiously as he stopped before them.

The figure closest to him was by far the largest person he had ever seen. He had unkempt dark hair and tanned skin, with leather and fur clothing partly covering his muscled body. His eyes were dark blue, like a deep pool. Handsome in a rugged sort of way, his face showed a few days growth, which failed to hide the faint discoloration of dirt hastily wiped.

The second figure was taller than Valdieron, but was slender, almost whip-like, with brown skin darkened by nature. Silvery hair hung to his waist. His angular features were sharp and handsome. His mouth was twisted in a grin, which seemed fixed, like a mischievous child's. Valdieron realized with an intake of breath that he was an Elf, mysterious long-lived people from the woodlands of the south. He was beautiful to look at, though in an exotic way.

The third figure seemed hardly older than Valdieron, though his face had the stern appearance of a seasoned guard. His short sandy hair was as dusty as his weathered leather clothes. With plain brown eyes, he would have been handsome if not for the large scar which ran along his left cheek from the point of his chin to his eye.

"Ah... may I have a seat?" he stammered, hoping he did not cause offence with his blatant staring, especially at the Elf.

"Nobody else is," barked the large man in a thick voice, turning back to his tankard of ale. He took a huge swig, his head low as he stared at the table before him.

"I can go elsewhere if you like," offered Valdieron, surprised at the big man's sudden coldness.

"No, stay lad." The dulcet voice of the Elf stopped Valdieron as he shifted to leave. "Forgive Thorgast. We are trying desperately to improve his social skills, but having little success on account of his sour demeanor." This brought a chuckle from the young man who shared the Elf's joke, until the big man called Thorgast turned to him and he muttered into his tankard.

"Aye, sorry boy. Your company is preferable to many here, and it seems there are no other seats." Propelled by the man's foot under the table, the chair closest to Valdieron slid out.

Valdieron dropped his pack and lowered himself into the chair. He noticed the Elf watching him intently, his darting green eyes straying to his right shoulder where the hilt of his sword protruded. He was forced to shift the great blade to the side to sit, and met with a friendly smile as he turned to regard the Elf.

"You already know our huge friend, Thorgast." The big man snarled a little but laughed as the Elf swept towards him with a flourish. "He's a little bad tempered, but you'll get used to that." Thorgast snarled again and narrowed his gaze, his large hand going to the haft of a huge axe at his belt. He winked at Valdieron as the Elf covered his face with his hands in mock terror.

"This here is the yet to be known Hafri of Minda, a young mercenary with a head full of dreams," he whispered behind a hand to Valdieron loud enough for all to hear "and not much else." The young Hafri darkened at the comment, before trying to imitate Thorgast's threatening pose. His sudden smile spoiled it as he tossed a nut from a small bowl at the Elf who caught it with ease and popped it into his mouth.

"Hmm. Not bad." He flashed a smile at the softly cursing Hafri before turning to Valdieron, who grinned at the humorous exchanges.

The Elf threw back his cloak with a dramatic swirl and bowed with his left hand pressed against his chest.

"And I am-"

"A buffoon!" Thorgast interrupted.

"Llewellyn son of Llewether, at your service," he continued without comment

Valdieron tried to hide a grin with his hand.

"Valdieron Ketherson."

"Well met, Valdieron Ketherson," nodded Hafri, moving Llewellyn's chair as the Elf began to sit down, though the Elf was ready for it.

"Are you thirsty, Valdieron?" asked Llewellyn, taking the last of his own tankard and smacking it down hard onto the table.

"No, thank you," answered Valdieron, but the Elf was busy calling over a nearby serving woman. She was cute with slight dimples in her cheeks, and her small eyes were a pale green. She smiled with unforced pleasure as the Elf threw a slender arm around her waist.

"Four more ales, my lovely lass, if it's not too much trouble." He pressed a coin into one of her small hands. Valdieron caught the flash of silver as she pushed it into the large pocket in the front of her apron. She began to fish around for change but Llewellyn grasped her wrist softly and whispered into her ear. She flashed him a thankful smile and did not flinch as he patted her on the bottom before she disappeared into the crowd.

"Ah, to be young again," lamented the Elf softly, though he appeared no older than Hafri.

Valdieron nodded his thanks as the serving woman returned with the drinks and Llewellyn pushed one over to him.

"That was some move against that rat, Kelgar," congratulated Llewellyn. "Where did you learn to do that?"

Valdieron took a slow drink from the tankard so that he could think of a suitable lie. He was surprised at the bitter taste, far different to that of 'Jahad's Fire'.

"My father taught me a few things."

"And your father, was he a warrior?"

Valdieron drew a deep breath. "No. He was a horse breeder."

Thorgast snorted in an attempt to keep down his laughter, while Hafri and Llewellyn doubled over with merriment.

"A farmer!" cackled Llewellyn, nudging Hafri. They sobered somewhat when they saw Valdieron's darkening face.

"And he taught you the sword too!" quipped Llewellyn, indicating the sword on his back.

Valdieron nodded, trying hard to stay his anger at their actions, knowing how foolish he must have sounded. He cursed himself for not thinking of a better response, but knew that it would serve his purpose.

"And I suppose you're going to Thorhus to participate in the Trial?" Hafri ran a hand over his mouth after a swig of his ale, wiping away the residual froth on his sparse moustache and beard.

"What if I were?" countered Valdieron. Taking another mouthful of Ale, he let his eyes slip from Hafri, so that the young man did not think he was challenging him.

It was Thorgast who answered. "You have barely the start of a man's growth on you lad, and you talk about taking part in a tournament against the best warriors in the realms." He raised his bushy eyebrows in disbelief. "Surely you can see how foolish that sounds?"

"Appearances can be deceiving," answered Valdieron. "I am not as naive as I seem. Combat is not new to me."

"Killing rabbits is one thing, boy, killing a man is another." Hafri drew out a dagger and slid its tip across the table in front of him. "There are worse things than men out there. Take a Troll for example. Ever seen a Troll, Valdieron? Fifteen feet tall and half as wide, with rough hide and a maw like a bear's. Just as soon eat you as rip your arms off."

"Kind of like these?" asked Valdieron softly. He removed his sword to show them the rough hide of his Troll-bound scabbard, and drew out from his coin purse a few Troll's teeth he had kept for no apparent reason. He had considered making a necklace out of them, but had decided against it, and was now glad he had kept them.

Hafri's smile disappeared instantly, and Llewellyn almost choked on a mouthful of ale. Thorgast regarded Valdieron with raised brows.

"And they're twelve feet tall, not fifteen," corrected Valdieron with a slight smile, "though it is true, they could rip you in half if they had a mind."

"Give me wings and call me a duck!" exclaimed Llewellyn with a chuckle, wiping the spilled ale from the front of his cloak. He fingered the curved Troll's teeth. His limited knowledge of the creatures told him that the six curved teeth had to be from three different Trolls. He needed no proof that the hide of Valdieron's scabbard was, by the color, a War Troll's.

"Looks can be deceiving." Valdieron leaned back, smiling at

their surprise. "Yet, no. I go to Thorhus to visit my sister. And you?"

Llewellyn laughed at this. "First point to you, Valdieron." He drained the last of his ale, giving his soiled cloak a rueful look before laughing it off. "My two companions are both seeking fame and fortune at the Trial of Combat. Hafri here is entering for the purpose of boosting his fame. Thorgast, however," he nodded towards his huge barbarian friend "just wants to show off his muscles to the young ladies of Thorhus."

Thorgast scowled while Llewellyn winked at Valdieron, drawing a chuckle from him.

"That's not true, you scoundrel." Thorgast paused then turned to Valdieron. "For many years now, my people have been at war with the Haruken, huge four-armed creatures somewhat akin to Trolls," he nodded towards the teeth on the table for emphasis. "Though outnumbered, we have endured their attacks thus far, yet they are slowly killing my people, for we do not have the wealth to finance such a drawn out confrontation. Our city, the great walled fortress of Chul'Haka, is falling into perdition, for we do not have the means to properly repair the damage. Therefore, I go to Thorhus to enter the tournament, so that I may win the prize money and aid my people." The barbarian's face slowly hardened as he spoke, as if remembering once again his responsibility to his people.

"Ah, I knew I had forgotten something," teased Llewellyn with another wink Valdieron's way.

"And you, Llewellyn?" asked Valdieron. "Are you not going there for the tournament?"

The Elf nodded with a smile. "Aye, lad, but not to enter, but to observe. I am a Bard by occupation, and a great tale I may construct from the trials and tribulations of the tournament. Perhaps each of you might also get a mention in it."

Valdieron chuckled, not really surprised that the charismatic Elf was a bard, though he could see no instrument on him.

As he drank, he silently wondered if he should enter the tournament. Perhaps it would assist him in finding the first piece of the Disk of Akashel. He realized that if he were to have any chance at the combat, he would have to learn far more than he currently knew.

"Are there any herbalists around here?" he asked suddenly. Llewellyn eyed him with furrowed brow, taken aback by the change of topic.

"There are bound to be a few in the market. Why, do you have need of something?"

"I was wanting something to help me sleep," he answered, wondering if he sounded foolish. "I have not slept well lately through illness."

"Then I suggest you go to the markets and check, lad. We have all day, and there is no rule that says you can't leave here, as long as you're back tomorrow at dawn when we depart."

Valdieron nodded and rose. "Which rooms are we staying in upstairs?" he asked.

"Number seven if you want to bunk there for the night. I will be sure to wake you in the morning if you are still asleep."

Valdieron thanked him and nodded farewell to the others before heading towards the exit, dodging the pressing crowd. He looked back at Fender and found the merchant in conversation with somebody. He pulled open the door, though he was forced to press against it as the wind caught it and pushed it into him. Dragging it closed behind him, he took a moment to let his eyes adjust to the morning glare before wading into the busy crowd of people heading south towards the market.

Chapter 18

The gentle shake of Llewellyn's hand woke Valdieron from a long sleep, and he cursed. He had been on the verge of overcoming a major obstacle in his current training. He had slowly worked through a few more combats against more strange creatures and men, gaining confidence and skill as he went. The fighting seemed to fly fast and furious towards the end, when he would eventually take a hit that invariably ended the combat. The Master seemed pleased with his progress, but had forced him to return again and again, concentrating on technique and execution rather than speed, saying that would come later.

Llewellyn's slender face peered down at him as he rolled over quickly, eyes screwed almost closed, though there was little light in the room.

"We are getting ready to leave, Valdieron. Gather your things. We must be downstairs soon."

Nearby, Thorgast and Hafri were packing, making sure they had not forgotten anything. Valdieron took a deep breath and rolled off the hard pallet, wishing he could have stayed asleep for longer. He had mixed a little 'Bark-ash Leaf' with water before he slept, having brought it from a stall at the markets the day before, and he had slept better than he had for many days.

His gear was mostly packed. He secured his belt around his waist and looped the baldric holding his sword over his shoulder, tightening it for fit and comfort. He looped his light pack over his shoulders and slipped into his worn boots. He had slept in his clothes.

Out front, a long line of wagons ran the length of the street, twice as large as Nagus' had been. Guards and teamsters wandered about, making last minute checks on horses, wagons and freight. Llewellyn led the four of them to the rear of the column, where a large group of guards milled near a line of horses. Unfortunately for him, Kelgar was standing among them giving out instructions.

"Each of you is given a horse. It is yours for the entire journey. Take care of your horse. If your horse cannot carry you, then you will walk, and pay for the horse out of your wage." There was a low mumbling through the group, and Valdieron was surprised at these harsh instructions. He even caught Kelgar glaring at him, his mouth twisted in a mocking grin.

Valdieron moved quickly to the line of horses. He searched for one that would suit him and last the journey. There were not many of good stock, and he chose a gray mare that looked to be reasonably healthy and resilient. Llewellyn had chosen a white gelding, while Hafri had a sorrel mare and Thorgast a slightly larger bay mare. Valdieron wondered how Thorgast's mount would fare, for the Barbarian was easily seven feet in height and must have weighted twice as much as Valdieron or the slender Elf.

After adjusting the stirrups and reins, Valdieron mounted. The others followed suit. Thorgast was surprisingly agile for a big man, but it was obvious to Valdieron that he was not an experienced rider.

A low, shrill whistle pierced the early morning. Wordlessly, everybody finished whatever they had been doing as the column slowly started off. A layer of clouds on the eastern horizon blocked the radiance of the morning sun.

Llewellyn drew his horse in beside Valdieron's as they walked after the last of the wagons. Thorgast and Hafri moved in behind them.

"You have never done this before?"

"No," he answered, though he had seen the guards of Nagus' caravan performing their duties.

"It is not hard to pick up. Just stay with me, and you'll be all right. Besides, I think Kelgar may have something in store for you that won't be to your liking."

Valdieron glanced to the fore of the column, but could not see the lead caravan of Fender and his brother.

"I don't think so, Llewellyn. Fender seems to be more or less honorable, and I have the suspicion he won't let Kelgar ruin his reputation entirely. He gave his word to Nagus, and I think he will keep it."

Llewellyn shrugged as his horse sidestepped slightly. "Just be careful, all right? Kelgar is nothing if not devious. It might be that he will do something and worry about his brother after."

Valdieron smiled over at the Elf. "Trust me!" he said calmly. Llewellyn smiled and shook his head, though his eyes did not carry their usual glint.

Although the streets were filling rapidly with people, all afforded the large caravan a wide berth. The road meandered to the southeast, where it finally broke the city's perimeter.

The southern region of Tyr was mainly rolling green hills and sweeping valleys. As the morning sun broke through the wind-swept clouds, it settled across the land, increasing its beauty. The wide dirt highway snaked through the valleys, making the journey longer but less strenuous on the horses and wagons.

They halted for a short time at midday. With the city left behind beyond the jagged horizon, they let the horses graze while they ate. The meal consisting of a hastily heated broth kept in a sealed cauldron on one of the supply wagons. There was water and stale bread as well, the quantity making up for the lack of quality. They saddled again and continued their slow journey.

By late afternoon, even Valdieron was feeling saddle-sore, and sighed with relief as the signal was passed back that they were making camp. All of the wagons continued forward before veering into a wide clearing. The wagons formed a large circle, inside which camp was made. Outside, sentries were posted. As the four unsaddled their horses and set their bedrolls, Kelgar walked through the group, giving out sentry times.

"You two, first watch." He indicated Hafri and Thorgast, who nodded and hastened their unpacking. "You two, second watch, midnight till dawn." He indicated Llewellyn and Valdieron. Valdieron heard the Elf groan. Kelgar moved on, giving the other guards first or second watch.

Hafri and Thorgast kept their weapons and moved to the outskirts of the camp. Valdieron and Llewellyn went to get some more food from the cook's wagon before returning to their bedrolls to eat. It was the same as the earlier meal, only the bread was more stale and the water warmer.

Llewellyn explained the sentry details while they ate.

"Two are picked together, for safety reasons. A single sentry is easily picked off. We can either walk around, or take up a post within sight of the teams to either side. As long as we stay awake and keep our eyes and ears open, we'll be fine. I do not recommend falling asleep on duty, either. Fender will half your daily fee if you are caught, and you will probably be given double duty the next night."

Valdieron nodded as he took out a portion of the dried Barkash Leaf from its small pouch and dropped it into his water canteen. He shook it slowly for several minutes before drinking it. It tasted bitter, almost like lemon, and left the taste in his mouth. He had selected only a small amount, not wanting to be sleepy for his sentry duty.

"Who are you, Valdieron?"

Valdieron turned to the Elf, eyes narrowed questioningly. "Excuse me?"

"I asked who you were." Llewellyn had taken a small flute from his pack and was fingering a silent tune on it as he stared unblinkingly at Valdieron. "I mean no offence," he continued quickly as Valdieron's eyes darkened and he frowned. "You are just an enigma to me, that is all."

"I am who I say I am," stated Valdieron shortly, wondering at Llewellyn's sudden questioning.

"Oh, of that I am sure," agreed the Elf with an offhand smile. "Yet there is more to you than meets the eye. For instance, you say you are the son of a horse breeder, which appears believable, given how well you ride. Yet you carry yourself like a warrior. You carry a sword the likes of which I have never seen." His green eyes sparkled with curiosity and wonder as he shifted his attention to the sword. "My curiosity is piqued, Valdieron. I am by trade a Bard, and my life evolves around knowledge. I am constructing an epic song concerning my life travels, and as your path has crossed mine, it is only fair that I learn a little about you so that your part in the tale is truthful."

"What would you have me tell you?" asked Valdieron defensively.

"Well. You say your father was a horse breeder. Where?" He blew a soft note on the flute, as if to test it.

Valdieron watched the Elf for a silent moment, but Llewellyn was concentrating on the flute as he worked through some more finger movements. Finally he sighed, wondering how many times he would have to dig up his past for the benefit of others.

"It was a little village called 'Shadowvale', in the

Dragonwing Mountains to the northwest."

"Was?" Llewellyn glanced at him with a raised brow.

"Aye. I was not lying when I told you I had fought Trolls. On Thirdday in the seventh week this autumn, Trolls attacked our village before dawn. Our farm was outside the village, but the attack came almost simultaneous. My father was killed." He struggled past the lump in his throat and wiped the beginning of tears from his eyes. "I escaped and fled north, seeing the village was being attacked and burned. I later found the village was razed."

"You returned to the village?" Llewellyn was leaning forward intently.

Valdieron shook his head. "Not at first. I could not take the risk of encountering the Trolls. I did not even know they existed up until the attack."

"You ran?" It was not an accusation but a question.

"Yes. I fled to the northeast; higher into the mountains, though I should have realized the Trolls were mountain creatures. I headed to a place called the 'Sentinel', a large mountain nearby which gave our village its name. Near there, I was spotted by Trolls and chased."

Llewellyn did not speak, but nodded as if taking it all in, and urging Valdieron to continue.

"I could not outrun them, so I turned to fight at a small rocky incline over a stream on the northern side of the mountain. During the fight, I was knocked unconscious and fell into the stream. When I awoke, I was inside a cave beneath the mountain."

"Such places are not uncommon," spoke up Llewellyn.

Valdieron shrugged ignorantly. He had not even spoken of the cave to old Hubert, but felt compelled to tell Llewellyn of it and its every detail.

"Yet this cave was more than just that." He glanced around to see if anybody was close enough to overhear. "What I am about to tell you is secret, so I leave it up to you how you use it. In good faith I hope you will tell nobody." He sighed, feeling the onset of the sleeping potion begin to take hold, and he was suddenly uncaring. Astan-Valar had told him sooner or later those who oppose him would confront him, and if that was sooner rather than later, so be it.

Llewellyn raised his brows in surprise. "My word is my life,

Valdieron, and nothing you speak to me shall pass my lips without your consent. I vow this as both your friend and an Elf."

Valdieron nodded, though only slightly more at ease. "This cave opened up into a whole underground complex, like nothing I had seen or heard of before. It was like a small underground city, the corridors wide and finely cut, and the caverns large and set with inscriptions and carvings. This one cavern was like a hall, with a raised stage and the remains of a chair, or throne set upon it."

Llewellyn was listening intently, his face stern. "There are tales of several such places on Kil'Tar. Not many know of them or their origin, though Elvish legend tells of a people who were master to the races and ancestors of the Loremasters. They rode the skies on the wings of dragons and none opposed them."

Valdieron nodded, remembering the tales of Astan-Valar and wondering at the extent of Llewellyn's knowledge of this. The Elf waited for him to continue. "Near the throne was this sword." He slowly unsheathed his sword and held it before him, basking in its beauty and latent power. Reluctantly he handed it to Llewellyn who grasped it like it was fragile and would break if he exerted too much force.

"Beautiful!" he breathed, grasping its dragon hilt and holding it before him. His eyes followed the tracings of the runes along its length on either side, widening as they did, as if he could understand their meaning. "Runes of power, by their appearance, yet in no language I know. Close to our ancient Tongue, yet different." He lightly brushed his slender fingers along the pale blade. "Not metal, nor is it Adamantium. It could be Mithril, but duller than any Mithril I have seen." He whispered to himself for a short time, Valdieron trying to understand some of what he said, but he could translate little into anything that could help him. That its origin and make were unknown to the seemingly worldly Bard did surprise him, however.

"A weapon of strange properties," mused Llewellyn louder, handing it carefully back to Valdieron, who placed it in his lap.

"As I was saying, I found the sword against the throne, and as I touched it, a man appeared in the cavern. He looked like a madman, and he spoke to me of strange and mysterious things. He told me of the Dragon Lords, called the Kay'taari, who rode dragons. He said they were enemies of the Demons who lived in the voids."

Llewellyn nodded. "Of Demons I know. I saw some in my youth before they were banished by the Loremasters back to their planes. These Kay'taari, did he tell you of them?"

Valdieron nodded. "He said they were the first beings, called Essence Lords, like the gods. They were split into two groups which led to the eventual confrontation between one group who were allied to the Dragons, and the other who sided with the Demons."

Llewellyn nodded with a twisting of his mouth, as if he were trying to piece together some puzzle.

"He also said that the Seals which bar the Portals to the voids are breaking!"

Llewellyn coughed with surprise, rocking back as if struck. "The Seals? The Loremasters created them to prevent their return. If they are breaking, then nothing can stop the return of the Demons, and there will be war again on Kil'Tar."

Valdieron nodded. He told him of Astan-Valar's warning, and even told him there was an artifact that could re-establish the Seals and bar the Portals, and that he hoped to find out more about it in Thorhus.

Llewellyn lay back in thought. He rose once to question Valdieron, but the young man was asleep already, his hand protectively clasping the hilt of the strange sword. To the Elvin Bard, who had seen many strange things in his six hundred years of life, the boy's tale came as a surprise. If the Seals were breaking, then the Loremasters must be told. He knew of their constant vigil over the Portals, so he could only assume they would know sooner or later, if not already. He remembered his people's last confrontation with Demons when they attacked his homeland. They had repulsed them then, but they had been aided by the most powerful of Loremasters. Now he knew there were few Loremasters, and his people were not as numerous.

Not needing sleep as others did, Llewellyn lay there lost in thought up until the time of their sentry duty was at hand, and Hafri and Thorgast appeared sleepily from the perimeter. Llewellyn rose and moved to Valdieron. He wondered if he were somehow linked to this strange lad, and decided he would follow him in an effort to unravel this mystery. One thing was for certain, it would make for a lot more passages in his epic, and if he were lucky, would probably alter its entire plot.

With a sigh, he took up his flute and roused Valdieron, knowing that to be late for their first duty would not go down well with Kelgar.

Chapter 19

Valdieron quickly found out that life as a caravan guard was both easy and boring. Seated on his horse for most of the day and doing guard duty every night left him with little time to do other things, not that he had a lot to do. He discovered that Llewellyn had a longbow, and the Elf offered to help him replenish his depleted quiver.

The Elf and he found themselves becoming fast friends, with the Bard willingly imparting his worldly knowledge to Valdieron as they rode. Valdieron was more than glad to listen, though at times even the Elf's dulcet voice grew monotonous.

They halted at one point when Llewellyn spotted a certain tree not far from the road. It was skeletal in appearance, its branches long and free of joint or gall, and would strip down well for straight shafts. That night, he showed Valdieron how to properly shed their bark and make the shaft even along its entire length. Valdieron, who had helped his father make his arrows, found that the Elf's knowledge of fletching was far greater than his.

The next night, with all of the shafts ready, Llewellyn took out a large fletching kit from his pack. The wooden box contained several items from thin sinewy thread to a leather bag containing pre-formed arrowheads. He emptied these onto the ground, and began to show Valdieron how to split both ends of the shafts to attach the feathered flights and heads. The feathers were predominantly white, but there were others mingled with them, obviously ones he had found along the way and tossed in.

By the end of the next night, Valdieron's quiver was almost overflowing with new white-fletched arrows, and he wished he could have strung his bow and let one fly to test it.

Where Llewellyn was extroverted, Hafri and Thorgast were silent and introverted, though in different ways. Valdieron guessed that like himself, Thorgast was not given to unnecessary displays of extroversion. Hafri, on the other hand, seemed to brood when alone, as if he was harboring painful emotions, something Valdieron could empathize with.

By the midmorning of the tenth day of the journey, they had long since passed from the rolling hills of Tyr into the flatter grasslands of Telargyr. Suddenly the piercing caterwauling of a desperate animal broke the monotonous rumbling of their march. Valdieron drew up quickly, his eyes darting to the north where the sound had come from. Llewellyn turned with him. Hafri and Thorgast drew up quickly so as not to run into them.

Once again the pitiful howling came. "Moorcat," explained Thorgast, turning his horse back as if to recommence their march.

"It sounds hurt," insisted Valdieron.

"Probably trapped," returned Thorgast. "Hrolth hunt them for sport and food."

Not knowing or caring what Hrolth were, Valdieron wheeled his horse at the creature's third cry. He urged it into a run, towards the peak of a small rise not far from the road.

"Damn!" cursed Llewellyn, turning to a guard who was riding past, his eyes raised in wonder at the boy's actions. "We'll catch up." With that, he spurred his own horse after Valdieron, and Thorgast and Hafri were soon in pursuit.

The rise gave way to a wide glen, stacked with tall alder trees, and split by a jagged stream. Valdieron, topping the rise ahead of the others, hardly paused to take in the beauty of the land as he guided his horse down the slope, snaking around the few trees. Having chosen the best horse amongst the group, he was drawing slowly ahead of the others.

The animal's fourth cry came louder off to the right and he altered course towards it. He was surprised he had heard it, for it seemed suddenly farther away than he had anticipated.

The stream came and passed with hardly a notice, the excited horse plowing through it without slowing his step. Water sprayed up around them. Shaking the water from his face and hair, Valdieron realized he was grinning.

He broke into a large clearing, circular and with a thick tree line to the north atop a small rise. At the base of the rise was a large felled tree, its branches devoid of leafage. Some branches stuck out of the ground like skeletal appendages, as if the ground had begun to consume it.

He found the Moorcat within the web of branches, and saw that it was not trapped by natural means. It was covered in a thin web of dark vine-like rope, cunningly camouflaged. The cat, obviously a kitten by its appearance and size, did not look like it was going to break free of the net quickly. Though its long teeth chewed desperately at the vines, it was doing little damage. As Val dropped from the horse it hissed and thrashed frantically.

Its color struck him as odd as he drew closer. It shone golden in the sunlight and had slender bands of crimson running along its flank and back. It was much like a domestic cat, only larger.

He heard the others arrive and dismount, and Llewellyn cursed his rashness. Thorgast approached cautiously to get a better look at the cat. He drew in a sharp breath at its appearance.

"Banded Moorcat," he explained to Valdieron. "Very rare, and extremely expensive to buy." He glanced at the makeshift net. "Though this is no poacher's net. Looks like Hrolth."

As if on cue, Llewellyn shouted a warning as an arrow sliced between Valdieron and Thorgast, striking deep into a branch. It was plain in appearance, its tip a flat rock rather than metal, though obviously as effective. Thorgast cursed and rose, reaching for his axe, while Valdieron remained in a crouch, hand on the hilt of his sword while scanning their surroundings. By its angle it seemed the arrow had come from behind them, and as he searched he spotted several dark shapes flitting between the trees and through the long grass.

"Ambush!" yelled Llewellyn, taking a step towards the horses. A sudden tumult of barking and roaring came from all around them as figures leapt from concealment, some barely twenty feet away. Some raised short bows and let fly, one striking Thorgast in the upper left arm and another taking down Llewellyn's horse, catching it in the neck. The other horses took flight instantly, despite Hafri's leaping attempt to catch the one nearest him.

"Hrolth!" Thorgast spat as he eyed the figures around them. Valdieron, having never seen nor heard of these strange figures, was not surprised by their appearance. He had seen worse in the combat ambit. They were human in appearance, with short, muscular bodies and hairy tanned skin. Their faces were akin to a pig's, with snout-like maws and small, beady eyes. They were camouflaged in leather and fur cloaks, several with the sun-gold pelts of the Moorcat. All carried weapons, though those with the bows did not fire again. Instead they slung them over their shoulders and drew out different weapons.

"Kturra ydarr!" shouted Thorgast, bringing flickers of understanding from the creatures. "Yak ghaharh xe zahkara." Valdieron watched the Hrolth intently, expecting them to attack, but they remained where they were. One who was slightly taller and more muscular took a step forward. He carried a spiked club. On his back he wore the pelt of a mountain lion, grayish brown with the darker brown of its main attached, whole right down to the clawed feet and tufted tail. He sneered at Thorgast.

"Hak atrik ka, Urak'Hai." Its voice was thick, as if it struggled with the words, especially the last. Its open maw revealed sharp teeth stained dark.

Thorgast, taking a step towards the creature, took his hands from the haft of his axe and crossed them against his chest. "Wek anakha, hikkenkhat." He turned slightly to emphasize the still struggling Moorcat, though its cries had died down to whimpering snarls of rage.

The Hrolth snorted with what Valdieron took to be laughter, joined by several of the others. "Ghu wakhar ug, takha." Thorgast frowned at the creature's words and began speaking to him again, this time quicker. The Hrolth smiled more and answered haltingly as Thorgast pressed him.

"What are they saying?" asked Hafri from the corner of his mouth to Llewellyn, who was following the discussion closely. His slender hands were against the long pommel of a Rapier belted at his waist.

"The Hrolth have been hunting the Moorcat for some time, now. They killed its mother yesterday and baited it into this trap today. I cannot quite follow, but it seems they are after it as a gift for somebody."

Valdieron scowled at the Hrolth's cruelty and turned to the Moorcat, which was still struggling slightly. One of the Hrolth stepped towards him in warning, leveling its short javelin, and Valdieron stopped.

The leader of the Hrolth had broken into a long tirade, gesticulating wildly with his weapon and eliciting cheers of joy from the others around him with his spirited words. Valdieron thought he caught the words Haruken and Chul'Haka thrown in, and he recognized them as being the names of the four-armed creatures near the Barbarian's homeland and the name of the Barbarian city.

Thorgast's face darkened as the creature continued. Suddenly his muscled arms chorded and snapped his axe free. The surprised Hrolth reacted for an instant before its head looped into the air to the side. A spray of blood accompanied it, splashing two others beside it. They froze in horror and shock, before Thorgast hacked them both down with successive overhand chops.

"If you haven't got anything nice to say, don't say anything!"

The Hrolth who had threatened Valdieron made to launch his javelin at Thorgast. Despite his shock at what Thorgast had done, Valdieron reacted quickly and drew his sword, and in a fluid sweep, severed its throwing arm with a crunching hiss. The hand and the javelin it clutched dropped to the ground trailing blood. The Hrolth screamed in pain and clutched at the dripping stump of its lower arm, oblivious to Valdieron, who ran it through.

Mayhem erupted in the clearing as Hrolth leapt up and threw aside their concealing hides, clutching weapons and crying in their guttural language as they charged. Llewellyn reached into the loose fold of his shirtsleeve, and with repetitive pumps of his right arm, sent flashing knives at the nearest Hrolth. Two went down, one pierced through the eye by a slender blade, the other taking one in the throat. Two others struggled forward with the hilt of a knife protruding from their chests. With a hysterical chuckle, the Elf drew his sword and urged the Hrolth forward.

A wave of javelins was launched from beyond the first line of Hrolth, and Valdieron took a stunned look around before diving out of the way. He came to his feet in a crouch, several Javelins scattered where he and the others had been. Hafri and Llewellyn had also escaped being hit, but Thorgast roared with pain and anger as one of the Javelins struck him in the right thigh. A hooting cheer ran through the Hrolth at the hit, but died instantly as the barbarian tore the shaft free and launched it at one of the Hrolth. The javelin caught it in the chest and knocked it back several feet before striking into the broad trunk of a tree, leaving the dead Hrolth dangling.

Valdieron felt the warm exhilaration of adrenalin coursing through him as several Hrolth closed around him. His eyes darted from one to another as they went to flank him, but he shifted to cut off each attempt. Two had short, thick bladed swords, while two others had ferruled staves as tall as themselves. One other had a spiked cudgel, and another a scythe-like implement attached to a short chain. Each snarled with mocking cruelty as they inched around him, but Val smiled coldly in return.

He let the Hrolth attack first. One Hrolth, armed with a sword, lunged at him with an overhead chop, which he intercepted and swatted aside. He noticed from the corner of his eye a second Hrolth step in behind him and raise its staff in both hands to chop at him. He kicked the first Hrolth in the chest, knocking it backwards where it crashed awkwardly to the ground. Spinning his sword in his hands, he reversed his grip and spun the weapon beneath his right arm with a backwards thrust, catching the second Hrolth by surprise as it attempted to brain him. It barely had time to scream as Valdieron's sword pierced its chest, impaled by its own lunging movement. Valdieron pulled the sword free with the familiar steely hiss.

As if in a non-stop dance, Valdieron retained the reverse grip on his sword and slashed backhanded at the first Hrolth, which struggled to its feet. He sliced so neatly through its throat that for an instant Val thought he had miscalculated and missed. The Hrolth continued to rise and took a step forward before its eyes glazed and its face drained of color. A torrent of blood leaked from the thin line at its throat and it toppled backwards.

A whirring off to the side caused him to spin cautiously, as the Hrolth with the strange chain and scythe swung the weighted end around its head. It feigned a throw and Valdieron rocked back in anticipation, but it spun the weapon again before loosing. Rather than aiming high, however, it lowered its arm to send it at Valdieron's legs.

It wrapped quickly around Valdieron's lower left leg as he began to lift it. With his leg caught, the Hrolth give the chain a hard yank, pulling him suddenly off balance, his feet flying out from under him. His sword slipped from his grasp as he tripped, and it bounced out of his reach.

The Hrolth began to drag him fiercely, his leg raised, forcing him to crawl on both hands and one leg. He planted his free foot firmly against an outcrop of rock. The Hrolth snapped his other leg taut with the force, but he reefed his leg back, biting back a shout against the tearing pain. The Hrolth gave a little ground as it tripped off balance. It was enough for him to loosen the chain and slip his foot free, so that when the Hrolth pulled at the chain again, it toppled from the lack of resistance.

Pushing off the ground with his shoulders, he snapped to his feet in time to duck a spiked cudgel, feeling one of its spikes graze his shoulder, ripping through his caftan. The Hrolth with the staff followed with a lunging thrust, but Valdieron swayed to the side and stepped into the Hrolth. Using the force of his lunge, he bent his arm and snapped his elbow upwards into the Hrolth's face, feeling its snout crack under the force. The blow dazed it and it toppled backwards, loose hands dropping the staff as Valdieron caught it with both hands.

He parried a swing of the cudgel with the staff before it brained him. The Hrolth chopped at him again, and he parried once more with a sweeping motion, which altered the direction of the weapon instead of stopping it. The Hrolth overbalanced as the club thudded into the ground. Stepping on the club, Val reversed the staff and snapped it at the Hrolth's head as it released its grip of the cudgel and stepped back.

The metal cap on the end of the staff connected with a dull crack against its cheek as its head snapped sideways. The Hrolth staggered on wobbly legs as blood trickled down its cheek, before collapsing to the ground.

Two Hrolth remained, the one with the chain weapon, and the other with a short sword. Neither bore the smiles they had worn earlier, but snarled at him cruelly.

The Hrolth with the chain swung it several times before releasing it at Valdieron as he turned to face the other who was behind him. The blade pierced the air with a shrill whistle, like a swooping eagle. Valdieron turned and swept his staff at it. The curved tip of the blade scraped his shirtfront. Bracing himself, Valdieron hooked the weapon and jerked the Hrolth forward with all his strength. It staggered off balance and flailed at Valdieron with the weighted end, but Valdieron crouched and grasped the loose chain. As the Hrolth's stumbled past he rose and looped the chain around its neck and jerked it back with a snap. He used its momentum to swing it around, right in front of a lunging attack from the sword-wielding Hrolth.

Seeing its sword pierce its companion's chest, the Hrolth drew back and lost its hold on the hilt, stunned. Valdieron dropped the dead Hrolth at his feet and took a step forward.

The Hrolth turned and fled with surprising speed over the grassy ground. Valdieron let it go as it disappeared into the thick foliage. Realizing that the din of battle was fading around him, he turned to find several other Hrolth fleeing also.

With relief, Valdieron saw that his companions were still standing, though Thorgast was favoring his wounded thigh. He stood amid a circle of bloodied corpses. His whole front was splattered with droplets of blood, and his leg was stained with his own crimson blood. He wore a grin however, seeming to take grim satisfaction in the carnage around him.

Llewellyn carefully wiped his Rapier clean on one of the Hrolth's fur coats. His mouth was curled in a rueful frown, as if he regretted the slaughter, but his eyes shone. He seemed free of blood, not even a drop staining his azure cloak or white shirt.

Hafri was not as lucky, clutching at his left arm below the shoulder. Thin trails of blood oozed between his fingers. His broadsword was caked in blood, the dead Hrolth around him a testimony to his skill. He was also smiling. "That was lively!"

Llewellyn nodded with a grin before turning to Thorgast with a questioning look. Thorgast seemed to understand the unspoken question and shrugged meekly. "You know I'm not one for conversation."

Llewellyn grunted. "If ever I begin to bore you with one of my tales, try not to take it personally." Llewellyn broke into a grin at his own humor before turning to Valdieron with another questioning stare.

"Although that was mostly enjoyable, it leaves us in a rather uncomfortable predicament. The caravan is by now way ahead of us. Even at their slow pace, we have little hope of catching them without horses, which I do not think we will see again." He cast a glance at the carcass of his horse, lying in a pool of its own blood in the long grass. "Although that does not dishearten me, it does leave us with few items in our packs and our own legs for transportation."

Thorgast grunted, as if to dispute that last point, taking a seat to inspect his thigh wound. Hafri moved to him to help clean and dress his wounds before attending to his own, which had bled heavily.

Moving to retrieve his sword, Val heard a whimpering snarl from the Moorcat. He had almost forgotten the reason for the battle. Returning to the tree, he maneuvered until he could grasp the inert kitten. Pulling the net free of the clinging branches, he stepped back into the open and took a seat on the grass, holding the wrapped kitten before him. Using his knife, he carefully cut away the clinging net. Finally it was free and struggled to pull away from him, but it was too week and gasped for breath in his lap. He removed his water bottle from his pack and poured small amounts into its mouth, which it gulped with some success. Finally it drifted off to sleep, hopefully still strong enough not to die from exhaustion.

With Thorgast and Hafri bandaged, Llewellyn returned to his musings. "What will we do?" He kicked absently at one of the dead Hrolth, its unblinking eyes seeming to glare at him. "We must get to Thorhus, of course. Thorgast, can you still walk?" The question was partly rhetorical, all guessing that the wound was more an inconvenience than hurtful to the big man.

"First things first, we need equipment. What have we got in our packs?" They all rummaged through their packs, uncovering little but personal belongings. Valdieron had some cookware, a lantern, his fletching kit and tinderbox, some extra clothes and a small hammock gained from Nagus, but he had no provisions. His belt held his pouch of Bark-ash Leaf and his other water bottle. The others were much the same. Thorgast had a side of mutton buried in his pack, but they were forced to toss it away, as it was beginning to turn foul.

"We have the horse." Valdieron rose and approached the dead animal. Although he had never eaten a horse before, his father had slaughtered sheep and pigs, and he had a fair idea on how they were cut up. He knew the meat would be worthless in a few days, so they would not need much of the animal. The others did not answer as he drew his knife and went to work on the creature's rump.

"We have your bows, and game is always plentiful along the highway," said Thorgast as he flexed his injured leg.

Llewellyn nodded. "Yet we will have to leave the Highway at some stage to cross to Thorhus, unless we want to head to Kethym and then to Thorhus. The road may be faster, but we'll lose many days from the extra distance."

"We can decide on that when the time comes," insisted Hafri, wincing as he clenched his left hand. "Besides, we'll probably be able to get horses at the next village. Who knows, we might even catch the caravan by morning if we hurry."

Llewellyn shook his head dismissively. "Maybe, but Fender would turn us away for abandoning the caravan, if he didn't just have us killed. He has yet to pay us so our loss means a bonus to his purse, even with the missing horses. I do not think he is ruing our departure."

Hafri sighed, as if expecting this but hoping Llewellyn would not pick up on it.

Valdieron finished the bloody work, finding the carving process more macabre than he had anticipated. Thorgast provided him with a large canvas bag to carry the meat in, and he tied it off securely, placing the smaller portion for the Moorcat in his own belt pouch.

"I am ready." As one they turned towards the highway, Thorgast groaning a little as he started up the slight incline out of the glen.

Valdieron carried the sleeping cat tucked inside his shirt as they walked. It stirred occasionally, but remained asleep until that evening when they made camp by the side of the highway. Thorgast limped against Hafri as a line of blood trickled down his leg from the blood-soaked bandage, and he sank with a grateful sigh onto the soft ground.

The Moorcat woke, squirming around as if frightened while Valdieron held it against him, rocking in his hammock strung between two small trees.

Thorgast chuckled from beyond the fire, his wounded leg stretched out before him as he leaned against the thin bole of another tree. "Kazakarum!" He nodded towards the squirming Moorcat. "In my people's tongue, it means 'Little Warrior'."

Valdieron nodded, suddenly cursing and sitting up as the cat pierced his shirt with its small claws. After several moments it quieted, and he peered down into his shirtfront to find it lazing contentedly in the darkness. He reached for his pouch containing the small roll of horseflesh, and drew out a small portion before holding it before the cat. Tiny teeth snapped at his fingers and he cursed again as the cat chewed hungrily. He dropped two more portions down to it and it ate hungrily, but Thorgast warned him against feeding it more.

"The kitten needs small feeds at regular intervals, not large ones."

Valdieron nodded and returned the meat to its pouch.

Llewellyn was out scouting for food and water, so the usual stream of conversation had ceased, leaving an uneasy silence amongst the three. Valdieron spoke.

"Thorgast, the Hrolth mentioned something about your people earlier. Was it bad news?" He had thought the Barbarian seemed a little more downcast than usual, but it may have been due to his injury and the obvious pain he was in.

The Barbarian nodded with a sigh. "The Hrolth said that the Haruken are more numerous in the northlands now than they were even a year back before I left. That is not good."

"It also mentioned Chul'Haka?"

Thorgast's stony silence warned Valdieron not to press the Barbarian. Whatever the Hrolth had spoken of, though, it was obviously not good news for Thorgast.

Llewellyn returned after some time, as Qantari was high overhead and Santari was beginning its night's journey over the horizon. The Elf, always cheerful, noticed the heavy silence but said nothing. In his hand he clasped a large fern-like leaf, splotched brown in color, along with several long tubular roots. The Elf dropped his Bow and quiver beside his pack before kneeling and slicing up the tubes with a thin dagger. Seeing as the others did not seem to notice him, Valdieron rose and retrieved his cooking utensils and moved to assist Llewellyn.

"Selwyn Root!" Llewellyn dropped the thin slices of the pale red roots into a small pot. "Half fill that pot with water."

The Elf passed Valdieron his large water skin and he half-emptied its contents into the pot. When the water struck the pieces, the pale red color seemed to wash from them, staining the water.

"That is only its pigmentation. It is mildly poisonous, so I do not recommend you eat them raw or drink the water." After he dropped the last piece into the pot, he stirred them around vigorously with his knife before straining the now crimson liquid from it and repeating the process. "Don't get the liquid on your clothes either."

Valdieron backed away from the spot where Llewellyn had strained the roots. "Can it poison you through contact with your skin?"

Llewellyn laughed sharply. "No. It stains your clothes and takes weeks to get out. It will also do the same for your skin."

Llewellyn refilled the pot and began to shred the large fern into it, but not before slicing away its stem. "Ikfael Fern. Don't eat the stem, or you'll be dead before you know it. The leaves are fine, however." This he added after Valdieron glared at him incredulously. He was starting to wonder if letting the Elf cook was such a good idea.

"Go and get me a large, flat rock, if you will?" asked Llewellyn, setting a small fire of dry leaf, moss and twigs. He had to borrow Valdieron's tinderbox to ignite it, and soon had a small blaze going. Valdieron wondered briefly why he did not use the other fire Thorgast had started, but just shook his head in confusion as he searched for the rock Llewellyn had asked for.

With Qantari's full brilliance above, he had no difficulties finding his way, though he was sure not to move too far from the camp and its light. He kept his hand near the hilt of his belt-knife just in case. After a brief search, he found a rock slightly larger than his outstretched hand, spherical and relatively flat.

Llewellyn was slowly feeding the cooking fire with larger branches to create embers, which would smolder for some time. He took the rock from Val with a nod of thanks and set it off to the side.

Valdieron watched with fascination as the Elf worked methodically through the cooking. The flat rock and pot he placed side by side in the fire's embers. When the rock was warm enough he placed as much of the horsemeat onto it as would fit, using his dagger to turn it slowly as it began to smoke.

"Have you any Bark-ash Leaf left?" Valdieron nodded and dug out his small pouch of the herb. At his waist, one of his water bottles contained a mixture of the sleeping potion, but he still had nearly a full pouch of it left.

Llewellyn took a pinch of the dried gray leaf and dropped it into the boiling pot with the Fern and Selwyn Root. "This should help everybody rest. We need it after today, I think." The leaf quickly evaporated, consumed by the warm liquid.

"Shouldn't we be keeping a watch?" asked Valdieron, glancing around. He knew too well the dangers of being this close to the merchant highway.

"I will stand watch."

Valdieron frowned, his brow furrowing in confusion. "How will you stay awake if you take some of the Bark-ash Leaf?"

Llewellyn stared at him for a moment before breaking out in a wide grin. "Sorry. I forget that you do not know of Elves. As a race, we do not sleep, Valdieron, so your sleeping potion will have no effect on me."

Valdieron chuckled softly, thinking the Elf was joking, but realized that he was not. "Don't you get tired? How do you rest?"

Llewellyn turned to stir the pot of roots and leaf and rotate the seared meat. "Instead of sleep, we slow down our bodies, so that we are in a sleep-like state, but our minds are still aware."

Val remembered his childish fascination with Elves and wondered what other details had been omitted from the books he had read.

The rousing Moorcat broke his thoughts as it stretched restlessly. He was soon forced to remove it from the confines of his shirt as it squirmed about.

At first, the cat stood dead still, his eyes darting about fearfully, as if it would bolt at any moment. Valdieron was ready to catch at it if it did, but it slowly calmed and raised its nose towards the meat sizzling on the fire, its ears pricked with interest.

"It seems our young companion is hungry," grinned Llewellyn, using the tip of his dagger to spear a small piece of meat grayed from heat. With a flick, he tossed the meat at the ground before the cat, which pounced on it quickly but recoiled as his nose touched the warm meat. Shaking his head angrily, he tentatively sniffed at the meat until it was cool enough to eat, chewing it hungrily in its large mouth before cleaning itself like a normal cat.

Llewellyn chuckled to himself and returned to the cooking, while Valdieron played with Kazakarum. The cat became more playful, though he tired quickly and allowed Valdieron to return him to his snug bed inside his shirt.

Meanwhile, Llewellyn finished preparing the meal and they were ready to eat. "Eat and rest. We will want to get an early start tomorrow, if we are going to get to Thorhus in time for the Trial."

Hafri and Valdieron nodded, and Thorgast remained broodingly silent, causing Valdieron to glance at Llewellyn questioningly. The Elf merely smiled, albeit wanly.

Valdieron's concerns faded as he began to eat, relishing the flavor of the meal. The combination of the Selwyn Root and Ikfael Fern was bittersweet. He glanced at it uneasily as he ate, expecting any moment to feel its poison taking effect. It did not, however, though the drowsy warmth of the Bark-ash Leaf did, and he had barely enough time after the meal to set up his hammock and roll into it before sleep consumed him.

Chapter 20

For Valdieron, each day of their journey brought him new understanding and knowledge. He developed a close camaraderie with his traveling companions and learned a great deal from each.

With Llewellyn he spent the most time, for the Bard was a wellspring of facts about many subjects, and his humorous view of things was infectious. He told Valdieron of cities and peoples, of places he had seen and heard of, and also of creatures, both great and small. He taught Valdieron some of the finer details of archery, which he was more than willing to learn. Although he had considered himself a good shot with the bow, the Elf was consistently accurate. He could put one of his white-fletched arrows into a slender tree trunk at fifty paces. Valdieron found his aim improving from the simple techniques taught to him by Llewellyn.

Hafri took more time to get to know, for he was silently secretive, for whatever reason. He would change moods in a heartbeat, turning from a smile to a frown at a wrong word. When he did open up, it was obvious that he had not traveled extensively. His knowledge of merchants and their business was deep, and Valdieron guessed he was probably the son of a merchant or shopkeeper.

Like Hafri, Thorgast had his mood swings and was slow to open up, but when he did, Valdieron could not help but be impressed with the big man's openness and trust. He told of his people and his childhood growing up in Chul'Haka. Valdieron was surprised to find he was the son of the city's War-Chief, and that his position among his people was like that of a prince. His knowledge of the Southern lands was as limited as Valdieron's, but his familiarity with the lands to the north kept Valdieron engrossed in his tales.

Far from being alone, the four found that the Highway had many travelers heading in both directions, though mostly northwest. Caravan guards would glance at them warily as they passed, and the four would prudently step from the highway, not wanting to cause any trouble. On occasions,

Llewellyn would converse with a few of the smaller groups who passed, gaining word of the south and east. It seemed that most of the attention was focused on the up and coming Combat, which drew more attention this year because of the favorite, a Warrior named 'Hagar', who was aiming for his fifth straight victory. Valdieron already knew of this Dak'marian warrior from Nagus. The others all seemed to know of him, and spoke with some concern about him.

"I watched him fight in last year's Combat," said Llewellyn one night. Hafri and Thorgast were both sleeping, and Valdieron lay awake feeding the ever-growing Kazakarum.

"Is he as good as everybody says he is?" From what he had heard, Valdieron understood that Hagar was strong, fast and cunning, and had hardly been pressed in his previous four appearances at the Combat.

"Probably," mused Llewellyn, his head bent as he listened to the tones of his lute strings as he tuned it meticulously. "But that does not mean he is unbeatable."

"An important thing to remember, whether you are a warrior, a Bard, a runner, or a fisherman is that there is always somebody better than you, no matter how good you are."

"Always?" Valdieron winced suddenly as Kazakarum bit softly into his finger.

"There will always be somebody who is said to be the best at something, whether it is Hagar the Warrior, or Llewellyn the Bard. Whether that is the case or not is of little matter. It is the reputation that creates these claims. This is what drives our young friend Hafri."

Valdieron frowned. "That does not help me much!"

"I know," returned the Elf with a mischievous smile, but he raised his hands to ward off Valdieron's rebuke. "All I am saying, is that no matter how much better somebody may appear, it is of little consequence if you believe in yourself. Those who think themselves the best usually aren't, and those who think themselves inferior are sometimes better."

"I suppose worrying about it will make it worse by tenfold," sighed Valdieron. "Thanks, though for what I'm not sure." Feeling the vague pull of the Bark-ash Leaves, he returned to his thoughts and was soon asleep.

All along the Merchant Highway, villages sprung up sporadically, little more than waypoints for the passing caravans. Each seemed to have a sizeable Inn if only a few houses. They often found themselves in one of these Inns as they traveled, finding the warmth and company preferable to the cold darkness outside. The Inns were not garish or pretty, and were hardly ever occupied by more than a few passers-by or locals. Llewellyn was able to get them food and board for the night in return for the plying of his Bard skills. A few declined his offer, but most were happy for his presence, to break up the monotony of their existence if nothing else. Val had the opportunity to see Llewellyn at work, and he was very impressed by the charismatic Elf's skill.

At each stop they bathed and rested, and asked for transportation in the form of horses. They only found one for sale, an aged, unshod mare, whose drunken owner asked for more than three times her worth. They declined and were forced to walk. Their progress was good and they knew they should reach Thorhus with time to spare before the tournament.

After a few weeks traveling, Llewellyn decided to move them from the Highway. "As it is, the Highway continues on to Kethym. Thorhus is more to the South-East, and although the Highway curves to meet it, we can make just as good time if we head cross country." The southern part of Telargyr was rolling grassland, making the terrain easily negotiable, though Valdieron still felt some trepidation leaving the protection of the Highway.

Kazakarum seemed to also agree with the change. The growing Moorcat was at home in the sweeping grassland, and would often leave Valdieron to dash about around them, caught up in the excitement of freedom as he chased insects or birds. Still, he would always return to Valdieron, who wished he could run free with the cat. He had little fear the cat would not return, for he knew it could not hunt on its own, lacking the skills its mother would have begun to teach it by now.

Although it had just turned over to winter, the few trees they saw were like skeletons against the parched grass. The weather stayed reasonably warm, although the clear days led to chilly nights. They always had a large fire to mill around for warmth. The clear nights were beautiful, though, and Valdieron often found himself lost in thought as he stared up at the star-filled heavens. Often he would go off alone and practice his swordwork. Thoughts of demons, dragon lords, portals and magic were held at bay during these weeks, where each day seemed to flow into the next, without care or worry, as long as they remained on track to reach Thorhus on time.

A cold hand pressed over Valdieron's mouth, and he started awake in an instant, the images of the Combat Ambit vanishing as his eyes snapped open. His hand was resting against the hilt of his weapon, and he tried to scream in fright as two glowing red eyes floated above him in the darkness. It took only a moment, however, for his night vision to register that it was Llewellyn, motioning for him to be silent.

"Your eyes?" he asked with a barely discernible whisper.

"Elvin night vision. It enables me to see heat patterns." Valdieron sat up slowly; remembering dimly that Elves could see in the dark, but he did not know their eyes glowed.

"What is it?" Valdieron rubbed his now cold face, feeling his skin shiver at the chill air. Overhead, gray clouds quenched the combined brilliance of the twin moons, which were both near their fullness. Val wondered what Llewellyn had woken him for. Hafri and Thorgast were still asleep and there was no sign of any danger nearby. Even Kazakarum was sleeping peacefully inside Valdieron's sleeping bag.

"I heard something in the distance. It sounded like chanting." Llewellyn had risen quietly and was staring off to the east. "I thought you and I might go and check it out."

Valdieron shrugged and rose, careful not to shift Kaz. He hastily grabbed his heavy ulster and boots, though even they did not seem to offer much protection against the cold. Strapping his baldric over his shoulder and securing it to his belt, he sheathed his sword and took up his bow. With a glance at the still sleeping Hafri and Thorgast, he followed Llewellyn with careful steps out of the camp.

"Here, I will lead you," suggested Llewellyn, reaching for Valdieron's arm, but Valdieron pulled away, and Llewellyn turned to regard him with raised brow.

"I can see well enough to get by," assured Valdieron with a wry smile.

"And if we have to run?" asked Llewellyn with matching

mock-arrogance.

"I'll keep up!"

Llewellyn's mouth turned up in a grin. Suddenly he turned and darted away, his long hair trailing behind him, his steps long and as silent as falling snow. Valdieron took only a moment to wipe the smile from his face before cursing silently and leaping after the Elf.

Although he could see as well as in a dim afternoon, he was hard-pressed keeping up with the fleet-footed Elf. To his own ears, his footfalls sounded like a stampeding herd of cows, and he concentrated on lengthening his strides and softening his footfalls as much as possible.

Val was not sure how long they ran, but it felt like some distance as the gray land flashed past him. He wondered dimly how Llewellyn had heard something at this distance. Maybe the Elf's hearing was as keen as his eyesight. Despite the desperate dash, Valdieron was smiling with delight. He had actually gained a step or two on Llewellyn, spurring him on even more.

Llewellyn suddenly stopped and dropped quickly into a crouch as he topped a small rise, pressing himself flat onto the low grass. Valdieron noted this and slowed also, coming up to the prone Elf in a crawl. Llewellyn turned to him, his eyes flashing brighter than before, and his mouth set in a wondering smile as he shook his head slightly. He was not even breathing hard, though his face was flecked with dots of perspiration. Valdieron was breathing heavily and felt his clothes sticking to him from the sweat of his body.

"Yet more surprises, Valdieron. That you have night vision, I cannot now deny, but it is like nothing I have ever seen, almost like that of your Moorcat." Llewellyn paused. "And then you chase me down like I am walking. Me! When young, I could beat any of the young Elves in Lloreander, yet I was hard-pressed to keep ahead of you."

Valdieron felt elated and proud at Llewellyn's words, but wondered if the Elf had even been exerting himself. He looked only to be pacing himself, and he also had the responsibility of choosing their path. His smile faded, however, as he turned to see what Llewellyn had stopped for.

A dark-stoned temple sat at the bottom of a small basin-like valley. It was large, easily as big as the 'Warrior's Way' back home, and as high at its peak. Its appearance seemed strange to Valdieron, until it struck him that it was shaped into the head of what he thought was a jackal, its entry the flame-lit maw of the beast. Its eyes, slanted and narrow, also burned with fire, mixed with strange hues of red and purple.

"What is this place?" asked Valdieron in a whisper. Although he could see nobody in sight, he kept his voice to barely a whisper.

"It seems to be a temple of sorts," mused Llewellyn, but it was obvious he had never seen one like it before, which made Valdieron suddenly uncomfortable and wary. His hand strayed to the hilt of his sword for comfort.

As if in response, the sound of many voices chanting broke the quiet of the night. The words were unknown to Valdieron, but their tone was one of morbid doom, and his skin crawled.

Llewellyn, however, stiffened at the sound of the choir, his hand also moving to the hilt of his rapier.

"What is it?" asked Valdieron again, his eyes darting around cautiously. Something about this temple gave him a feeling of foreboding, and he could not help but feel he was being watched.

"Devil cult," answered Llewellyn with a sneer. "Godless heathens who know not what they do. I wonder if-." He suddenly quieted and pointed off to the right, but Valdieron was already turning there, having glimpsed something from his periphery.

A line of figures, two abreast, crested the ridge of the valley. Each carried a pole topped by a lantern save two in the center of the line. These two bore between them a long pole, on which was suspended a prone figure covered in heavy furs like the carcass of a beast, tied by wrist and ankle. The figures were dressed in dark robes, concealing their appearances. They moved hastily, as if pursued.

Valdieron turned to Llewellyn questioning, but the Elf shrugged.

The column, numbering fourteen not counting the tied figure, made their way to the temple's entry, slowing as if afraid, but not daring to halt. Nobody emerged from the temple to greet them, and the chorus from inside continued with its mystical chanting.

Once before the temple, the two lines parted, allowing the

two figures carrying the figure to approach. Standing under the upper jaw of the jackal, they lifted the pole from their shoulders and set it atop the two lower protruding fangs at waist height. The two figures bowed low before scrambling back quickly, still bent in obeisance, but obviously eager to be away. Once back in line, the column reversed and retraced their steps from the valley.

Valdieron followed their progress, but was alerted by Llewellyn's sharp intake of breath and returned his gaze to the Temple. At the opening, two figures had appeared. They were human in appearance, but their heads were in the shape of jackals, and seemed to be masks of a dull black metal. He turned to Llewellyn to question him, but decided that it may be better if he did not know, and turned back.

The two jackal-men lifted the captive from the fangs, easily hoisting it onto their shoulders and retreated into the Temple. Inside, the choir was gaining volume and pace.

"Llewellyn, what is going on here?"

Llewellyn turned, his eyes burning with a fury, his face set like stone. "The Temple worships a Devil, and like all cults, they make sacrifices to appease their Devil. It seems that bound figure is the next sacrifice."

Valdieron gasped, stunned by the barbaric practice. "And those jackal-men, are they real men or monsters?"

Llewellyn shrugged. "I do not know."

"And the robed people who brought the captive?"

"Villagers, probably. A nearby society could well come under the Temple's influence. They are probably given the task of providing sacrifices every month, so that the Temple lets them live or doesn't spoil their crops."

"Harmless?" asked Valdieron, concerned about their situation. The Temple was bad enough, but having a village of fanatical Devil-worshippers close by was something that made him edgy.

"I cannot guess. Maybe they would appreciate the destruction of such a sect. Maybe they believe the Devil brings them protection. They might protect him with their lives, especially if the Devil has some hold over them."

A sudden, piercing female scream broke the cold night, sending shivers over Valdieron's body. Valdieron found himself rising and drawing his sword. Llewellyn also rose, but only to grasp him by the forearm to prevent him from charging.

"That was a woman, Llewellyn!"

"I know, Val. There is little we can do for her, though!"

Valdieron whipped his sword up before him. "Little is more than we can ever hope for!"

Llewellyn regarded him intently for a moment before nodding slightly and releasing his arm. With a swift motion, he drew his own slender sword and smiled grimly at Valdieron.

Llewellyn took the lead, picking a course around the rim of the valley before crawling down the left bank, flanking the entry. Valdieron could not see any guards, but was still watching intently for any signs of danger.

They were approaching the stone wall of the Temple when Valdieron noticed movement before him against the dark wall. He grasped Llewellyn by the shoulder, halting the Elf who turned to him questioningly. Valdieron stepped past the Elf as the outline of a figure sprang at them.

It was one of the jackal-men, taller than Llewellyn and lean, lower body covered in thick leather and its upper body a metallic corselet. What he had thought were masks looked more supple than metal and more lifelike than helms, and Valdieron realized these were not men dressed as jackals, but half-men, half jackals. It was armed with a staff of sorts, made of a dark metal and tipped with a wicked, curved blade, like a saber but thicker. Valdieron raised his sword in a horizontal parry and stopped the weapon in its deadly path towards Llewellyn's unprotected head.

The jackal-man withdrew, impossibly fast and swung again, this time at Valdieron's torso. Rather than parry, Valdieron threw his sword high and bent back, feeling the blade scrape across his heavy cloak, slicing it like it was grass. The jackal-man then sent his weapon thrusting at Valdieron's stomach in a backhand thrust.

With sword high, Valdieron brought it down in a sweeping parry, clutching the sword in both hands as it connected with the weapon. The thrust went harmlessly wide, and Valdieron knew the creature had thought him beaten. Valdieron spun, coming around full circle with sword extended. Despite its speed, the jackal-man could not defend, and as it attempted to bring its weapon to parry, Valdieron's sword sliced into its right arm, slicing through the metallic skin. The keen blade severed the arm and continued into its chest. Valdieron jerked it free as the jackal howled. The howl grew softer as the jackal-man toppled to the side.

Llewellyn cursed behind him and he turned to regard the Elf. "I could not detect him," he whispered wonderingly. "Surely they are creatures of evil manifestation. You lead us. I will be fine when we get inside the temple." Both were looking around, wondering if there were any other jackal-men about, but the rising chorus inside had hopefully deafened the howl. As if on cue, however, the voices halted abruptly, and there was silence.

Without further delay, Valdieron ran to the Temple wall and followed it around to the entry, looking back occasionally to see if there were any jackal-men creeping up behind them. They reached the entry unchallenged, however, and sidled along the wall where they could peer in.

The entry was a large, arched corridor running fifteen feet into the temple before opening into the main hall. Four metal sconces, crafted as clawed hands, held burning torches, which bathed the hall in dancing light. From his vantage point, Valdieron could make out little inside the hall, but what he could see made him gasp with wonder.

The very center of the room was raised in a circular pillar, only a few feet in height. It glowed with an effulgent heat, fading and pulsing, almost like a heart beating. Around the circumference of the pillar's wall were runes and sigils. He did feel his hackles rise, as if he could sense their evil nature.

Atop the wide pillar lay the inert form of the captive, though he could see little save their shackled feet from where he stood.

A single gong, like the rolling thunder of a storm, reverberated through the temple. Several moments of deep silence ensued, until a single voice rose up throughout the huge room. Valdieron strained to catch a glimpse of the speaker, but he was hidden. His voice made Valdieron's breath catch in his throat. Dulcet and hypnotic, it was snake-like in its venomous lure. He could not understand the words, but recognized the urgency in the frenzied rise in tone.

"Summoning!" whispered Llewellyn at his side, and Valdieron felt the tension in the slender Elf's body as his eyes blazed. His sword glowed with a pale luminescence, like a bright star on a clear night.

Valdieron felt himself inching forward, oblivious to the warmth of his own sword in his hand, and the tension and anticipation that made his nerves tingle. As the voice rose in its frenzy, the captive seemed to come awake. Closer now, Valdieron could see the captive was a naked female, her body covered in detailed runes. In the instant Valdieron saw her he knew that he would remember that face for the rest of his days.

Her young skin glistened with sweat as she attempted to scream. Platinum-blonde hair clung to her sweaty face and shoulders, whipping around like miniature snakes as she shook her head to and fro in frenzy. Her face, finely boned with wide, large eyes, upturned nose and slender mouth, was twisted into a bestial snarl as she strained against her bonds. Trails of blood, glowing golden from the torch-fire and the pulsing pillar beneath her ran along her arms and legs. The gold-lined pillar seemed to pulse brighter with the spraying blood and the drops evaporated as if consumed.

Valdieron was rising without thought, but felt the restraining hand of Llewellyn on his shoulder. He whirled, shaking his head to clear it. He saw Llewellyn turn toward the right of the room and he spun quickly, expecting to find more jackal-men charging them. There were jackal-men, but they were lined before a tiered stage against the far wall, their huge pole-arms raised before them like a barrier. Above them, arms outspread and head held high in exaltation was a lone man. Llewellyn hissed vehemently.

"Sable Elf!"

Valdieron had only heard of the wicked dark-skinned Elvenkind from books and stories. The anti-thesis of their lighter-skinned cousins, Sable Elves were believed to sacrifice or eat their own young to appease their deities.

Valdieron knelt transfixed as the Sable Elf continued his chanting. His skin tingled as if there were a chill in the air, though he was sweating profusely. Gesticulating, the dark Elf worked his spell while the room quieted to a deathly stillness.

Llewellyn gasped at his side and Val turned quickly. Above the prone woman, the air was beginning to shimmer like swirling stars against the dark sky, though the stars were of fiery red. They swirled quickly, growing wider and faster with each circuit, until a giant ball of fiery diamante floated above the pillar. The woman watched wild-eyed but fascinated, as if captivated by every tiny particle, until a slender appendage broke the glittering field, and grasped her by the throat, choking off her attempted scream.

Chapter 21

The arm was long and slender and was covered in dark serpentine scales, which glowed fiery red. The clawed hand had six hooked fingers. It grasped the woman fiercely, but with just enough pressure that she could still breathe. She struggled desperately to tear herself free.

Valdieron was stunned. He looked over at the dark-skinned Elf, and found the figure had his eyes closed and was concentrating, his dark skin glistening with sweat.

Like a blurred dream he found his gaze returned to the pillar, and found a figure stepping wholly from the Portal. It bore a remarkable resemblance to the dark Elf who had summoned it, only taller and more muscular. Its feet clawed as they clicked on the stone of the pillar as it straddled the woman. Its head was slightly bulbous, with eyes that were narrow and deep-set, like pinpoints of darkness. It had a small upturned nose, like a child's, and its pointed ears were large and flared. If not for the malignant sneer it bore, it may have looked almost cherubic.

As if compelled by some force, Valdieron was up and running towards the pillar, sword in hand. He half expected Llewellyn to pursue and halt him, but sensed the Elf also rise and dash off to the right, towards the dais.

"The Elf is the key," he heard him shout, but Valdieron gave it no heed as he was suddenly confronted by two more of the jackal-men.

With hardly a pause, Valdieron batted aside the lunge of the jackal-man on the left, its pole-arm flying harmlessly to the side. He had a moment's opening, but was forced to hold his killing blow as the second jackal-man slashed at his head from the other side.

Valdieron spun in a crouch, his sword held out before him as the dark blade passed inches above his head. Turning full circle, he came around at the creature's unprotected flank and legs. Using the momentum of his spin, he sliced across the leg closest to him, feeling his sword bite in just below the knee, slicing through flesh and bone with ease. Blood spurted and the jackal-man howled with pain as he toppled, writhing in agony as he clutched at the dismembered stump.

Valdieron left him for dead and turned. The first jackal-man recovered and thrust at him again, slicing at his chest. Without hesitation Valdieron spun once more. The cruel edge flicked his heavy cloak as he turned fully away from the jackal-man. Reversing his grip on his sword, he thrust it back behind him, beneath his right arm, grimacing cruelly as it pierced the side of the jackal-man and tore into its lungs. With a twist he yanked it free and continued towards the pillar. The jackal-man toppled in a pool of purple blood in his wake.

Screams and shouts rose from the chanters who scattered from the melee, seeking the exit. Valdieron gave them no heed.

Atop the pillar, the Devil crouched over the woman, and Valdieron gaped as he realized the purpose of the summoning. The woman was not to be sacrificed, but was part of some sexual ritual. Horrified, Valdieron screamed something incoherent, and the Devil turned toward him.

Those eyes, now pinpoints of intense fire, struck Valdieron like a barrier and he found himself slowing. The Devil shrank away from him also, as if in shock. It hissed, showing feline teeth, stained with the blood of the woman.

Val felt compelled to flee but he slowly approached the Devil, scowling.

The Devil stood in a flash, leaving the motionless woman beneath him. Valdieron noticed for the first time that it had a tail, long and sinuous like a cat's, but barbed at the tip. It brought its clawed hands up before it, ready, as Valdieron crept inexorably forward.

A faint flicker of movement from his peripherals warned Valdieron that more of the jackal-men were stalking him and he almost grinned. The Devil, as if to draw his attention from the closing jackals, began to laugh balefully and spread its arms, goading him into attacking.

"You are dead!"

Whether the Devil heard or understood him he could not tell. His words seemed to act as a catalyst for the jackals, and they attacked without sound.

Acting on instincts gained from endless hours in the Combat Ambit, Valdieron spun and lunged at the jackal on his left, moving away from the one on his right. His movement caught the jackal off guard, enabling him to sweep away the desperate lunging attack of a pole-arm. Reversing the momentum of his sword, he slashed the jackal's unprotected chest, cutting deeply as it sliced across, and bit deeply into its right arm above the elbow. With a howling cry that sent shivers down Valdieron's spine, the jackal reeled back, loosing its grasp on the pole-arm before toppling backwards.

The whistling of a weapon's flight alerted Valdieron of the next attack from behind him. Without thought he pushed off to his left, diving into a roll straight at a third jackal. He had hoped the jackal would not react to this unusual move, but the jackal leveled its pole-arm at him as he came to his feet.

Unable to parry, he tried to twist away from it as he rose. Its tip scraped painfully across his right thigh and a shock ran through him, but he was too focused on the jackal to be slowed by the wound. The jackal barely had time to draw back in alarm before Valdieron's sword pierced its chest, driving through lungs and catching its spine before punching through the back, dripping purple blood. With an exultant cry, Valdieron wrenched the sword free and turned to face the last jackal.

The remaining jackal seemed to realize that it was in trouble and hesitated before its attack. It thrust at Valdieron's legs. Val swept his sword low in a parry, but found the pole-arm already reversing, its other end sweeping towards his head.

For the second time he rolled away, desperate to gain time and ground. He rose but stumbled as his right leg gave way. Sprawling on his side, he twisted to see the jackal hovering over him, weapon descending in a blow Valdieron knew would not miss.

The weapon faltered in its descent, as if caught by some unseen force. The jackal strained, almost convulsing as it fought against it. Valdieron rolled and pushed himself to his feet, using his left leg for strength, his right leg bent and shaking. He raised his sword, but found the jackal was still shaking uncontrollably. It began to howl and the despairing sound caused Val to lose heart. Not wanting to run the creature through, he found he did not have to. The jackal's form wavered like a reflection in a rippling pond, growing fainter and fainter before it vanished completely, like a shadow overwhelmed by darkness.

A clicking of claws on the floor alerted Valdieron and he turned as the Devil took a step towards him, smiling malignantly. He risked a glance at the dais and found Llewellyn engaged in combat with the dark-Elf, his slender rapier being met with an equally slender sliver of darkness. Their fight was brutal in its beauty as the two hacked at each other in anger, a dance of death in its purest form.

Valdieron wrenched his attention from the dazzling fight, his eyes narrowing as they settled on the Devil.

"Who are you, Dragon-man?"

The Devil's deep, echoing voice caught Valdieron by surprise and he halted, stunned. He had not expected the creature to speak, let alone question him. His query bemused Valdieron.

In answer, he flicked his sword at the Devil. It was only a testing strike, to see the Devil's reaction. It surprised him when the Devil darted away from the sword, very fast. He easily evaded the strike, but its eyes stayed on the sword, as if it feared it.

Valdieron's second strike was more forceful, but still testing, a low, lunging thrust with his weight still under him so he could dance away if necessary. As if recognizing the attack for what it was, the Devil swayed back only slightly, the weapon coming to within a hand span of its abdomen. It merely hissed defiantly at him.

The sword, however, flared suddenly, a golden aura shimmering warmly along the blade. It flickered and pulsed, like a living creature, and a tendril of the scintillating light lashed out at the Devil and whipped across its chest like a tiny bolt of lightning.

The Devil screamed, a shrieking, pain-filled sound and was thrust away by the jolting strike. A slender gash ran across its chest, showing pale red flesh beneath, blackened by the cauterizing heat of the attack. Valdieron almost dropped the sword, stunned. The Devil leapt at him.

In the first blurring exchange, the Devil scored two minor hits on him, easily getting through his defenses with its unnatural speed. One clawed hand opened tiny blood-trails across his chest and another rent his left shoulder more seriously, slicing across bone as it passed. Fighting for control of the pain, Valdieron managed to evade several more attacks before the Devil drew back, watching him intently.

Valdieron gulped down deep breaths, struggling to fight the pain of his injuries as he sought a plan to fight the Devil. He was not fast enough to swing his sword effectively in defense and had no time to formulate his own attacks without being wounded.

With a growl of frustration he sheathed his sword. Although the weapon, with its surprising magical ability, was able to hurt the creature, he knew he had a better chance of deflecting the Devil's attacks without the weapon.

Seeing its new advantage, the Devil hissed triumphantly and attacked without hesitation.

Val was struck again several times in the first few attacks, and blood ran freely from new wounds on his thigh, arm and cheek. Although he had been given sound combat training, he felt unable to cope with the Devil's speed.

Valdieron retreated before the Devil's next onslaught, waiting for an opportunity to strike. He turned away most of the attacks and dodged the others, taking only a glancing blow in the next sequence. This seemed to drive the Devil into a greater frenzy.

Although he could feel his strength ebbing slowly from the tirade, Valdieron continued to wait for his chance, which finally came.

The Devil feigned a low slash at his legs, crouching and lunging, but then rose up and slashed at Valdieron's chest and throat. Valdieron leaned away from the attack and followed through with a kick at the Demon's leg. He connected solidly with the knee, a dull crack signifying he had done some damage, and the Devil howled as it spun back around, slashing with both claws at his head. Val raised his forearms to block as he retreated, taking a stinging graze across both arms. The Devil limped back a step, showing surprise and fear in its blazing eyes.

Pressing his sudden advantage, Valdieron considered bringing out his sword again but thought the better of it.

The Demon met him and lashed frantically. One clawed hand sliced Valdieron's ribs and the other darted forward to pass within an inch of his face as he dodged to the side. The thrust reversed into a slash at his head, forcing him to crouch under it.

Punching the Devil's knee made it howl furiously again,

giving him the time to rise. As he did, he bent his right arm and lifted his elbow to strike the Devil in the face. The blow sent the Devil sprawling backwards to land heavily on the stone.

Shakily it rose. A trickle of dark blood ran from the corner of its mouth. It snarled, whether from pain or outrage he was unsure, but it once again set itself to attack.

A piercing scream cut the heavy air. Val watched stunned at the scintillating ball of flickering diamante dimmed and began to fade, growing smaller and smaller. As it did, the Devil howled in agonizing pain, as if being crushed by a great weight. As the ball faded to a pinpoint, the Devil shrieked one last time, causing Valdieron to press his hands over his ears to blot out the sound. It ended abruptly, however, and the Devil pitched forward limply, landing on the floor.

Llewellyn was at Valdieron's side then, leaning heavily on his sword and favoring his right leg, which was cut deeply above the knee. His left shoulder was also gashed, though not as bad, and a few minor grazes trickled blood down his arms and legs. His hair was matted with sweat and blood.

"It is done," he assured Valdieron, glancing down at the still form of the Devil. He thrust his Rapier into the back of the creature's neck. He cast a lingering look over the still woman who was bleeding from several wounds to her chest and neck before he turned and limped from the hall.

Valdieron took a moment to take in the macabre scene. All around were the bloodied forms of the jackals, felled by both he and Llewellyn. A few lay seemingly untouched though obviously dead. Atop the dais, the dead Sable Elf lay amid its crumpled lavender cloak. Its dark weapon lay nearby, or at least half of it, shattered a foot from the tip. In death the Elf appeared less dangerous, his face almost serene and as comely as Llewellyn's, despite the dark skin.

He followed Llewellyn from the temple. He was breathing deeply and shaking slightly from shock, and his blood was racing. His wounds felt like fire, sending warm pain through his body with each limping step.

The climb from the hollow was agony for them, but they finally reached the peak and dropped to the ground to rest. Llewellyn tore a strip of cloth from his cloak to wrap his leg, slowing the bleeding which had coated most of his leg. He winced as he pulled the bandage tight, but levered himself to his feet soon after.

"The sooner we leave this place behind, the better!"

Valdieron merely nodded and painfully rose, using his sword for leverage. His thigh wound had reopened, fresh red blood running over the dried blood. When they returned to camp he would bandage the wounds, for now he just wanted to be away from the Temple as quickly as possible.

They had barely taken two steps when a long, agonizing cry broke the cold night, causing Valdieron to shudder with pure terror. Both he and Llewellyn turned as another, less voluminous cry rang out.

"The woman!"

Llewellyn grasped his arm tightly as he started back towards the Temple.

"She is dead!" The Elf's voice was without tone, and his eyes bore a steely glint, though rimmed with teary sorrow.

"What are you talking about? She is still alive. Listen!"

Llewellyn shook his head adamantly, despite the gurgling cry that echoed around them. "She was a sacrifice, Val. She has been chosen to bear the Devil's offspring. Even now, the Devil is preparing to be born. She will die with it. The Devil will tear her apart, but will also die shortly after, with the link to its homeland severed."

A hesitant note in the Elf's voice made Valdieron pause. Was he unsure of the truth of his words?

With a twist he broke free of Llewellyn's grip and limped quickly back down the slope, not bothering to see if the Elf followed.

"The best you can do for her is to end her misery, Valdieron!"

Llewellyn's words followed him as he staggered through the archway, letting the eerie light guide him. Although he knew what to expect, the sight before him stunned him momentarily and he screwed his eyes closed in sorrow.

The woman, still secured over the pillar, was strained taut against her bonds, her fingers curled and white. Her back was arched impossibly and her head was thrown back as she cried out and whimpered with convulsive pain. Her stomach glistened with sweat in the firelight, swollen and distended.

He started forward with the echoing words of Llewellyn in his mind. Her head swung up as she sensed his presence. Her face was flushed from pain, and she silently implored him for help. Her hair was matted across her cheeks and forehead, and her lower lip was cut and bleeding from where she had bitten through it in her agonized convulsions.

He knew then that he could not help her. His ignorance had forced him here, confident he could do something, but Llewellyn had been right. She was dying, and he could do nothing but stand there and helplessly watch.

A choking cry burst through clenched teeth, one of great agony, and he saw a rending gash across one side of her swollen stomach, hardly breaking her skin, but bleeding profusely. As he watched, another gash appeared, this time near her naval, a small claw tearing through and disappearing. He knew the Devil was tearing itself free, and wondered how the woman was still alive. That was probably part of the Devil's intent, not to kill quickly, but make it last: its first malign act.

Valdieron was determined to make it its last. Turning his gaze to the woman, he found her looking vacantly at him. Her face was set, and her eyes flinched with every slash of the Devil, but she was oblivious to the pain, now. That imploring, almost accusing stare struck Valdieron like a blow, and tears came unbidden to his eyes as he raised his sword.

He did not know whether or not she could still see, but her thin lips stretched into a brief smile, and her head nodded once, slowly. Watching her struggle against the Devil's attacks, Valdieron felt himself wince. Hoping he was doing the right thing, he raised his sword and set its tip against her rent stomach, both hands grasping the hilt.

As if sensing the weapon's presence, the Devil's head broke the slashed skin of the woman's stomach, its tiny eyes turning to him angrily. It was so like a human child that Valdieron felt his fortitude waver briefly, but when it hissed at him, revealing cat-like teeth, his will hardened. With a whispered apology, he drove his sword down, through the woman's stomach and into the Devil. It halted when it struck the pillar with a rasping hiss.

The woman was still almost instantly, for which Valdieron was grateful, but the Devil howled furiously, tiny, tormented screams before it too was silent. Only then did Valdieron pull his sword slowly free, his eyes closed so as not to see the growing pool of blood. He knew he should do more for her, cut her free and bury her, but the cloying atmosphere of the room pressed at him suddenly, and he reeled away towards the exit. Flashing images of the carnage assaulted him, until he was flat against the dew-cold grass, and his stomach revolted and heaved. He took it as penitence, and he was glad for it.

Llewellyn's hand upon his shoulder brought him back to the present. He looked up into the eyes of the Elf, seeing there a proud, sorrowful gleam. He tried to speak but could not, and Llewellyn shook his head for silence, knowing what had happened inside the Temple was what he had expected. Helping Valdieron rise, they began the slow trek back to the camp, each silent in their own thoughts, but knowing somehow that their thoughts were shared.

* * *

The Demon's eyes turned from black to milky white as it finished its commune with Hammagor. Its smooth, featureless face turned to the other Demons around it. The four Hunters and two Shadows watched him intently, eager for news that they could kill. During their weeks in this new plane, they had killed little, despite having passed many cities and villages. On Hammagor's instruction, they had also passed through the land of their hated Elvin enemies, quickly and without incident.

"We have new objectives."

The mental communication sent the Demons into a near frenzy, for they assumed they would kill soon.

The Soul Seeker would have smiled if it had a face. How eager these Demons were to kill, for the pleasure and the glory of Hammagor, their Master.

"You four," he indicated the Hunters, jackal-headed Demons of great speed and killing instincts, "are to remain here and await my return." The four Demons were instantly upset with the new command, but were appeased shortly after. "However, if you happen to catch anybody nearby, they must not discover your presence." The Hunters took that to mean they had a small amount of hunting area, and knew it was better than nothing.

"You two," the Soul Seeker turned to the Elf-like Shadows, vicious killers with an affinity for darkness and killing. "You are to return to the Elvin land and make sure no Elvin messengers enter or leave. It will most likely be the Elves who first learn of our presence, so it will be there that we begin our assault. Other forces will join you there."

The two shadows silently took their instructions and left, while the Hunters skulked away, leaving the Soul-Seeker to his own evil thoughts. He turned to where the city lay below him. It was a beautiful sight, perched on the shores of the great silvery lake.

With a short step he set off towards the city, shifting slightly as his form changed to that of a simple farmer he had slain several days earlier. With this guise he hoped to gain entry to the city. If all went as planned, his disguise would fool even those who had the ability to sense his true nature.

Long enough for him to tear their throats out, silencing them forever.

He grinned, for he could now, knowing that soon he would be in control of the city. The Astral City, as it was now called, held the greatest threat for the Demons, so he was to slowly destroy it from within using every possible means.

He smiled all the way to the city, confident of success.

Chapter 22

The old man straightened, glad for the rest after lugging the heavy chest through the ruins. It now stood beside several others inside a large metal vault in one of the larger buildings still standing in the city. The building used to be a Tavern, and a portion of the redwood bar was still erect to one side. Around the chests were several rows of shelves, stacked with odds and ends, but mostly with books and scrolls or wads of paper in cases.

Behind him, he heard heavy footsteps and turned as a large figure stepped through the doorway, carrying another chest by its straps. The chorded muscles in his arms indicated that he was straining. His face was free of the grime that covered the old man.

"This is the last, Ka'Varel." The large man lowered the chests gently beside the others, marveling briefly at the collection before him. Although he had only known the old man for a few decades, he was surprised at the extent of his life's work and belongings. Considering Ka'Varel's unique heritage he should not have been surprised.

"That is good, Tyr." Ka'Varel grinned almost sheepishly, for he had only carried a small portion of what was before him. "I had forgotten how much I had acquired over the years."

The Barbarian grunted sourly. "Five thousand years is a long time to hoard things."

Ka'Varel frowned ruefully, feeling every second of his age. Where once he had thought he would live eternally, he now numbered his life in years, as his mortal companion did.

Yet he would not have lived differently if he had the choice over again. As a Loremaster, he relished his responsibility as guardian of the realm of Kil'Tar, a task he held in the highest honor. His thoughts turned to his brethren, who were no longer of this realm, and would never return. Of this he was sure, feeling they were somehow lost to this era, even if they had survived the many dangers of the universe.

"Thinking of the past again, old friend?" asked Tyrun softly, his large and tender brown eyes taking in the old Loremaster.

"Aye. Wondering what might have been is one of the perils of growing old. I wonder yet where I may be now if I had not chosen to remain on Kil'Tar."

"Probably somewhere far more beautiful and peaceful," confirmed Tyr with a smirk, but Ka'Varel shook his head in denial.

"Probably dead," he whispered, though he knew the old barbarian had heard.

"Let us be gone from here. There is no more we can do before we ride out tomorrow." He ushered the barbarian from the room, taking time to swing the half-rotten door closed behind him, though there was no latch for it and it swung open several inches after he released it.

"Are you sure it's safe?" asked Tyrun skeptically. He eyed the run-down building as if it offered little protection against the very air, let alone the eyes and tools of bounty-seekers.

"It will hold. Wards will prevent any but a few from entering. Illusions will also hide it in our absence."

The barbarian merely shrugged at this, knowing the old Loremaster knew far more than he where magic was concerned.

Their own dwelling was a short walk away. A spacious single room it was, though a cloth petition divided one end from the rest, housing the kitchen and bath area. There were two bunks set against one wall, while the other was set with now empty bookshelves and tables. Several traveling bags were set near the entry: a stone archway once set with a fine doorway but now hinged with a simple iron door. Two narrow windows ran along each wall, covered with wooden shutters, and between the bunks was set a large hearth, in which embers burned low.

Tyrun tended the fire as Ka'Varel shuffled to the bags of gear, running again through his items in case he had forgotten something.

"So we are still bound first for Lloreander?"

He turned at Tyrun's question, finding the barbarian standing with hands outstretched to the fire.

"Yes. Of all races, the Elves are most hated by the Demons, and as such are in the most danger. It is they who will most likely believe us, for their histories are long stained with Demon blood."

"Will they believe us, though? From what you have said, these Demons have not been seen for over five thousand years. That is time enough for truths to become legends, even for the long-lived Elves."

Ka'Varel shrugged at Tyrun's worrying question, one he had asked himself many times before. How indeed would the races react to his claims that Demons were again loose in the realm? He hoped he would not have to back up his claims with living proof.

By then it would be too late.

"And this Chosen One, are we not to find him before the Demons do?"

Ka'Varel shook his head again. "We dare not. My presence may be enough to draw the Demons, so he would only be in more danger. We must hope his own presence remains hidden from them, as it is by me, so that he can fulfill his part in this."

"And what part is that?"

Ka'Varel frowned. "Of that I am not sure. It could mean the end of the realm as we know it, or the destruction of the Demons once and for all, as some prophecies foresee. There are too many possibilities to consider an ending yet."

Tyrun nodded grimly and returned to his thoughts, leaving Ka'Varel to his own. The ancient Loremaster knew his reason for being was close at hand. He vowed to use whatever powers he had to see that the memories of his brethren were not forgotten.

* * *

Valdieron awoke the next morning stiff and sore, feeling worse rather than better. Fitful dreams had marred his sleep. He had removed the Dragon's tear so as not to enter the Dream Plane, but wondered if he should have, if not for the more peaceful rest.

The others were already awake. Hafri tended the small fire, while Thorgast sat nearby, silent and grave. It was obvious he was angry at something. He noticed Valdieron's waking and flashed him a frown, but it passed quickly as he addressed Llewellyn.

"I just wish you had woken me." A tight smile crossed his stern face. "You had to have all the fun though, didn't you?"

Llewellyn nodded; though his equally grave face showed what had happened the previous night had been far from fun. It was obvious Thorgast was angry over not being woken by the two.

"Like I said, all I heard was some chanting from afar. As you and Hafri were wounded, I thought Val and I should investigate. Neither of us had any idea we would encounter such a scene. Next time, I'll be more than glad to wake you," assured Llewellyn with a groan as he stretched. His right thigh was bandaged, as were the other few scrapes and cuts he had received. Remembering his own wounds, Valdieron rose slowly.

"Here," warned Llewellyn, tossing him a small bundle of wrappings. "There's warm water near the fire. Wash your wounds before you wrap them, and put some of that paste on." Llewellyn referred to a small ceramic pot of salve beside the water pot, its contents a sickly green and acrid to the nose.

Using an old cloth, he dampened his wounds and wiped them free of the dried blood as well as he could, careful not to re-open them. His thigh wound was the worst, long yet shallow, but he was able to strap it tightly. The green salve was surprisingly cool against the wound, though it stung furiously. He cleaned and applied some to his other minor wounds, wondering if they could have been worse than they were.

He used the remaining water to wash his face and hair and then rose and began to work the stiffness out of his body. It was close to mid-morning, with a large bank of dark clouds moving in from the north. The sun was trying its hardest to warm them. It was probably snowing back home, and he wondered if the snow would have obliterated all trace of his home and the village.

"From what I can remember, there should be a small town not far from here," advised Llewellyn, scanning the distant Southlands. "There we should be able to have a decent night's rest and a bath."

The prospect of this drove them throughout the morning and early afternoon. Valdieron felt his aches and pains dissipate somewhat, but knew they would return twofold the next day.

The town Llewellyn had spoken of was called Sembria. It was only small, some three times larger than Shadowvale. A large fence of picketed wood surrounded it, slightly dilapidated in places but on the whole, sturdy. Two grated metal gates barred travelers from the west and southeast. Two guards manned the western gate when the four arrived with an hour or so remaining until dusk. They snapped to their feet when they spotted the weary group, grasping rusted Halberds.

"What is your business in Sembria?" asked the elder of the two, his voice neither stern nor meek.

Llewellyn stepped to the fore, flashing the two men a smile, sighing as if grateful for the stop.

"We are but simple travelers, good sir, seeking bed and rest for the night. As the weather seems to be growing foul, a roof over our heads is preferable to sleeping in a downpour. As your humble town was nearby, we decided to impose upon your hospitality if possible."

The old man, glancing long at their weapons and recent injuries, was silent for some time before motioning for his companion to let them in. The other man, who was probably his son by his similar features, frowned but moved to obey.

The four entered with thankful nods. The gate closed more silently beside them, though the latch was thrown into place with a forbidding crash.

"Are you a Bard, Sir?" asked the younger of the two guards, motioning to Llewellyn's harp case slung across his back. His eyes also took in the Elf's weapon, and his hand tightened a little on his halberd.

"I have been known to play a tune or two," replied Llewellyn modestly, flashing him a smile. "Is there an inn nearby which might appreciate some entertainment for maybe a meal and drink?"

The young man shrugged and turned to the other who replied. "Try the 'Singing Breeze', two blocks down and to your left. Old Jakob is probably your best chance." His tone told that it was not likely, but Llewellyn thanked him none-the-less before starting off.

The houses were of sturdy construction, of wood and stone, mostly single-level. Doors and windows were narrow, and most were closed and barred.

"Looks like they're set for a siege," whispered Thorgast, motioning down the street. It was deserted save for a small dog that trotted into a side street ahead.

"Set in for the night," guessed Llewellyn, pointing to the

many smoking chimneys.

The 'Singing Breeze' was a large, single level Inn of neat appearance. Its shuttered windows flanked a large set of swinging doors in the front. With a shrug, Llewellyn pushed through them, and led them into the dim interior.

The room beyond was large, with a small bar set in the center of the far wall. Round tables surrounded by high stools were set around pillars, which supported the roof. A fire burned at either end, where the few people present were gathered for the warmth, huddled and silent as if scared. All heads turned as the four entered, and most brows furrowed. Nothing was said as they settled at a vacant table near the door. A man behind the bar, bald and middle-aged with a lean, sharp figure, eyed them suspiciously, but donned an apron and skirted the bar to tend to them as they settled down.

"Too damn cold to be out," he snarled affectionately, nodding to the doorway and the chill gloaming beyond.

"Aye," agreed Llewellyn with an equally distasteful scowl. "But not too cold to drink."

"Just as well or I'd be out of business," cackled the barman, motioning to the other patrons who had returned to their silent drinking. "Business is not that good. Those guys are too bloody scared to drink, it seems."

"Trouble?" asked Llewellyn softly, averting his gaze a little, guessing what kind of trouble it was.

The barman raised his brows a little, as if studying them. "You could say that, but more from hag's tales than anything. Word is there is a beast roaming free nearby, ravaging livestock. One old farmer even said he saw it, like a huge wolf or dog. It killed a dozen of his sheep in one night."

"Scared of dogs?" asked Thorgast incredulously.

"Easy to criticize when you're a foot taller than most," barked the man affably, though his frown deepened as he shrugged. "There is more, but only stories, mind. Still, we are simple people with simple beliefs. Such things are enough to make us lie low."

Llewellyn nodded understanding, though he knew these were more than simple stories the barman was talking about. Farmers would be used to dealing with far worse than just large dogs.

Tugging at the chords of his Lute case, Llewellyn took out

the worn instrument. "I think they might just need a little cheering up, that's all."

"You any good with that?" asked the barman inquisitively.

Llewellyn shrugged with a wry smile. "I've been known to pull a crowd or two in my time. What's it worth for me to liven this place up a bit?" He glanced shrewdly at Valdieron and winked, though Valdieron merely shifted his lips in a half-smile. The banter between the two was of only passing interest to him as he battled his resurfaced inner turmoil.

"Free drinks every time one of my kegs empties." The barman turned and motioned towards four small wooden ale barrels set atop the bar. There was perhaps enough in each of them for thirty or forty mugs of ale, more than two for every customer currently present.

Llewellyn screwed his face in thought for several moments. "Throw in a room for the night if all are emptied and you've a deal."

"Agreed," smiled the barman with a nod. "What'll it be?"

"Just four ales," suggested Llewellyn, to which nobody objected. "And some warm food, if you have any."

"You'll be paying for that, until I see the benefits from your playing," reminded the barman with a sly grin. Llewellyn merely winked back, sure of his craft.

"Jakob's the name. Just holler if you need anything. I'll be back directly."

Llewellyn smacked the table victoriously as Jakob left. "That was easy, wasn't it?"

Thorgast raised an eye at him questioningly. "Yeah, easier than it will be to get these people drinking, to be sure."

"Trust me!"

Llewellyn moved to an adjacent table against the wall, moving a stool before it so that he could sit on the table with his feet on the stool. He rested his lute beside him while he began to flex his fingers.

His actions brought strange looks and whispers from the patrons. When he plucked at the strings in a high-pitched chord, heads turned and the whispering stopped momentarily before being taken up again.

His first song was a sad but bawdy one about a sailor who finds the pleasures of women and cheap wine in every port until he meets a young woman with whom he falls in love.

Unfortunately, men who are owed money by the sailor kill her. Despite the dismaying turn, the patrons in the bar warmed to the song.

Food and drinks were brought to the table during the song. Jakob was grinning like a cat in a milk pot. "He can really play."

"Aye. You'd better keep those ales coming, man," assured Thorgast, draining his first tankard in one hit and passing it back to Jakob with a grin. Jakob, far from being offended, clapped him on the shoulder before taking the tankard and returning to the bar.

Valdieron hardly touched his food and a mouthful of ale was almost enough to turn his stomach, so he pushed himself back and watched silently as Llewellyn played. Neither Hafri nor Thorgast made mention of his silence, though occasionally Thorgast cast him a brief glance.

Llewellyn had the crowd milling about him after a short time with his captivating stories and almost magical lute-playing. It was obvious he took great pleasure in his craft, and his smile was wide at each break when the crowd applauded enthusiastically. He cast them slight bows or nods of thanks after each, before breaking out into another tune.

With the noise in the room increasing with every song, and a pall of pipe-smoke growing, Valdieron began to feel the need to leave, and to bathe. His skin itched as if burning slightly, and he rubbed absently at his wounds.

When Jakob brought the next round of drinks, Valdieron asked if there was a washroom or somewhere he could clean up.

"Sure. Down the end of that corridor and on the right," advised the smiling barman. "There's warm water in the tubs."

Valdieron thanked him and rose, taking up his pack. Kaz, asleep inside his pack, stirred from his slumber and he removed him, setting him on the table, still wrapped in his fur-lined blanket. He shifted about but settled back after Valdieron dropped a few scraps of meat from his plate beside him. Thorgast nodded briefly to him as he left. It was a strange gesture, and he realized it was to inquire if he was well. He gave a weak smile in return to show that he was fine, hoping the Barbarian did not see it for the lie it was.

The washroom was large, dominated in the center by a

raised platform surrounding a large metal tub. It was half filled already, and as he dipped a hand into it, he found it warm. Three smaller metal tubs held warmer water, and he scooped several buckets from them into the bigger tub until it was more to his liking.

There was nobody else about, so he stripped off his clothes quickly and dropped them into the tub so he could give them a scrub also. He sat his pack on a wooden bench along the rear wall, but placed his sword beside the tub within easy reach before slowly lowering himself in.

With a grateful sigh he laid back, his arms looped over the side with his head thrown back, letting the warmth slowly infuse his body. His wounds smarted at the water's cleansing touch, but it passed quickly. He started to doze off, but rather than fight it, let himself be carried away.

A soft clicking and a screech of hinges brought him awake with a strangled cry of alarm before he remembered where he was. His hand whipped to the hilt of his sword and he stood in the now cold water.

A young woman stood wide-eyed in the doorway, holding a towel and a bundle of clothing to her chest with one hand, the other pressed to her mouth to suppress a cry of fright. She was small but womanly in figure, pretty in a way with strawberry colored hair loose about her face and shoulders.

"Who are you?" blurted Valdieron hotly, startled and angered by the woman's presence. "Why do you sneak up on me so?"

The woman's face flushed briefly before darkening with anger. "I did not sneak up on you. I tapped on the door twice and nobody answered, so I entered."

Valdieron realized suddenly he was standing naked before her in the tub, holding his sword and scowling. He must have looked a menacing sight, bedraggled and wounded as he was. He mumbled an apology as he sank deeper into the tub hiding his nakedness, setting his sword back in its scabbard.

The woman was silent for a moment before smiling in forgiveness. "No offence taken. Often have I fallen asleep in the tub. My name is Jelika."

"I was just getting out," offered Valdieron, feeling his body shiver at the water's chill embrace.

"Do not leave on my account," apologized Jelika, stepping in and closing the door behind her, forcing Valdieron back into the tub. It was obvious she was intent on joining him in the tub as she dropped her bundle onto a bench and began to strip her clothes off. Valdieron felt his face redden and he turned away, caught in a very compromising position.

Jelika giggled when she turned towards the tub, but said nothing as she stepped lightly onto the platform. "Argh! That's colder than my grandmother's cooking," she cursed, pulling her foot from the water quickly. Valdieron chuckled at her remark, and heard her fumbling with the water bucket before scooping several loads of warm water into the tub. She hurled the bucket into the corner when she was finished, eager to be in the warm water.

"That's better," she breathed as she settled in behind Valdieron. Her foot brushed his leg briefly as she did and he flinched, causing her to laugh again. "You can turn around now."

He did so reluctantly, keeping his eyes on her face as he settled back against the tub's wall, knowing the water was clear enough so her body would not be completely hidden if he looked. He flushed when he noticed her admiring his body shamelessly. Rather than let her see, however, he rested his head back against the tub, staring at the ceiling with eyes half closed.

"Where you from?" she asked abruptly, causing him to glance quickly at her.

"Far away," he whispered with a sigh, realizing for the first time how far and how long he had traveled from his home. He wondered briefly how much further he would travel.

"Never been there," quipped Jelika sarcastically. "Where is it?"

"Tyr," relented Valdieron, knowing the name of his village would mean nothing to her.

"The northwest?" Her curious tone made him glance at her again. He found her staring at him in surprise. "Did you pass by the town of Aspen, a day's ride from here?"

Valdieron shook his head, and she breathed easier. "No. This is the first town we've seen since leaving the Merchant's Highway."

"Lucky you are, then."

"Valdieron," he offered, realizing he hadn't given her his

name, and she smiled in thanks. "This Aspen, is there trouble there or something?"

Jelika frowned suddenly, glancing about as if to check they were not being overheard. "Indeed there is. Strange goings on, it is rumored, and none of it good. The Devil resides there, it is said, though by whom I don't know. None have returned from there in some months."

Valdieron squeezed his eyes shut at the mention of the Devil, wondering if his reaction was what Jelika had been expecting, and when he opened his eyes, he found her regarding him questioningly.

"We must have passed close," he acceded. "We saw a dark temple there a ways back. It looked forbidding, with strange lights beyond its walls."

Jelika gasped, looking upon him with a mixture of fear and awe, her honey-brown eyes gleaming. "You went past the temple!"

That she knew of the Temple surprised him. "You know of the Temple?"

She drew back suddenly, eyes closing momentarily as if silently berating herself. "Aye," she conceded. "Though only I and a few others do. We heard tell of it one night, so we went to investigate. We know what goes on there, but we fear to tell the Council or our parents, in case we end up like Aspen or worse."

"To visit there was dangerous," warned Valdieron, visions of another young woman, bloodied and broken, flashing through his mind. "The Temple will pose a threat no longer, however."

Jelika pursed her lips briefly, wondering at his words, but gawked as the revelation struck her. "You can't be serious!"

He nodded with a sigh, resting back again against the tub.

"You must tell me!" stated Jelika with awe, leaning forward again.

He could have told her something to appease her, but she would probably visit the Temple herself to make sure of his tale. Sighing pensively, he nodded but stood. "More water, first." He flushed when he remembered he was naked, but glanced away from her as he stepped from the tub. His cheeks burned as he felt her eyes on him, but could not deny the strange pleasure he was feeling.

With the warm water creating a pall of steam in the room, for which he was silently thankful, he sank back into the water across from Jelika, wincing as he put his weight on his right leg. The water had washed the wound of any remaining blood, and was raw to the touch. He knew this was due to Llewellyn's healing unguent, and reminded himself to ask the Elf how to mix the ointment in case of future emergencies.

Jelika prompted him into speech quickly, and he smiled thinly at her enthusiasm. He took his time to put his reeling thoughts into words. As he spoke, his telling was broken with pauses where he wrestled with half-remembered actions, but knew his retelling was more or less how it had happened.

Jelika's face captured the gamut of emotions as he spoke, from awe to fear as he told of the jackals, then to anger and horror as he told of the young female captive and the Devil conjured by the Sable Elf. She was even teary-eyed when he recounted the pain and agony of the strange birth. She clapped her hand over her mouth as he told her how he had driven his sword through her and the Devil-child, ending both of their lives. She recovered, however, when she realized the struggle behind his choked words.

"You did right. She would only have died a far more painful death, if you had left."

Her words were not lost on Valdieron, but still he shrugged, wondering if his action had been warranted.

"You did more than anyone could ask for. Beating the Devil and killing the Dark elf will surely end the threat the temple posed. For that you have the unspoken gratitude of many hundreds of people, and who knows how many other women will be spared a similar fate." She drifted over to his side, catching him by the shoulder and wiping back wet strands of hair from his face. He flinched at her contact, so warm and focused, but smiled gratefully at her. He could not deny her words, but still there was the lingering doubt in his mind.

Her fingers, slender and soft, traced the wounds on his shoulder. He stared down into her eyes with a joyful sadness and found her staring up at him unblinkingly. Her face was so close to his, it seemed, and he could feel her warm breath on his skin. It would be so easy to lean forward and kiss her.

He found the opportunity passed, however, as she drew back suddenly with a shake of her head.

"Wait here. I'll be back shortly to dress those wounds for you." She rose and stepped out of the tub, and he forgot himself momentarily, turning away after a glimpse of her browned body, supple and gleaming.

She dried herself and dropped her towel beside his gear and draped a pale green robe around herself, securing it with a slender chord.

"Wipe yourself down with my towel while I'm gone," she ordered, before disappearing out the door. He heard her soft footsteps receding down the hall and rose, drying himself quickly and wrapping the towel around his waist. She returned carrying a handful of bandages and set to work, neither speaking nor questioning him further. He remained quiet throughout, save for a sharp intake of breath when she wrapped his thigh.

"There!" she said, standing after she had finished. His thigh and shoulder were wrapped. She turned to leave, but he caught her softly by the upper arm, turning her with a soft gasp of surprise.

"Thank you."

She smiled warmly before pulling from his soft grasp.

"I'll see you around." She gathered her gear quickly and left, leaving Valdieron wondering silently, his mind clearer and his shoulders no longer bowed with strain. With a sigh he gathered his own gear together, dressing in his spare clothes and fishing his others from the water. He found them slightly cleaner, and set them on a bench to dry. Belting on his sword, he made his way back to the common room. The sounds of Llewellyn's singing and playing greeting him as he entered, and his spirits lifted as he sat. He picked up his refilled mug of Ale with a smile at Thorgast and turned to listen to Llewellyn play.

Chapter 23

Nortas walked the deserted corridors of the Blade Academy, his long strides echoing softly off the marble walls. His face was stern, lined with worry from endless days and nights trying to organize the Council and set into motion the deployment of men to the eight Portals. He was tired and angry, so his impromptu meeting with Valkyra concerned him. What did she want that could not wait for their next meeting in two days?

The Horse-Maiden of the Fire Stallion Clan had her quarters on the upper level of the four-story structure, a level designed to house the Masters and officials. Her room in the northeast corner overlooked the lake, and by chance it was the farthest part of the complex from where he had been when the message had arrived.

He rapped on the brass-lined door then tapped again, softer. Several moments of silence passed and he shifted anxiously. Muffled footsteps came from within. A soft clicking of the lock preceded the door swinging silently open, revealing Valkyra.

The morning light through her room outlined her figure with remarkable clarity and Nortas gasped softly, for she was clad in only a silken nightgown. Her crimson hair looked like fire around her sleepy face, as if she had just awoken.

"Nortas. Come in." With a sweeping movement, which accentuated her figure beneath the scanty outfit, she swung the door open and allowed him to step inside. Pursing his lips in stunned confusion, Nortas stepped into the room.

Valkyra pressed the door closed and then threw herself into his arms, clasping him passionately and kissing him. He took only a moment to respond to the surprised move. She was pushing him towards the bedchamber, urging him with her enthusiasm, but he pulled away from her briefly, more than a little stunned by her actions.

"Valkyra, what are you doing? I have important business to attend to."

She traced a fingernail across his cheek and lips, staring into his eyes with a passionate gleam. "Business that cannot wait?"

she purred, loosening her robe to let it fall away from her supple body.

Nortas stammered as he sought to reply, but could not fight her power of persuasion and found himself catching her up and carrying her into the bedchamber.

* * *

Nortas sat with his hands clutched against his forehead on the side of the soft bed. He knew he should be up and back to work, but he relished the time to think and rest. Valkyra stirred behind him and her soft hand caressed his shoulder.

"Tired?"

"No. Just thinking," he lied, rubbing at his blood-shot eyes. He had not slept more than a few hours straight in many nights and he was feeling the consequences of it. He silently cursed his advancing years. Although not yet forty, a decade ago he could have resisted sleep five days straight and fought for half that time without fatigue. Now, he felt the strain in his bones each morning.

"About the war?"

He shook his head briefly, though he had been in part. "The chosen one. By all accounts we are approaching the time when he will return to aid us." He had told Valkyra of his people's beliefs and prophecies, of the Chosen One who would return to lead them against their ancient enemy. His people lived in hope that one day they would be chosen to fight alongside this reincarnation of their forefathers.

"Then where is he?" asked Valkyra lightly.

"I don't know," was his only reply.

She sighed behind him and he knew her well enough to know she was about to speak.

"I have been thinking. The Trial of Combat is about to start in Thorhus. Shouldn't we have a participant?"

Nortas snorted derisively. "We have no time for games, Valkyra. Our men are needed elsewhere. Our numbers are already so low that we need all the people we've got. Besides, when the King of Thorhus learns of this possible threat, it is likely he will cancel the Trials."

"Maybe not," returned Valkyra challengingly. "This threat is not yet verified though our men surround Mount Drac, waiting for news. King Kelvor will continue with the Trials unless first-hand proof is given to him. He has too much to lose by canceling them."

Nortas nodded slowly. It was true that the Demon threat was as yet unverified. The disappearance of first the Squad of men and then the search party was no coincidence, however. He thought the worst, but an Essence Storm could have destroyed both groups as readily as Demons. Indeed, the uncontrollable Essence Storms were powerful enough to loose lightning capable of flattening mountains or rain enough to flood lowlands in minutes. Even more dangerous was the Essence shifts, which made using magic unpredictable and unstable. The simplest of spells could be distorted to cause cataclysmic consequences. If the storm had hit Mount Drac, it could have destroyed the first squad without word, and if Saratholeus had teleported them into the midst of the storm, it may have simply obliterated them within moments.

Yet a feeling deep within told him otherwise.

"All right. I'll test the students myself and see who will represent us."

"Why not you?"

Nortas began to laugh but realized she was serious. "Me! I've other things to be worried about than stupid games."

"But shouldn't we send someone who represents us and our cause? Besides, none in the city can better you with the sword or axe, despite your complaints. It would do you the world of good to be free from all this strain for a time."

Nortas began to argue that another should go, but was quiet. It was true that the very thought of entering the games made his blood race, but his commitment to the realm and the people of the City was enough to give him pause.

"I will give it some thought," he relented. "There is still much time before the Trials, and if all goes as I think it will, I will have other worries by then."

Valkyra ran a hand through his tangled hair. "Yes, think on it, my love. We can gain much by your participation."

Nortas rose finally, pulling his clothes on quickly. "I must go now. I will see you later?"

Valkyra nodded and he leaned forward to kiss her on the forehead before wheeling and leaving the chambers.

After his departure, Valkyra lay on the bed, smiling slightly and staring up at the ceiling. After a long time, her features began to warp, like a reflection in a still pond suddenly struck by a pebble.

The Soul Seeker chuckled maniacally. In this guise, he had already set the wheels of destruction into motion. With luck, Nortas, the powerful Dak'marian would be slain in the Trials, maybe under treasonous conditions, fouling the academy's reputation. He would have to devise a plan, maybe even the possession of the warrior, but that would be some time away. For the moment, he needed to concentrate on disrupting the plans Nortas was setting in place.

With the proud Horse-Maiden's knowledge, however, the soul seeker could goad the proud Dak'marian into entering the games. Then, with one of the Masters out of the way, he could turn to destroying the others by whatever means possible. Then Hammagor would have free reign in the lands without the threat of the Loremasters, and the Demon hosts would conquer all who stood to oppose them.

* * *

The further South-east into Ariakus the four traveled, the more populated it became. They followed dirt tracks and rugged paths along the boundaries of farmlands and riverbanks so as not to trespass, though many farmers allowed them passage with scarcely a sideward glance. In general, the people were tall and light of hair color, with skin a lighter shade than Valdieron and Hafri's.

"Are they all like that?" asked Valdieron skeptically, indicating the mounted farmer they had just passed heading northwards in search of a missing cow. He had allowed them free passage in his lands, and had even offered them lodging if necessary for the evening. As it was only early afternoon, Llewellyn had declined apologetically.

"Not all, but mostly, at least out here," responded Llewellyn, throwing his arms wide to take in the rolling farmlands before them. "In all the realms, the people of Ariakus are probably the most courteous. They are hardy and practical, with a stubborn core. They are skilled in all endeavors, especially farming and commerce."

Valdieron shook his head doubtfully. "I keep expecting one

to kick us off his land or set his dogs on us."

As chance would have it, that happened not far down the road. Nearing dusk the next day a haughty man of middle age galloped up to them, demanding their business on his property. When Llewellyn tried to explain to him that they were just passing through, he spat on the ground and told them to turn back and find another path. With a mocking bow Llewellyn apologized and they retraced their steps to the man's border before following it around, under his watchful eye until it became too dark and he disappeared.

"At least he didn't have dogs," whispered Valdieron, as he sank into his hammock later, to which Llewellyn chuckled briefly. With a grin, Valdieron rolled over to sleep.

There were horses aplenty, and with a little searching they could have bought a couple, but they knew at their present pace they would make Thorhus with many days to spare before the Trial.

Kaz found the transition to farmland harder than most. The now tame Moorcat saw the many animals around it as food or threats, and many times Valdieron had to physically hold the cat back from chasing down a sheep or goat. That was not the easiest of tasks, as Kaz had grown at a rapid rate. He responded only sometimes to Valdieron's commanding shouts or whistles when he was about to do something wrong.

They rejoined the Merchants Highway some sixty leagues to the northwest of Thorhus, where Llewellyn explained that it ran from Kethym to the north. It was wider here but perhaps less worn than it had been near Ranil, but its traffic was no less frequent. There were many single travelers and those with small wagons. Valdieron realized they were mostly either contestants or spectators in the upcoming Trials.

Troops were also not uncommon along the road, obviously trying to keep the roads free of trouble. Their presence alone may have accomplished this. They were clad in ocean-blue tabards over bright chain hauberks and armed with heralded lances and swords.

"Light cavalry, the King's own guard," explained Llewellyn as Valdieron stood in awe of a group of four such horsemen.

As the days passed the weather turned rainy, a cold, sleety downfall, like a droning lament that mourned the passing of winter. For the four, it meant slow travel, with moods shifting to less than humorous.

Whenever a roadside tavern came along, they happily stopped there, if not for the night at least for a chance to dry and have a warm meal. The food and drink was markedly better than in the northlands. Llewellyn had little trouble finding places that would allow him to trade several hours of barding for food and lodging, such was the whispered reputation preceding him. Many of the bartenders knew him by name and asked where he had been for the last few years.

Thirty leagues to the West of Thorhus, the Merchants highway turned east towards Thorhus and west toward Brek, a large trade-city in the Western Arkanth Ranges.

"We should reach Thorhus in a little over a week," said Llewellyn, which surprised Valdieron. They had made good speed in the five weeks since leaving Sembria; some hundred leagues back to the north.

With their spirits buoyed by their better than anticipated pace, they forced themselves to greater speed with the lure of the city before them. More and more people were on the roads as they grew nearer to Thorhus. Most were waiting for the games but were too poor for city accommodation, so they rented small patches of land along the way for camps. It proved a boon for the local landowners, who made themselves a goodly amount of money in the several weeks leading up to the Trials.

On one occasion a young thief crept into their camp after money or loot, but Llewellyn, ever vigilant, sent one of his arrows thudding into the ground at his feet, causing him to flee in panic. Wakened by the singing of the arrow's flight and the thief's sudden curses, Valdieron saw it was a young boy.

"Vagrant," said Llewellyn with a little pity in his voice as he retrieved his arrow and inspected it for damage.

"From the city?" asked Valdieron, though by the kid's look, he was probably a farmhand nearby. The city was a little too far away for the boy to be out by himself.

"No. The city thieves are a more organized lot. No doubt we will have our trouble with them when we get there."

"What sort of trouble?" asked Valdieron. "You make it sound as if these thieves run the city."

"They probably do to a certain extent," returned Llewellyn with a chuckle, and when Valdieron frowned he crouched beside him, leaning on his bow. "The Thieves of Thorhus are like a whole community unto themselves. Their organization is run well from within, and they have more control over the city's workings than many believe. It is best to get on their good side if you can, else they make your stay in Thorhus uncomfortable, to say the least."

"Why doesn't the King do something about this?" asked Valdieron. "Surely he knows about it, and may even know who is behind it."

"Of that I have no doubt, but if you think about it, it is in his own best interest for the Thieves Guild to prosper and remain. Organized crime is a lot more efficient and effective than unorganized crimes, which lead to more deaths and injuries. As long as the Thieves remember their place and follow the rules, the King accepts them for the job they do for him."

Valdieron shook his head in wonder. "You mentioned that the King might know who runs the Thieves Guild?"

Llewellyn nodded. "It is rumored to be a man of the King's own choosing, maybe even a former minister of his who knows the city well. They are too well organized, however, for any but one or two to know whom the leader is. I have had a few run-ins with the Guild in the past."

Valdieron felt ill at ease with this unfamiliar territory but trusted Llewellyn knew what he was doing. With a shrug he rolled up in his blankets and tried to go back to sleep.

Kaz proved a continual source of silent amusement for Valdieron over the closing stretch of their journey. At first, the cat had been frightened by strangers, especially those on horseback, and would run from them and cower, usually behind Valdieron. As he grew and became more accustomed to them, he became more playful, and would dance around the occasional horse or traveler, growling low and menacingly from a distance until they passed. It reminded Valdieron so much of Ruff, who herded the sheep back on their farm much the same way. The likeness brought a smile to his face, despite the sad memory. Most times, the traveler or rider would react with a mixture of surprise and alarm, looking to Valdieron or one of the others to see if the cat was serious in its antics. Valdieron realized that Kaz was imposing in a way, being already as large as a dog. He need only whistle sharply to Kaz, however, and most times, though somewhat reluctantly, the cat would cease its playing and return to his side.

Valdieron knew he would remember his first view of Thorhus for the rest of his days. The road that brought them inexorably to the city topped a sparsely wooded rise a league away. When they cleared the woods, he drew up in amazement at the sight of the third largest city in the northlands.

Its dark stone walls rose thirty feet into the clouded sky, seeming higher atop the low mesa of land, like a insuperable barricade capable of stopping wind, rain and anything nature and man could throw against it. Its battlements were crenulated all around, with wide pilasters spread evenly along its length. Two small barbicans were set above the gatehouses, their projecting walls held by bastions as with the other towers. On top of each fluttered a huge flag of pale gold inlaid with the insignia of the King: a blooming rose standing amid a gleaming diadem inset with a diamond, ruby and emerald in a triangular pattern.

"It's beautiful," breathed Valdieron, awed by the enormous structure. He had never imagined that something as large as this existed.

"Aye," breathed Thorgast, equally impressed with the city, having only his own city of Chul'Haka to compare it to. Hafri and Llewellyn were seemingly unimpressed by the sight, having been here on numerous occasions, but still Valdieron noticed Hafri regarding the city with delight.

"One of the wonders of the world," assured Llewellyn with a grin, but turned to regard the darkening sky around them. "And one which we should be inside before this night descends upon us. There is rain on this cold wind, and I for one do not intend to sleep under it with the protection of the city walls in sight, mocking me."

The others nodded, and with a whooping cry Llewellyn raced down the road. Any who saw him must have thought him mad, but the others quickly followed him. A few whom they passed watched them with caution and suspicion.

A wide, deep moat surrounded the immense mesa, some thirty feet across and lined with stone. Above them, like a behemoth, the walls rose on the acclivity, dark and forbidding in the failing light. Two tall pillars rose on the other side of the moat, flanking the road, to which thick chains descended to the metal-lined drawbridge that spanned the dark waters below.

There were no visible levers or pulleys in the pillars, the chains disappearing into narrow cuts in the gray stone.

"The drawbridge is raised from the gatehouse yonder," advised Llewellyn, motioning to the gates some fifty feet away up the slope. "The chains run from here to there underground, so it can be drawn and lowered without putting anybody in danger. Anybody approaching the city is easily seen from up there, so it can be lowered whenever necessary without leaving the gatehouse."

Valdieron marveled at such a simple yet ingenious device and wondered how many other wonders he would find in this city.

They crossed the lowered drawbridge carefully. Although it was a good thirty feet wide, the drop to the dark waters below was a good distance. There was no sign of handholds to crawl from the moat up the smooth stone walls, ten feet above.

The road leading up to the gates was cobbled with the smooth macadamized surface looking recently patched. As the ground leveled, they came under the gloom of the barbicans. Huge double doors, bound with iron and doubly secured with braces, were swung inwards, flanking the road through the gatehouses. A raised portcullis whose pointed spars looked like gigantic spear-tips in the fading light, was set to drop preceding the massive doors.

A second set of gates was set at the far end of the second walkway, with another portcullis set at the fore.

"A brilliant design," complimented Llewellyn, indicating the entirety of the entry. "These doors themselves," he nodded at the first set of doors, "would take some time to break open. The second set of doors, though less resilient, are no doubt braced from beyond, and the portcullis can be dropped at any time, locking men between it and the doors." He pointed overhead as they passed under the second walkway, some twenty feet across. There was the vague outline of casements set in the stoned underside. "They can be opened, and archers can fire upon those trapped below, or boiling pitch can be dropped through those grates." Narrow grates were set every few faces across between Portals, covered from above. Valdieron even noticed the narrow slits for archers in the guardhouse walls on either side, on three levels, where arrows could rain down without mercy. He felt suddenly vulnerable there, wondering how many guards were watching them even now with bows or crossbows drawn. He could make out only a few on each battlement, carrying halberds and wearing light armor with tabards bearing the King's emblem.

The dark road ran beyond the gates, flanked by patchy grass for a distance before houses began to spring up. The buildings were large wooden structures with shingled rooftops, often two or three stories high. They appeared well tended and were some distance apart, with grounds marked off with wooden fences.

"The middle-class suburb," declared Llewellyn, spreading his arms to take in the warm surroundings. Fire-lit interiors could be seen through dark curtains and shutters. "This part of the city is predominantly so, though the castle lies yonder." He nodded ahead but the afternoon gloaming had turned too dark for them to make too much out. The castle was indiscernible, even to Valdieron, though he thought he could see a hint of high walls above the rooftops. "The upper-class people live in the north, while to the south lay the slums of the lower class along with the industrial area and markets."

The main street ran off towards the castle to the west, but at a crossroads not far ahead they turned southwards, navigating by the light of occasional street lamps and house lights. Valdieron could see quite well and knew Llewellyn could also. He did not know where Llewellyn was leading them, but they traveled some distance through the city before he slowed. The streets were far from empty even at this late hour.

Taverns and eateries were very popular along the main road. Laughter, song and shouting were predominant with each, and occasionally the breaking of a tankard or the barking of a nearby dog.

Another sound, incessant like the wind's moaning could be heard. Valdieron started as they crossed a metallic grate across the road, under which flowed a torrent of dark water many body lengths below.

"The River Orin," spoke Llewellyn suddenly, startling Valdieron. He wondered if there was anything about the city the Elf did not know. "It is the river which fills the moat, and cuts the city almost in half. A constant source of water and a natural defense."

They came at last to an Inn, on the border between the

markets and the slums. The outside of the Inn was pleasant and clean, made of smooth stone set with dried mortar, with a second level of dark wood. The roof was constructed of split bamboo strung together and overlapping, so the water drained from it in easy rivulets. The windows were bracketed with narrow wood and shuttered with adjustable louvers, and several chimneys could be seen above. A wooden rail surrounded a narrow veranda, where three entries were evenly spaced in the front wall. A picket for horses was set up out front. In large writing on the center door were the words 'Hangman's Noose', with a symbol of a noose above them.

Llewellyn did not tarry out front and strode up the single step onto the wooden porch. He hung his bow over his shoulder and unslung his lute case, as if expecting to walk straight in and play. The others grinned and followed him as he pushed open the heavy door with a loud creak. A torrent of noise washed over them.

The interior of the Inn reminded him a lot of the 'Singing Breeze' in Sembria. Long and narrow, it had a bar set against the far wall, with kitchen and storage areas beyond. Wide pillars of square stone were set in a pattern through the room. There were high tables of dark wood on metal frames with thrice as many stools, all occupied. The room nearly overflowed with people. Barmaids scurried about with trays of ale, expertly dodging well-placed grabs at their behinds from the more bold or intoxicated patrons.

Shouldering his way through the press, Llewellyn sided up to the bar, scanning it shortly. He shifted a little way to where a tall, slender barman worked furiously trying to keep up with the onslaught of orders.

"Four Ales, and make it snappy," cried Llewellyn sharply at the man.

"Get in line, Mister, like-" he halted and his head snapped up from where he had been pouring a tankard of ale. He stared wide-eyed at Llewellyn and cursed as the tankard overflowed in his hand. He slapped it onto the bar before him and accepted coins passed to him without so much as glancing at them. He vaulted over the bar to stand before Llewellyn. Valdieron tensed suddenly, suspecting trouble, but the barman grabbed the Elf in a quick embrace, one hinting at long friendship, and he came away with watery eyes.

"Llewellyn, you old scoundrel. So, you haven't gone to that big music hall in the sky, huh. Where the hell have you been for the last six years?"

Llewellyn sighed, as if what he had to say was too burdensome and long for simple explanation. "Where haven't I been, you mean?" he countered, and the barman roared with laughter.

"Damn good to see ya," he said with a slap on the shoulder. "Welcome home!"

Chapter 24

"Home?" mouthed Thorgast and Valdieron simultaneously, while Hafri tried to hide a smile.

Llewellyn spoke briefly with the barman before leading them thru the kitchen area into a large dining room, furnished with ornate chairs and tables and lined with smooth darkwood walls inset with bookcases filled with leather-bound volumes and scroll cases of bone and leather. A huge chandelier hung above the table, gleaming from a thousand crystal teardrops lit by the single internal lantern. Ornate silver sconces were set beside the entry and the single door at the rear of the room, all set with freshly lit torches, their smoke rising and dissipating through slender grills in the roof.

"Of a sort," shrugged Llewellyn, dropping his heavy travel gear beside the table and opening the rear door. A small corridor ran away from it, a single doorway set in either wall and at the far end. "An Elf has to have somewhere to call home, and Thorhus is where I spent most of my time over the last few decades, so I decided to buy this Inn. Besides, the money is good and I can at least say I own something when its time for me to pass on."

"You could have told us, you old rogue," cursed Thorgast with a haughty laugh, relieving himself of his own gear, as did the others. Servants entered to gather them up. One young boy tentatively reached for Kaz' collar, which Valdieron had kept a tight rein on up until now.

"What of Kaz?" asked Valdieron.

"He will be fed and kept in your room," advised Llewellyn, "though I hope he doesn't get out. He would cause quite a stir."

"He wouldn't harm anybody," assured Valdieron, as much for the young servant's good than Llewellyn's.

"No, but he would be a sight, especially for ale-affected eyes." Valdieron had a brief thought of Kaz frightening a drunk from his chair, and could not help smiling.

"I'll keep an eye on him, though I think he would rather sleep and eat lately."

"Come!" urged Llewellyn, stepping through the doorway at

the rear of the room, and beckoned them to follow. "I have instructed Gerkar to bring us supper, but we shall bathe first."

Llewellyn paused at the first doorway along the corridor beyond and pushed it open on silent hinges. The quiet, rhythmic gurgle of running water told Valdieron it was the bathhouse. He gasped in wonder as the steam-filled room came into focus.

A huge tub was set in the center of the room, square shaped and large enough to hold a dozen people or more. It was set in the floor so that it could be entered easily, and a wooden deck ran around it for safety of footing. In the far wall, an angled metal chute ran from mid-wall, opened at the top. Valdieron could see water rapidly cascading from it, striking the bath with small waves. A wide bench ran around the walls, and wardrobes were set in each wall for storage.

Llewellyn quickly undressed and stepped into the tub, and the others followed suit. Valdieron could tell by the steamy air that the water would be warm, but he was unsure as to how it was made so. He asked Llewellyn.

"The water exits through those pipes," he nodded to three small holes in the end of the tub. "The water is siphoned back through the pipes, which are heated as they pass through ovens, and dropped back into the tub through the chute. It is a marvelous invention, one which a passing Dwarf showed me in exchange for several nights accommodation." He sighed as he sank deeper into the warm depths. "I wonder who had the better of the deal."

This brought a laugh from the others. Valdieron was stunned at the mention of Dwarves, but conceded that if Elves and Trolls were real, why not yet another of his childhood myths.

Conversation lapsed into trivial chat as they soaked. Valdieron noticed Llewellyn staring at the Dragon's tear hanging around his neck. Valdieron had not told him about the pendant or its magical powers, and he wondered if the Elf had some knowledge of the item. He said nothing of it, however, and the others seemed not to notice.

After bathing, they changed into dry clothing that the servants had brought in, carefully folded and smelling of sweet fragrance. Valdieron tried on a loose pair of dark blue trousers and a white shirt embroidered with running horses along the sleeves and cuffs. He was also brought new boots of soft leather, folded below the knee where his trousers were tucked. He felt a little foolish in the finery, but he was refreshed and happy.

When they were all dressed, Llewellyn led them back into the dining hall, not surprised to find the huge table topped with steaming platters of food. Llewellyn bade them be seated and took the chair nearest the corridor facing the entry. Valdieron sat on his left, Thorgast on his right and Hafri at the far end. Plates of silver were set along with matching cutlery and wine goblets filled with a dark liquid.

"A toast," declared Llewellyn, raising up his goblet and catching each in turn with his eyes. "To a safe trip with friends, and to our future." He closed his eyes and drank deeply.

Valdieron tingled with the sudden solemnity of the toast. He gulped down the chilled wine, finding it bitter but not unpleasant.

"Don't let it get cold," advised Llewellyn, referring to the banquet before them. He started piling generous portions onto his plate.

For Valdieron, the meal was an experience in itself. Never before had he seen so much food in so many varieties. The midsummer festival back home had been a time for feasting and revelry, but the food was mostly local fare. Here, he had several different types of meat from beef, chicken, venison and fish, along with vegetables he could not begin to name. There were sauces and herbs to garnish every mouthful. He ate and ate until he could not stomach another mouthful. The others copied him, and none seemed sorry for it.

With the meal over, servants re-entered and cleared away the table, refilling the wine goblets before they left. Llewellyn skidded his seat back and lifted his feet onto the edge of the table with a contented sigh. Valdieron was of a mind to copy him, but was mindful of the polished table and stood instead, striding to the nearest bookshelf.

"You can read?" asked Llewellyn as he saw Valdieron scanning each book, mouthing the titles as he passed. Valdieron almost jumped at the sudden question, and felt suddenly foolish.

"A little," he lied, for he had probably read more books back home than all of the other villagers combined excluding old

Bart Letterman. A pang of sorrow struck him as he thought of the old scholar who had deserved better than the fate he received at the hands of the Trolls. "My village had a small library. It had a number of books, probably as many as you have here."

"A treasure indeed," nodded Llewellyn sincerely. "I have a great collection here, and it has taken me many years to amass it."

Val spotted a few titles he had read back home, along with others Bart had told him of which he had always desired to read.

"Have you read them all?" he asked with interest.

"Alas, not all of them," sighed Llewellyn ruefully. "I intend to, however, probably when I am too old to travel, and I can sit in here with a pipe and a fire and read to my heart's content."

The regret in Llewellyn's voice made Valdieron pause. He wondered once again at the Elf's age, and if the time he spoke of was not soon coming. He seemed tired which was most uncharacteristic of the normally energetic Elf. He suspected that his encounter with the Sable Elf had changed something in him.

"They are yours to peruse at will," continued Llewellyn with a wave, taking in the whole room. "I think, however, that there may be other things on your mind." He rose and stretched, carrying his half empty goblet. "Come, I have something else to show you."

He led them back down the corridor, past the bathroom and a few other doors until they reached a heavy ironbound door at the end. Llewellyn unlocked it with a large key on a chain from around his neck. Valdieron had not noticed it before and wondered where he had picked it up. Perhaps it had been brought with his clothing earlier.

With a soft push, Llewellyn let the door slide open, casting a long shadow into the dark room with the silhouette of his slender body.

"Wait here." He disappeared inside the dark room for a moment. A pale light sprang up, and he reappeared holding a hooded lantern. He ushered them into the room and pushed the door closed with a soft click.

Valdieron's breath caught as he took in the great room. Growing firelight illuminated the room in a soft candescence, almost mystical with its dull flickering. Thirty foot across and twice again in length, a dark lattice of wooden beams cast a web across the ceiling. The walls and floor were of polished timber, an oak by its grain, with the floor a darker shade. Wooden buttresses, semi-circular and perfect in their symmetry, ran from floor to ceiling at intervals along each wall. In each, at chest height was a marble sconce in the shape of an eagle's head. Tiny flames glowed thru parted beaks, while faceted ruby eyes glowed from the fire behind.

The room had no furnishings save a small sitting area against the left wall, almost like a shrine. A fine tapestry covered the whole wall, flanked by glowing eagles' heads. The scene on the tapestry was sylvan perfection, towering trees of hemlock, araucaria, birch, alder and abele. Each was woven with great detail, showing the fine tracery of branches beneath an ocean of leaves.

On the opposite wall hung a collection of weapons, perfect in their detail and craft, and gleaming in the building light. Each was of simple design, yet showed immaculate workmanship and craft.

"Welcome to my training hall," boomed Llewellyn, his voice clear in the spacious room, with no reverberation from the smooth walls.

"It is a sight to behold," breathed Thorgast, awe evident on the big man's face. Even Hafri viewed the room with a gaping mouth, approval written on his face. For Valdieron, however, it felt as if the room had a spirit of its own, and he felt truly at ease within it.

"Use it at will," offered Llewellyn, striding to the wall where the weapons were hung, gleaming in the light. Valdieron was painfully reminded of his own sword on the night of the Temple fight, something he had not thought about since witnessing the strange magic of the sword. As if his mere thought was a call for it, it seemed to warm and hum against his back.

"You have bathed and eaten. Rooms have been prepared for you and you may come and go as you please. I have important business to attend to, so I must be away for the evening. If you wish for anything, one of the servants can get you what you want. My home is your home. I will see you tomorrow. Good night!"

So saying, Llewellyn spun and was gone before anybody could speak. With a baffled shrug, Thorgast took one last look at the hall and turned to exit. "Wine is all well and good," he mused with a lift of the empty tankard in his large hand, "but there is nothing like a cold ale to warm the blood. Who is with me?" Hafri nodded quickly, starting towards the doorway even before Thorgast had finished the question, but Valdieron declined.

"Maybe a little later. I will check on Kaz first." Thorgast nodded and followed Hafri from the room. He did not know why he felt so at peace here, but surprisingly he felt no tiredness in his body, even after so long on the road.

After a time lost in thought, he crept to the door and stepped outside, pulling it softly closed behind him. He wondered at the lights, whether they would burn out after a time or whether a servant would come later to extinguish them. If he had been able to see beyond the doorway, he would have found the fires already extinguished.

Gerkar was still behind the bar when Valdieron re-entered the taproom, and the old barman smiled warmly at him. Valdieron asked him about his room and was told it was number eight, first on the right up the stairs. Valdieron thanked him and climbed up to his room.

Kaz almost bowled him over as he stepped into the lantern-lit room. He dropped into a crouch to wrestle briefly with the cat. Kaz warmed to the play, dancing around him and growling deeply, pouncing suddenly and planting large paws on Valdieron's shoulders and licking at his face. With a laugh, Valdieron rolled back and the cat fell on him, still trying to lick his face and neck, until he rolled free.

"Did they feed you well?" he asked rhetorically. He knew the cat could not answer but wondered if he somehow knew what was being asked of him as he sat licking his paws. There was a large bowl in one corner, which smelled of meat while another beside it had been tipped over, and bore the residue of milk contents.

He found his pack emptied and his belongings laid carefully out in a small chest at the foot of a large bed. There was a small pile of gray bedclothes at the foot of the bed, and a washbowl and washcloth on a small table off to the side. It was a wonder Kaz had not been up there drinking it. His other clothes were packed into a small wardrobe beside the door, neatly folded among small pouches of scented herbs.

"Here, let's take you outside for a bit, and then it's off to bed for the both of us. It's been a busy and exciting day." Kaz rubbed past him as he pulled the door open and danced around him as he led the cat downstairs. Rather than go through the taproom, he made his way through the kitchens and out the back door. The door was latched but not locked and he let himself out, placing a piece of wood against it to keep it ajar.

The city seemed peaceful at this time of night, shining like the moon with its many lights under the dark blanket of night. He turned to the north where Llewellyn had said the castle was. He wondered where in the city Kalamar, the spy from the brigand camp might be. He knew the road to Thorhus was long and fraught with many perils, but hoped the spy had made it back, especially with Shakk.

Kaz finished his business in a patch of bushes that Val hoped was not part of the cook's garden, and came padding back, his tail flicking sharply as if feeling the cold. Despite his thin shirt and trousers, Valdieron did not feel the chill in the air, or the bite of the wind as it pushed across the city like a tide against a beach. The warmth of the Dragon's tear pressed against his chest, a reminder of its presence and Astan-Valar's words that it would know when they were close to a piece of the Disk of Akashel. He wondered if it would glow or become warm when they were near, or if even a piece was even here in Thorhus. His doubts resurfaced but he pushed them back to their place in the back of his mind, knowing that hope was his life now.

With these thoughts he returned to his room and extinguished the lantern before settling into the bed. As usual, Kaz leapt up with him and he made room under the blankets for the moorcat, flinching once as the cat stretched one paw against his legs and dug his claws in.

His thoughts as he drifted off to sleep were of the Combat Ambit, where he knew he would be in only a short time. For the past week they had been moving towards left handed fighting against single foes, something Valdieron found he was somewhat adept at. He could remember learning to juggle at an early age and throwing rocks with either hand into the river, and wondered if these activities had aided his balance and coordination. He knew the test would come when the Master had him battling with two weapons simultaneously.

As usual, the shift to the Dream Plain came suddenly, as if he was there before sleep fully overcame him.

With a renewed spirit, he turned and made his way towards the hall where the Combat Ambit was, where he knew he would find the Master and his lessons would continue.

Chapter 25

The buzzing of city life brought Valdieron from his sleep, and he rolled over with a groan of complaint. The morning sun filtered into the room through the curtained window. His stirring wakened Kaz deep beneath the bed sheets, and as usual the cat came awake and clawed its way free, most likely hungry again.

The sharp angle of the sun's rays showed him without rising that the morning was well under way, and that he had slept longer and easier than he had since his supply of Bark-ash leaf had run out. Throwing back the covers, he rolled to his feet, careful not to step on the stretching Kaz, and padded to the window, eager for his first view of the city under the revealing light of day.

It awed him with its simple enormity. The high Inn afforded him a better viewpoint, but he saw nothing but rooftops and walls. Like a sea covered with thatched and shingled rafts it sat, the slender thread of roads not easily traced as they snaked around small declines and hills. He made a quick calculation and realized he was looking over the southern portion of the city, where Llewellyn had told him the markets and slums were situated. He could just make out the widening area which was the markets to the left, a maze of simpler structures intermingled with stands and tents.

The noises that had awoken him came from the river of people passing along the road below. There were wagons drawn by horses, their hooves cracking on the cobbles and the metal-lined wheels creaking over the loose pebbles. An occasional shout would go up in greeting or curse as somebody got in another's way.

With a smile he tugged off his bedclothes and pulled on his new clothing. He washed his face quickly, and ran a brush through his hair. It had grown considerably in the past weeks and hung down past his shoulders. Using a piece of cloth, he tied it back in a tail, out of his way. He shivered slightly, but knew he would warm up quickly in the warm winter sun outside. He pulled on his boots and strapped his belt around his waist, then secured his baldric to it. He passed a quick eye over his funds, finding he had spent nothing over the course of their journey. With the money Nagus had given him, he had four Gold Sovereigns and a mixture of Silver Crowns and Copper Marks. In his village, such a fortune in coin could buy several cows or sheep, but here in Thorhus it was likely a very small amount.

Kaz scratched at the door and darted out into the corridor when Valdieron pulled the door open. He heard a sharp intake of breath accompanied by the rattle of a pot cracking against the floor. He stepped out quickly to find one of the servants, a young girl, standing in wide-eyed shock, nervously looking down the hall at Kaz.

"Sorry," stammered Valdieron, bending to retrieve the pot. Luckily it had been empty. The girl took it with an appreciative nod before passing by quickly, with one final glance back down at the impatient Moorcat.

"Now that wasn't very nice," scolded Valdieron, trying to hide an amused smile. He wondered how many others would react in a similar way to the appearance of the Moorcat. "Stay beside me, now."

Kaz padded beside him, head lowered slightly, but only for a short time before he was skipping ahead again. He bounded down the stairs so that Valdieron had to chase after him. He caught him at the doorway leading to the kitchen. With a grin he pushed the door open, but held Kaz back with his foot, knowing what sort of havoc the cat may wreak upon the place. He was surprised to find the room abuzz with activity, with cooks and servants running about in a frenzy. Shouts and commands were given freely, and curses were exchanged for sloppiness or slowness, so Valdieron closed the door and decided to return to Llewellyn's private dining hall.

There was nobody present as he entered, but as if his appearance was a call, Gerkar stepped through the doorway from the kitchen.

"Greetings, young sir. What will you be partaking of this morning?"

Valdieron almost laughed aloud at the man's formality. "Just some bread and meat will be fine, Gerkar, and maybe some cheese and a bit of water to wash it down, if you aren't too busy."

Gerkar nodded. "And your little companion?"

Valdieron had almost forgotten Kaz, who had disappeared behind him. "Better make that a double order, and maybe some milk, please." Gerkar nodded and excused himself, but was back shortly with a large tray of food.

"Are the others here?" asked Valdieron as Gerkar placed the tray before him, mindful of Kaz who was turning circles at his feet.

"Master Llewellyn is still out on business, and Masters Hafri and Thorgast have gone out for the morning to look around."

Valdieron thanked him then turned to his food. He did not think he would be hungry after the huge meal the previous night, but as the smell of the meat permeated the room, he found he was ravenous. First things first, however, he took a small plate of meat and some bread and set it on the floor for Kaz, along with a shallow bowl of milk. Kaz growled low then pounced on the food and ate as if he were starved.

With a smile Valdieron sliced cheese and meat and sat them between two thick chunks of bread. He stood and paced as he ate, using the time to scan Llewellyn's library some more. He found the tomes titled in the common tongue, but a few he opened were written in a language he could only guess as Elvish, with its alien tracery. One row of books caught his attention. They were untitled and bound in leather. A single sigil was printed on the front of each, and he guessed them to be numbers of the texts.

Swallowing the last of his food he flipped the book open, the slender sheets opening almost to the center of the tome. His eyes darted to the writing, and as they did, he shuddered and his eyes blurred briefly. It passed, but he was left shocked and curious. It was like a chill from a sudden cold, only more intense, and his brow beaded with perspiration, despite the chill room. He shook his head, wondering if he had eaten something he shouldn't have the previous night.

The writing was the same Elvish hand, only more flowing and connected, as if words were joined to others to form single-word sentences. He flicked back through the pages, startled to find thin drawings on the creamy paper. He wondered if it was a book on combat, from the warrior figures depicted. There were detailed drawings of stances, movements and weapon-angles intermingled with others less obvious. He assumed the five others were the same, and reminded himself to ask Llewellyn later. He returned the book to its place just as Kaz was finishing his milk, pushing the bowl across the floor with each desperate lick to draw more from the already empty container.

"Let's get out of here," he called, taking a moment to drain his cup of chilled water. He placed the plates and bowl back on the tray and left it on the table, not wanting to enter the kitchen. He circled around to the taproom to search for Gerkar, and found the man polishing empty tankards at the long bar.

"Ah, going out, young Sir?"

Valdieron sighed. "Please, Gerkar, I am no more a Sir than this cat here. Call me Valdieron, or even lad, but Sir does not become me, I'm afraid."

"On the contrary, you are looking much the Sir in your attire, but if you so desire, Valdieron it shall be."

"Thanks," returned Valdieron, casting an eye over the busy room, where people were enjoying their morning meal. "I seek a craftsman to make a baldric and sheath, Gerkar. Do you know of any who may be able to help me out and not deplete my modest purse?"

"There are a few to be found, Si-Valdieron," spoke Gerkar, smiling at his near slip. "There is one, however, a new smithy on the corner of seventh and twenty-first street, not far from here. He is said to be as cheap as any, for he has no guild affiliation as yet."

Valdieron repeated the directions given to him and thanked Gerkar.

The mass of people passing by seemed more daunting to him at ground level. He was able to get a better glimpse of them as he halted at the steps. A more diverse range of people he could not imagine, old and young, large and small, he marveled at each and wondered how so many people could coexist in one place. He knew he was a long way from home, but was determined not to be out of place here.

Like a tide the line of people seemed to drag him away as he stepped into it, but he found he could move freely if he needed to. Kaz was having a slightly more difficult time, dodging the multitude of feet. He stayed close to Valdieron and after a short time they were moving easily through the throng.

The streets were marked with large wooden poles, ferruled

and marked with both numbers and cuts. Twenty-first Street was narrower and not as well tended as the larger one, but it had fewer people, so he was able to maneuver more easily. He found that despite the conversations that passed between many of them, none spoke or even acknowledged his presence, though many did veer clear of him and especially Kaz.

With more room to move and see, he was able to concentrate on his surroundings. He found the houses growing steadily more ramshackle and unkempt the further south he walked. Litter and debris marred the streets and alleys, and poorly dressed people loitered, obviously with little to do. They eyed Valdieron as he passed, and he was suddenly conscious of his own dress. What he thought to have been average dress to those back at the Inn must have appeared almost lordly to these people of the slums.

He found Seventh Street with little difficulty. It was a narrow, winding street almost dark, between rows of high yet worn structures that seemed to overhang it like eerie sentinels. Valdieron felt more than a little out of place here, and could feel eyes upon him every step of the way. As it happened, the Smithy was situated at the far end of the street, in a large block a little away from the other nearby houses.

A high metal fence surrounded it, topped by barbed wire. A single large gate was swept inwards, showing a small muddy yard with a roofed overhang where the smith started. It was like a large shed was built onto the front of a house of decaying wood. It had two levels, but the top level seemed in bad condition, and the roof looked as if it was being mended. The chimney also looked like it was recently mended with metal plates over it to cover holes. The work was well done, however, showing an attention to detail not usually seen on such a menial task.

The smithy was centered under the conical roof, the small forge's hood rising to deposit smoke at its peak. Three worn bellows surrounded it like guards, and before the center bellow was a large anvil, spotted with rust. A rack of utensils was set up on either side of the anvil, and the walls held tools. The smell and warmth brought back familiar feelings to Valdieron as he entered under the low roof.

A small but solid lad of around twelve or thirteen tended the forge. His sandy hair was matted with ash and grime, as was his skin. An oversize apron hung around his neck, though it appeared more of an inconvenience to him as he swept the dirty floor with an old broom.

"The smith is currently out, good sir," apologized the lad after he spotted Valdieron and shuffled over, obviously relieved at the short break it afforded him. "He won't be back until this afternoon."

Valdieron cursed silently. "I need a sheath prepared for me, along with a baldric and buckle. Can you let your Master know of this for me?"

The boy screwed his mouth in thought for several moments before setting the broom down and wiping his soiled hands on his equally soiled clothing. "I will need your weapon's measurements so the Smith can make it for you." He pulled out a lump of charcoal and a scuffed sheet of parchment.

Valdieron tentatively drew his sword for the lad to measure with a small length of string tied in knots at regular intervals. He could not help but grin as the lad gazed upon the weapon. He needed a little prompting before he actually began measuring it. When he was done, Valdieron sheathed it promptly, feeling suddenly vulnerable.

"The Smith has several jobs to be done ere the week ends, good sir, but he should have it ready for you in no more than a week, if you wish to return then."

Valdieron nodded. The influx of people into the city provided more work for smiths especially from those entering the tournament. He nodded and pressed a copper Mark into the lad's hand. "Tell your Master there is no hurry, as long as it is ready by the tournament."

The lad nodded and turned. With a final glance around the smithy, Val departed. Memories haunted him as he strode from the yard, head downcast and feet dragging slightly.

Back inside the smithy, several moments passed before the door to the house opened and a large figure stepped from the dark interior. "Is he gone, lad?"

The boy peered about a while longer before nodding.

The smith snarled and cursed. "Damned guild members. How many times do I have to tell them, I've already paid up for the month!"

The boy shuffled between feet, obviously concerned. "I don't think he was a Guild member, Sir. He was too young, and there was no suspicion in his face. I think he was an honest client, a warrior, maybe a lord by his weapon." He handed over the copper Mark.

The Smith grunted sourly. "If he is a Guild member, I hope the Thieves catch him and rob him. Serve him right for wasting his time and mine." Still, he took up the measurements from the boy and studied them for a short time. "It is not a hard job. I will have it ready tomorrow, just in case he does return."

With a shrug, the boy returned to his chores. He tried not to concern himself much with the workings of the Guild of Smiths, though he knew of their practices from conversations he overheard in the streets. After several minutes he was whistling merrily. The stranger was all but gone from his youthful mind.

Valdieron almost returned to the smith after he realized Kaz was missing. The Cat had entered the smithy before him, but he had not seen him leave, so he must still be back there. He waited for several moments before whistling a call that would normally have brought the cat running back. There was no sign of him. He took a worried step back towards the smith but stopped as a muffled cry issued from a narrow alley nearby. It was Kaz; he had no doubt, and wondered what sort of trouble the cat had gotten itself into.

Probably stuck somewhere and couldn't get out.

The surrounding buildings made the alley dark, but Valdieron's keen eyes had little trouble picking his way through. He gave a wide berth to the piles of rubbish and rubble strewn about, but he could see no sign of Kaz. He pressed further into the alley, and his hand strayed anxiously to the hilt of his sword.

He rounded a sharp bend with barely room for three to walk side by side, and found a cloaked figure holding Kaz in his arms, silent and lolled as if dead or asleep. Valdieron tensed and grasped his sword. The figure made no move nor was there any sign of others.

"What have you done with my cat?" he asked harshly, feeling his anger build.

"Your cat?" stated the figure as if confused. "Such a rare thing he is, but you are misled. He is mine."

Valdieron cursed. The figure obviously knew of the banded Moorcat's worth. "His worth cannot be more than what is in my purse," he bargained, drawing his money pouch out and rattling it in his hand. "A trade?"

The figure drew in a breath as if in thought. "I think not!"

Dark forms appeared from places of concealment around him, both in the alley and above on the rooftops and catwalks. Weapons were drawn with a hiss and they stepped around him threateningly. "Drop your sword, your purse and any jewelry you have, and you may leave."

Valdieron doubted the sincerity of the figure's words as soon as they were spoken. He wondered if these brigands were members of the thieves' guild. He remembered Llewellyn's advise about buying them off. He had already offered them all of his money, an amount they could not guess at, so it was obvious they were more concerned with his sword.

"I have an offer also. Give me back my cat and return to your Guild master before you get hurt, and maybe I won't tell him of your little job on the side."

His hastily spoken words had a better effect than he had hoped. Several of the figures drew up short with gasps of surprise, but the figure holding Kaz merely chuckled. "Stupid and empty threats, young Lord." He nodded and the armed figures, faces hidden by veils, stepped around him again.

Valdieron knew he was in trouble, though he could sense these thieves did not wish to kill him, or they would have tried already. Still, he drew his sword with a steely hiss, an unspoken promise of death that rang through the alley and hung over them like a foreboding of doom.

The thieves were not as skilled as he had expected, but they were quick. Their weapons were predominantly short and, concealable, though a few had staffs and clubs. Valdieron had the benefit of a longer weapon, and his experience in the combat ambit, facing off against many opponents who were faster.

After a brief but lively exchange, two of the thieves found themselves bleeding from shallow cuts and another was groaning as he rolled to his feet after having them swept out from beneath him. A fourth cradled bruised ribs from the flat of

Valdieron's sword. It only angered them, however, and they returned twice as ferociously.

With his sword a blur, Valdieron spun, content to parry the onslaught of attacks rained down upon him from all sides. A dagger snuck past a parry and grazed his hip, while a staff cracked against his right shin as he stepped away too late. The thieves broke away again, as if to sally their strength. Two were without weapons, and two others had cuts - Valdieron had been hard pressed to keep his temper in check.

The third attack from the thieves was more intense. Blows came from every angle, sometimes twice or three times in rapid succession, so Valdieron had to parry many attacks with arm or leg. One attack sliced open his forearm, another struck him in the side with a club he could not evade. He felled two thieves, one with the flat of his sword to the back of the head, and another with a kick to the face, breaking his nose and sending him reeling to the ground. Their numbers did not seem to dwindle, however, and soon he was overwhelmed. A dagger sank into his shoulder as he tripped on a body, and almost instantly something cracked against the back of his head, bringing a moment of dizziness and numbness before darkness fell.

Chapter 26

It began as a soft tapping, a distant echo that beckoned Valdieron from the darkness, which clung to him like a fog. His memories flashed back to the dark, cold water of the stream in the Dragonwing Mountains, into which he had fallen during his fight with Trolls. He tried to claw his way free of the depths, his head shaking in denial and anger and his lips voicing low cries.

His eyes snapped open and awareness consumed him as the dark waters vanished. He almost cried out in alarm as darkness still surrounded him, then he realized he was blindfolded. He was seated on a wooden chair by its feel, and his arms and legs were bound to it. Though he felt pain from his new wounds, he could feel they had been tended to and dressed. He heard a brief shuffling to his right and turned. Through the veil he saw the dim light of a torch or lantern, and a door rattled open and closed briefly as several people entered the room. He sensed someone step before him and he tensed.

"Who are you?" The gruff voice was muffled slightly. It was deep and commanding, however, obviously a man who was used to being in command.

"Where am I?" he countered, his anger beginning to build at his predicament. The room around him was cold and damp, and his head throbbed incessantly.

There was movement and a stinging backhand snapped his head to the side. The pain passed quickly, leaving a tingling against his cold skin and a trickle of blood running from the corner of his mouth. He turned his head towards the figure. His look would have forced the man back a step if he had not been hooded. The first figure repeated his question.

"Valdieron!" he spat in response.

"Valdieron. You are in a safe place at the moment, but for how long depends on you. Now, what are you doing here in the city?"

Valdieron paused, which brought another slap. He was feeling rather abused, and groaned with anger and frustration.

"Do not seek to mislead us, Valdieron. Answer us honestly

and quickly and it will go better for you. Now, what are you doing here in the city?"

"I am here in the city to enter the Tournament."

A light buzz of whispered conversation sprang up through the room. Valdieron judged there were between six and ten figures in the room.

"You say you are here for the tournament. Where are you from?"

"Shadowvale, a village in the mountains of Southern Tyr." He was trying to draw out his answers to give him more time to think as the interrogator pondered each response.

"You lie. Your dress and your weapon mark you of higher station. A Duke's son, perhaps, but no farmer."

"Its true, I swear it!"

The punisher shifted at his side and Valdieron waited for the blow to fall, but it was held in check.

The interrogator was silent for a moment, before continuing. "How came you here?"

"From Ranil, the merchant city in Tyr, I traveled with three others, one of which is from Thorhus himself, Llewellyn by name, a Bard by profession."

Once again those around him broke into soft whispering, and the name Llewellyn was mentioned. It was obvious the Elf was well known.

The interrogator stood suddenly, the conversation obviously at an end. "You may leave, Valdieron. You will be guided to an exit, and given your cat back."

"What about my sword?" he asked softly, his voice taut with anger. He could feel the warmth of the Dragon's tear against his chest. He wondered why they had not taken it.

"Your sword will be your payment for safe passage in our city. A hefty price, but one which I think you are more than willing to pay."

Valdieron cursed aloud, straining against his bonds. "You cannot do this. How will I fight in the tournament without a sword?"

The man's voice answered from the doorway as several men began to loosen Valdieron's bonds. "You will find a way, I am sure. Farewell, Valdieron."

Rough hands grasped him and he was lifted from the chair and borne more than led out of the room, through a twisting maze of passages. He tried to measure the distance through steps and the direction, but there were so many twists and turns he was soon lost. He let himself be dragged along. After a long while, they were above ground in the city.

He was thrown onto the ground unceremoniously and footsteps departed quickly. When he ripped the hood from his head he could see nobody. It was evening, the day having passed while he was knocked out. By the look of the filthy alley, he assumed he was in the slums. He rose angrily. His purse and dagger were gone. Kaz was also missing, as he had expected.

Tucking the hood into his shirt, he left the alley and began to navigate his way home. He decided to head north, keeping the fading light of the sun on his left. Eventually he stumbled onto Twenty-first Street without further incident. A few who were still on the streets watched him with interest as he passed gloomily.

The patrons of the Inn were in full voice when he returned, so he decided to use the back door. He rounded the corner, and was stunned to find Kaz resting beside the door. He leapt at Valdieron with glee, and Valdieron scooped him up. "I had thought you gone, my friend, but it seems you have a better sense of direction than I." With his spirits slightly lighter, he let himself in and mounted the steps to his room.

The cold reality of the day's events struck him and he began to shake with repressed fear and anger. His sword had been taken from him. Its worth was of no importance to him but he felt somehow attuned to the weapon, and had grown comfortable with wielding it. He vowed to get it back, even if it meant infiltrating the Thieves Guild. He drew out the dark hood and found it was one his attackers had worn, and placed it with his other clothes. It may come in handy in the not too distant future. He was going to need information, however, if he was going to retrieve his sword from the heart of the Thieves Guild, and Llewellyn seemed the obvious place to start.

Unfortunately the Elf was away again on some business, and rather than seek out Hafri and Thorgast, he decided to bathe and eat. This drained some of the tension from him, and after that he drew out the strange book from Llewellyn's library he had opened before, and began to flick through it.

Many of the diagrams he could follow, so he made the brief

trip down the corridor to the Training Hall. It was unlocked and lit when he entered. He moved to the low mat beneath the tapestry on the left wall and resumed his reading.

With his thirst for retribution driving him, he lost himself in the thrill of discovery and learning. The book showed different stances and how they could be shifted into others, along with different forms of attack and defense.

Some time later in the evening, Llewellyn entered the hall. Valdieron had removed the ceremonial Longsword from the far wall and was running through different techniques, surprised at the perfect balance of the weapon. He was running through the movements slowly, sword in one hand and the open book in his other hand, and Llewellyn's warning shout broke his intense concentration.

"Valdieron, NO!"

He started and almost dropped the book.

He turned as Llewellyn leapt across the room and grabbed the book from his hands. He regarded Valdieron with surprise.

"Llewellyn, what is it?" asked Valdieron with a light smile. The Elf seemed pale and without breath, as if something terrible had happened or just been averted.

"How can this be?" he whispered softly, his green eyes passing from the book in his hand to Valdieron. With his other hand he grasped Valdieron's chin softly and turned his face so that he could scan it. A sudden understanding seemed to come over him. Valdieron wondered if he was studying his bruised mouth and cheek where the thieves had hit him.

"How can this be?" he whispered again. He lowered Valdieron's chin and shifted drunkenly to the matted area and sat, lost in thought. Valdieron joined him, feeling the Elf's eyes on him, deep in judgment, it seemed. He was loath to break the silence.

"Who are you, Valdieron?"

Valdieron stammered, not understanding the reason for the question, the same one the Elf had asked shortly after they had met. "What do you mean, Llew? What's the matter?"

"Just when I think I have you sorted out, something else crops up and you become a bigger enigma to me than before."

"You said I could read the books, Llew. If I have given offence, accept my apologies and know it will not happen again." His words were not bitter, but spoken from confusion.

"And lucky I am, it seems that you are the inquisitive type, not Hafri or Thorgast, else I would have lamented my offer for the rest of my days."

"What in the Voids are you talking about, Llew?" asked Valdieron angrily. His day had been one he would rather forget, and now Llewellyn was raving like a madman. He wondered if the Elf had perhaps had a little too much to drink.

"This book!" indicated Llewellyn, lifting the now closed book. "It is an ancient text given to me centuries ago. It, and the others, tells of the fighting techniques of the 'Wind Dancers', of which I was the last taught. There is a powerful ward set on it, which prevents any not of the blood of my ancestors from opening them. Yet here you are, studying from it like you would any other book."

Valdieron gasped. "I did feel a slight tingling when I first opened it," he confirmed, "but I thought it was only the cold. How can this be?"

"It is simple enough to answer, now that I have seen. For any not searching for it, the traces are small and easily overlooked."

Valdieron frowned, but then comprehension dawned on him. He shook his head in denial. "It cannot be. My father was a normal man, a farmer, and my mother-" His words trailed off. He knew little of his mother, but was sure she was not of Elvin background. "My mother also, of that I am certain, Llew."

"Not even a slight portion?" asked Llew softly. "It must be so, Val, or else the ward would have caused you a great deal of harm. It is too powerful to be broken or dispelled."

Valdieron dropped his face into his hands with a confused sigh. If one of his parents had the Elvin strain, it would have to have been his mother. His father he knew too well. He wondered why his father had never spoken of it, and remembered the cryptic letter his mother had left for him with the Dragon's tear.

Llewellyn was silent beside him, and rose after a while. A startled gasp brought Valdieron's gaze to him to find Llewellyn glancing down at the ceremonial sword at Valdieron's side.

"Where is your sword?" His green eyes scanned the room, for he knew Valdieron would not part with the weapon by choice.

"It is gone," sighed Valdieron. A grim determination caught him and he rose, clutching up the sword. He quickly told

Llewellyn of the ambush and the interrogation, the Elf silently angry through it all.

After Valdieron had ended, Llewellyn cursed furiously and turned towards the door when Valdieron caught his arm, turning him.

"Don't do anything to compromise your position in the city, Llewellyn. I told the Thieves I was with you, and that caused a stir among them. You hold some weight around here, and I cannot let you jeopardize that. You have too much to lose. If you wish to help me, tell me how I can retrieve my sword."

"I will tell you all I know, but even with that knowledge, your chance will be slim at best."

"That is more than I can ask for," smiled Valdieron thinly. Llewellyn nodded and turned back to leave.

"Meet me for supper later, and we will go over a few things."

"Llew!" The Elf turned, the door almost closed behind him. Valdieron had bent to retrieve the tome Llewellyn had left. He regarded it with a measure of fear and reverence. "Can you teach me the ways of the Wind Dancer?"

Llewellyn regarded him intently for several moments.

"Why not. It was my belief that the ways of my people would be lost with my passing. Now I see an opportunity for it to continue through you."

"But in all chance you will outlive me, Llewellyn," argued Valdieron, wondering at the Elf's tone. "You have plenty of time to pass them onto another."

"Maybe not, Valdieron. Remember, if you have Elvin blood in your veins you may very well live longer than the usual span of human life."

The shock on Valdieron's face made the Elf smile as he closed the door behind him, leaving Valdieron to his thoughts. He pondered the strange turn his life had taken of late, with the coming of this strange young man named Valdieron. From the first moment they had met he knew the boy was different. He had met many people through the years who had shown great potential and gone onto great things, but this unassuming young man seemed beyond anything he had ever witnessed.

The boy's unknowing introduction to the ways of the Wind Dancers was a revelation to him. He had been taught the ways of the Wind Dancer as a young Elf, and carried the secrets with him. He had diverted from the paths of his people and become a wanderer, destined to roam the lands as a Bard, forsaking his people and past life. He rarely returned to the place of his birth, finding other races more accepting of him as a Bard.

And yet it seemed his past was catching up with him. He had borne the burden of being the last carrier of the secret ways for centuries, and had had every intention of passing them onto a child of his loins. His wandering lifestyle had not led to a lasting relationship so he had never known any of the children he may have sired. Now, however, there was one, more human than Elf, who could be taught the secrets of the Wind Dancers.

The matter of Valdieron's lost sword irked him, however, and he wondered which of the Guild's Taskmasters had taken it. No doubt they would seek to sell it after a time, making enough to pay off those who had assisted him, as well as reap a windfall for themselves.

There was the chance, however, that he would keep it. Llewellyn had never seen a weapon of such strange qualities. He had witnessed its magic against the Devil at the Dark Temple, and knew that its magical capabilities could not be limited to that.

Returning to his own quarters he sat and wrote several notes. They were addressed to several men he knew well, who would keep an eye on the trade quarters for news of the sword's sale. More than likely the Taskmaster would seek to sell it to a Lord or even someone in the royal family here in Thorhus. He wrote another note to an even older friend for information on recent changes in the Thieves Guild. Although he was familiar with their ways, and knew some of their hideouts and passages, he had not been in Thorhus for some time. Some vital areas of the hierarchy may have changed, or their secret places shifted for security. He sealed the letters and called on one of his servants to take them to their appointed destinations. The evening was getting away from him and he had need of bathing and food.

Valdieron did not join him for supper, but Llewellyn was not offended by his lack of attendance. He knew the young man had much on his mind, and it would take some time to sort through. He ate slowly and after that took a wine bottle from the kitchen and returned to his room. He would have liked to have returned to the taproom and join Hafri and Thorgast, but he had things that needed to be done. At the door of his room, which was opposite the bathroom, he paused and cast a last look down the corridor, seeing a flickering light beneath the door of the training hall. He knew Valdieron was beyond the door, or the fires would not be lit. He smiled at the magic of the room, placed there by a wizard and lifelong friend of his from his home in Lloreander; he could not remember seeing the fires so intense.

With a sigh he entered his room and bolted it closed behind him. He moved to his desk, situated at the foot of his large canopied bed. Papers were organized on it in piles, reports he had to read in the next few days, but instead he drew out a faded book, its leather cover showing signs of age. It was his life's work, a tale of every event worth noting in his three and a half centuries of life. Of late he had written often and long, of meeting Valdieron and more recently the fight against the Sable Elf and Devil at the temple. He added the discovery of Valdieron's unusual heritage and the decision to teach him the ways of the Wind Dancer. When done, he waited for the dark ink to dry and closed it again. He knew he would soon be back to tell of other things.

Taking his wine flask, he moved to his bed and rolled back, kicking his boots off as he did. He drank and pondered, a dangerous combination he knew. He was awake for many hours, the lanterns burning out before he decided even he needed to rest and drifted off into his trance-like slumber.

Chapter 27

Llewellyn's whistling rapier flashed past Valdieron's face, glimmering a pale gold in the bright firelight of the training hall. The Elf had just completed a dazzling set of spins, striking out with great precision with both feet and weapon. Even his cloak, after the first spin, slashed out like a weapon, breaking Valdieron's tentative thrust, as he envisioned his sword catching in the heavy folds and being pulled from his sweaty grip.

He stepped back momentarily, declining the invitation to strike as Llewellyn came to a stop. He knew how soon the Elf could reclaim his balance and counter. This equipoise was something the Elf stressed on many occasions as vital to a Wind Dancer's style. To be able to shift an attack at any time required perfect balance, muscle control and timing.

"Why do you pause?" asked Llewellyn almost tauntingly, though Valdieron knew it was not.

"Your momentum was too much. I could not get a strike in without it carrying me away."

"Then you must use that momentum to your advantage."

Valdieron nodded as he ran the previous set of movements through his mind, trying to figure out counters to the Elf's spin. There were many options he could choose from, but he knew that the wrong one would be costly. Llewellyn noted the young man's reflections and launched another attack, forcing Valdieron to react.

"Why do you reflect so?" asked Llewellyn airily after he finished a routine of high and low thrusts.

"To remember your moves and to think of counters to them," answered Valdieron a little angrily.

"To what end?"

"To better understand their workings, and to know for next time how to react."

"How will you know next time?" asked Llewellyn urgently, as if willing Valdieron to greater comprehension.

"I will not, in most likelihood, but it is the subconscious thought which is a precursor to action. If my mind knows of the possible reactions, it has something to work on."

Llewellyn regarded him silently. What Valdieron had spoken made sense, and he marveled at the young man's innate understanding of combat. He seldom needed to explain himself fully, the young Warrior acutely aware of what was needed of him.

In his next attack he repeated the spin that had turned Valdieron to contemplation. Valdieron half expected the attack, and was ready for his counter.

Llewellyn's cloak swung around first from a flick of his wrist to propel it, and Valdieron swayed back out of its reach, waiting for the horizontal slash he knew would come. He swayed back into him as the Rapier came around, starting low but rising, so that it was at head level when it came at Valdieron.

He would have ducked under it, but Llewellyn may have realized the direction of his parry, so he raised his sword diagonally so the slender blade skimmed off its flat side with a hissing clang.

Llewellyn's arcing kick came next, perfectly executed as if Valdieron's high parry had not affected his poise. Valdieron knew it was coming, however, and dropped into a spinning sweep, his right foot snaking out beneath Llewellyn's high kick at his supporting leg.

His timing was a little off; for it was the first time he had attempted such a move. He would have connected with Llewellyn's knee if the Elf weren't so skilled and agile. With a slight coil of muscle, the Elf leapt off his supporting leg, the momentum of his kick carrying him around in another circle and lashing out again with a snap as Valdieron rose, catching him solidly in the chest, propelling him backwards. His sword flew from his hand and he rolled to his feet in a crouch, though he was laughing softly, amazed at the Elf's maneuver.

"A counter counter," he whispered dryly, and moved to collect his sword. The Elf waited, a wide smile spread across his face as Valdieron cursed.

"Do not be perturbed, Valdieron. I suspected such a move, and I knew how to turn it against you. Now, however, you know that I know, and now you know yourself, which is after all the reason we do this, is it not?"

Valdieron nodded, though his bruised chest was wishing the

lesson had been a little less painful. He took up a towel and wiped the layer of sweat from his face and arms. Llewellyn had already sheathed his weapon, his breathing only slightly labored.

"I have more business to attend," he explained ruefully. Valdieron frowned and followed him to the door. In the three weeks that he had been learning the ways of the Wind Dancer and plotting to retrieve his sword, Llewellyn seemed to be spending a lot of time away from the Inn. Val lamented the lost time. "I have something for you, however."

He disappeared momentarily into his room before returning with a small roll of parchment, which he handed to Valdieron. "It is a map which you may find useful."

"I'll be back before the evening," he explained, but Valdieron was already shuffling down the hall, towards the dining room.

The parchment was a crude but invaluable map of the sewer and drainage network beneath the city. Valdieron wondered where Llewellyn had got it. He thought it could only come from somebody in the Castle or somebody closely associated with the Thieves Guild. He rolled it back up and shoved it into his shirt, meaning to study and remember its every twist and turn that evening.

He was about to rise and return to his room when Thorgast strode in. The Barbarian was dressed in his new clothes of brown and black, which seemed to match his mood. His stern face was lined with worry. He spotted Valdieron and made to turn back.

"Thorgast, wait!" The big man turned at Valdieron's call and Valdieron rose and took a step towards him. "Is something wrong?"

The Barbarian shook his head "I do not know, Valdieron."

His unusual reply confused Valdieron for a moment. In the past few weeks he had been so caught up in his own affairs that he had not given a thought to the Barbarian's plight. He knew the big man worried for his people and for his family.

"Can it be that bad?" he asked with sudden concern. He knew little of the problems of the Barbarians, only what Thorgast had told him during their journey. Even then he had been reluctant to speak of it.

"That is something I cannot tell, Valdieron, and that is what burdens me," sighed the big man, running a large hand over his worn face. "Chul'Haka was not in the best of shape when I left it, which was at the end of last summer. I fear that with the winter coming to an end, the Haruken will press my people even more. I wonder if we can hold until...."

"You have to keep believing, Thorgast."

The big man turned and regarded him silently. "It is hard to hope when I am ignorant of what is happening in my homeland. One thing I know, however, is that my kin will fight to the very last."

"What did the Hrolth we encountered tell you? I heard it mention your city, and by your reaction it was not to your liking."

Thorgast nodded. "Aye. He told me that the Haruken clans were amassing in greater numbers than ever. This is not good news, for Haruken are as a rule very nomadic and rarely band together, even under a banner of war. They must have a new leader who unites them under the common cause of fighting my people."

"I thought these Haruken monsters, akin to Trolls?" Valdieron asked with a grimace. He had seen many things in the last season he would not have previously believed possible or real. He wondered what else existed in this land that he was unaware of.

"They are only like Trolls in their brutality, I fear," answered Thorgast after a long silence. "I am loathe to tell you that the Haruken may be kin to us, Valdieron, though they may appear as monsters in their four-armed appearance. They are unmistakably human, however, no matter how crude their language or lifestyles. They are both cunning and dangerous, and more than a match for even our best warriors."

"Is there no reasoning with them?" asked Valdieron. "If they are as intelligent as you say, maybe you can bargain with them."

Thorgast shook his head, and Valdieron was reminded of the antipathy that existed between the Woodland and Sable Elves.

"Do you think you can gain any support here in the Southland's?" he asked.

"I do not know. I do not think I have the time to waste waiting for the tournament to begin, yet I must if it will help me become known."

"Well, you have at least one who will aid you," he said with a smile, causing the big man to turn to regard him intently.

"I have business which must be taken care of, but when that is seen to, I promise that I will help you as I can. I have no home, no family, and I know of no better cause than what you fight for."

Thorgast regarded him for several moments, his face an unreadable mask. "You are serious!" he whispered at length.

"Of course. You are a friend, and I wish to fight for what you fight for. Is that not what you desire, aid?"

"Yes," breathed Thorgast. "But I did not expect your offer, is all. What I fight for, I fight for knowing that it is more than probable that it will bring my death." He sounded resigned to this fate.

"Why fight for something if you aren't prepared to pay with your life?" asked Valdieron, suddenly serious. He liked Thorgast, had grown fond of his quiet, friendly demeanor, and was more than willing to help him in his fight. He, Llewellyn and Hafri were the only ones he could call friends now.

"I could not ask for better aid, Valdieron. Your offer touches me, and I will gladly accept it. May my people learn soon that strength and honor still presides in our southern neighbors." His big hand grasped Valdieron solemnly by the shoulder, and he nodded thanks, his eyes rimmed with moisture.

Valdieron rose, seeing Thorgast retreat back into his thoughtful shell. He could say nothing more to him that would raise his spirits. With a look at the hunched man, as much a stranger to this place as he, he left the room.

It was only midday, and his mind was too jumbled to concentrate on practice. He decided to see a little more of the city. He knew that to carry out his plan to retrieve his sword, he would need a greater knowledge of the workings of the city and its layout. He was weaponless when he stepped from the Inn, feeling more than a little vulnerable without one. He figured it was best not to attract any more attention to himself, so he left Kaz inside.

His few forays into the city had been to the slums, where many of the guild's refuges and safe houses were located, as well as the access tunnels to the underground level. Llewellyn told him that many of the upper class houses were also fronts for the Thieves Guild, as were, Inns, houses of pleasure, warehouses and shops.

The stream of people bore him away to the north, and he let himself be swept along, content to ride the wave where it took him. He passed many places worth noting, and he tried to take them all in, despite the fact he was lost within minutes.

The forest of dark buildings dropped away like a falling screen, giving way to a large meadow. Its undulating green surface was meticulously kept and dotted sporadically with trimmed trees. It was like an oasis in the middle of a desert. People walked casually through there, soaking up the peaceful atmosphere, so close to the mayhem yet miles apart. He was drawn into the park, welcoming its soothing touch. The city clung to him like a shroud, choking him slowly with its difference. He welcomed this place that reminded him so much of home.

A shadow fell over him then, dark and oppressive, causing him to shiver. He was standing at the base of a huge gray-stoned wall, lined and marred over time with the corrosion of rain and wind. It was crenulated at its peak, some twenty feet above him, like a huge crown. This was one of the walls that encircled the palace.

On top of the ramparts he could see shadowy figures, dressed not in the usual blue tabards of the city, but the more regal lavender of the Kings own guards. Silver-tipped pole arms emblazoned with the King's insignia of rose and crown danced above the walls, like narrow puppets bearing long pennants.

Beyond the walls rose two spired towers of the palace, a burnished marble in color, which seemed to draw in the sun's warmth. Narrow windows were set around the upper level probably arrow slits for archers.

With a sense of awe beneath the hulking power of the walls, he began to follow it, fascinated. He knew that beyond the walls lay the arena where the tournament would take place. The castle would be overrun with people milling to view the spectacle.

The Castle gates were closed, not surprisingly, huge grated arches flanked by square barbicans and topped by a rampart, much akin to the outer gate of the city. There was no portcullis, but he could see the edges of two immense metal slabs on either side of the gates. How such huge things were shifted he did not know, though surely not by manpower.

A line of armored guards stood along the paved boulevard beyond the gates, lavender tabards covering their metal breastplates of silver and hauberks of fine chain. Pennants lay curled around the shafts of their halberds, and each had their gaze locked onto the figure across from them.

The arena dominated the left of the interior that he could see, a huge, circular structure supported by a wood and metal framework and raised almost as high as the walls. Flags atop tall poles shifted loosely in the high wind. A large portion was cut away, allowing access, and he could see the many rows of wooden benches and stairs. How many people it would hold he could not tell. He knew that once inside the arena, it would be daunting.

The marble and sandstone palace, topped by its blue spires and pyramid roofing, sat majestically in the distance. Low buildings in the foreground concealed most of it, but that which could be seen made him stand agape. He did not know what he had expected but its towering beauty and solid presence made him feel privileged to see it.

He stood there for a time, soaking up the atmosphere. Doubts began to creep into his mind. The tournament was coming up and many of the greatest fighters in the realms would be competing for the one prize. He, on the other hand had studied the martial arts for not even half a year, albeit intensely and using the mystical assistance of the Dream Plain.

His mood turned sullen. Shadows lengthened eerily across the streets as he passed. His peripheral vision watched the shadows, though he expected no more trouble from the Thieves.

He could smell the burning wood from the hearths and hear the din from the taproom as he approached the Inn. The sky around the city broiled with dark clouds, and he could feel the air changing around him, despite the myriad of other sensations the city brought. Rain would fall before the dawn, bringing another cold change after the week or more of cloudless, warm days. *'So much for winter being gone,'* he sighed. Though he was raised in the cold climes of the highlands of Tyr, he was more comfortable with the warmth and heat of summer. Pushing open the solid doors, he stepped into the dim interior of the taproom.

Chapter 28

Heavy rain fell like small stones on the shingled roof of the Inn. Through the upper level and over the noise of many people could it be heard, like an unending portent of doom. Outside, the streets ran with water, tiny streams all interconnected. Others became quagmires of mud and slush, where only the more foolhardy or brave ventured. Patronage at the Inn was at a maximum this night, and Valdieron was thankful they had their own table at the end of the bar where he sat with Hafri and Thorgast. The blazing fire nearby gave little heat through the throng of people crowded before it, trying to dry off.

"Damn fine evening!" hooted Hafri, eyeing the crowd around them with a predatory stare. He was well on his way to being known for more than his feats on the battlefield, if the amount of female attention he was receiving was any indication. It would not be long before he rose to mingle; he was just seeing what there was to go after when the time came.

"This weather is at least good for something," cursed Thorgast, grasping his large tankard of ale, his head bowed as if under an oppressive weight.

"As long as we don't have to fight in this," mused Valdieron softly. He had not counted on battling in rain. He reminded himself to use the wet conditions to train outside a few times while it lasted, just in case it lingered for the tournament.

"Aye, it'll be hard enough as it is," agreed Thorgast moodily. Like Valdieron, he had been keeping himself occupied studying the opposition they would face during the tournament. He was not very hopeful. He had even heard that one of the Masters from the Academy at Astral City was here for the games. Many were already saying that he and Hagar would likely meet in the final battle, and bets were being made on the outcome. This betting had amused Valdieron, especially when Llewellyn told him he had a small wager on him winning.

"Wish me luck," Hafri said with a wink before draining his tankard and rising. He wound his way towards a young woman he had spotted earlier. Thorgast watched him disappear into the crowd with a wry smile, but said nothing.

Llewellyn arrived shortly afterwards, stepping from the kitchen area behind the bar. He paused to speak to Gerkar, his face grave. His usual smile appeared as he skirted the bar towards them, offering greetings to some as he passed.

"I see Hafri is already terrorizing my female patrons," he joked as he took the young man's vacated seat. He was carrying a tankard, and one of the barmaids approached before too long to refill it. She was middle aged yet still slender and pretty, her dark hair flecked by strands of gray and white. Her eyes were bright, a deep blue that seemed to reflect her maturity, and she flashed both Thorgast and Valdieron a warm smile. Valdieron found himself blushing slightly. Llewellyn turned to him after she had moved away, studying him in his open manner. "Have you decided when you'll get your sword back?" he asked. He saw Thorgast regarding him, and knew the big man wanted dearly to help him with his plans. Valdieron had told him that it would be easier alone and that his size would make them conspicuous.

"I was going to make it in the next few days," mused Valdieron, "but I think I'll wait a little longer. I would have liked to do it before the tournament, but I'll have a better chance once the tournament is under way."

Llewellyn nodded agreement. "The Thieves Guild will be a hive of activity with the tournament on, and they may be more careless than usual. Anyway, you can borrow that sword in the Hall for the tournament if you need it."

He was referring to the sword Valdieron had been using over the last few weeks. Val found it an excellent weapon, well balanced and of solid construction.

"Thanks, Llew." He rued the loss of his own sword, but knew the practice he had had with the other sword would be an advantage.

"What's that?" asked Valdieron as a loud murmuring ran through the crowd. Heads were turned to the Inn's entry, and as the crowd parted momentarily, they spotted a small party of newcomers standing at the door, looking about. Valdieron did not recognize any of them, though Llewellyn cursed vehemently and rose to get a better look, using his height to peer over the crowd.

"It's Hagar and his cronies!"

"Hagar?" breathed Valdieron. He also stood, using his chair to lift him even higher so he could get his first glimpse of the infamous young warrior.

He had no trouble picking out Hagar amongst the small group. He stood at the center of the close group, tall and lithe. He was dressed in a leather vest and brown trousers of heavy wool. At his waist was belted a curved sword, like a single edged rapier but broader. He also had a long dagger on his opposite hip. Long bracers ran along his forearms.

His face told Valdieron whom he was, cold and calculating with unblinking eyes darting around the crowd. His hands rested near the hilts of his weapons, ready. His narrow mouth was pressed in a wolfish grin.

The others around Hagar appeared nondescript, bodyguards or thugs using the Warrior's prestige to bring attention to them. All were armed and looked as though they could use them. Two, however, were noticeably different.

"That one on the left," Llewellyn indicated, a short, slender man with wispy, gray hair, "is his trainer, Adakar." He was dressed in garish green trousers and shirt with a white overcoat. His face was searching, almost worried as he took in the crowd, as if expecting trouble at every turn.

"Like Hagar, he is a Darishi."

Valdieron noted that both were of darker skin, but the similarity ended there.

The other at Hagar's left was tall, almost gaunt. He wore thin robes of dark blue trimmed with black, secured by a shoulder-brace and belt. Small pouches were set at his waist, and his left hand clutched a slender staff of black wood carved with an array of symbols and runes. His hood was thrown back, showing a skeletal face with high forehead and pointed chin. It was a strong face dominated by deep eyes that looked over the crowd. His mouth twisted in a sneer of condescension. He urged Hagar into the press with an extended arm, which seemed to part the crowd like a wind shifting leaves.

"That other is his chief adviser, Myrtti," sniffed Llewellyn, his eyes hard. "A conniving son of a mud crawler if ever there was one. He's the one behind most of the stories you hear, multiplied tenfold. I know not his background, but I'd be surprised if it didn't involve backstabbing and murder."

"I just hope nobody decides to offend any of them, or there

could be bloodshed." Llewellyn returned to his seat and finished his ale with a flourish that seemed to dismiss Hagar and his group from his mind. His eyes were still stern.

"I doubt anybody would be that stupid," returned Thorgast with a sniff, "but who knows what may happen after a few too many ales." Llewellyn nodded agreement as he motioned for the same barmaid to bring him a refill, which she did with a favorable smile and alluring sway of the hips.

Hafri had all but disappeared in the crowd but appeared now and then in the arms of different women as they floated amongst the throng. They were all strangers to Valdieron, but Hafri knew many of them. Hagar and his group were seated around a large table at the far end of the hall, out of sight but not out of mind.

At one particular point the crowd quieted enough for them to hear the clear straining of a harp. Llewellyn spun sharply, seeking its source.

"I did not know we were hiring a performer tonight," he admitted.

A dulcet female voice was snatched away by the sudden rise in volume of the crowd.

"Beautiful," breathed Valdieron, hanging on to the distant voice.

"Aye, it is indeed," agreed Llewellyn, high praise indeed from the Bard. Valdieron had not seen many other Bards perform at the Inn, as Llewellyn provided most of the entertainment. He had heard none who captured his attention as much as that single snatch from the unseen Bard tonight.

"I would see this Bard," said Llewellyn, rising quickly and taking up his tankard.

"Me too," offered Valdieron and rose with him. They looked at Thorgast, but the big man waved them away.

"You go. Music is lost on me."

The two snaked through the crowd to the small dais in the corner near the bar. Valdieron caught a glimpse of Hagar and his companions nearby.

In his mind he had pictured the Bard to be a beautiful young woman, though why he did not know, but he was surprised to find that although she was young and pretty, she was far different than he had expected. Her body was hidden beneath a flowing cloak of faded gray and a velvet dress cinched at the waist by a silver belt. Her hair was purple, which he assumed was from a colored dye of some sort, having never seen nor heard of such a natural hue, cut short to her shoulders. Her face was wide, with slender chin and full mouth, narrow nose and widespread eyes of sandy brown.

Her fingers swept briskly across the strings of the Harp as she sang a slow, sad ballad. Valdieron was not focused on the content of the song, however, as he was awed by her voice. Llewellyn moved to the front of the stage, leaning forward to listen with his head angled and eyes half closed, nodding slightly, seemingly oblivious to the woman. When she had finished, his applause was loudest of all those nearby.

"You play well, Miss," he congratulated with a slight nod. This caused her to blush.

"Thank you, Master Llewellyn. One day I hope to be as well known as you." She cradled her harp carefully in her lap as she drank briefly from a tankard of water beside her chair.

"That will not be long in the coming, I should think," returned Llewellyn with a broad smile, and the girl flushed again. "I do not think I know your name, however. I have been away of late."

"Cari-Ann, Sir," she replied curtly, seeming nervous by the attention of one of the greatest Bards in the realms.

"A name we shall no doubt hear more of in the future. Tell me, are you from here, Cari-Ann?"

She shook her head, causing her hair to swirl briefly about her shoulders. "From Brek, Sir, although my Mother and I moved here last year."

"Brek's loss is our gain," he laughed. "You sing and play with feeling. That is rare."

"My music is my life, Sir. It is how I express myself."

Llewellyn nodded, sharing the same feelings as her. For him, music had been his life, so much so that he had forsaken his people and the honor of becoming the last Wind Dancer of his people.

"Well, if ever you need work, come here. I am always ready to help those who would seek perfection at our craft, if such a thing exists."

Cari-Ann thanked him warmly.

Valdieron did not join in the conversation, content to stay at the side and listen, entranced by the sound of her voice and laughter. He did not notice her cast several glances at him. After a time he caught movement off to the side, and turned slightly to see Hagar saunter through the crowd toward them, Adakar at his side. Hagar wore an angry scowl, as if offended, but his trainer was smiling as if he'd been handed a present.

"Get away from my woman!"

Llewellyn turned his head slowly to face Hagar, brows arched in displeasure. "Go back and sit down, son!" He turned back to Cari-Ann with an apology.

"I said get away from my woman, prick-ears!"

Dropping his head with a sigh, Llewellyn turned again to Hagar, his eyes now ablaze from the insult. Hagar stood unblinking, his eyes holding Llewellyn's with an equal intensity. Tension built like an afternoon thunderstorm, quaking as if ready to explode. Those closest to the two stepped away.

"Dare you enter my Inn and insult me, boy?" hissed Llewellyn, his brow furrowed in anger.

"I dare what I will, Troll-kin. Keep away from my woman!"

Llewellyn turned to Cari-Ann who looked at Hagar with scarcely concealed anger. She spat at him: "Keep away from me, you animal!"

Hagar moved to grab at Cari-Ann, but she skipped back as Llewellyn knocked his outstretched hand away. With a wry smile, Hagar turned on the Elf.

"Never touch me, again. This does not concern you, Tree-dweller."

Llewellyn flashed him a contrary grin. "It does when you come into my Inn and bother my workers. Leave, now!"

Hagar exhaled. With an almost imperceptible shake of his head he lunged at Llewellyn.

Although Valdieron had expected an attack, the suddenness and speed of it stunned him. Hagar's fist was at Llewellyn in a flash, and if the Elf had not been as fast, he would have been struck in the face. As it was, he ducked and swayed away at the last moment. Hagar's sword flashed out as quickly as his fist, but Llewellyn's Rapier met it with a loud clang, which caught the attention of many nearby. Valdieron pulled Cari-Ann away gently as she cried out, but she saw who it was and moved with him.

"What is this?" asked Llewellyn angrily, more to Hagar's

trainer than to the warrior, though his eyes never left Hagar. Adakar merely shrugged, as if surprised at what was happening. His smug expression showed he was not concerned.

Hagar's sword snaked out again, but Llewellyn batted it aside easily. Off to the side, Valdieron was at an impasse. He did not know how to deal with such a thing, and wished for Hafri's presence or even Thorgast's. Neither was to be seen, however, and he was loath to interfere. He sensed that more than insult was at work here, and maybe some honor was at stake. He knew Hagar could not stand down here; such was his renown among the people that doing so would discredit him. He knew Llewellyn well enough to know he too would not be the first to stand down.

Hagar exploded into motion again, sword held in one hand and flashing before him in diagonal slashes which rained down upon Llewellyn's upper body. With Rapier pressing left and right, the nimble Elf was able to deflect them, though he could not get in a strike of his own.

Hagar halted his attacks suddenly, reversing with a horizontal slash from right to left. Llewellyn stepped into it, reversing the grip on his own sword so the blade was pointed to the floor and intercepted Hagar's blade and he continued to spin, angling his bent elbow at Hagar's head. The Darishi was not there, however, dancing back out of reach with the slightest of smiles.

The two parted, and Llewellyn was smiling also, like they were part of a game, albeit a deadly one. Valdieron hazarded a glance about, suddenly aware of the warm presence of Cari-Ann beside him, and saw Thorgast step through the crowd opposite. His face was grave, but it was obvious he was not going to intercede. He could tell why, too. All of Hagar's companions were spread around the two combatants like guards, hands resting on weapons not yet drawn. Would they halt anybody attempting to break up the melee?

It did not seem they would have to, however, as Llewellyn sheathed his weapon and stepped back.

"Leave!"

It was spoken in a whisper, but all who stood there heard it. Hagar made to move forward, but Adakar rested a hand upon his arm. A silent communication passed between them before

Hagar inclined his head to Llewellyn and sheathed his sword.

A murmured buzz ran through the crowd and Valdieron sighed with relief, exhaling loudly when he realized he had been holding his breath. He began to smile as Llewellyn turned to him.

Hagar had moved impossibly fast before, but his next move came even faster and without warning. As Llewellyn turned, the Dak'marian lunged at him, a stiletto coming to hand from somewhere concealed. Catching the movement at the last moment, Valdieron stepped forward, but he knew he was too late.

The stiletto pierced Llewellyn's shirt with ease, beneath his ribs in his left side. Llewellyn arched painfully, his eyes wide and mouth agape in shock. Valdieron's hand struck Hagar's forearm with a numbing blow, freeing his hand from the blade. Valdieron was clutching Llewellyn then, face to face, and the agony he expected to see in those emerald depths was not there, only regret and a sudden deep sadness. He made to speak, but his breath was rasping. His eyes closed, and his mouth turned up in a slight smile as the life faded from him.

Valdieron crouched under the weight, laying the Elf on the ground. He looked asleep, so much so that he wished he could just nudge him and bring him awake. Images of his own dying father flashed in his mind and he winced, bringing his bloodied hands up before him. Around him, all was pandemonium as the crowd pressed against Hagar's guards. Thorgast bellowed wildly from somewhere, but Valdieron did not notice as he turned to Hagar. The blank expression on Hagar's face was a direct contrast to Adakar's, who was staring at Valdieron with a look of surprised shock.

"You are dead!" he vowed, and he knew the two heard or at least understood him, for Adakar reeled back as if struck. Hagar remained impassive.

Grasping Llewellyn's Rapier, Valdieron rose. He caught a glimpse of Cari-Ann crouching beside Llewellyn's body, but did not draw his gaze from Hagar.

The Rapier felt alien in his hand, but he advanced on Hagar with a cold grimace, his anger slowly giving way to controlled aggression. It would not do to end up like Llewellyn.

His first attack was a fast measured thrust. Hagar's flashing sword knocked it away before it even got close to his body. He repeated it, inching closer to Hagar who remained still. Adakar had retreated, his face cruelly set in a sneer. The ring of his guards was thinning as the crowd drew them away and none interrupted Valdieron as he pressed Hagar.

He thrust again, high and level with Hagar's throat. The barest of movements preceded a dazzling riposte. One! Two! Three thrusts, high, low then high, which Valdieron barely saw. He stepped away with a silent curse, oblivious to the pain of the cut to his shoulder and oozed a stream of blood down his arm.

He swung in a double-handed slash, diagonal from high, but Hagar crossed in a sweeping parry to drive it across his body. He loosed one hand from his hilt and swung his elbow back at Valdieron's head, but Valdieron was able step to the side and spin, bringing his sword around in a crouching sweep, just out of reach as Hagar leapt up and away, his mouth twisted in a mocking grin.

Pressing the attack, Valdieron drew tall and lunged at Hagar's shoulders. He saw Hagar's lightning vertical parry sweep across to meet the thrust. His sword stopped seemingly in mid-air, then he saw Hagar's sword blocking it, almost resting on his head. His right foot lashed out simultaneously, catching Valdieron in the ribs, driving the breath from him.

With a groan of anger and frustration he attacked again with single-handed strikes in a flurry, high, low then wide, hoping to find that elusive gap in Hagar's defenses. It did not come, however, and he found himself tiring quickly. He sensed Hagar was toying with him a little, though his smug smile was gone and his face was now a mask of concentration. Valdieron grasped the rapier with both hands as his right hand, sweaty and bloodied from his shoulder wound, began to slip. Sensing this, Hagar pushed the attack with powerful blows, driving Valdieron back. The two weapons locked up after a flurry of parried blows as he anchored his stance. The weapons met with a clang and Valdieron locked gazes with Hagar.

As if engaged in a mental struggle the two remained locked, swaying slightly as both sought to push the other off balance.

"I'm sorry for your friend."

Hagar's whispered words came as a blow to Valdieron, and he was nearly thrown back but steeled himself quickly. He almost spat at him. How could he speak such lies?

Shifting his weight he levered his hands and spun his Rapier, the suddenness catching Hagar by surprise. He spun his sword, and the two locked and formed a circle between them before Valdieron forced Hagar's hands low. With a snap he pushed Hagar's sword away and low, while beginning a spin, his left leg circling. The move was desperate, and he expected Hagar's sword to bite deep into his unprotected back. His heel caught the back pedaling warrior in the side of the head with a dull crack.

Stumbling to the side, Hagar reeled and almost toppled over a table, but righted himself with a steady hand that smacked against the heavy furniture. His left hand slowly rose, wiping at his ear. It came away stained crimson, and he stared at it, stunned. His gaze flicked imploringly to Adakar before returning to Valdieron, eyes ablaze with a renewed fury.

Valdieron moved to meet him as he stepped forward again, feeling more confident now. A surge from the crowd split them, and in the tumult he saw Adakar and his adviser grab Hagar and guide him away. The warrior bellowed angrily at them, shaking his head and pointing his weapon towards Valdieron. Brief words from Myrtti appeased him and he allowed them to guide him from the Inn, unhindered as if the crowd did not see them. Valdieron moved to follow, but strong hands grasped him by the shoulder. He spun quickly and dropped to a crouch, Llewellyn's Rapier coming up between him and his opponent. He saw through blurred eyes that it was Thorgast, and halted the weapon.

"It's me, Val." The big man was puffing laboriously, and his shirt was torn at the front, though he appeared unwounded. His axe remained in his belt, obviously not brought out in the fight.

Valdieron looked imploringly into his eyes but saw no answers there, only the deeper sadness he was used to seeing in the pained Barbarian. He could sense the crowd thinning around him, and saw the fallen bodies of several people strewn about, some moving slightly, but his eyes saw nothing but the body of Llewellyn, lain out on his back with arms folded across his chest. There was no sign of the Bard, Cari-Ann.

The Rapier slid from his hands as he leapt to the Elf's side. Tears returned, but he did not cry as his hands settled above the Elf, as if not daring to touch him. He bowed his head and grasped the Elf's hands in his, finding them still warm and soft.

"Farewell, friend. You most of all knew me for what I was and gave me support when I could not ask for it. May you ever live on in our minds, gone but not forgotten. I shall remember you always."

The distant shrill of whistles caused him to lift his head. He guessed what they were, and wished for something more fitting for the Elf's passing, like the dirge of a harp. It was then that he spotted Cari-Ann's discarded instrument, forgotten as she fled the violence. He shifted to pick it up. If only he could have played it then, he knew Llewellyn would have liked that.

Armored figures poured through the door. He saw see the blue tabards of the city guard, each armed with sword or axe as they spread out through the room, catching up those who remained while their eyes scanned the room, evaluating what had happened. One man who was large and burly with an air of authority barked orders, his sword still sheathed.

"Get those men secured. Check the wounded."

At one point, Gerkar, bloodied along his side and sporting a black eye, raised his voice to plead their case, but the commander cut him off.

"You'll have your chance to tell what happened tomorrow. Tonight, you will spend the night in one of the King's cells, just to cool you off and sober you up." He turned his nose up as he shifted to the mutilated body of one of Hagar's guards near the door. "Gather up the bodies."

Valdieron was grasped by the arm and allowed himself to be manacled by the wrists by a young soldier, who did not protest to him keeping the Harp in his hands. He was checked briefly for weapons. At his side Thorgast was also secured, though the soldier seemed to shrink away from the huge man, probably expecting him to protest. He hesitantly reached for the huge axe at his waist, but Thorgast offered no resistance as he took it.

Two soldiers filed them out of the room one at a time, connected to a long rope through a ring in their manacles held at either end. The others, battered and bloodied and mumbling darkly, were wishing they had been quicker to leave the Inn. Many asked where Hagar had gotten to and why he was not being dragged off to the dungeons also.

The Commander led them through the dark streets, wet from the rain, which had thankfully ceased. The spectacle attracted the attention of many people looking out windows and doors at the line. Valdieron walked with head bowed, feeling like a criminal before their gazes.

The shaming journey took longer than he expected, winding through the streets at a good speed, but the castle was further away than he remembered. When they did arrive, he found himself sweating despite the chill air and his every muscle seemed to ache, along with his bloodied shoulder. He hardly noticed the gates swinging with a great groan of protesting iron. He managed a brief glance at the flanking guards.

They passed the arena, dark and menacing in the dim light, and the palace towered over them. They were taken through the arched entry of a large building opposite the castle, which must have been the cell area. Another grated door was opened before them, and they were ushered through slowly, unhooked from the rope at the door and led individually to a cell, standing opposite one another all the way along the long building. Some were already occupied by dark figures lying on pallets or yelling renewed protests to the uncaring guards.

Valdieron was thrust ungraciously into the last cell along the line, the door swung shut behind him with a resounding clang. He was tired and numb as he sank thankfully onto one of the pallets. The metal frame creaked and the soft padding was not thick enough to mask the hard frame, but it was more comfortable than the floor. He cradled his head in his arms, pulling the heavy dark blanket over himself to ward off the chill coming through the tiny barred window. He clung to the delicate harp like a lifeline.

He was asleep before long, but his rest was troubled and he awoke many times to darkness and loneliness and a profound sadness he could not shake.

Kitara sat on her bed, clutching her knees to her chest. She was still dressed in a heavy cloak, the Mask of Disguise dropped carelessly at the foot of the bed, staring up at her with eyeless accusation. She clenched her eyes shut and cursed, feeling the flaked blood on her hands from the dead Elf. The events of the evening had passed with such speed that she was left stunned and shocked at Llewellyn's death. She remembered now with clarity what had happened, and she shuddered with horror.

The menace of Hagar had surfaced, and she had been foolish to allow herself to be caught up in it. "How did he know it was me?" she asked herself angrily. She had constantly told herself there was no harm in what she did. Now she realized it was her fault the Darishi warrior had killed Llewellyn, the greatest Bard in the city and her childhood idol.

How she had wished that the Elf's gleaming blade had stolen the smug smile from Hagar's face, humiliating him in front of the large crowd. She had almost choked on her own tears when Hagar had thrust his dagger into Llewellyn's side, and the light of the Elf's eyes dimmed like a lantern running out of oil. She had seen the pain in the eyes of the other young warrior who had been with Llewellyn, and had feared he would join the Elf's fate as he turned to avenge his death. She saw the first exchange of the fight but could not stand to see the finish, fleeing from the mayhem through the back door. In her haste she had left her harp.

She lay awake for some time, feeling the tension drain from her body as the cold surrounded her. She accepted its cleansing embrace, though she knew it would not reduce her guilt. After a time she cried, something she had not done in a long time, but it was from sadness at the passing of a great man whom she had admired and respected since childhood. In the early hours of the dawn she crept beneath the warm covers after shirking her stained clothes, and sleep came, but little reprieve from the pain.

Chapter 29

The clinking of thin metal chains woke Valdieron from a deep sleep. He had sought refuge in the solitude of the Combat Ambit, not lingering for the Master to arrive. The globe allowed him to vent his pent up anger, and he had launched himself into the combat with a berserk frenzy. Foes fell before his sword like blades of grass to a scythe. He scarcely noticed as the tempo increased to a pace he had not experienced. He had no thought for form or balance, only for conquering, defeating, defending his life against those who would take it from him. Not a weapon touched him. Images flashed before him after a time as he fought on instinct alone until finally, exhausted, he raised his sword with a roaring cry as a dozen weapons pierced and cut into him.

His eyes were leaden. He raised his head from the hard pallet, the dark cell dimly lit from the small barred window. His head throbbed with an ache that seemed to start at the base of his neck. He groaned as he swung his legs off the bed. Every muscle seemed to ache even more than the night before. He wondered dimly if it had anything to do with his action in the Combat Ambit, though it had never affected him thus before.

A jailer was shifting along the corridor, unlocking each cell with a ringing click. Muffled groans and whispers came from the other prisoners as they woke. He saw Thorgast and Gerkar led from their cells with their wrists manacled. As the jailor unlocked the door of his cell, Val rose and slowly raised his hands. The cold metal burned his skin as the manacles locked into place.

The day was bright and clear outside. The early morning was cloaked in the cold bite of a receding frost, leaving icy shadows beneath the shaded buildings. It would be a beautiful day, but Valdieron hardly noticed as he followed the shuffling line of dejected captives.

The gates of the castle loomed to either side of him as they were led between the round barbicans. The ramparts overhead were topped by armored figures of the Castle Guard. None were visible inside the gates, but the barbicans probably housed dozens of guards waiting for orders to storm out if necessary.

A broad field opened beyond the gates, split down the center by the cobbled path. The walls to either side were sectioned into buildings, and he glimpsed a blacksmith, furrier, guardhouse and a tailor. Above them, the wide ramparts teemed with guards also.

He marveled at the amazing architecture of the palace, its whitewashed marble walls of intricate style, and the pale blue roofs. Great doorways were lined with sandstone backed by metal for support, the doors a heavy redwood and braced with gleaming silver. They passed guards and others who were probably members of the castle staff.

They were led through a large courtyard running beneath a large square building, with huge wood and marble stairs rising to either side. At its center bubbled a large fountain with dolphins rising from the water. Thin jets of water sprayed from them to land in the crystal waters beneath. Its beauty was lost on Valdieron, who felt an increasing sense of dread the further they went.

They passed through a large garden, with great thorny hedges forming a boulevard through it. Patches of flowers were set ornately throughout. The most visible of these was a banked formation of roses depicting the crown and rose symbol.

The towering double-doors of the throne room were swung open. Guards bearing huge Halberds flanked them. A well-dressed man stood waiting for them. He stepped forward to consult briefly with the commander. He wore puffed pants of yellow and a shirt of tasseled white. His face showed him to be of middle aged, with short hair brushed forward to hide his balding. With a grave nod he turned and entered the hall, and his echoing voice heralded their arrival.

The commander led them into the hall, which was dark compared to the daylight. Valdieron lifted his head cautiously. Even in his dejected mood, he was awed at the sight of the Throne room; far different than anything he had seen before.

Rows of gold and silver pillars ran through the room, from the checkered floor to ceiling thirty feet above. Each pillar was inset with silver sconces holding flickering torches, while the walls held lanterns on small projections. Guards stood at every pillar like silent sentries, nothing shifting save their cold eyes.

The entry was offset to the left, so they were directed to the center of the hall before they had a clear view of the dais on which rested the Thrones. It was tiered, with a row of smaller seats set in a semi-circle on the lower tier, and a single Throne set above them. This one was huge, crafted of silver and gold, inset with gems of varying hues and size. On it sat a large man with arms resting at his sides. He was middle-aged also, with a slight stain of white through his sandy hair and beard, barely concealing a regal and hard face. His eyes were deep and unblinking as they scanned the captives. There was wisdom and intelligence in that face, and his large frame showed what must have once held the strength of a warrior.

The lower seats held mostly aging figures dressed in gray robes, silently watching. Val assumed they were advisors. One bore a large quill, set to document the proceedings.

Guards and assistants lined the edge of the stage, standing patiently with the practiced ease of servants.

"The charge, Commander?" asked the King in a deep voice, his eyes flashing to the Commander off to the side. The scribe began scribbling furiously, the quill flying in his hand.

"Brawling, Majesty. At the Inn called 'Hangman's Noose'. There were six dead sir, one the owner, the Bard Llewellyn."

The King's eyes twitched briefly at the news, and he sat back in his throne as if stunned. His eyes turned to the captives. "The other deceased?"

"One citizen, sir, and four hired guards, by their appearance."

"And the Elf's killer?"

The Commander shrugged and motioned to Gerkar who stood at the front of the line nearest him. Gerkar stepped forward and made a constricted bow to the King.

"Llewellyn was killed by Hagar the Darishi, Sir. Those here merely reacted to the heinous act of the brute."

There was a gasp of surprise from some in the room, but the King remained impassive at the news. "Your name?"

"Gerkar, my Lord, part owner of the 'Hangman's Noose'."

The King nodded and turned to one of the gray robed men beneath him who nodded briefly, as if clarifying Gerkar's claim. "Hagar, you say. Did you see this or any sign of Hagar, Commander?"

The Commander shook his head in denial. "No, your

Majesty. Hagar's adviser also denies those who died were employed by him."

"That is not surprising," sighed the King, pausing to take a clearer look at the captives. "Names and business in Thorhus?"

Each captive stepped forward to state their names and why they were in Thorhus. The King raised his eyes when Thorgast stepped forward, obviously stunned by the big man's presence. He nodded when Thorgast told that he was there for the tournament. Valdieron was last. He and Thorgast were the only outsiders, the others being laborers or craftsmen from the city. The king was silent, and after a time spoke, his deep voice tinged with regret.

"Those who are of Thorhus return to your families and pray do not let me see you back here soon. Those others, here for the tournament, are required to quit the city, to forfeit the tournament and not return for a cycle of seasons. Those who are deceased shall be given proper burial."

Valdieron felt his knees weaken. "But you cannot-" he started, stepping forward, but the clang of armor beside him warned him that he had erred. The haft of a halberd took his knees out from under him and he dropped to the hard floor.

"I can, and my order is final, Valdieron of Tyr. A long way from home you are, and unless you have somebody to vouch for your well doing, you will leave the city on my order. Have you such a person in mind?"

Valdieron shook his head. With Llewellyn dead, there were no others in the city who carried enough weight for the King to listen. Hafri was missing, yet even he did not carry enough weight for the King to change his order. Then he remembered one who might be able to help him. It was a slight chance, but one he had to take.

"Kalamar, your Majesty. A, ah, member of your staff." He did not voice aloud that Kalamar was a spy, for he did not think the King would like it known, but his hesitation had let the King know that he knew. The King knitted his brow in surprise and turned to the side as a low whispering swept through the room. He motioned for a guard to bring Kalamar to him.

"What know you of Kalamar my Chief Adviser, young man?" asked the King sternly. "Know that if you said that for a reprieve, and Kalamar knows you not, your punishment shall be greater than that already passed."

"He will tell when he arrives," assured Valdieron hopefully, but he prayed this Kalamar was the one he had saved.

Val waited impatiently, trying to hide from the King's gaze. A door opened and he heard footfalls echo across the marble floor. He did not look up but closed his eyes and waited.

"What is this about somebody claiming to know me, Your Majesty?" came a youthful voice, strong and commanding in its own right.

Valdieron felt his skin tingle with relief as he recognized the voice of Kalamar. He looked up and stood erect as the King inclined his head his way and Kalamar turned.

Cleanliness was the only major difference in the spy's appearance. Before he had been unkempt, dirty and unshaven, but now his face was smooth and his hair combed straight. He wore clothes of black silk. A fine saber hung at his side, and his fingers were adorned with rings. A flicker of uncertainty crossed his face and his brow furrowed in thought, causing Valdieron's heart to skip a beat. Had he forgotten?

Then Kalamar's eyes grew wide and flickered with shock as he took a hesitant step forward and grasped Valdieron by the shoulders. Valdieron returned the gaze, and saw recognition in the man's eyes. "Valdieron, is that really you?"

Valdieron smiled wanly, knowing his appearance would probably have deceived his own father at first sight. In the months since the two had parted, Valdieron had grown a little, gained some weight, his hair was longer and he no longer carried his strange sword on his back. It was little wonder Kalamar had not recognized him at first.

The King was staring at them in open disbelief. He raised his brow questioningly to Kalamar. "This is he?"

"Yes, your Majesty. Do not forget that appearances can be deceiving." Having said that, he motioned for a nearby guard to loose Valdieron.

"So be it," boomed the King, a mark of his character that he did not sound disappointed by the outcome. "Valdieron shall enter the tournament as a free man. My other orders remain, however."

"My friend..." whispered Valdieron urgently to Kalamar, not forgetting that the King's orders would still keep the Barbarian from the tournament. Kalamar's gaze shifted to the big man, but if he was surprised he did not show it.

"Your majesty. If it pleases you, I shall take Valdieron's friend into my care, as well, so that he may enter the tournament."

The King had obviously expected this, but he paused thoughtfully with a barely restrained grin. "It seems that he has made quite a journey to get here, it could be cruel of me to deny him that. Thorgast of the Urak'Hai, you are free to enter the tournament at your will."

Thorgast stepped forward and bowed respectfully, as much as his bonds would allow. "It seems word of your wisdom was not unfounded, your Majesty. Thank you."

The King merely nodded graciously as the jailer unhitched Thorgast from his manacles. The guard passed him back his War-Axe with almost an apologetic nod. Thorgast clasped it with a grin and looped it back into its sheath at his waist. Valdieron was passed Llewellyn's rapier, which Kalamar spotted and raised a questioning eye.

"It's a long story," sighed Valdieron. He felt the sadness of his losses begin to creep back, despite his gladness at this reunion.

"One I would hear over a meal and a drink," agreed Kalamar, turning. "Come, Thorgast. Join us, please." The big man stepped over to join them.

"By your leave, Your Majesty?"

The King nodded dismissively, and motioned for the others to be taken away. The commander barked an order and the captives were led from the hall. Kalamar motioned for Valdieron and Thorgast to join him. Valdieron turned, and saw the person Kalamar had walked in with and stopped still.

The young woman's beauty struck him like a blow. He stared openly at her; glad she was not watching him but looking with interest across at Thorgast. She was tall and athletically built, with raven-dark hair hanging loose over her shoulders as she leaned against a pillar. She wore a long dress of morning blue, cinched at the waist with a wide leather belt. A silver bracelet entwined with a serpent encircled her left wrist, and her right hand bore a thin ring of plain gold.

"My lady, let me introduce to you to an old acquaintance of mine and his companion". Kalamar drew up beside the woman. From the way he addressed her, Valdieron guessed she was the Princess Kitara.

"This is Thorgast of the Urak'Hai." The big man bowed again at the waist. Being the son of the King of Urak'hai, formality was in his blood. She responded with a curtsy and a smile.

"This is Valdieron of Tyr. Nobody else but your father knows this, but he saved my life last autumn. Gentlemen, I present to you the Princess Kitara, Jewel of the House of Temorial."

"A pleasure, Lady Kitara," stammered Valdieron, feeling at such a loss for words that he wondered how he got through that simple sentence. Her wide blue eyes held him paralyzed. He waited for her full pink lips to mouth words.

"The pleasure is mine, Valdieron. Anybody who saves the life of Kalamar is always welcome here."

Kalamar laughed at her side and placed a hand on her arm as she flashed him a mocking grin. Valdieron almost lost the strength in his legs and choked on his own breath as he recognized the voice of the Princess. He studied her face, and knew it for the one he had imagined belonging to the female Bard, Cari-Ann. The voice was the same. He remembered its every tone and inflection, having been entranced by it the previous night. But how was this paradox possible? Some magic, he guessed, but potent if it disguised her features in such a way.

"Please excuse me, gentlemen. You obviously have some catching up to do, and I have pressing business to attend. Farewell for now." With the twirling of dress and hair she turned to go. Valdieron called after her as she went and she turned in surprise.

He stepped towards her, fumbling at his belt where he had hung her harp. He handed it to her with a wistful smile. "A present for you."

She took the Harp slowly, her face set in a thankful smile, but her wary eyes betrayed more as they darted to the throne where her father sat. "Your gift is appreciated, Valdieron," she said with a curt nod before turning again and leaving the hall. Valdieron watched her leave and felt Kalamar's hand on his shoulder.

"A marvel among women that one, Valdieron," he whispered, and Valdieron could only nod. Yet why had she been alarmed by his knowledge? He assumed she had hidden her identity to protect herself while in the city. But was it circumstance that brought Hagar to the same Inn? He had heard the Warrior's threat to Llewellyn, but had passed it off as drunken thuggery. Now he realized Hagar had recognized the princess. But how?

"Come, we have much to talk on, and you need a bath and some food by the looks of you. Come!"

With a lingering gaze after the disappeared Princess, he followed Kalamar from the room.

Kitara leaned thankfully against the door of her quarters and bolted it closed behind her. She trembled as she clutched the harp to her breast. Her eyes were closed, but she could still see the face of the young warrior, Valdieron.

How had he recognized her? She had asked the same question of Hagar the previous night, though she suspected his adviser had informed him. It was rumored he was a sorcerer of some power; so it was likely he could see through her magical guise. But the young man, Valdieron, had had no such help.

There was a soft tapping at her door. Through the looking hole she saw it was her father and quickly unlocked it to allow him entry. His face was clouded with thought as he shuffled in, and he pushed the door carefully closed behind him. His eyes scanned the room quickly before settling on her. She tried to meet his gaze with a smile.

"What was that about the Harp?" he asked softly.

"A present, no more," she answered, hoping he read nothing in her thoughtful pause. "Kalamar mentioned that I liked to play, and the young man gave it to me as a gift. I think it may have belonged to Llewellyn."

The King nodded and sighed heavily, running a large hand over his tired face. He reached out and grasped her hands warmly. "Times are changing, my daughter. That such a man as Llewellyn is slain by a brute like Hagar. Never a better man than Llewellyn you will find, as you know. His passing will be mourned for many a day."

Kitara remembered several years back when Llewellyn had been a regular entertainer in the palace, usually at feasts or other festive times. Then he had gone on one of his trips and been rarely seen until recently. Kitara had missed his vivacious and charming presence, and blamed herself for his death at Hagar's hands.

"Is there nothing you can do to bring Hagar to justice?"

The King sighed with a shake of his head, his white hair flicking over his face like a shadow. "I wish there was, my child, but there was no credible witness who could identify Hagar as the murderer. Besides, the people have become so infatuated with this warrior that such a charge would more than likely lead to rioting in the streets."

Kitara bit her lip angrily. She had only to admit to her trips under disguise into the city, and Hagar could be charged for his crime. She could not admit to her actions, however, having sworn to him that she would do it no more, after he had found out the first time. She was his most cherished child, for she reminded him so much of her mother, dead since her childhood.

"We can only hope he will be beaten in this tournament," mused the King softly. "It is very possible this year. There are many who can match him, including the Master from the Astral City. Thorgast the Barbarian will also prove more than a match for Hagar, I am sure."

Kitara could not argue, but silently wondered if Kalamar's other young companion would not also prove his match. He had survived a pass against Hagar the night before, and was still alive this day.

"Anyhow, time will only tell. Keep well, my child. I shall arrange the funeral for Llewellyn tomorrow if you would like to attend. I will understand if you do not. He was a dear friend, to you most of all."

Kitara smiled wistfully but found herself crying softly as her father's figure receded through the doorway. Kicking the door closed with a crash, she ran into the bedroom and hurled herself onto the bed, wishing Andrak was home, not in Brek. He would console her and tell her that what had happened was not her fault, and probably make her laugh.

"Please come home, Andrak. Please."

Chapter 30

"*Now* that is a tale in itself," warned Kalamar with a wry smile. Valdieron had asked how he had managed on his way to Thorhus from Tyr. "I must admit, however, that without your horse, I would never have made it. He kept me out of trouble and kept going when I wanted to give up. We traveled for three days non-stop after you left us, until we came across the first village where my wounds were tended."

"And Shakk?"

"Getting lazy in the stables here," assured Kalamar. I fear you may have trouble budging him from there. The Princess has grown fond of him and rides him regularly, so she will miss him."

"Well, I am not going anywhere until after the tournament and Llewellyn's burial."

Kalamar nodded. "I spoke briefly with King Dhoric, and he has in mind a ceremony on the morrow for Llewellyn. It may surprise you to know that Llewellyn was once the court Bard before he took his most recent sojourn into the north."

Valdieron turned to Thorgast in surprise. "He spoke little about his past," answered the big man with a shrug.

"Well, to say that he was well received would be an understatement. His music was special, no matter how much he played it down, and many were touched by his talents."

"Can we be there?" asked Valdieron hesitantly.

"Of course," smiled Kalamar quickly. "In fact, the King would have you rest here the night again. He has sent men to assist with the cleaning of the Inn."

"We do not want to impose, Kalamar," began Valdieron humbly. "We already have these clothes," he motioned to the new clothes Kalamar had arranged for them while they bathed.

"Nonsense, Valdieron. If we were to turn you away with a wash and some clothes after what you did for me, then I would be ungrateful to say the least. Do you have any idea what you helped me do?"

Valdieron shrugged.

"I told you I was a spy when we escaped, and that I was

investigating the theft and sale of poached horses throughout the realms. The group who captured you were terrorizing horse breeders throughout Ariakus, but we could never infiltrate their group. I was able to gather enough documentation to bring them to justice, but if they had thwarted my return to Thorhus, they would still be abroad, and I would most likely be lying in a shallow grave somewhere."

"Was it that bad?" asked Valdieron. He had heard little of such groups, and had known of nobody from the village losing horses.

"Aye. This group was located in Tyr, not far from where we were camped that night, though they had only recently moved there."

Valdieron was surprised at this. He had heard or seen nothing to indicate this group's presence. He wondered if the Trolls' attack on his village was not indirectly related to their existence.

"Well, I am glad to have been of assistance," assured Valdieron. Although his father had not sold many horses, any loss would have come as a great blow to him. Knowing what it was like without Shakk for the last half year, he wondered how he would feel if the horse were taken from him without warning.

"That is one threat we are well rid of, and I am certain others will follow." He clapped Valdieron warmly on the shoulder. "I know that is little recompense for you, considering what you have suffered, but many will be in your debt, especially me."

Valdieron felt uncomfortable with talk about debts, so he concentrated on his food for a time, savoring the many exotic tastes. That which he had eaten at the Inn had appeared fit for a King, but this before him was even more lavish.

After a time, Kalamar shook his head as if in disbelief, a wry smile playing across his face. "I would never have believed this if I hadn't seen it with my own eyes. Many times I have hoped you would find me, yet when you do you are even more of an enigma than when we first met. That you are here to fight in the tournament should come as no surprise. I think I may even have a little wager on the result."

"Yeah, well I wouldn't bet too much of your money if I were you," smirked Valdieron. "I fear I overestimate my skills, and will not have much success. Besides, I don't even have my sword."

"I noticed that earlier. What happened to it? It was a weapon of unsurpassed quality."

Valdieron sighed, wishing he had not mentioned his stolen sword. "It was taken from me."

"By whom?" asked Kalamar, incredulous. "Brigands on the road, perchance?"

Valdieron shook his head. "If only it were," he whispered. "No. It was taken from me by one from the Thieves Guild here in the city."

Kalamar appeared stern though not greatly surprised. "How can this be?"

With his background, Valdieron knew the Spy would probably know the workings of the Thieves Guild better than most. He told the story of his ambush and the taking of his sword, during which Kalamar sat in stony silence. "I intend to get it back, however, even if I have to tear down the city to do so."

Kalamar was silent for a time, then a wide smile broke his face and he laughed. "And I dare say you would," he barked humorously. "There is no need, however."

"How so?" interjected Thorgast sharply, suspecting something in the spy's words. "Can you help somehow?"

"Possibly," answered Kalamar thoughtfully. He looked about the empty eating hall. He was pensive for a time, then rose. "Come. I have something to show you."

Bemused, Valdieron and Thorgast followed him. The hall was in the lower level of the sleeping quarters, and up one flight of stairs were Kalamar's quarters, at the eastern edge overlooking the garden. It was one large room divided by partitions for his study, bedroom and personal bathing area. He led them to a large wardrobe, which was locked. The spy unlocked it with a key from around his neck and pulled it open.

"A ladder!" breathed Valdieron, seeing a dark Portal in the floor with a ladder reaching down in the darkness. "But where..."

Kalamar retrieved a nearby lantern and lit it. Realization dawned on Valdieron.

"You're a member of the Guild!"

"You could say that," said Kalamar, not denying the statement. Valdieron baulked briefly as he motioned for them to precede him down into the darkness, handing the lantern to Thorgast who stepped forward. He guessed that Kalamar would not bring them here unless he had good reason, and he assumed the spy would let no harm come to them.

The shaft was deeper than Valdieron had guessed, and he wondered where it passed through the lower level of the building, probably the kitchen somewhere. He counted the smooth rungs, seventy-eight in total before his foot touched stone floor.

Thorgast stood to the side of the ladder, his hand clutching the haft of his great axe as he raised the lantern above them, but his face was calm as he waited for Kalamar to descend. They were in a square room fifteen feet in diameter with a wooden door set to either side. Kalamar led them to the left door and pulled it open.

A dark passage led away from them, fading into darkness as the lantern danced across the smooth walls. At regular intervals unlit torches were set in plain sconces. They passed through one door, which Kalamar unlocked and continued to follow the passage for many minutes until it opened into a larger chamber.

"A sentry chamber," indicated Kalamar, looking down the three other passages, as if expecting to see some others. "Our presence will be known by now."

Whether that was good or not, Valdieron did not want to ask. Kalamar led them down the largest of the exits, passing other passages and rooms. Figures skipped past, dark and hidden, obviously Thieves who flashed Kalamar hand signals, which the spy returned wordlessly.

"Isn't it a little dangerous to have passages right under the palace?" asked Thorgast after a time, obviously ill at ease in these cramped passages, the low roofs causing him to stoop slightly for faster passage.

"Danger or convenience?" asked Kalamar in turn. "The Guild knows the rules. The passages are particularly good for others and myself. I do not have to leave my chamber to come here."

Valdieron did not doubt news of their presence was being spread as an expectant buzz preceded them. They entered another two sentry chambers, and Kalamar guided them unerringly into new passages. Valdieron thought they were going around in circles, and was totally lost.

"We must hurry," urged Kalamar as he ushered them along. Valdieron looked to Thorgast who shrugged with no answers.

After a short time they came to a door at the end of the corridor and found it locked.

"Would you do the honors, my friend?" asked Kalamar, turning to the big Barbarian. Thorgast nodded and stepped to the door. With a single powerful kick, the door crashed inwards, accompanied by the splintering of wood and surprised curses and exclamations from those beyond. Kalamar nodded his thanks and led the two into the room.

It was a personal chamber, markedly different from the oppressive corridors without. Wood-lined walls covered with paintings and tapestries adorned it, and it had several pieces of furniture throughout. It was a single room, with an area for sleeping set at one end. A large fire burned in a mantled hearth in both left and right walls.

Several figures occupied the room, a mix of young and old men, standing around another figure who stared in disbelief as the three entered. He was dressed in puffed leather pants of gray and green and wore a shirt of dark gray. He was young, though some years older than Kalamar. His hair was a sandy brown, long and tied at the back and his face showed the stubble of a few days unshaven. His hand rested on the familiar hilt of a sword hanging at his waist.

Feeling his anger boil, Valdieron almost stepped forward to attack him. Kalamar laid a restraining hand on his shoulder. The other figures around the room had hardly moved at their arrival, but he sensed their alertness as they stood with hands close to weapons.

"Going somewhere, Kalel?" inquired Kalamar softly, looking around the rooms at signs of packing.

"Kalamar. I had not known you were back in the city," answered the man, a wide smile sweeping his handsome face.

"Why? Have you been awaiting my arrival? You must know I come and go as I please, Kalel."

"Why, of course. There are things which must be discussed between us."

Kalamar nodded with a smile. "You are right. One such matter concerns the sword you wear. May I ask where you got it?"

Kalel paled briefly. "It concerns you not, but suffice to say I came upon it from a friend."

"You lie!" accused Valdieron with a snarl, stepping forward again. Two of the Thieves closest to him squared off and drew slender sabers. Valdieron halted and pointed at Kalel. "That is my sword, and I want it back."

"What is this?" stammered Kalel, showing surprising recovery. He had not recognized Valdieron, and it was obvious he had not seen Valdieron's face on the occasion when he had taken his sword. "You cannot come here and accuse me of theft. Where is your proof?" He turned to Kalamar with a questioning sneer. "You of all people know that such claims need proof to be even heard."

"And you should know that keeping booty for yourself without consulting the other leaders is against our code, Kalel."

"Like I said, Kalamar, the sword was given to me by a friend. I could have this boy flogged for his accusation."

"Only if there is proof on your behalf that the sword was indeed given to you," Kalamar stated. He looked to the other thieves in the room and left the words hanging, though none of the others spoke in Kalel's defense, despite the looks Kalel gave them. It was obvious that although they were Kalel's cronies, they did not want to side against Kalamar.

"Which leaves us but two options," continued Kalamar. "The first one is for you to confess your wrongdoing and give the sword back, accepting the punishment of our order for your crime." He smiled mockingly, knowing Kalel would do no such thing. "Or, you can accept the challenge of ownership by martial superiority."

Kalel grinned maliciously. "You are serious? And who will I fight, you or his big companion?"

"You will fight me!" interceded Valdieron calmly. "Unless you fear to face me when my hands aren't tied and my face visible?"

Kalel darkened as the insult struck a nerve. He grasped the hilt of the Dragon Sword and pulled it free. "Come, let us see who deserves to wield this."

Kalamar shook his head. "That is not allowed, Kalel. Fight with another sword, as honor demands."

"To the voids with honor," snarled Kalel and leapt forward, lunging at Valdieron. Kalamar and Thorgast danced away as

Valdieron drew Llewellyn's rapier from his belt and barely pushed the attack aside.

The speed of his parry caught the thief by surprise, and Kalel stepped away with a trickle of blood running from a narrow gash in his shoulder. He laughed it off and swung the sword around him with the élan of a show-off, the blade slicing through the air like a whisper of death.

Kalel was a skilled fighter, but he was no match for Valdieron. The thief had speed, reflexes and a cunning mind, but Valdieron was fighting with passion and determination. Seeing his own sword used against him and with Llewellyn's death so recent, Val was fired up to the point where he became oblivious to all save the fight.

To his credit, Kalel fought well, but he knew from the start he would not win. He made desperate maneuvers, hoping to catch the young warrior out, and they did to a certain degree, but not enough to bring him any opportunities to end the fight.

Having no intention of killing the man, Valdieron started to look for ways of disarming or knocking out the outmatched thief. He tried once to slam the pommel of the rapier into his face as they locked together in a close parry, but Kalel twisted like a cat and his sword snapped around the rapier, slicing cross Valdieron's ribs. Snarling against the pain, Valdieron watched the thief dance away with a cruel smile on his face.

The thief thrust next, trying to press the advantage while Valdieron was wounded, but Valdieron saw his chance instantly. Stepping into the thrust he pushed it away to the right so the thief was suddenly side on to him. His left hand clamped down on the hilt of the Dragon Sword, and simultaneously swept his left leg around Kalel's ankle, seeking to throw him off balance.

The thief could not recover from the surprising sweep, and felt his feet spinning out from under him. With a twist of the sword hilt, Valdieron set the blade spinning out of the thief's hands, catching it before it struck the ground. He stepping back as Kalel rolled cautiously away, expecting to be struck while down. He came to his feet, twin daggers coming into his hands from concealed places. His face was a mask of anger, but there was unconcealed fear in his eyes. He cast a quick glance at the other thieves in the room. All were standing with weapons drawn, but none had made a move as yet to help Kalel.

"Well, what are you waiting for?" he snarled at them, but his eyes turned to Kalamar, who was staring calmly around the room.

The thieves looked from Kalel to Kalamar, weighing the pressure from their leader against the influence and power of the Spy. Four of the thieves lowered their weapons and stepped away, but the two others stepped forward with defiant sneers. Thorgast reached for his axe and took a step forward, but Kalamar restrained him with a hand on the arm.

"This is his fight," he said solemnly, though his hand was also resting on the hilt of his saber.

Valdieron lifted his eyes from Kalel for a moment and turned to them. Seeing them still standing there made him pause, but he realized that what he had started, he must finish himself. He saluted them with his sword and turned as the thieves closed in, surprised to find Kalel hanging away from the melee, waiting and watching.

The two thieves, both armed with sabers, flanked Valdieron, and he spread his arms so his swords faced both of them. He stepped back to give himself a better angle, but they moved further around so that they were on opposite sides.

Knowing he could not let the Thieves make a concerted attack, he turned to the left thief who was closest to him. The thief snapped his saber into a thrust and stepped back quickly as Val's swords came over in a double parry. Val spun to face the other thief who came in from behind. Fast and agile, the thief was already slashing at him with a huge overhead chop. Valdieron arced his Rapier, catching the slender blade in its descent and swept it to the side. Out of the corner of his eye he saw the flickering shadow of the second thief with sword raised high for a chop at him.

He distantly heard Thorgast yell as he stepped back, reversing the dragon sword in his left hand down under his shoulder so that the point thrust backwards as he pulled his arm back. He heard the thief gasp with shock and then scream in pain as the dragon sword pierced his chest, grinding against bone. Blood lined the sword as he jerked it free, its tip coated with crimson as he stepped to the side. The thief toppled where he had been standing.

The second thief stared momentarily at his fallen companion as Valdieron wavered. He had reacted instinctively, but had not intended to kill the thief. He slapped the next attack aside, wishing the thief would surrender. The thief seemed unconcerned by being outmatched, happy to dance out of Valdieron's reach after each attack. Valdieron wondered dimly at the tactics. When a stabbing pain erupted in his lower back he realized the tactics had been a diversion. He staggered forward in surprised pain, almost impaling himself on the thief's lunging sword. He batted it away and punched the hilt of his rapier into the thief's face. The thief stumbled back and collapsed, but Valdieron did not notice as he looked around at the dagger protruding from his back. He knew Kalel had not advanced to attack, but launched the dagger from where he stood off to the side.

Thorgast was bellowing a cry of outrage and Kalamar streaked past him as he stumbled to his knees. He could feel the wound like a cold touch against his skin, and it spread a numbing pain through his every nerve. He fought its embrace, urging his muscles to respond, but he found himself slipping into darkness as his vision blurred. In the distance he heard shouting and a clang of steel, but then he was floating and wondered with his last consciousness, if he was dying.

Chapter 31

The incessant tugging of a haunting dirge stirred Valdieron from the dark forgetfulness of sleep. He blinked through weary eyes as the sunlit white room surrounded him, but he soon grew accustomed to it and looked around warily, the events of the fight coming back to him.

This was no room in the thieves' Undercity, and he guessed it was the palace. The room was large, with carved furniture of stained wood, the bed itself large and canopied with a silk curtain. There was a window on his right, and outside the bright morning light was visible, though the sky was dark and foreboding. A fire was burning low in the wall at the foot of the bed, a large steel mesh set before it to catch any stray sparks.

The low music of many instruments echoed from outside and he sat up, groaning as his sleeping body stirred and he felt his injuries. He shrugged aside the heavy blankets, feeling the cool air on his naked body and he swept his legs over the side to stand. He felt at the wound he had received in his back. A heavy bandage encircled his abdomen, so he could not see the extent of his injury, though it felt good if not a little tender. The gash across his ribs he found surprisingly healed, a long, white scar the only indication it had existed.

He padded to the window and gazed out over the rain-splashed garden, which looked more like a maze of hedges and patches of flowers from his height. Guards stood forlornly around the perimeter, and a larger group of figures was gathered in the center of the garden near a marble statue. It was carved in the figure of a man with strong, proud features and wearing a heavy crown. A huge sword was strapped across his back, and a wreath of real flowers hung from his strong shoulders. Worn with age, Valdieron felt awed by its nobility.

A large wooden coffin was set on the ground at the base of the statue, half covered by a large white shroud. In a semi-circle around the coffin stood several musicians, playing lute, harp and flute in a mingling tune of somber tone. At this distance he saw the Princess Kitara was one of the musicians, dressed in a large coat and playing the old Harp she had been playing at the

Inn.

With a curse he realized this was Llewellyn's funeral. Casting about the room he spied his clothes and dressed hastily, unmindful of his wounds. He tucked Llewellyn's rapier through his belt and pushed his own sword under the bed before exiting and searching for the way to the garden.

A cold, soft rain drizzled from dark clouds. Two guards flanked the doorway, but hardly noticed him as he stepped past them. He noted the music had faded and a deep, powerful voice was rising through the thick air. He recognized it as that of the King, but more emotional and strained than he had heard the day before in the Throne room.

"...and although he was not of Thorhus and counted the open land his home, I know he held something in his heart for this city and its people."

"That Llewellyn of Lloreander was one of the greatest Bards of our time is undisputable, as is his reputation as a friend and companion for those who were not necessarily deserving of it. His love for people, whether kin or of the other races, was surpassed only by his love for his music."

As Valdieron closed on the ceremony, the King paused and he looked up to see him smile wryly. "I remember as a youth, I was in awe of him, and he would always pause to speak with me at my will, not because I was the heir to the throne, but because he wanted to speak with me. For that I have always held him in the highest regard, and will always remember him."

Valdieron stopped at the edge of the crowd; his head bowed solemnly as he listened to the King's stirring words. He was glad for the light rain to mask the tears running down his face. He tried to smile for he knew Llewellyn would not want him to mourn his passing. He noticed two stone doors opened in the base of the statue; leading underground to where he guessed was a vault. He felt eyes on him and turned to see Kalamar gazing at him with a concerned frown, his own dark hair dripping and his dark cloak clinging to him.

"Therefore," continued Dhoric, "I have decreed that Llewellyn shall rest in the vault of Temorial, with my ancestors. So shall his memory ever be remembered with the house of Temorial."

Valdieron staggered forward as several guards moved to the

coffin, feeling the eyes of many on him. As the guards bent to hoist the coffin he dropped to his knees before it, laying a tentative hand on the cold wood. Tears ran unashamedly down his cheeks as he choked on his words. "You were my friend for only a short time, and you understood me and supported me when I needed it. I will always remember you, my friend. Sleep well!"

He took a step back and another figure shifted past him. He lifted his head slightly, smelling faint rose-scented perfume, and recognized the Princess Kitara, her head also bowed so her long, soaked hair hid her face. She carried her harp protectively against her chest but held it out and rested it on the casket. Valdieron stepped back further, watching the Princess but giving her privacy. If she said anything he did not hear. When she was done, she spun and strode quickly back to her father's side and he rested an arm around her shoulders as she buried her face against him.

The guards shifted after the pause and marched towards the vault. The entry was immense, so they did not have to stoop to enter. They marched down the stairs into the dim interior. The low music started up again, and Valdieron wished it had been a livelier tune, which the Elf would have appreciated more. After a short time, the guards returned and eased the heavy doors closed and sealed the vault. With a hushed murmuring the crowd drifted away, and Valdieron felt a soft hand on his shoulder. He turned to find Thorgast and Kalamar there.

"Valdieron, you should be abed," warned Kalamar softly, showing concern that he was up and walking.

"I couldn't miss this," returned Valdieron sternly, for he did feel well, if not a little tired.

Kalamar merely nodded and Thorgast spoke.

"I will be returning to the Inn now. Are you coming?"

Valdieron shook his head slowly. "I wish to see Shakk first, but I will be there later."

Thorgast nodded and turned to Kalamar. "Farewell."

Kalamar bid him farewell and the big barbarian strode from the garden.

"I too have business which cannot wait," explained Kalamar, his gaze lingering on the closed vault doors. He laid a comforting hand on Valdieron's shoulder. "The guards have been instructed to let you walk the palace unhindered. If you need me for anything, do not hesitate to find me."

Valdieron nodded as Kalamar drifted away, his footsteps leaving a trail on the damp ground. He did not stay long, not wanting to linger on his lamentations, and turned back towards the palace. The garden was silent and there were no more guards at the doorways.

The quarters were not busy, with only several maids and cleaners moving about, so he stopped briefly in the room he had awoken in to swap Llewellyn's rapier for his dragon sword.

The stables were set under the ramparts of the inner bailey they had been led through the previous day as prisoners. It was large, with a single large door reinforced with iron. Inside it was clean and well kept with a long row of wooden stalls. It was probably for the horses of the royal family, he mused, seeing some of the stalls empty. Other stalls housed horses of quality. Usually he would have marveled at these great animals, but his gaze dropped on one of the horses down the line and he stopped with a great smile. He whistled sharply, and the dark horse wheeled.

There was instant recognition in his large red eyes as he reared as much as the high stall would allow, his whinnying causing a stir from the other horses before Valdieron managed to quiet him with a hug. Shakk almost threw him to the ground with his antics, and he slapped the big horse firmly but joyfully.

"You haven't changed a bit, have you?" he joked, stepping back to cast a critical eye over Shakk. It was obvious he was being treated well in the royal stables, something he knew the horse would not soon grow weary of.

He set his sword down and vaulted into the stall, pushing the excited horse away so he wouldn't get crushed. He gently ran a hand over Shakk, checking him thoroughly. He appeared more muscled than Valdieron remembered, probably as a result of the long journey from Tyr to Thorhus. His hide was glowing, an indication of his health, and his tail and mane were braided and intertwined with delicate silver ribbons. His hooves were also new, and appeared softer, probably to compensate for the hardness of the cobbled roads here in the city.

"Well, at least they take care of you here, boy" he said. Shakk had returned to his food after the joy of being reunited had worn off. "And I see you get plenty of exercise."

There was a silvery peal of laughter from nearby and he whirled, feeling suddenly self-conscious speaking to a horse. His surprise turned to nervousness, however, as he saw Princess Kitara standing at the stable's arched entry. A fur-lined gray cloak covered a long white dress beneath. She wore high boots, slender and traced with silver, and her hair was tied back in a tail. A small bag hung over her shoulder, and he could not be sure but the hilt of a weapon seemed to bulge at her left hip.

"Do you always speak with animals suchlike?" she asked, her pale lips pressed into a tight smile.

Valdieron coughed in embarrassment and turned back to Shakk, who shifted forward in the stall as Kitara entered, neighing as if in greeting. The princess strode forward with a fond smile, raising one slender hand outstretched, holding a small cube of sweet sugar, which Shakk carefully lifted between his teeth, and chewed.

"I spend most of my time with them," answered Valdieron softly, remembering his childhood days when Shakk and Ruff had been constant companions. He knew few other young people from the village, and the farm's isolation made it difficult for him to see them more than several times in a year.

"Well, at least they don't tell you what you can and cannot do," sighed Kitara wistfully. She ran a hand through her bedraggled hair, wet from the rain. "If I hear another member of my family tell me what I should and should not do, I will scream until they all think I am mad and stay away."

Val guessed that with the sudden insurgence of people into the city for the tournament, the Princess was limited in her freedom to leave the palace. He knew she had needed the magical mask to let her escape the other night to play at the Inn, and realized her father had most likely forbidden her from leaving the palace at all. Yet by her appearance, she was intent on going riding. Although the castle grounds were large, she would not need the traveling bag or weapon that he was sure was hidden beneath her cloak.

"Going for a ride?"

The princess started and turned from where she was stroking Shakk's long mane. Her blue eyes darkened like a pool shadowed by cloud. She looked around briefly, as if frightened he had spoken too loud or somebody was within earshot. She frowned briefly and narrowed her eyes, but merely sighed ruefully. "I need to think, and I cannot do that surrounded by doting family members or dutiful servants. It has been some time since I have ridden, and I thought what better way for me to get away for a while?"

"I take it your father doesn't warrant leaving the grounds without permission. Surely he has some reason for this?"

Kitara began to scowl, but instead nodded acquiescence. "He thinks that with so many strangers in the city, some factions not loyal to him may seek to grab an upper hand. He fears that every dark street holds an ambush for me, or every turn an arrow."

"And Hagar?"

Kitara cursed vehemently, making Valdieron rock back with shock. He had heard worse over the last few months, but never had he expected such from the Princess. "I do not think he has concerns for Hagar stealing me away." She sighed disdainfully. "Why should he when Hagar may have my hand anyway after he wins the tournament?"

"*If he wins,*" whispered Valdieron. His resolve hardened again as he remembered the silent vow he had made to avenge Llewellyn's heartless slaying. He would do that at the tournament, before the amassed populace. He saw the incredulous look Kitara cast at him, however, and realized he must have spoken out loud.

"You aren't really entering the tournament are you?"

He nodded gloomily.

Kitara chuckled softly, but his stern gaze made her cease. "You aren't joking?" He shook his head. "But, you are so young. Why? This is not a game, you know. People have been killed in this tournament."

Could he tell her the reasons for his entry? He had only wanted to enter the tournament at first because it had been a marvel to him. To be present with some of the greatest fighters in the realms would be an awesome experience. It would also enable him to match his newfound skills with more experienced and powerful warriors. He guessed that many trials and tribulations would stand between him and his goal of finding the pieces of the Disk of Akashel, and his martial skills may need to be enough to carry him through, and out of, trouble.

But could he also tell her of his newest reason? Tell her that he would never let her be taken by Hagar?

That the Dak'marian had ignoble intentions for the Princess was almost assured considering his actions the other night. A sudden thought struck him.

"How did he know you?"

Kitara turned to him questioningly.

"How did Hagar know you the other night at the Inn? Did he recognize your voice, as did I, or did he see through the power of the mask?"

Kitara frowned as she shook her head, brushing wet strands from her face. "I do not know, to be honest. I have asked myself that selfsame question many times."

Valdieron frowned, but Kitara turned away. She moved to a bench nearby and bent to grasp a saddle. "Coming?"

"You can't be serious?" asked Valdieron bemusedly. If her father had forbidden her to leave the palace and she did, if they were found out it would be he who would be frowned upon. Considering his earlier run-in with the King, that was something he didn't need.

Kitara laughed, and it was without the undertone of sorrow he had noticed earlier. She hefted the saddle to one of the stalls nearby and fussed over it momentarily before turning back to him. He gasped involuntarily, seeing now the face of Cari-Ann before him, and he realized she had donned the magical mask. She laughed again at his shock, and it was the same laugh, but her skin was paler, and her features almost completely different. "The guards will merely think you are riding with Cari-Ann, the serving girl from the kitchens."

With a disbelieving chuckle Valdieron rose. He had not expected this. He would rather have been back at the Inn, helping clean up, or concentrating on his training. He was never comfortable with strangers, and had always been the quiet type, who would listen and learn rather than speak. Now he was in the company of the daughter of one of the most powerful men in the realms, and he felt totally inadequate. Her very presence made him nervous.

Kitara was almost done saddling her own horse, a tall dapple mare of only a few years. He hurriedly moved to Shakk and set the saddle in place, securing it quickly. He had no blanket to put under it, though he hardly ever used one.

Leading Shakk from the stall was a task unto itself as the big horse tried to shuffle past. He followed Kitara, trying not to stare at her athletic body beneath the heavy cloak. He did keep an eye on people passing, however, waiting fearfully for the call from someone who recognized Kitara. He copied the Princess as she mounted her mare and walked her slowly from the palace.

Valdieron could not guess at how he looked as they exited the palace under the close scrutiny of the guards. They began to cut the two riders off, but the recognition of either Valdieron or Cari-Ann seemed to appease them. Kalamar had said he would spread the word that he was not to be accosted on exiting the palace. Kitara looked at him and winked as they passed under the towering parapets. He almost fell from the saddle, fearing it had been witnessed by one of the guards and recognized for what it was. There were no shouts of alarm, however, and they passed from the palace without pause.

"I knew we could do it," whooped Kitara as they moved far enough away from the gates not to be heard. Not that they were free yet, having yet to clear the castle gates.

Once free of the gates, Valdieron began to breathe a little easier, though he did glance over his shoulder occasionally or start when he saw the ocean-blue tabards of soldiers in the King's livery. At his side, Kitara laughed at his apprehension, but he saw her also studying their surroundings warily.

They followed the road to the north first, wide and less populated as it wound through the wealthier suburb. Valdieron found that the houses were built more for purpose than for show. Although many were expensive and beautiful, with plush gardens, marble pillars and silver-gilded walls, they were made for strength. He also noted the right-angled streets, which Llewellyn had once told him was a basis of defense. The buildings were high, most with rooftop balconies where archers could wait in ambush, while doors were strengthened by flanking beams of stone or hardwood. He wondered if war had ever ravaged the city, and if so, when?

With the rain clearing, the streets became more crowded as they skirted to the east and turned south. They passed the great academy, a wide, narrow building some several stories high and built of huge sandstone blocks. Its weathered appearance indicated an age beyond even that of the castle and palace, though many places showed reconstruction and repair. It was plain, with many narrow windows and railed balconies. A wide, clear lawn was set before it, with several arrays of statues, their arrangements holding no meaning for Valdieron. Llewellyn had told him that people were taught many things there, from poetry to economics. He wondered if it might hold something he would be interested in. He assumed their library must be vast, and wondered if he would see it one day.

The east gate, like its western counterpart, was a heavily fortified portcullis and gate arrangement surmounted by twin barbicans and wide ramparts for archer positioning. It lay open, allowing passage for the populace. The few who entered or left beneath it were mainly farmers and outlanders coming and going on business or those entering for the tournament. He realized there were seventeen days remaining until the trial. He had much to do to prepare himself, but looking across at the princess, he would not have been anywhere else at that moment.

The shadow of the gate passing over him made him think of the gallows. The road from the gates turned to dirt and rock as it sloped sharply down to the drawbridge. Dark waters rushed below, slightly tinged with brown as a reminder of the recent rain. Droplets of rain rested on the grass, like an ocean of glistening diamonds split by the winding brown road.

With a sigh of relief, Kitara looked back over her shoulder at the looming city walls. There were few people about, and she peeled the mask away, revealing her beautiful features. She secreted the mask beneath her cloak.

"Where are we going?" asked Valdieron skeptically. Although he felt more at ease out of the hustle and bustle of the city, he realized now that Kitara had revealed herself, they were susceptible to being caught out. He could almost feel the eyes of the parapet guards on his back as they walked the horses along the road.

Kitara merely flashed him a roguish smile and spurred her horse forward. The gray mare leapt forward, long-legged and strong. Shakk trembled and started, pulling at the reins sharply as Valdieron took a deep breath and sighed. "Well, don't you think they've gone far enough?"

Shakk turned his big head and eyed him coldly, and it made Valdieron think of happier times. The stallion snorted, derisively it seemed, and then leapt forward, nearly throwing Valdieron whose laughing curses only spurred the great horse on.

Their chase followed the widening river as it wound languorously to the southeast through several hollows and ravines, which were cleared of trees for an uninhibited view from the parapets. Further on, sparse trees sprang up, until an almost constant line flashed between him and the slow, sparkling water.

Shakk pursued the long-legged gray as if it were a game. He zigzagged between trees and over sharp inclines, hurdling small obstructions such as bushes, boulders or felled trees. He drew level with the mare after a time and slowed to keep pace, drifting and drawing near as the terrain allowed. Valdieron marveled at the beauty of the princess as she rode. Her long hair trailed behind her, and her tanned face was alive with glee as she urged her mount to greater speed. Her smile was wide as she turned occasionally to look over at him.

Water erupted around him and he gave a start, not realizing she had led them to a wide fiord in the river, neither deep nor fast flowing, its bottom more sand and mud than rock. He shook his face free of spray as they topped the small rise on the far shore, and laughed. Shakk, as sure-footed as ever, was ahead of the mare and Valdieron wheeled him to the left where he spotted a shallow glade surrounded by fir and birch. A single willow leaned over to trail, its slender branches trailing into the slow-moving water.

Kitara was also laughing as she drew up alongside him in the glade. Her hair and face were flecked with water, and the bottom of her long cloak was soaked, but her pale blue eyes flashed with joy. "Whew! I wish I could do that every day."

Valdieron vaulted from Shakk, and stepped to her horse to help Kitara down, but she slipped easily from the mare, landing lightly. She removed her cloak quickly and draped it over the mare's flank before slapping the mare softly. The two horses wandered away slowly, looking for the fresh grass that lined the glade.

"I had almost forgotten what it was like to ride," lamented Valdieron softly, turning away to look at the river. "There was a time not too long back when I wondered if I would ever see Shakk again, let alone ride him."

"Shakk? Is that Elvish?" Kitara was at his side, wringing her hair free of excess water. He glimpsed the hilt of a weapon at her hip, a carved hilt in the form of an eagle's head atop the slender blade of a saber. Removing the small bag from her back, she knelt and drew out her old harp, checking it for moisture.

Valdieron shrugged. "I don't know. I read it in a book somewhere, I think."

Kitara pursed her lips in thought. "I think it is Elvish, though abridged from its extended name. I think it means Wind Dancer. If I am correct, your horse is aptly named."

Valdieron gasped at the translation. Was this some coincidence? What had he read that would speak of Wind Dancers? A lot of what he had read had been snatches of volumes during brief visits to the library, so he had little idea. It was ironic he had named Shakk thus, with him having begun to learn the fighting style of the Wind Dancers, yet its link with Llewellyn pained him.

"Is something wrong?" Kitara regarded him with a slight frown, and he realized he was brooding.

"No, nothing," he replied, managing a dismissive smile. "Where did you learn to ride like that?"

Kitara had produced a fine bone-handled comb and was running it through her hair. Even wet and unkempt she was beautiful, and he was glad she did not see him studying her briefly before she turned to him.

"It was part of my upbringing. I was required to ride from an early age for public appearances and marches. Besides, I have always loved horses and the freedom riding allows. My brother Andrak and I rode often, before he became old enough for father to use him as an envoy." She sniffed sadly, her voice distant with thought. "You?"

He gave a brief start, thinking she had lapsed into a pensive silence. "My father and brother taught me. I grew up on a farm, and my father bred horses, so it was a matter of course, you could say."

"Bred?" The princess had caught onto his words, and he winced with previously suppressed pain. She did not continue, maybe glimpsing his unease, or maybe the single word had been a question in itself.

"He is dead, now. They both are." Though the words were

strangled, they passed more easily than they had when he had spoken of his ordeals with Llewellyn. He wondered if he would ever become so detached that he could speak of it without pain? He hoped not. Slowly, with a little prompting, he told her his story. Though little time had passed, his story encompassed many deeds. It was hard to believe all that had really happened in a season and a half. All through it, Kitara was silent, though she gasped with shock and sorrow when he told of his father's death and the death of Nagus' granddaughter. He saw her eyes moisten and become flecked with gray.

Of course he did not tell her of the things he wished to remain secret, like the Dragon's tear, the pieces of the Disk of Akashel, and the Demons. She smiled briefly when he told of his meeting Llewellyn at Ranil, but was stunned at the telling of their battle at the Devil's temple. She bit her lip, to keep from crying he thought, when he told of the young woman held captive. He had trouble continuing as he recalled the painful moment at which he had ended her pain. He half expected her to accuse him of murder, but she grasped his hand warmly and in support as he struggled for calm.

When he told of the loss and subsequent reclaiming of his sword from the thief, Kalel, she frowned. He wondered if she had been unaware of the extent of the Thieves guild. "I wonder why Kalamar did that?"

Valdieron frowned and shrugged. "He did what he could."

Kitara's peel of laughter surprised him. "I think Kalamar could have had this Kalel kneel before you and hand it to you on a gold tray." She bit her lip as if to cut off any further words or repent what she had just said. His wondering look made her sigh and look away briefly. "Kalamar is not only my father's chief spy, he is also the leader of the Thieves' Guild."

Valdieron stammered before rocking onto his back. He knew many, especially the lesser members of the guild, would not know this information. From the reaction of Kalel, the higher-ranking thief had known. He did not blame Kalamar for not doing more, knowing his identity could not be given away, especially in front of other thieves and two foreigners.

"How can this be?" he asked. He wondered how the King could warrant the Thieves' Guild being run by his own chief spy. He remembered Llewellyn had told him the guild was necessary. He guessed it was preferable to have it run by someone he could trust and compel. That way, he was able to regulate the laws and actions of this underworld group.

Kitara silently fingered the slender strings of the Harp, and he was content to listen, such was the mood of the quiet glade.

"Can you beat him?" The question came after a brief silence.

He did not have to be told of whom she spoke and he wanted very much to reassure her as she regarded him with hopeful eyes.

"No." He remembered the lightning fast attacks of the warrior at the Inn. He had held his own, but had been charged with anger and revenge. He saw her face darken, and the glimmer in her eyes fade, and he wished he had been able to lie to her. "Can it be that bad? I have heard stories..."

She sighed deeply in resignation before nodding. "I cannot think of a worse fate. You saw what he is capable of, and yet he would see me marry him. Something about a vague prophecy his people believe in. They have so many prophecies, I think most are just made up."

Valdieron felt his interest piqued by talk of prophecy, but he refrained from speaking more of it, seeing how pained she looked and how she felt about it. "Surely your father will not let it come to pass," he said instead.

Kitara scowled. "I hope so. Still, there are many who see it as only fitting, and cannot see beyond the fraudulent screen that surrounds him. The greatest warrior in the lands marries the beautiful daughter of the King of Ariakus." She looked as if she would spit, but did not.

"Well, if it makes you feel any better, I'll be trying my hardest in the tournament."

She turned to him with a smile that threatened to melt him. "Thanks." She turned her attention back to her harp and began to strum dreamily, a slow, pensive tune suited to their mood, free yet tinged with sadness. Valdieron lay back on the soft grass and closed his eyes. Her playing was excellent, and although he was not musically inclined, he had heard enough from Llewellyn in the past season that he could tell quality from amateurish street trash.

He dozed sleepily, his wounded body still recovering. When he awoke, long shadows had settled across the ground and a cool afternoon breeze swept low from across the river, softly rustling the leaves. He was not sure what had woken him. He sat up cautiously. Kitara lay dozing beside him on her side, facing him with her head on her arms. Her harp rested against her stomach. He would have been content to stay there and watch her for all time, and wished he could smooth the hair from her passive face. As if feeling his eyes on her, she shifted and woke, her eyes slowly opening, pale and flawless.

"We had better get back," he advised softly, turning away. Shakk and the mare were close by, the dark stallion keeping the mare from wandering off. "I have things to do at the Inn."

Kitara sighed, obviously wishing they did not have to return. "They'll probably have the whole guard looking for me by now." She giggled childishly, obviously seeing some humor in the thought, though it would probably mean more trouble for her.

Valdieron called Shakk over with a sharp whistle, and the mare followed slowly while Kitara packed her harp. He held the reins while she mounted. He leapt easily onto Shakk and followed her from the glade. Their pace was slow as they returned to the city, and he frowned. He had hoped the brief respite from the city would help settle his thoughts, but it had not. He escorted the now disguised Princess to the castle gates, where she entered without incident. She paused momentarily and turned to him.

"I had a pleasant time today, Valdieron. I hope we can do it again soon."

"We may be able to, if you aren't locked up by your father." He smiled at her and wheeled Shakk.

The vision of her remained with him, but it shifted and changed to another image he had of a platinum-haired young woman. They shifted back and forth, merging as often as not, and it seemed to hang on his mind for many days afterwards. Try as he might he could not shake it.

Chapter 32

The day of the tournament arrived, bringing with it an air of expectation. When he woke, the sun had not yet shown itself and was just a pale threat over the horizon. He rose, feeling refreshed and ready, though he knew many others in the city would not feel as he did.

The previous day, New Years Day, had seen the city transformed into a dazzling, energetic festival that had lasted well into the night. Food, wine and ale had passed freely, while people roamed the streets in costumes and varying guises, many carrying instruments and leading crowds in song. Valdieron had partaken of it to a small extent, though he steered clear of ale, seeing the effect it and the warm spring sun had on many others.

Despite Llewellyn's death and the rumors that had spread, The Hangman's Noose was filled to the rafters. Many rooms had been used for entertainment to accommodate the revelers. Servants scampered everywhere at a frenzied pace, carrying trays of wine and ale as well as food and other exotic treats.

Valdieron had spent almost all of his time over the last several days in the training hall. He had shifted a bed in and slept there when he remembered to, or when tiredness overcame him. Kaz slept in there also, and during the day he was kept in Llewellyn's old room where he seemed content to remain.

Throughout the city on the night of the Festival, pavilions and marquees were set up wherever there was room. Great feasts were prepared and shared, with many toasting the King who had paid for a lot of the festivities. Valdieron had wandered aimlessly through the streets, in awe of this festive spirit, which seemed to bring everybody together in good cheer. He passed the slums where the partying continued well into the next morning. He also looked towards the castle, wondering what Kitara was doing at the time. She was probably taking part in a grand ball or feast, which he would have loved to attend. He had returned to his bed feeling alone and homesick.

As he stepped carefully through the mass of sleeping bodies in the commons, he was surprised to hear some revelry still continued in the streets. He stepped into the warm morning air to the sound of drunken shouting and singing, though less boisterous than the previous night. He smiled at these people who were obviously enjoying themselves, but would probably not be feeling the best for the next day or two.

Luckily for many, the tournament did not start until midmorning. After a short walk he returned to the training hall. His sword, and Llewellyn's rapier, rested together beside his bedroll. The dim light seemed to burn brighter than usual, as if recognizing the importance of this day to him.

Kneeling before the Elvish tapestry, he wondered at the road that had brought him to this place. All thoughts of finding the pieces of the Disk of Akashel had been forced to the back of his mind of late, and he wondered if that was wise. He had been told time was an important factor in their retrieval, yet he had spent several weeks simply training and concentrating on the tournament. He did not even think he had a chance of winning, despite his ever-improving skills, but he wanted to do what he could to aid Kitara and avenge Llewellyn's death.

He stretched slowly and worked himself into a sweat running through forms and patterns he had learned over the weeks. He focused his mind, taking in everything from his weight distribution and the effort each move required. He had learned that swordplay was more than a brutal hack and slash game, but involved a complex array of interconnecting actions, like a dance, at least for those who wished to survive. He found the Wind Dancer techniques were only slightly different from those he was taught in the Dream Plane.

With the morning passing slowly he ceased his practice and changed clothes. He had been sent clothing from Kitara, which had surprised him, accompanied by a short note. It read:

Valdieron,
I have arranged for these clothes to be made for you. I hoped that you might wear them in the tournament. I will understand if you do not, but I helped design them with you in mind. It may appear gaudy to you at first, but I think they will suit you.

The clothes were indeed bold at the very least. They included a new pair of high boots. They were turned down, with the fold in the shape of semi-spread wings, like a bat's, only he knew she had meant them to be dragon's wings. The trousers were of strong yet thin material, not silk but somewhat akin. They were light gray, and stitched with silvery thread. The lace-up shirt was of matching material; the same color as her eyes, and the thread was golden instead of silver. Sinuous dragons wound their scaled bodies along the full sleeves, their heads resting on the shoulders. There were also two finely crafted silver bracers, bearing matching dragons of gold and bronze. He could feel their cold metal forms against his skin.

    He did indeed feel uncomfortable wearing them for their finery, but he conceded that the fit was more than comfortable. The loose material did not hinder him, but stretched to allow extended movement, and it seemed to circulate the air around his body rather than keep it in. The boots were a little loose, but he strapped them tight and found them surprisingly light.

    He had purchased a new thin belt some days ago, from which hung Llewellyn's rapier. A slender chain secured the tip of its scabbard to the belt at his back to keep it from dragging. Simple latches allowed for quick removal if necessary, but were strong and cunning enough not to be knocked loose.

    He intended to get the scabbard for his sword this morning, so he used his old scabbard and baldric. Its weight was reassuring on his back. He had his hair brushed back, secured by a chord in a large tail which extended some way past his shoulders. He had considered getting it cut, but he had come to like having it long, despite the inconvenience it sometimes caused.

    When he passed by the kitchen again it was alive with bustling movement. Gerkar noticed him almost instantly when he stepped through, the now owner of the Inn busily overseeing the preparations for the many morning meals that would be needed. He took a moment to have someone organize something for Valdieron before being called away on several other errands, though he did offer Valdieron luck before departing.

    Valdieron ate quickly; some meat, bread and cheese washed down with water. There would be vendors around the arena where he could purchase some food if he got hungry during the day, though he had survived on less than what he had just eaten when alone in the mountains. He patted the small purse of silver around his neck, the safest place he had found to carry money when walking the crowded streets. There should be plenty left after he purchased his scabbard and baldric. He returned his plate to the kitchen and asked one of the younger cooks, Alven, to see that Kaz was fed as well. The boy, some years younger than Valdieron, agreed with fear and excitement, having had the duty to feed the voracious cat on several occasions.

He did not see Thorgast before he left, but would meet him at the arena. Stepping out into the street, he became conscious of his appearance and donned a light traveling cloak of Llewellyn's he had borrowed. It covered him enough to hide his flashy clothing, though it was itself of excellent quality and cut. He wondered if he would be accosted for the coat, especially where he was going.

Thankfully, the morning was bright and clear, with few sparse clouds on the horizon. The streets were already packed and alive with excited overtones as the majority of people headed north to the castle. He skirted the main stream, winding his way to the slums, still not entirely at ease in the streets. City life was definitely not for him.

It may have been his imagination, but it seemed that many who passed seemed to study him, especially as he went further into the slums. He felt their eyes on him, and those he did see shied away when he locked gazes with them. He realized things had changed markedly since the last time he visited. This time he was dressed more guardedly, and his demeanor was less anxious and intimidated, indeed he was more intimidating, his cool gaze studying everything as he walked.

The gates to the smithy were slightly ajar when he arrived. He tapped politely on the thin metal and waited, hearing soft curses and scuffled footsteps approach before one of the gates creaked open some more. The young boy who had tended him previously, appeared.

"Are you closed, lad?" he asked mildly. The boy was dressed in his work clothes and apron, but was free of grime.

"Yes, sir, except if you have something to be picked up." The lad sized him up warily, not seeming to recognize him at first until his eyes spotted the hilt of Valdieron's sword over his shoulder.

"I have a sheath and baldric to pick up, if it is ready," he said softly, trying not to intimidate the boy.

"Ah, yes sir," stammered the lad. "Let me fetch it for you. Please, wait here!" That last bit came out in a youthful squeak, and Valdieron wondered why the lad would be afraid of him.

There was movement inside the Smith, movements too heavy for the boy, and then muffled talk before the boy skidded back into view, clutching a baldric and sheath wrapped in new leather belt with buckle.

"Sorry to keep you waiting, sir. Your equipment is ready." Val reached for it but the boy stepped back. He realized the boy was waiting for payment.

"Sorry. How much for the Smith's services, lad?"

"Ah… three, um, three Crowns sir, if it pleases you." The boy was obviously reluctant to name the price, as if it was something Valdieron might strike him for. It was steep compared to what Kyle and his father charged back at Shadowvale, but it was one of the cheapest he had seen in the city. He detected movement from behind the gates again as somebody beyond drew closer; probably the figure the lad had spoken with before.

Carefully, so as not to alarm the boy, he withdrew his purse and counted out five silver coins, half his total beside the five gold sovereigns needed for entry in the tournament and for emergencies. He pressed them into the boy's shaking hand before taking up his new equipment.

"For your service and your Master's," he whispered, loud enough for the figure behind the gate to hear. The boy gasped as he counted the coins, and managed an awkward bow before darting back inside the smith. Valdieron did not linger as the gate was pushed closed. He turned to walk back down the street and heard the beginning of whispered conversation beyond the gate as he left.

He was keen to be away from the area without showing himself further. Watching his surroundings intently, he made out several young vagrants watching him. He cast some of them smiles that caught them off guard, making them dodge back into the crowd or behind shelter.

When he drew near the castle, people were queued for some distance, waiting to file inside. The large gates were divided into two arches, one for the spectators and the other for those participating in the tournament. This line was shorter as competitors filed through slowly. He joined on the end, behind a short, muscular man of youthful appearance with a voluminous beard. He wore a long leather jerkin with a broad bladed axe looped through his belt. Val smiled as he was reminded of a lumberjack.

A small shaded table was erected just inside the gates, at which sat a stern old man in a white cloak, who confronted each warrior in turn. He spoke briefly with each, and money changed hands. The old man dropped the coins into a large chest at his side. The chest was chained to a stake in the ground and watched by two large castle guards.

Beyond the gates he could see the activity around the arena. The arena itself was huge, nearly as high as the castle walls themselves. Tall poles held various wind-whipped flags and pennants. One large archway led into it, through which a steady stream of people passed. Tents of all description were set up around the arena. Some appeared to be stalls and shops, and others personal tents for higher-ranking entrants in the tournament. Armed men and castle guards walked everywhere, and many glances between them were lingering and wary.

"Name?"

He gave a start at the voice and found that he had come to the old man's table. "Ah, Valdieron of Tyr, sir." He had decided to use that address, having no other titles or personas by which to be recognized. The old man scribbled briefly on a large list before taking out a sheet of parchment. On this he wrote Valdieron's name at the top.

"Will you need medical insurance?"

Valdieron frowned bemusedly. "How much is that, Sir?" He had not heard of this nor been told about it, but realized it was a healing arrangement of some sort.

"Ten Sovereigns," stated the old clerk, as if tired of having to speak of it. "Half is refunded if the service is not used."

Valdieron gave a choking grunt. He began to say no, but a voice cut him off.

"Yes, Master Letch." The old man peered askance at the figure who had spoken and Valdieron turned, surprised to find Kalamar walking towards them. He was dressed in tight breeches of dark green and a fluffed shirt of creamy white. A rapier was belted at his side, and a dagger opposite it.

The old man nodded without pause and scribbled again on the parchment before taking out a stamp and setting the King's symbol onto the bottom of it in red wax. He passed this to Valdieron and ushered him through without asking for payment.

"I don't know what to say, Kalamar," stammered Val as he greeted the spy.

"Then do not say anything, Val. It is the least I can do. Besides, if you win your first match, I will be repaid in full. I have a small amount resting on your win."

Valdieron shook his head. "You would have been better served placing a bet on Thorgast." Kalamar merely smiled, and he knew the spy had done that also, and he could only laugh.

"Come. Let me show you where you have to go." Kalamar led him across the lawn towards the arena, skirting the long line and moving to the rear of the new structure. They approached a large archway guarded by several guards who gave Kalamar a brief nod. The archway was dark but not deep, opening into the large oval of the arena. The ground was grassy, though cut short, and there were no obstacles to speak of. Towering stands opened around it, as yet only half packed with people. He wondered how much louder it would get when every seat was occupied.

Kalamar led him to a section divided from the rest, with palace guards lining the rising stairs at each end. The seats here were of better quality with more space between each. Several seats at the fore were raised on a platform that projected from the stand. Val realized these seats were for the royal family. All were large and padded, with an angled roof providing shelter from all save the midday sun. Nobody was present on the platform yet. Well-dressed courtiers and commoners of high standing filled several dozen seats behind it.

"Many of the contestants sit in the first row of seats around the arena." Valdieron saw that the first row was clear of the next and divided by a small barrier. Many of the seats were filled, and he guessed there were probably three hundred seats in that row alone. "You can sit back here, though, if you like." He indicated a line of seats before the royal platform. He saw Thorgast and Hafri talking with a young man Valdieron did not know. He had shoulder length sandy hair, and was tall with a lithe frame. He was handsome, with large eyes and a flashing, disarming smile.

"I had started to think you were locked in that hall," greeted Thorgast with a laugh as the two moved closer. "Its a sight, aint it?"

"It is indeed," agreed Hafri at his side, his eyes scanning the growing crowd. Valdieron wondered if he was in search of young women, which made him smile.

Hafri was dressed in dark trousers and a brown vest, with leather bracers on his forearms and legs. Thorgast wore gray trousers and a dark blue shirt, and also had thick leather bracers on his forearms. His axe rested at his left hip within easy reach.

Valdieron was introduced to the young man who turned out to be Andrak, Kitara's brother. There was some resemblance there, in the mouth and nose, but his eyes were a dark brown.

"Are you entering the tournament also, Valdieron?" asked Andrak, maybe a little surprised. Valdieron nodded and sat beside him while Kalamar moved to the end. He untied the new sheath and baldric he had been carrying and began replacing his old gear. The fit was excellent, and the sheath was cut low so that he could draw the long blade easily.

"As am I," said the Prince, his eyes tracing a line around the arena where the other warriors were assembling. "Though I think my father will throw me in the dungeon when he finds out."

Valdieron chuckled slightly. "Maybe you should have borrowed Kitara's mask." The words were meant as a quip, but Andrak turned on him with alarm, and he could hear Kalamar chuckle softly at his side.

"You know of the mask?" he accused softly, looking around. He was not angry, but concerned.

Valdieron, realizing he had a little explaining to do, told Andrak of the events of Llewellyn's death and his castle visit afterwards.

The Prince's face twisted with sorrow, but he marveled at the story. "I had been told of Llewellyn's death. I just returned from Brek. He will be sorely missed."

Valdieron nodded grimly but tried to shake it off. "What are those?" he asked curiously, pointing to twin metal arches over the only two doorways leading to the arena floor. Both were silver, and rose eight feet in height. A robed man stood by each, black and almost invisible, and they seemed to him to emit power with their very presence.

"Those are the arches of truth," advised Andrak with a grin. "They are used to uncover any magical properties an entrant has. Magical weapons are acceptable, but any other magical items are forbidden. Those men are Alchemists from the Astral City, who study all forms of magical items and their properties."

On closer inspection, Valdieron saw that their robes were in fact a dark gray, but still seemed to draw in the shadows around them. He was relieved to hear magical weapons were not forbidden, remembering the electrical properties his sword had shown when fighting the devil.

They talked amongst each other for some time, while the crowd gathered. After a time, with the sun just peeking over the looming stands, a booming gong was sounded from somewhere outside. The crowd caught their breath as a single entity.

Kalamar motioned to the arena entrance and saw the King enter with his family, flanked by guards. Valdieron spied Kitara, as tall and beautiful as he remembered, wearing a silken dress of ocean blue with a circlet of gold and silver in her hair. She seemed to notice him as she was led past onto the platform. She flashed a smile and winked, and he wondered briefly if it were to him or her brother at his side.

Once the royal party was in place, the gong sounded again three times and the crowd hushed as the King's voice resounded through the arena.

"People of Thorhus! Visitors from abroad! Warriors of Kil-Tar! Welcome to my city!" A deafening roar erupted as the king paused, but it died quickly as he continued to speak.

"Today marks the commencement of the annual Tournament of Champions. As patron and founder of these games, I welcome you all and thank you for your attendance."

"I am sure we will be witness to a great many combats over the next three days, and I hope the spirit with which they are fought is both magnanimous and honorable. This Tournament might see a feat yet to be witnessed, the fifth consecutive victory by one warrior. Will Hagar the Dak'marian prevail, or will some other warrior best him at this test of skill, courage and strength? Three days from now we will know. Let the games begin!"

The King's words brought another tumultuous cheer from the crowd, which lasted for many moments. The blaring of trumpets from both sides of the arena heralded another hush as all eyes turned to the announcer who stood below the royal seats.

"The first combat is being introduced," advised Andrak softly, his eyes wide with anticipation.

"Javin the Darishi, of the Water Seekers clan!"

A roar erupted from every mouth at the first name but quieted again almost instantly for the second calling.

"Keitel of Cartyl!"

Whether these warriors were known or not, the crowd became a hive of shouting and cheering. Valdieron saw many red-clad figures moving through the stands, with people milling around them excitedly.

"Brokers," advised Andrak. "They take bets from the people. There are stalls outside for the placement of bets also. Small slips of paper are exchanged for money for each person betting, showing contestant number one or two, determined by the colors red or white they wear in the battle. Their chances of winning are also put down, which can affect how much return you get if you win. The likes of Hagar will not get as much return as the likes of you or I, for instance."

It was puzzling to follow, even had he the desire to, so he watched as both contestants entered the arena. Both passed through the archways with no apparent effect, and met in the center of the arena where a white-robed man waited. He carried two pieces of ribbon of red and white, and two matching flags. He tied a ribbon to each warrior's arm and stepped away, lowering both flags between the two combatants. After a long pause, he blew a shrill whistle in his mouth as the flags raised, as did the roar of the crowd.

The battle was over quickly.

Keitel of Cartyl, a slender man of youthful appearance wielding a falchion, was easily beaten by the Darishi whose twin sabers flashed with great skill and speed, disarming him after a short time. Keitel was forced to submit then, kneeling before the warrior with his head bowed. The flag-carrying official stepped forward and raised the red flag, which

333

coincided with the Darishi's ribbon. The crowd roared, but there were many who were not so happy and booed, obviously having placed bets on the Cartyl warrior.

"Lowering yourself onto one knee is a sign of yielding," confirmed Andrak at his side. His face was flushed with excitement as he watched both warriors leave the arena to boisterous cheers.

Many battles were fought during the morning. The crowd did not seem to tire, growing louder with each fight. Nobody left his or her seat unless nature overcame excitement.

On the whole, the fights were without incident, though one middle-aged warrior did get sliced across the stomach and was carried from the field on a stretcher, hopefully to receive medical attention. Like sharks in a feeding frenzy, the crowd erupted from their seats and cheered loudly at the spilled blood.

Thorgast was the first of their group to be called, and he rose with his face set in determination. He gave them a smile as he passed, skirting to the closest archway. His opponent was, to Valdieron's amusement, the axe-wielding man who had preceded him at the queue outside. The crowd, seeing both axe-wielders, began a chant, as if expecting a bloody contest.

The lumberjack did not last long against Thorgast's superior strength and size. Axe combat proved to be very strategic, with the larger weapons requiring great skill to wield, and the haft was used often for parrying the great crescent-shaped blades. Thorgast managed to maneuver his axe inside the other man's after coming together in a parry, slicing across his opponent's right hand before striking him across the face with the haft of his great axe. The man dropped flat on his back and did not move, and another stretcher was brought out. The crowd erupted, not displeased at the display, and Thorgast's name was chanted through the crowd, who seemed to have found a favorite.

Hafri and Andrak both fought soon afterwards. Hafri showed the effects of too many hours in the Inns with a close victory over an older and slower opponent.

Andrak's flashing saber was more than a match for his opponent, another youth from Thorhus who used an iron-shod staff. Valdieron congratulated the young Prince on his return, surprised at his victory, though he should have known his training was of the highest standard.

"Valdieron of Tyr!"

It was probably one of the last matches, but none in the crowd had left, though more than a few throats were raw and dry. With a sigh he rose and removed his light coat. He also removed Llewellyn's rapier and rested it against the seat.

"Wish me luck," he whispered as he left, and he was given reassuring smiles. He had not heard of the warrior he was up against, and many thoughts ran through his mind as he passed the seated warriors on his way to the nearest archway. They studied him as he passed, but he looked ahead and did not let them see his discomfort. The crowd was chanting again, sending a wave throughout the arena and he could feel it shaking the very ground like an earthquake.

To his surprise, his sword did not register as he passed under the archway. He felt the gaze of the alchemist on him, and the aura of power he had felt earlier was more tangible at this range.

His opponent, Dravin, was a tall and athletically built Darishi from the Clan of the Fire Walkers. His dark skin was even darker than most of his kin, and his head was shaved save for a single lock extending from the top and flowing down to his lower back. He wore a crimson vest cut to show his chiseled stomach, and his light pants were of pale gold. A thick chain carrying the symbol of a running deer encircled his neck. He twirled a gleaming broadsword in his slender hands, and his white smile seemed to beckon to Valdieron.

The official, a hard-faced man who was probably a veteran of the guards, tied the white ribbon around Valdieron's arm and secured the red to Dravin's upper arm before crossing the flags in front of him, preparing for the start. Valdieron slowly drew his sword, taking comfort in its cool touch. If the sight of his magnificent weapon had any effect on the Darishi, he did not show it as he pranced around eagerly.

The flags dropped, and on cue the crowd erupted with a deafening cheer. Dravin leapt at him with an arcing attack, the heavy weapon almost a blur. His mouth was twisted in a snarl, but any sound he made was swept away with the crowd's tumult.

Shifting backwards, Valdieron let the weapon pass him, the keen blade hissing as it cut the air. He hoped the heavier weapon would lead to the warrior tiring himself, and the less contact with his own sword the better. Still, the tall man's reach was longer than he thought, and he suspected that any closer and he might have needed a new shirt.

Dravin reversed the attack without a pause, sending the point at Valdieron's groin. Swinging his sword down with a flick he turned the heavier blade easily, but Dravin spun with cat-like grace into a spinning attack, his sword arcing high as he leapt from his feet. Valdieron spotted the feint at the last moment, throwing his sword low and rolling away a split second before Dravin's lashing foot swept across where his head had just been.

Rolling to his feet, Valdieron found the Darishi watching him intently, like a predator, curiosity and appreciation evident in his eyes, though his sneer remained. Valdieron knew he had been drawn against a skilful warrior, probably a veteran of the tournament the way he signaled to the crowd for more noise with his free hand.

Taking a step forward, Valdieron decided he could not let the Darishi determine the pace of the fight. Any rest aided the Darishi and helped build the crowd behind him. He thrust testily, then again and again in quick succession, forcing the Darishi back slowly as he parried. The dark-skinned warrior managed a low riposte, but Valdieron batted it aside before pressing another array of thrusts, low then high. He repeated this again, but first high then low and another high, just so Dravin could not find a pattern. Feeling the momentum swinging, he began to feel his way through several sweeping chops and cuts.

The fight shifted into a circling melee as blades flashed in attacks both high and low. Hands and feet snaked out on occasion when the blades were pushed wide, and a few of these connected, for both warriors.

Valdieron felt truly alive as he let the battle take him. His blood felt like fire coursing beneath his skin and his senses tingled. The crowd's shouting was a distant drone as he concentrated on the fight, but it seemed to charge him with its power. He slipped slightly, taking a thin slice to the left thigh. He turned the blade away with his left bracer as he regained balance, snaking his own sword forward in a thrust, which caught Dravin on the upper left arm. In a stalemate, the two backed away again, assessing and planning. How long they had been fighting, Valdieron could not tell. It seemed both like an eternity and an instant.

He had hoped Dravin would tire, though his own sword weighed heavy in his hands. The Darishi was sweating profusely and his moves did not come with the speed or strength they had earlier. Sensing his chance, Valdieron pressed him again.

Dravin swept a savage horizontal cut at waist height as the two stepped together. Grasping his sword with both hands, Valdieron met the blow. The ring of pure steel seemed louder to him than the bell had earlier. The muscles in his arm numbed at the shocking impact, but he held his ground and threw his weight behind it, which surprised the Darishi and threw him off balance. Pivoting on his right foot, he spun a kick, aiming high, and caught Dravin in the chest. The breath blasted out of his lungs like a silent scream and he stumbled back a few paces. Following the kick, Valdieron dived forward daringly, coming up in a crouch before the winded warrior. He raised his sword blindly to protect his head and somehow managed to parry as Dravin chopped at him. The angle of his sword caused the heavier weapon to slide harmlessly to the side, digging into the ground with a soft thud.

Valdieron brought his sword around quickly in a blow that would have sliced into the Darishi's side had he not halted it short of the man's shirt. The dark warrior, wide-eyed and panting heavily, looked down at the leveled sword, his face already twisted in the pain he had expected. His sword still lay embedded in the soft ground. He stepped back carefully, releasing the grip on his weapon before dropping to one knee. His snarl was replaced with a wry smile, and his eyes showed relief.

The sudden increase in crowd noise told Valdieron that they had hushed for the outcome, and tumultuous applause assaulted him. He raised the hilt of his sword to his forehead, honoring the Darishi's valiant battle before sheathing the sword. He waited as the official removed the ribbon from his arm then turned to walk from the oval. The crowd cheered and clapped, and his body felt like wildfire, trembling like a newborn foal. He was glad when he almost drooped into his seat, and the others gathered around to clap him on the shoulder and congratulate him. He had not glanced at the royal pavilion as he neared, but he knew he had been keenly watched.

"That was incredible, Valdieron," breathed Andrak, awe mixed with wonder crossing his fair face. "I have never seen a combat like that before. I bet old Hagar is pissing himself right now."

"Well, he wouldn't be the only one," breathed Valdieron. He was relieved at having completed the first battle, and overjoyed at winning. He knew if he fought too many like Dravin he would not progress much further without a lot of luck.

The others laughed and he joined them. That each had won their fight gave them a common bond, and their spirits were high as they watched the final fights.

It was perhaps not a coincidence that Hagar fought in the final battle. His opponent was a large, grizzled old man who looked to have been a skilled warrior in his day. He had neither the speed nor skill of Hagar, who moved like living lightning, his sword weaving a death-web into which the old warrior fell after moments. His stomach was pierced with a cruel thrust. As the flagman stepped in, Hagar sliced his blade across the dying man's throat, and any strand of life was severed instantly.

The crowd watched this with macabre cruelty, cheering the vicious display in such a way that Valdieron felt sick to the core. He felt nothing but sorrow for the old warrior who lay dead on the ground. Healers rushed out with the stretcher to assist him, but he knew they would be able to do nothing.

The chant of "Hagar! Hagar! Hagar!" swept across the arena in waves, and the mocking warrior saluted them all with a raised blade before turning to the royal platform and performing a mocking bow. He even had the temerity to blow a kiss toward Kitara, and the crowd cheered louder. The warrior left the arena slowly, and the crowd was as loath to file from the arena after they realized the entertainment was at an end. Valdieron had to almost pinch himself before he was able to move. There were similar stunned expressions on the faces of the others, though Kalamar was shaking his head sadly, as if what had happened had not been unexpected.

"I will see you on the morrow," whispered Andrak, joining the royal party as they filed past. The young Prince's face was grave and his eyes held unshed tears, his words almost choked.

Kalamar followed him, giving them a parting nod, his face lined with sadness. Valdieron noticed Kitara as she passed. Her face was ashen and tears rimmed her eyes. She met his gaze and shook her head, whether from sadness or as a warning he was not sure. She linked arms with Andrak as he caught up, and she was gone.

Thorgast's heavy hand rested on his shoulder then, and he knew they were leaving. No words were spoken on the trip home, and none were needed. All now knew the danger they faced, which before had been an unseen reality. Death loomed over them like the fast-approaching night, and Hagar's face seemed to ride it like the wind.

Chapter 33

The Dream Plane surrounded Valdieron, so clear and tangible it felt like he was awake. There was no smell, no breeze, and nothing living beyond himself, he knew, but it felt like reality. The haze, which had been present on his first appearance, had dissipated to the point where he saw only a vague swirling, like the last wisps of fog carried away by an eddying breeze.

The dark city surrounded him, bleak and harsh yet he felt at ease here, almost as if it were his home. The towering roof of the Combat Hall, with its huge spire topped by the needle-like projection and statue, looked jagged and torn. Yet it seemed somehow familiar. He felt he had trodden every square of the huge plaza thousands of times, yet he had walked around on only a few occasions while not training. He did so now, however, needing a reprieve from the rigorous workouts.

His meandering brought him to a stairway, which descended into darkness. He knew there were thirty-seven steps without counting them, yet he had never descended. How did he know that? Walking them, he found he was correct.

He alighted onto a wide passage flanked by steep walls, covered with indistinguishable carvings and reliefs. There were sigils and runes, and again he felt he knew their meaning, like the words to a song never sung.

A large arched doorway was set at the end of the walkway. The gloom darkened as he walked towards it. The doorway was of a black material, neither metallic nor wooden, but possessive of a reflective sheen, like the dark surface of a deep pool. There were no handles or hinges that he could see. Tiny writings were etched across it at eye-level, though he could not read them. A circular indent was pressed into the surface above this writing, in the center of which was a small hole, not quite circular in shape.

There was an invisible aura about the door, a tangible permeation of power which seemed malevolent yet kind at once, which bemused him.

"What do you hide?" he whispered softly, words hardly

breathed. He felt that a vast maze of knowledge and danger lay beyond the door.

"Beyond lies your destiny."

As usual, he had neither heard nor sensed the approach of the Master.

"How so?" asked Valdieron tentatively.

"Knowledge and power lie beyond that door, as do death and torment. It can tell you of things past, present and future, some things you may wish to see and others you would rather not. It is the test of all tests, and there is no failure other than death."

"Can I take this test, Master?"

"All must take the test, Valdieron. As for when, you will know when the time comes."

"And how will I get past it?" he asked skeptically as he turned towards the door without hinge or handle, but the Master was gone. His words floated to Val's mind.

"You will know!"

Giving the door a final glance, he retraced his steps to the plaza and crossed to the Combat Ambit. The doors opened slowly to allow him passage and closed silently behind him.

As he battled in the Ambit, his mind was afire with thought of what test awaited him behind that dark Portal.

* * *

In the still of the morning, in a large manor in the north of Thorhus, a shadowy figure shifted through the still darkness, as silent and imperceptible as a shadow. Outside was quiet and peaceful, save for the distant howl of a dog.

The Soul Seeker moved through the dark hallway without fear of being spotted by any of the house staff or inhabitants. The spell it had placed over the dwelling would ensure that all slept deeply until morning.

With a motion of its pale hand it swept a door open and passed into a dark bedroom, split by a pool of moonlight through a large window. A canopied bed was set off to the right, surrounded by a curtain of silk. On the bed, covered by a thin sheet, slept Nortas. Normally, the warrior would not have slept so soundly, even after a day of battle, but his sleep was not natural. He shifted as if tormented by dreams as the Demon floated to the bed, though he would not wake.

The Dak'marian warrior looked dangerous, even asleep. His face was stern and his heavily muscled body was barely concealed by the thin sheet. The Demon hissed. Its hatred was exceeded only by its duty, or it would have slain this mortal already, but he had another Dak'marian who needed to be killed.

In the guise of Valkyra, the Demon had spotted the other Dak'marian at the tournament, exuding power like no other. He was young, yet to come to his full strength. The Demon knew the youth had the looks of a Dak'marian, but his blood was alive with the blood of the Dragon Lords.

And soon he would die. It was inevitable the two would meet in the tournament, for the youths skills were far superior to the others, even the giant Barbarian. In the form of the Blades master, he would see that this threat, however minor, did not grow.

The silk curtains parted before the Demon as it rose onto the bed, though anybody who saw him would simply have seen a pair of disembodied flaming red eyes. It moved a hand over the sleeping warrior's head and lowered it until it touched flesh. Nortas thrashed as if caught in a nightmare, but remained asleep. Slowly the Demon transferred itself into the body and mind of the Master Warrior. In the next two days, it would see that not just one Dak'marian would die, but two, and along with them one of the few threats which remained for the Demon host.

* * *

Blood rushed from Hafri's leg. He sat with a groan and a curse, though his smile remained as he cherished the reverberation of his name throughout the arena. His beaten opponent was only just being assisted into the healing chamber across the arena, his arm broken and his side gashed by Hafri's sword.

"That was a little close," mused Thorgast grimly, studying the wound. In fact, there was a point in the fight where Valdieron was sure Hafri would be beaten by his taller and stronger opponent from Kethym. Luck seemed to smile on him, however, and he remained to fight again.

Andrak frowned beside him; perhaps disappointed that Hafri had won. The prince had lost his second fight earlier to a Darishi Maiden of the Stone River clan, her slender staff and speed too much for his flashing saber. His wounds were not bad, merely bruises which he would not allow to be tended. '*A mark of my defeat*', he called them. His pride was hurt more, though there was no shame in it. The warrior maiden was as skilled as many of the men they had seen over the last day and a half. She was the only woman warrior competing, and as such, had become one of the crowd favorites as it allowed them to jeer the men she defeated, and that it had been the son of the King only seemed to spur them on.

A honey-robed figure appeared before them. He was one of the healers, the one Andrak had waved away earlier, and he knelt to examine Hafri's wound. He was a slender man, not old but with a stern visage. He said nothing to them as he placed his right hand, fingers spread, above the wound, not touching it. Valdieron felt the skin along his arms and nape tingle briefly. This figure had the same aura as the Alchemists. As the wound closed, Valdieron realized he was witnessing magic. The bleeding slowed to a stop and disappeared from the wound. Both edges of the wound closed together to form a pink slash, then darkened slowly until only a scar remained, smaller and less obvious than had the wound healed itself over time. The Healer rose without comment. Valdieron was too stunned for words. These people had power beyond anything he had ever witnessed or believed. He would have liked to ask the man how he came by this power and if it could be taught.

"One more to the collection," whispered Hafri, running a finger along the scar, whether he was referring to the scar or the previous battle Val did not know. His thoughts were interrupted as Thorgast's name was boomed across the arena.

"Time to go," quipped the big man, hefting his axe. He gave them each a wink and a smile, and cast one look at Hafri's bloodied leg before departing.

He was back in his seat before it had cooled, his face split with a satisfied smile and hardly broken into a sweat. His opponent, smaller and armed with a halberd, had been like a blade of grass before a hurricane to Thorgast. He had yielded shortly after the Barbarian tore the weapon from his hands, tripped him with it and split its shaft in two, tossing both away with a roar. The crowd's roar had echoed his, but he did not salute them as Hafri had done as he left.

"The easiest four sovereigns we'll ever get," whispered Kalamar with a chuckle, and Valdieron smiled. The Spy had placed bets for both of them earlier, irrespective of opponent.

Fight after fight passed throughout the day. Each one saw another warrior drop out of contention, and the stronger warriors continue. Valdieron's second and third fights were much easier than against Dravin, and he progressed after hard but brief struggles. Both his opponents had yielded after they realized they could not beat him, and he was even closer to his objective of meeting Hagar.

Hafri's luck ran out in his third combat. Ironically, it was also to the female warrior Maiden of the Darishi, Al'kariva. This galled the young mercenary no end, and he sat with a disgusted frown, at least until she was defeated in her next combat.

Failing light came with the last of the battles, and Valdieron knew his name would be called even before it echoed through the arena. He rose and removed his mantle, but gave a start when his opponent was announced.

"Javin, of the Darishi Water Seekers Clan."

Javin's flashing twin sabers had become a talking point of the Tournament. The Darishi's skill was matched by his speed and determination, and he had not taken a hit from a weapon in any of his battles thus far. The crowd took up chanting his name, watching him as he circled the Arena.

"This is the last battle of the day, Val. Win this and you are through to the final eight tomorrow." Kalamar rested a reassuring hand on his arm, though his tight grin warned the fight would not be easy.

Andrak gave him a victorious gesture and Thorgast nodded encouragement to him. The barbarian was already through to the next day's combats, after crushing victories over his last two opponents.

Val removed his baldric, increasing his mobility, which would be vital during the fight. He knew through previous combats that Javin could not be fought with a single weapon, so he pulled Llewellyn's Rapier from its ivory sheath and rested it on his shoulder. Kalamar's eyes showed his surprise, but he said nothing.

He could see Javin from his periphery as he skirted the arena. The Darishi carelessly juggled his weapons between hands, sending them into a dazzling array around him with practiced skill. This only made the crowd more boisterous, chanting for blood. Valdieron carried his two weapons as he stepped through the magical arches without incident and approached the Darishi, his own sword spinning as he tossed it into the air and caught it. This only made the crowd eager for the contest to begin, and they began stamping their feet impatiently. Brokers dodged between them frantically, trying to meet every bet thrown their way.

Javin eyed Valdieron with what seemed to be respect as the two faced off in the center of the arena. His dark skin glistened with perspiration, and he smiled. His dark eyes flashed to the two weapons in Valdieron's hands, but he only smiled more as he raised his own twin sabers.

Valdieron did not even notice the red ribbon being tied to his arm, nor did he hear the whistle that started the battle. Their staring was broken as the official raised his flags between them, all that was needed for the crowd to roar again. Valdieron hardly noticed Javin's sabers flashed straight for his throat behind the rising flags.

Instinct and reflexes prevailed as he leant to the side. His longsword batted the first saber aside while the rapier intercepted the second. He leapt back, arching his stomach just out of reach of a lunging side-kick, and then was forced to roll backwards as twin sabers spun at his head. It had all happened in an instant, yet the crowd took slightly longer than that to react with another burst of cheering and stomping.

Without wiping himself down, Valdieron settled into a stance, feet close and left side slightly forward, leading rapier high and his longsword low. Javin circled him slowly, like a predator, showing no surprise that Valdieron had managed to evade the perfectly executed routine.

The two met again. Weapons clashed as feet shuffled from one stance to another and arms pumped furiously, working for speed and strength. Fighting with two weapons was a lot different to singular weapon combat, and twice as fast. Weapons flew one after the other, hardly ever at the same time, so the clang of metal on metal came in almost a constant stream, except when the two drew apart momentarily to plan or catch breath.

Valdieron's arms felt leaden after the first exchanges, though he felt confident his skill at fighting with two weapons extended beyond the combat ambit. Timing was of the utmost importance now, and his mind had to work overtime to remember such things as movement, speed and purpose for two weapons, not one, and he had to come up with moves and counters of his own. It was like a blur, a subliminal awareness that went beyond instinct.

Javin worked him through another routine, sabers pressing high and wide. He was not surprised by a sudden double thrust low at his groin, though the speed almost caught him. He crossed sword and rapier in an 'X', forcing the sabers low. Both stepped back after the stalemate, breathing heavily. Valdieron wore a slight smile, finding the fight an exciting challenge.

The next exchange erupted again, swords arcing and slicing high and low, seeking a hole in defenses. Valdieron felt a slice of pain across his ribs as one of the sabers darted past a parry that was a fraction too wide, and another dug a shallow gash in his thigh as he stepped away too late. He felt his rapier dig along Javin's arm, leaving a narrow cut and a line of dark blood.

Surprisingly, he realized Javin was again forcing him high and wide, and wondered if the double thrust low would come. He expected a ruse, therefore he was not entirely caught off guard when one of the sabers darted in low, and the other struck like a coiled snake at his throat.

His longsword swept high, flashing to intercept the saber, while the low rapier barely deflected the other as it sliced his thigh again, though not deep. The parry saw Javin exposed momentarily, and he launched a straight kick at his stomach.

His foot connected solidly below the ribs, hard enough to drive the breath out of the dark warrior, but not enough to force him backwards. Recoiling his leg, Valdieron spun slightly and lashed out again, this time at Javin's face.

The Darishi saw the blow coming and tried to fall away, though it was obvious he had not expected the second kick. His head snapped back as Valdieron's foot caught him on the side of the face. The blow, coupled with his own retreat sent him sprawling back onto the hard ground. One saber flew from his grasp, landing several paces away, but he retained the other. He tried to roll to a crouch, blood trickling from the corner of his mouth, but Valdieron's leveled longsword at his throat made him pause. It took him only a moment to lower his saber and nod, signaling his acceptance of defeat.

Another deafening roar filled the arena, and Valdieron felt his skin crawl with excitement as he extended his hand to Javin. The dark warrior accepted it, allowing himself to be pulled to his feet. His face showed no anger, only a deep disappointment. He retrieved his other saber while Valdieron turned, and under the stares and shouts of thirty thousand people, made his way back to his seat.

Kalamar was nowhere to be seen when he returned, though he had not glanced up at the royal platform. Andrak, who hopped around as if caught alight, clapped a hand on Valdieron's shoulder.

"That was incredible. I never thought you would defeat Javin, and by the looks of it, I do not think many in the crowd did, either."

"Not even I did, Andrak," laughed Valdieron, dropping onto the seat. His arms felt leaden as he dropped his weapons beside him, and the brown-clad healer knelt before him to tend his wounds. His skin tingled again as the man worked his healing magic, and the cuts to his thigh and ribs were soon nothing but pink scars which would fade after a few days.

The others were rising, and Valdieron had not noticed the royal party departing. Andrak smiled almost apologetically before he sped after them. Thorgast offered him a hand back up as the healer bowed his head and left without word.

"Well, we live to fight another day, Val!"

"So it would seem. Only eight left." He did not have to mention the chances of them meeting each other were growing with each fight, nor did he have to remind himself that Hagar was still there.

The Dak'marian had wreaked bloody havoc during the day, seeming to grow stronger and crueler with every fight. Thankfully nobody was killed, if not for lack of trying on his behalf.

There was also the Blademaster, Nortas from the Astral City. He had proved even more awesome than Hagar, dispatching his opponents with an array of stunning and powerful moves which had the crowd pumped up to a fevered frenzy. Few escaped without bad injuries that even healing could not fully fix.

As the three returned to the Inn, there was hardly any conversation between them. Even the despondent Hafri had nothing to say, obviously still furious at his loss. Valdieron looked to the sky, dark and pale with the oncoming night, and wondered what the new day would bring. He did know that whatever he had experienced over the last two days, would pale in comparison.

A cold uncertainty gripped Valdieron as he stood in the center of the arena, oblivious to the tumultuous booming of the crowd around him. Before him stood Nortas: Master of the Astral City Academy, and Heir to the House of Cal'Tor. As imposing as his title, the Dak'marian stood a hand taller than Valdieron, and his muscular body showed hardness and strength. His face was stern, impassive, and his gray eyes stared unblinking, without emotion, which made Valdieron shiver despite the warm morning air. Nortas carried a weapon similar to Val's Dragon sword, double-edged with a tapered point, though his was plainly hilted with a wooden grip and a round golden counterweight for the pommel.

Flags appeared between them, though they continued to stare at one another. Straining to hear the whistle, Valdieron felt his every nerve tingle and tense. Already he knew both Hagar and Thorgast had won their opening matches for the day, and he was determined to join them.

The two weapons met overhead as the flags dropped with an almost imperceptible whistle. Valdieron's arms tingled from the shock. He almost expected one of the weapons to break, but his strange blade held fast, as did Nortas' dark-hued weapon. Without strain, the heavier bladesman heaved Valdieron backwards and waded in without pause.

Valdieron knew he could not beat Nortas with strength. His only chance lay in speed and maneuverability. Although the big warrior was fast, Valdieron was faster. He parried using the other man's momentum to turn away strikes, or just evaded them by turning away. This was perhaps not the wisest option, but he knew he had to give himself time to figure out how to counter this Master's moves.

Unfortunately, Nortas did not seem to tire as he wielded his weapon in a continual flood of strikes. Sweat covered his tanned skin, but his face remained expressionless as he fought. Valdieron knew he could not defeat Nortas by being defensive, as he was tiring quickly without even taking a swing at the warrior.

Throwing caution to the wind, he stepped in to meet Nortas. Again and again the darker blade met his with a crystalline ring as he tried to parry every attack. It was all he could do to get in a soft strike, but he could not read any pattern in the man's fighting. His left arm was tingling from a deep gash, while he thought one of his ribs might be broken from another hit, but he pressed on doggedly.

With alarming certainty he knew he would not win the fight unless he took some real risks, and the price for those risks could be fatal. Nortas was unrelenting and ferocious. All could see that the attacks he performed had the intent of killing Valdieron. If he slipped up on a risky maneuver...

His mind was suddenly filled with the images of his past. First there was his father, not as he had last seen him but laughing and full of life. Then there was Kyle, his best friend, who seemed to enjoy life's every minute until he had been killed. There was Llewellyn and Nagus, and old Hubert the teamster. There came also Master Letterman, then Thorgast, Hafri and Gerkar. Natasha's beautiful face there was also, but that changed into Kitara.

He spun suddenly, performing the move he had seen Llewellyn perform several times in training. He led with his weapon spinning faster than his body. His blade met with the other, even as he was spinning, as he had hoped, for the weapon was not his attacking option. His foot lashed out, catching the Dak'marian below the right armpit, connecting with a dull thud. The crowd had become a surging cacophony on the edge of his awareness.

Nortas shifted slightly to the side, though his face showed no sign of the pain of bruised or cracked ribs. He recoiled and thrust upwards, double-handed. With a cry, Valdieron stepped into it, spinning again with a double-handed parry of his own, forcing the other blade aside. Continuing his spin, he arced the sword around, expecting to feel a sword enter his back as he did, but completed the turn to find Nortas stepping away. Too slow, Valdieron's sword sliced across his chest, opening a deep cut. Blood flowed, and Valdieron knew he was hurt as his mouth flashed into a painful scowl.

Taking a rasping breath, Valdieron stood there watching, blinking away the sudden sweat in his eyes and the knot clutching his stomach. A drop of blood fell from his lowered sword-tip and he raised it, watching a thin trickle run along the edge. He expected Nortas to yield then, for the wound must have been burning with pain, but he roared and leapt forward.

This time their swords met in a thunderous clash. Like a bolt of lightning from clear sky, a chime echoed through Valdieron, so loud that it reverberated for what seemed an eternity. Pain lanced his face and chest, like fire-warmed needles, and his hands rose before him, empty. Staring down dreamily, he saw his sword protruding from Nortas' stomach, the hilt almost hidden in his shirt fold.

The Dak'marian warrior's face contorted with pain and his hand dropped the hilt of his broken sword, and he clutched at Valdieron as if trying to embrace a lover. Valdieron caught his shirt, trying to keep him upright, his face only inches from the dying warrior's face.

"The Prophecy." The rasping, choked words were nothing more than a whisper that Valdieron almost did not hear, and would not, had he not been so close. He looked deep into the man's eyes and saw awareness there, and a closeness that had previously been a dark wall. "Be strong, Cousin!"

Valdieron would have dropped him then in shock, but a hissing exhalation from the man preceded a popping sound, and his eyes were suddenly filled with an incandescent screen as orange flame engulfed him. Heat as intense as a forge-fire struck him in the chest and he was lifted and thrown by a great force into a dark fog. He was not aware of landing, but instead floated in a state of agonized awareness, fighting the pain which flowed through every fiber; growing from his pores and building in intensity to flow straight into his brain like molten fire.

He was screaming. The sound drifted through his subconscious like a wave, but intermingled with it were other sounds, distant voices and noises. Above these echoed the dying words of the Warrior, Nortas. *"The Prophecy. Be strong,*

Cousin! The Prophecy. Be strong, Cousin! Be strong... Strong...Cousin!"

Suddenly it felt like he was dropped into a cold pool and plunged deep into its dark depths. Light faded from his awareness as he was drawn into the soothing clutches, tired of fighting. Sleep was what he needed. Sleep and dreams and.....

Chapter 34

A coarse, dry scraping across his face woke Valdieron from the timeless clutches of sleep. His mind was free of thought, as if purged, and his blurred vision cleared to find the furred face of Kaz looming over him. He gave an unexpected start, but soon began to chuckle. The large cat pawed at him softly. More than likely he was just hungry.

The room came into view as he glanced around. A deep numbness made him groan as he shifted his head, though it passed quickly. The room was large, with white plastered walls and flowered cornice. Bowls rested in niches set into the walls, and from them exuded a myriad of aromas from rose and lavender to mint and rosemary. Arched windows with shutters ajar let in a tinge of fresh air, which bore with it the heat of a summer's day, and along with it the brightness of a cloudless sky.

He was lying in a narrow bed. A heavy sheet covered him, and his head rested on a feathered pillow. At its side was a small table, on which sat a wooden bowl of water and a cloth. Near one of the windows stood a small stool, and on it a large book left upturned with the pages pressed down to keep it open. A strong wooden door was set in the wall to his left, and it reminded him of a dungeon's door, with a square grate in its upper half for looking through.

Feeling suddenly alone he sat up, dislodging Kaz who leapt down from the bed and padded about, tail flicking as he searched for something to prey on. He raised a hand to brush the sheet away so he could rise, and stopped, staring at his arm with wonder mixed with dread.

Around his right wrist was the burnt impression of a Dragon. It did not take more than a moment to realize it was the exact duplicate of the bracers he had been wearing for the tournament. It was marked into his skin like a symbol, of a darker hue like a bruise. The whole lower half of his arm was tinged with pink, as if newly healed. Raising his other arm he found the same dragon mark and tender skin. Memories flooded back, as if the sluice gates had been thrown open, and he remembered the fires bursting before him as he clutched Nortas.

Looking himself over he found his chest similarly hairless and pale, but his legs and face were free from the fire's effect, though some of his hair was cut shorter. He recognized the signs of healing and wondered how bad his injuries had been, and why the healer had not been able to rid him of the bracer's markings. He raised his arms again, and found that where one Dragon had been bronze, and the other gold, so were each marks tinged with this color, as if the metal was grafted into his flesh.

He began to rise when the door swung inwards, and a middle-aged woman in a flowing silk gown of pale red entered. She carried a packed tray on a small pile of clothing. She was tall and pretty with a generous figure hardly concealed by the loose, almost transparent gown. Valdieron felt himself flush at the image and the thoughts that flashed through his mind, then flushed again with greater embarrassment as he threw the sheet back over his naked body.

"It is good to see you awake, young Master. No doubt you are hungry." She carried the tray to the small table and deposited the clothing on the bed, frighteningly close to him and he nearly shied away. He whispered thanks as the new aroma of freshly cooked meat and vegetables swept over him. Kaz had also caught the smell, and came padding over, but the woman bent to catch him up smoothly. "You, my furry friend, are going outside." Surprisingly, Kaz did not struggle as she carried him to the door and left.

Val scooped up the tray and began shoveling food into his mouth, hardly taking the time to appreciate the succulent taste.

The clothes the lady had brought for him were finely cut silk garments, thin and loose. The shirt was of lavender, and the pants black. His boots were tucked under the bed, along with his weapons, which he quickly strapped on. He made a quick inspection of his sword, remembering the impact with Nortas' dark weapon, and found it unmarred and as sharp as ever. Slipping it back into its sheath, he made a step to the door when it swung open again.

Prince Andrak's handsome face broke into a wide smile when he saw Val.

"I did not expect to see you up so soon." His eyes flicked

over Valdieron. "Are you well?"

"I am fine, though tired. And curious. What happened? All I remember is Nortas' sword breaking, then there was a fireball and I was falling."

Andrak winced, as if the memory pained him. He shifted to the window, standing in the warmth of the sun, setting his foot on the small stool.

"Taranar, my father's adviser, seems to think somebody in the crowd worked a spell as you defeated Nortas, trying to stop you from winning."

Valdieron frowned thoughtfully, his brow knotted. "He's dead, isn't he?"

Andrak nodded grimly. "Aye. There was nothing we could do for him. The wound and the fireball..." he trailed off, remembering the charred remains of Nortas.

"I did not mean to slay him, you must know that." Valdieron turned to Andrak desperately, his voice a hiss. "When his sword broke, I was dazed and confused. The next thing I knew he was clinging to me, with my sword in his stomach, and then the fire erupted around me."

"I believe you, Val!" There was empathy in the young Prince's voice and his eyes brown eyes were sad. "He impaled himself on your sword trying to grab you."

Valdieron sighed again, squeezing his eyes shut as images of the battle flashed through his mind. "How long was I asleep?"

"Two days."

"Two days!" Valdieron gasped. "What happened with the tournament?"

At this, Andrak shook his head wistfully. "Unfortunately, it was decided that you could not continue, so you were forfeited from the next combat. I am sorry, Val."

"Thorgast?"

The Prince's smile widened suddenly, and he fondled a large pouch of coin at his belt. "Victorious!" He took a deep breath, as if reflecting. "You should have seen it, Val. It was incredible. Thorgast took the best that Hagar could hand out and then some, but he fought through the pain and triumphed. Hagar is probably now riding as fast as he can to get away from the city. Many in the crowd were not happy with his loss, especially after his boasting."

Valdieron stammered in disbelief. "Thorgast? Defeated

Hagar?" He cursed that he had missed it.

"Aye. The ceremony is to be conducted tonight, at my Father's request. You will come, won't you?"

"Of course," breathed Valdieron. "Why wouldn't I?"

Andrak shrugged dismissively. "I thought perhaps you would be bitter that you were scratched from the tournament."

Valdieron laughed at that, and the Prince reddened slightly. "Why should I be bitter, Andrak? Thorgast deserves the victory, if what you say is true, and like you said, I was in no state to fight, so I had to be withdrawn. Besides, there is always next year."

"Yes, but you had better watch out for me next year. I intend to go all the way." With a laugh, the Prince clapped Valdieron on the shoulder. "Have you any plans for the day?"

Valdieron shook his head. "No. I thought I might see Thorgast, first."

Andrak nodded. "Do as you will. I will see you later, before the ceremony." With a smile he departed, and Valdieron was not far behind him.

The corridors of the castle were alive with activity, and he nodded greeting to many he passed, though most were servants. A few lesser courtiers whispered at his passing, and he heard the soft words "Nortas", "killed" and "Dragon sword." It made him wonder what rumors were being spread about him after the strange events of the tournament.

After asking several guards and servants for assistance, he found Thorgast outside the castle, giving orders as he helped load several wagons with bags and boxes of supplies. Hafri was there also, shirtless and dripping sweat as he hauled freight. Thorgast spotted him and hoisted him by the waist, though mindful of his injuries as he did. "Val. It is good that you are well. Did you hear the news?"

Valdieron smiled at the big man's joyous demeanor. Only days earlier he had been darker than a thundercloud with worry. He nodded. "Aye, congratulations. I am just sorry I wasn't there to see it." He saw the bandages circling the big man's stomach, chest and arms, obviously wounds inflicted by Hagar, and he wondered why the barbarian had not had them healed. He knew Thorgast was reluctant where magic was concerned, but surely he would not resist attempts to heal him?

"I'm sure you will hear about its every detail in the days to come," quipped Hafri from atop the wagon, wiping a dirtied rag across his brow. He looked as if he was paying the penalty for too much ale the night before. Thorgast bellowed at this.

"But do not believe half of what you do hear. Already I have heard that Hagar fell to a single blow, and undoubtedly it will get worse as the days pass and the ale flows."

Valdieron laughed with him. "When are you leaving?"

The Barbarians face became suddenly stern again. "On the dawn, tomorrow. I have left it long enough as it is, Valdieron, but the King would not bring the ceremony forward, saying you would want to be a part of it. Still, it gave me time to get the weapons and supplies I needed."

"How could you afford all of this?"

Thorgast flashed him another smile. "Twenty sovereigns bet on myself soon turned itself into another fifty at the end of the tournament. Also, Llewellyn," he made a respectful signal in the air with a downcast look, "left me some money in the event of my leaving. It was not a lot, but more than I needed. So, I have been busy this last day buying what I could."

Valdieron shook his head. "Still, there is too much."

Thorgast nodded, and his smile widened even more. "The King has given me the services of a hundred of his Soldiers. They will return with me to Chul'Haka. He says he can't have one of his neighbors being victimized, so he has sent his men on 'Official business of the Crown'."

"That is great," said Valdieron, relieved his friend had found the aid he required. The big man looked at him then, a questioning hope in his eyes.

"I cannot, yet, Thorgast." The big man smiled wistfully and nodded. "There is something very important which I must do. I promise, however, that one day I will be at your side, fighting your fight."

Clapping a big hand on Valdieron's shoulder, Thorgast thanked him. "I know, Val. And may our enemies come to rue that day." He turned and began tossing bundles up to Hafri, who cursed as he continued stacking them.

Valdieron began to help, but Thorgast waved him away. "You are not fit for this, yet. Go and rest." With a thankful nod, Valdieron departed, saying he would see them later that evening.

Rather than return to the palace he decided to go to the Inn.

There were still some of his things there, which he needed to gather. He also wanted to leave on the morrow, and would need some supplies.

Gerkar was pleased to see him enter the common room. It was sparsely filled this morning, the city having had more than their share of ale in the last week. He guided Valdieron out back, and offered him something to eat, which Valdieron accepted. The walk to the Inn had taken some time, and he was surprisingly famished, even after his earlier meal. He was feeling stronger, however, as if the walk had helped remove some of his fatigue.

He chatted with Gerkar for a time, and notified the barman he would be leaving in the morning.

"I will have rations prepared for you, Val. Feel free to take what you will of Llewellyn's. He would have wanted you to, you know that." He cursed then and excused himself momentarily before returning with a large purse that jingled with coins. "I almost forgot. It seems Llewellyn placed a sizeable bet for the tournament and won. I have more than I need, so I leave the rest for you."

Valdieron almost choked as he tipped the contents onto the table. There was mostly silver in the pile, but some gold also. It was a small fortune, more than he had ever seen. He thanked Gerkar many times.

"Just take care of yourself, lad."

With the new purse weighing heavily around his neck, Valdieron took time to scout through Llewellyn's things, cleaning up his room and putting things in order. He knew Gerkar would not throw things out, but there was no need for many of the Elf's belongings, especially his clothes. Valdieron borrowed several shirts and trousers, along with another weatherproof mantle of dark gray. He felt uncomfortable taking his dead friend's clothing, but knew Llewellyn would have given him the clothes freely. He found a small traveling bag to replace his old pack, and began filling it with things he would need. He placed the Wind Dancer books on top, and would use his saddlebags for provisions and other gear he could not carry.

When he was done, he left his gear in Llewellyn's room so he could retrieve it in the morning.

Leaving from the Inn, he squinted at the mid afternoon glare.

The warmth of the new spring day made him sweat almost instantly, though his clothing was light and airy. He almost rolled up his shirtsleeves, but remembered his burned markings and left them rolled down. He stepped from the high patio, when he caught sight of something through the crowd that made him start.

Kyle!

He looked as the figure disappeared into the press of people, down the street heading south. It could not be. Kyle was dead, or so he believed. Yet he had survived the attack, so chances are others might, especially Kyle. But had it been his childhood friend or somebody whose likeness merely pricked his awareness?

He darted into the crowd, using his height to peer over the sea of bodies. Although the figure he thought was Kyle was tall, he had disappeared.

Desperate for truth, he pushed through the people, intent on catching glimpse of the figure again. He wondered if he was not letting himself become too hopeful at the thought, but it was a chance he had to take.

He did not gain a good sight of him again until they had wound further to the south, where the streets narrowed, though the press remained as tight. He was further away than before, and they were heading deeper into the slums.

He struggled to bridge the gap between them, but still he could not get a proper glimpse of the figure. He began to think something else was happening, however, when he sensed he was being trailed. He spied several figures paying him close attention, though none remained with him. It was as if each was assigned a certain area and then another took over. He assumed they were thieves, but whether it was Kalel's doing or another's, he could not tell.

He was almost within reach of the figure when the man ducked into a block, and Valdieron drew up in shock as he realized it was the smithy where he had brought his baldric and sheath. The gate was pushed closed. He looked around briefly, not wanting to draw attention to himself as he stood before the closed gates, and wandered across the street, ducking into a narrow lane where he thought few would be able to see him, and he concealed himself behind a broken crate.

The two figures who had followed him were no longer visible, and he waited and watched intently for some time, half expecting a rush of opponents down the alley. He loosed his sword, vowing that if they were after his sword again, they would find him a harder man to steal from. The rush did not come, and he began to rise when a figure near the smithy caught his attention.

A vagrant, shabbily dressed and unkempt with a tattered hat pulled over his face, was propped against the wall. A close examination saw he was not asleep, his eyes showing beneath the dark hat as he glanced around occasionally, and his right hand flexed a few times, as if stretching to keep it from falling asleep. It could also have been a signal, because he guessed the vagrant was really a thief. Val glanced around again, suddenly fearing he had been led into another trap.

Then it occurred to him, what if he wasn't the one they were following? The vagrant was obviously a sentry of sorts, and the few who he thought were following him could easily have been following the figure he had taken for Kyle. But why would they be staking out this poor smith's dwelling?

Wondering if there was some other way into the Smithy, he began looking around. Shadows were lengthening across the dim suburb, and fewer people were about, but the vagrant remained. He could pick out several others who seemed to be loitering aimlessly, but they could have been people who lived nearby.

The most likely route into the yard apart from the main gate was the surrounding rooftops. Many of the buildings were two or three levels in height, with rusted ladders or rungs allowing access to the rooftops. Most roofs were pointed and made of sheet metal, with square gutters for rainwater collection.

He took time to plan his route and let the shadows deepen across the streets. He then climbed silently onto a roof further down the alley. This roof, and many of the adjoining ones, ran down the narrow street across from the smith. He carefully stepped across them, watching every shadow around him and listening for any noises that might herald unwanted attention.

Luckily for him the roofs were sturdy for the most part, and he managed to skirt the street with a minimum of noise, though it did take longer than he expected. By the time he was sitting in the shadows of the roof adjacent to the smithy, the sun's rays were arcing above his head. A few pale lamps were lit in nearby buildings, but there was little other light, and probably would not be until the full illumination of Santari and the brighter Qantari.

But Valdieron did not need greater light to properly see his surroundings. His enhanced vision allowed him to check the street below. He saw many of the people were gone, but a few remained, as did the vagrant. There was a young man selling rotting fruit from a small cart a few buildings down. Another youth sat on a footstool he used for polishing shoes, the wiping cloth settled over his face as he leaned back against a wall.

The smithy's dark interior was also visible from here. He saw a small window in the side of the building's dilapidated roof. The broken shutters were rusted open and he knew that with a small leap he could be inside. One room on the floor below it was illuminated with warm firelight. There was shadowy movement within, and he detected the faint smell of burning oak.

He almost jumped as a shadow moved across the roof ahead and to the side of him. He saw it was a figure, clad in black to blend in with the night. It moved silently, creeping towards the roof's edge closest to the smithy, with footfalls no louder than a cat's.

Valdieron knew the thieves were up to something here, and guessed it was something he should stay out of. Maybe they were exacting a punishment for the smith not paying his dues to the guild or some such matter he had little understanding of.

Still, the figure's likeness of Kylaran had him wondering, and he could not walk away with the possibility that these poor people would be victimized by the guild, for whatever reason. He had some weight with the guild, now that he knew Kalamar was the guild leader, so maybe he could help the smith somehow.

Cautiously he moved behind the dark figure who had halted momentarily at the edge of the roof, perhaps awaiting a signal. Unfortunately for Valdieron, he was three paces away when the aged metal beneath him groaned under the pressure. Not loud, but the thief spun quickly, dropping into a crouch and a knife appeared in his hand. He did not hesitate, and lunged at Valdieron.

Valdieron stepped into the unexpected attack. Weapon-less,

he swept the thief's forearm with two extended hands, knocking the knife from its path to his stomach. Using his right hand, he grasp the thief's arm and spun it sharply around as he stepped past him, so that the arm was pressed behind the thief's back. He clutched him around the neck with his left arm.

"Not a sound," he whispered, as he tightened the grip on the thief's arm. "Drop the knife."

The thief resisted momentarily, but then the knife fell from his grasp. Using his booted foot, Valdieron deadened the knife's fall, so that it clattered with less noise against the roof.

Now that he had the thief, he did not know what to do with him. He had no desire to kill him, but he could not let him go, or he might rejoin his comrades below. Kicking his feet from under him, he lowered him to the roof on his stomach. Grasping both of his wrists behind his back, he removed his belt and used it to fasten his hands and feet together behind his back. It was painfully uncomfortable, but he reasoned that a decent thief would be out of it in a few minutes.

He also tore a strip of cloth from the man's cloak and gagged him, just in case.

Looking down into the now dark street, he saw the vagrant had disappeared, along with the other two he suspected were also thieves. A soft noise like a scraping footstep inside the smithy grounds caught his attention, and he guessed where the vagrant and his men had gone.

Without glancing back at the bound thief, he leapt softly across the dark void to the window, clutching the sill for support as it wobbled beneath his weight. Inside was a large room, which ran the length of the upper floor. It was obviously a bedroom with a large bed off to one side with wardrobes and a table and a smaller pallet against the far wall. A web of dark rafters ran below him over the room, and he stepped onto them.

Suddenly a cry came from below, accompanied by a piercing scream. He heard a thud and a crash of cookware, before shouting drifted up the narrow stairway in the far wall. Cursing, he almost dropped down when booted steps sounded on the wooden stairs. Lifting himself back up, he waited.

A young woman, who was glancing behind with concern and calling for somebody downstairs to hurry, ushered a smaller figure into the room. Valdieron recognized the young boy he had met on the two occasions he had been to the Smithy. There was another crash from downstairs and a cry of pain, before heavier footsteps were heard on the steps, and another figure appeared.

Valdieron's gaze locked onto the young woman as she spun back, searching the bedroom as if expecting others to be waiting. She was dressed in a thin gray sleeping gown. Her long hair was like blazing sunlight as if caught by the light from below. His breath caught in his throat and his stomach cramped into knots as he recognized her, and tears rimmed his eyes as he unconsciously fingered the pale rose-scented scarf around his neck.

Natasha.

He swayed and almost fell from the rafter, but steadied himself. He was not dreaming, he knew that.

So that meant-.

Kylaran crashed into the room then, struggling with a dark-clad thief who clutched a dagger in one hand, which Kylaran held away from his face as they tumbled. With a flick, the big man tossed the smaller thief away. The lithe figure rolled to his feet like a cat as three others entered the room, armed with daggers and short swords.

From a side window, two other veiled figures appeared and Natasha screamed as she clutched the boy tightly. Kyle was unarmed as he stood before them, but nobody moved. Then one of the figures dropped his veil and stepped forward. Valdieron almost cursed aloud as he recognized the young thief, Kalel.

"Well, Smith. Where is your duty this month? I have asked politely for it twice, and I have not received it." The sandy-haired thief bore a mocking smile as he confronted Kylaran.

"I told you. You will get the money when I have it. How was I to know the amount was treble with the advent of the tournament?" Kylaran's voice belied his calm as he tried to appease the thief.

Valdieron marked how his friend had changed over the few seasons, being taller than he remembered him. His hair was thicker and he wore a rough but suiting beard.

"It is common knowledge, smith. It is your duty to find out these things. Alas, you cannot pay, and you know the punishment for that. Perhaps in the lonely nights to come you might have a chance to figure out how next to pay on time, and maybe then we will return your wife to you."

Kalel's words rocked Valdieron with their implication. Wife? Had Kyle and Natasha married in such a short time, or had the thief mistaken their partnership? He growled low in his throat at the thief's threat, remembering how it hurt to lose something you cared for, even for a short time.

Stepping lightly to the next rafter he dropped easily into the bedroom between Kalel and Kyle. The thieves gave a start as he landed, but Kalel's eyes widened with shock as he saw who it was.

"You. What are you doing here?"

"I could ask the same thing of you, Kalel. I am sure Kalamar will, when I tell him of this. No doubt he will be more than delighted to hear of it. I would have thought you learned your lesson last time."

Kalel sneered contemptuously, then smiled. "I could say the same for you. Surely you haven't forgotten what happened when last you confronted me?" He flipped his dagger in his hand and smiled as some of the other thieves chuckled softly.

"Of course not. That is why I will let you walk out of here now, and maybe Kalamar will go lighter on you than you deserve." A sweat broke out on his brow, though not from fear. His body tingled in anticipation of a confrontation. He would have liked to repay Kalel for his backstabbing attack during their last confrontation, but still he preferred they left. His strength hadn't quite returned, and his wounds still ached a little.

"I think not. Besides, Kalamar will not punish what he does not know about."

Valdieron gave a resigned sigh as Kalel signaled and the thieves began to spread out around him. He turned to the side and motioned for Kyle to stay back. Obviously the big man did not recognize Valdieron in the dim light, for he looked at him curiously.

"This is no longer your fight, Kyle. Stand back."

Kylaran nodded slowly and stepped back, throwing a protective arm around Natasha and the boy who both sobbed faintly. He wondered how this stranger knew his name?

The thieves opted for their longer weapons: sabers, rapiers, a falchion and Kalel with a gleaming new longsword. Slowly

Valdieron drew his sword. Despite the gloom, the thieves gave a start at the sight of the weapon.

Kalel sneered. "So the sword will be mine again, huh. Thank you for the gift."

The thieves rushed forward in a concerted attack, though only three could press at him effectively. Valdieron spun in a blur, his sword knocking away two thrusting strikes and he stepped past the third. His foot lashed out and dropped one of the thieves, catching him on the jaw, while a punch with the hilt of his weapon caught another, who fell back dazed. Not surprisingly, Kalel had dropped back out of the fight.

The melee became unorganized then, as thieves pressed at him in waves. He smiled, for together they could have overwhelmed him, but now he began picking them off one by one. One saber slipped past a parry but he arched away from it, and it sliced his shirt, which was the closest any of their weapons got to him.

Two thieves remained against him after only a few exchanges, and they looked as if they may flee at any moment. The other thieves writhed on the ground in various degrees of agony from smashed noses and jaws to broken arms or legs. He had not used the blade to strike, not chancing the possibility of seriously injuring any of them. They were merely pawns. Kalel was the one he would hurt, if necessary.

All through the fight he expected Kalel's sneak attack as before, and this time he was ready for it. He lost view of the thief as he dodged an attack but he spun as he sensed the attack, and hammered the spinning knife from the air as it flew at him. Simultaneously he arced a kick backwards, catching a lunging thief in the face and dropping him like a rock, his saber rattling to the floor. The last thief did the only thing that would save him. He ran. He was down the stairs in a flash, but Valdieron let him go as he turned to Kalel.

The thief was not smiling now as he clutched his sword tightly. Valdieron stood between him and the doorway, but a window lay opened behind the thief, and he was edging back towards it. Valdieron grinned at the thief's discomfort. "I would not be too close to the city by the morning, if I were you, Kalel. Your luck doesn't seem to be holding out lately, and I daresay Kalamar will not be so easy on you this time."

Kalel fled. He hung in the window momentarily, giving

Valdieron a look that promised ramifications. He disappeared then, dropping to the ground below and fading into the night. One by one, the thieves on the ground stirred and also fled, helping their other companions who were not so well off. Soon, all the thieves were gone and Valdieron sheathed his weapon. Kylaran gave a grateful sigh and stepped forward.

"We are thankful for your intervention, friend. You are...?"

Valdieron turned to face him and swept his hair back to clear his face, and he could barely contain a wide smile. "Surprised to find you here, Kylaran Jackson, and you as well, Natasha Peterson."

Recognition dawned on both faces then. Kyle's face became ashen and he fought for breath, while Natasha's face went even paler, and she fainted with surprise. Kyle stepped to her side before she fell, but Valdieron was quicker, and they set her down on the bed gently.

"Who is he, Kyle?" The young boy was staring up at Valdieron with a mixture of awe and terror, and his lower lip quivered with fear.

"An old friend," whispered Kyle with a choking laugh. "An old friend."

Chapter 35

Kyle stared across at Valdieron, his face a mask of wonder and awe as Val related the events of his past half year. He spoke little as Valdieron went along, apart from commenting on something or another. His brow knotted with concern and disbelief as Valdieron described the Dream Plane and the quest he had been given to discover the pieces of the Disk of Akashel. He expressed his sorrow at the death of Llewellyn, whom he had never met.

"I had heard your name whispered around the city," marveled the big smith, taking a large gulp of his ale. Valdieron sipped at his, his head lifting occasionally to the roof where Natasha rested above, still passed out from before. "But I heard it belonged to a great Warrior from some far away land, so I did not give it much thought. Had we the money, we would have been to the tournament and seen you, but as you can see, we are not really settled as yet, and the guilds are still hassling me."

Valdieron smiled wistfully. "You probably wouldn't have recognized me from afar, anyhow. I almost did not recognize you at first. You have changed over the months."

Kyle frowned with a weak nod. "It hasn't been easy, Val. When we left Shadowvale, we had no money or possessions other than what we could scrounge from the remains of the village or nearby farmhouses. Every house in the area was razed, so we couldn't find help close by. We stopped to see my aunty Marna at Marsh Point, but she could not support us. We decided that we should head to Thorhus, where I thought I could get a smithy or become an apprentice."

Kyle's moist eyes drifted to where Natasha slept above.

"You love each other, don't you?"

Kyle turned his gaze to meet Valdieron's, and there was shame there, but he was honest as he nodded. "I have always loved her, Val, though I never told you. We were the only survivors, because I was up early in the smithy, working on a present for my ma, and then Natasha rode past, and she stopped to talk. The next thing we knew, Trolls were everywhere. I grabbed my father's axe," he motioned to the axe resting now at his side, the double-bladed weapon Val had seen hanging in the Smithy many times, "and then I knew we had to get out of there. Houses were burning and people were scampering through the streets with weapons, but the Trolls were tearing through us like we were nothing. Some of them set fire to the houses, though I could tell they did not like the flames."

More tears flowed down his cheeks and he cupped his face in his hands briefly. "I saw my father get hurled into our burning house by a Troll, and he was dead before I could save him."

Valdieron could only reach over the table and lay a soothing hand on his friend's arm. He had thought he had seen chaos, but Kyle had seen many people slain, people he had known and grown up with. How much worse were his nightmares or memories, he wondered? "I know, Kyle. My father is gone too."

"I know how she felt about you though, Val. She told me about the meeting at your house." The big man's words were slightly choked as he pressed on. "She did love you, she expressed as much, and she did not speak for days after we found the burned remains of your farm. We thought you dead also." There was regret in his voice now as he eyed the scarf around Val's neck. "She will go with you again, if you ask her. I know she will."

Valdieron smiled with thanks, realizing the sacrifice his big friend was making for him, though he shook his head. "Kyle, I could not ask her that, even if I wanted to. I told you, I am no longer the person you knew. I have a perilous path ahead of me now, which I feel pulling me down darker and more dangerous paths. I fear that any who accompany me will only be lost to these perils." He sighed deeply as he rose and shifted to the cold hearth. Pressing his hands to the worn stone mantle, he stared down at his feet. "I cannot even decipher my feelings towards her now. If things had stayed as they were, who knows, but now she needs you, as you need her."

Kyle shifted in his seat awkwardly. "You mean to say I cannot help you with your quest?"

Valdieron turned and found the big man wearing a sad frown, as if he was a child having his favorite toy taken from him.

"There is no need, Kyle. I have chosen this path for myself, come what may, but you have another life, now. I cannot ask you to accompany me any more than I could Natasha."

Kyle nodded, maybe a little thankfully as well, but he remained pensive. "Then we must part again?"

Valdieron nodded and returned to his seat. "Yes, but do not think I won't return. When I do, I expect you to be the best known smith in the city."

Kyle huffed with disbelief. "Chances are I'll be run out of the city by the guild after this."

Valdieron chuckled and gave him a slap on the shoulder. "Don't worry about the guild, Kyle. I have my connections, and I don't think Kalel or any of his cronies will harass you after I'm through."

Kyle shook his head in wonder again. "You amaze me, Val. I always thought you were different, destined for something great, somehow, and here I find you after I think you're dead, and you have done things beyond belief in two seasons. You have fought a devil and befriended an Elf, and you are one of the best fighters in this year's Tournament." He shook his head again. "I wish I could help you."

"So do I, Kyle! So do I."

Natasha was there then, standing in the stairway, her face sleepy but her eyes rimmed with tears. Kyle rose and helped her to the table where she sat.

"Kolin is asleep. He's a little shocked, but he will be all right."

Kyle had told him the building had previously belonged to an old smith, who had taken Kyle on as an apprentice when they got to the city, in the hope the youth would take over after his death. The old man had passed away only recently, and with no other family in the city, Natasha and Kyle had adopted Kolin in memory of his dead grandfather and all he had done for them.

Valdieron rose and went to her then, and she smiled at him, like meeting an old friend. He embraced her briefly, marveling at her warmth and beauty.

"Are you well?"

She nodded, though she appeared shaken up still. "Yes. We missed you. We will miss you again."

He realized she had heard him speaking of his quest, and

wondered what else she had heard. "I must go."

She nodded understanding and patted him on the cheek. "I know. But you will return."

He wished he could be so sure, but he merely nodded with a forced smile. He remembered suddenly that the ceremony was taking place at the palace, as he realized it was well into the night. He cursed silently and rose.

"The ceremony for my friend Thorgast is under way at the palace tonight. Why don't you come with me?"

Kyle laughed and Natasha gawked at him in disbelief. "We could not possibly go, Val. That is not our scene, and there is Kolin, plus we have nothing to wear."

He was surprised she had not mentioned that about clothing first. She was a woman after all.

"Kolin can come. He will be well looked after if he has to sleep, and clothing is no problem. I am sure there will be somebody who is still open and ready to trade at this hour." He brought out his full purse and shook it meaningfully. "Besides, I'm sure the Princess has something that would fit you. You are about the same height."

If the two paled at the sight of the coin-filled purse, their jaws dropped in amazement at the mention of the Princess. Kyle was laughing then, and Natasha looked stunned.

"Settled then. Whenever you're ready, we'll get going."

Still stunned, Natasha went to gather Kolin and change while Kyle also took the chance to change into something else. Kolin eyed Valdieron with sleepy curiosity as Kyle carried him on his shoulders.

It was not very difficult to find a tailor open late who dealt in both men's and women's clothing. After claims of having swindled the tailor out of funds for his daughter's education by getting such a low price, they left with a slender dress of pale green and white slippers for Natasha; a rose-colored shirt and black trousers with fine leather boots for Kyle, and white pants with a brown shirt for Kolin along with dark leather boots. All were of silk and well cut.

Getting back into the castle and palace was not difficult. The guards were familiar with his description now and he was allowed passage. The presence of the others made them curious, and the Captain of the guards sent a runner through to Kalamar to tell him that Valdieron had arrived with others.

Kalamar was waiting in the lobby of the main building, beside the fountain, and he waved as they entered and crossed to them. He was dressed in a gray outfit striped with crimson, and he wore a studded earring and a plain gold ring on his right hand. He carried a silver goblet of wine, and it was obvious he had come from the ceremony.

"Thank the stars you're here, Val. I began to worry for you. What happened?"

Valdieron briefly described the events of the evening, and Kalamar frowned at the mention of Kalel.

"I will see he doesn't bother you again, friend Smith." He gave greeting as Valdieron made the introductions.

"I thought it would be all right if I brought them along. I could not leave them in case Kalel returned."

Kalamar waved it off. "Of course its all right. From what you have said, it is a night of celebration for you all. Come, I will show you where you can get cleaned up and changed."

He took them to the guest quarters where he had several servants prepare hasty baths and press the clothes ready for wearing. He even took the liberty of bringing out a silver necklace and earrings for Natasha. "It would be a shame for a woman of your beauty to go without ornamentation." Where the Spy came up with them Valdieron did not know nor did he particularly want to know. He wondered if somebody would be missing some jewelry on the morrow.

Valdieron was also provided with new clothes; a blue silk shirt with white trousers striped with gold, and high boots. He was self-conscious about his strangely burned forearms, so he was glad for the coverage provided by the long sleeves. He was surprised to find the Tear glowing a strange golden hue, and was unusually warm against his skin. It was the first he had noticed it since arriving at the castle.

Kalamar led them back to the hall. Valdieron was forced to leave his weapons with Kalamar who had them locked away for safekeeping.

There were over three hundred people inside the great hall, and he saw the expressions of awe set on the faces of Kyle and Natasha when they entered. Kolin took it all in with youthful surprise, clinging to Kyle at the sight of the many strangers.

Long tables were set throughout the room. Each was topped with silver cutlery and tableware over white silk tablecloths, while people sat in finely crafted wooden chairs, which were padded for comfort. The royal family sat at the largest table in the room, each dressed regally and talking among themselves. Thorgast and Hafri were at a table to their right, seemingly on their own, but a place beside them was obviously where Kalamar had been, and another spot was set up for Valdieron. They looked up in surprise as the five approached, and Kalamar motioned for a servant to make another three places for Kyle, Natasha and Kolin. Food was already being eaten, and as they were seated and the introductions made, more food was brought. Talk was made between mouthfuls of food and drink. Kyle seemed more than a little nervous, but Natasha looked as if she were enjoying the public appearance, while Kolin stared around him in wonder.

Bards were playing music throughout the room. Valdieron found himself thinking of Llewellyn, who would have enjoyed this evening greatly. He would miss the Elf, he knew, and every time he heard sweet music he thought of him.

At length the meal was finished, and everything cleared away. King Dhoric rose to address the gathering.

"Friends and guests. I thank you all for your presence here tonight, with the purpose of presenting this year's winner of the Tournament with his plaque and prize. I am sure you will all agree with me when I say that this year the Tournament was an even greater success than we have seen in many years." He paused as the crowd cheered. "It also saw the unveiling of a new champion. Make welcome and give praise, to Thorgast, Warrior of the Urak'Hai and Prince of Chul'Haka."

The crowd applauded and cheered then as Hafri nudged the red-faced Barbarian to his feet. The King stepped away from his table as Thorgast approached him, welcoming him with an extended hand.

"In tribute of your honor and courage, we give to you the coveted Shield of Thorhus." This was a miniature tower-shield bearing the King's etched emblem on its polished surface. Beneath it was etched Thorgast's name and his victory in the tournament in the year of 5119 of the Third Era. The King had already given him his five hundred Sovereigns so that Thorgast could buy his supplies.

Thorgast bowed as the King placed the shield around his neck on a fine silver necklace. When he rose, his face was puffed with pride and emotion, and there were tears in his dark eyes as he returned to the table.

"Now. Let you all enjoy yourselves for the rest of the evening." So saying, the King waited for the rest of his family to rise, and the crowd rose also to see them leave. Surprisingly Andrak and Kitara stayed, breaking away and heading to the table where Valdieron and the others stood. On cue, servants rushed in and began to shift the tables to the outside of the room while the Bards gathered on the lower level of the dais and began to play again. Servants wandered about with trays of wine and fine ale.

"Valdieron! We were wondering where you had gotten. I am glad you made it!" Andrak was dressed in gray leggings tucked into high black boots, and wore a loose shirt of lavender and crimson. A loose gold chain encircled his neck, hidden as it hung behind his shirt.

"Better late than never, that was what my Pa used to say." With a smile he glanced past the Prince to Kitara, who was standing aside looking around the room. She was wearing a sparkling white dress with a sweeping gown and frilled bodice. A diamond circlet was set in the swell of her dark hair, and from it hung a small silver chain, connected to a dark gray symbol about the size of a coin, though thicker.

Valdieron introduced Kyle and Natasha to them both, with Kolin staring wide-eyed at the two royals, like a rabbit ready to run. Surprisingly, Kitara and Natasha got along well, and the two drifted away after a short time to talk and mingle, while the men drank and chatted.

Hafri and Kalamar drifted away shortly after. Kyle and Thorgast also seemed to take a liking to each other as the two sat to talk to each other, in between Thorgast being congratulated by those passing by. Valdieron knew the Barbarian spoke of his return to his homeland, and Kyle listened with rapture, like a child being entertained by a story. Valdieron realized his friend had probably only heard of the Urak'Hai in stories, as had he before meeting Thorgast in Ranil.

Suddenly a woman was standing before him, the sweep of her long black gown caressing the floor. She was tall and pretty, some years older than him with curled brown hair past her shoulders. Her low-cut dress clung to her slender figure, accentuating her womanly gifts. Her full-lipped smile revealed sparkling teeth. Pale gray eyes regarded him as she would regard something she was about to buy. A long necklace with a ruby pendant hung between her bosom, and Valdieron wondered which drew the eye more readily.

"Would you care to dance, Valdieron of Tyr?"

It was an invitation more than a question, though she gave him no chance to answer as she grasped his hand. He realized there was no pain in his hands or arms where he had been burned, and even the scarred dragon sigils on his wrists felt like they were not there.

They entered the throng of dancers and dug deeper into their midst. Valdieron would have preferred hanging on the fringes, but it was obvious this lady wanted to be seen dancing with him. He tried not to blush under the gazes of those nearby as she turned and pulled his body against hers. He was sweating slightly at her touch. Her perfume, light and smelling of rose, made him think of Natasha. He was taller than her, but she peered up at him in a way that made him feel shorter somehow. He tried not to peer down the front of her dress as he looked down at her, though he did slip occasionally.

"I do not dance well, Madam," he confessed as she led him through a few steps, and he clumsily followed. In truth he had had few occasions to dance, and only then during the festivals in the village.

"That can be amended, Valdieron." Her smile was without guile and her intention made clear as she took a deep breath that swelled her chest. He flushed again and looked away, though he almost kicked himself for it.

Salima was her name, the daughter of one of the King's advisers, and she let it be known that she was unmarried though looking desperately, which made him nervous. She asked in a roundabout way if he was related to the King or a nobleman himself. When he told her he was the son of a Horse Breeder, she laughed and slapped him softly as if she thought he was joking.

She chatted with him intimately as they swirled about slowly, whispering up into his ear as she pressed against him, adding to his awkwardness. Though it was not a displeasing predicament to be caught him, he felt trapped. She was obviously trying to tempt him with her sweet words, and had he been like Hafri in any way, he would already have succumbed to her dulcet seductions and been led away.

"May I have this dance?"

Salima cursed softly as she spun to see who had interrupted. Her scowl turned to a wide smile as she beheld Princess Kitara standing there. She curtsied slightly as she released Valdieron, though her slender fingers caressed his hands as she released him, and she flashed him another smile before departing.

"Having fun, were we?"

He had half hoped that Salima would refuse Kitara as the Princess stepped in to him and caught him up in the same embrace. Obviously it was normal to dance this close here, and he sighed softly as her warm body pressed against him. She was almost at a level with him, so he did not have the problems he had with Salima with regards to her bosom, not necessarily a good thing.

"I felt like a rabbit caught in a snare, with the Hunter bearing down on me," he confessed with a relieved chuckle, to which she smiled.

"Salima certainly has her charms."

The emphasis she placed on charms made him blush again as they danced. His chest grew warm and he drew away slightly, realizing it was the Dragons Tear. Its touch was almost unbearable against his skin.

"Is something amiss?"

Kitara regarded him, and he could not help but notice how beautiful she was, which made him wonder why he had thought that at that moment. He saw, the Coin-like pendant against her forehead, its surface etched with the symbol of two miniature dragons clutching a globe in their clawed feet, their tails tracing the smooth edge to meet head to tail.

He knew suddenly this was a piece of the Disk of Akashel.

He reeled away from her then, and hardly heard her gasp of surprise as he pushed through the crowd. Suddenly he felt overwhelmed and suffocating, and the noises around him intensified in volume. He bumped past people, bringing soft curses and looks, but he paid them no heed as he searched for the nearest exit.

He stumbled into the garden, collapsing onto the grass with a groan.

Silent footfalls on the rich grass did not cause him to raise his head. He smelt the Princess' rich perfume as she sat beside him in silence. Her arm encircled his shoulders and she pressed against him comfortingly.

"Are you all right?"

He was shivering, whether from the cold or the sudden fear he could not tell. He took a rasping breath and looked at her. The pain in his eyes must have been clear, for she gave a start.

"There is something wrong. Tell me!"

It was no command. The concern in her voice was evident as she grabbed his hand. Her skin felt warm, where he himself felt like ice, and he wondered how she could not feel it.

Reaching inside his shirt he brought out the Dragon's tear, and she gasped at its illuminated beauty. It was a pale crimson color now, different than he had ever seen it. He knew it was a result of the presence of the piece of the disc. With his other hand he reached out and touched the pendant on her forehead.

The eye blazed on impact, and he released the Disk instantly, hoping he had not caused her any harm. His skin tingled, and he wondered if it was because he was so close to the Piece or because he'd touched it.

Blinking, the Princess was staring at him with disbelief. "Who are you?"

"If only I knew," he whispered.

"What is going on Val?"

He regarded her fearfully, wondering what danger her knowing might put her in.

"You are beautiful!"

She gave a surprised start at this comment, and blushed. He had spoken aloud, and he blushed more furiously than he had all night, even while catching glimpses of Salima's bosom.

"I'm sorry. I should not have said that."

Kitara laughed as he stammered though the apology. "Why be sorry, Valdieron? I took no offence from the comment. It was just surprising, that is all."

Desperate to change the subject, he began to tell her the secrets he had omitted from the original telling of his life. Her face darkened and she looked thoughtful, though shocked as he continued.

"And this?" she unsecured the pendant from her tiara and held it in her hand, almost like a spider. "This is part of a Symbol which will help recreate these Seals?" Her voice wavered as she shook her head in denial. "How can this be?

This pendant has been part of my Mother's heritage for many generations."

"The Seals were created thousands of years ago, and their creation broke the Symbol. Thus was it scattered, thought worthless. It is not impossible that your mother's family came by this piece. Maybe they even have more." He wondered at this. He knew that Kitara's mother had been Dak'marian, and he would check out this lead when he went to Dak'mar in search of his own identity.

Kitara clasped the pendant in her fist and held it to her breast, biting her lip as she closed her eyes. Then she pressed it to him. "Then you must take it."

Valdieron stammered as he searched for a reply, seeing the pain in her eyes. Obviously it was something she held dear, as he did his own Dragon Tear pendant. It was a link with his mother, as this was for her. Gently he closed her fingers around it.

"Keep it for me. I will return for it one day if I can. For now I know where it is."

She gave a choking sob and embraced him with relief. "Thank you," she whispered in his ear, and he felt light-headed again by her presence and smell. He was loath to release her. "I will keep it safe, always."

A tightening of his stomach and a tingling along his skin he almost passed off as nervousness at her embrace. He spied a figure exiting the hall, walking slowly as if savoring the garden's solitude. The man was tall and slender, with flowing white hair, though he appeared youthful and fair. He was dressed in a flowing black cloak traced with silver. He was smiling, and his eyes darted around the garden as if cherishing every sight from the dim moonlight, though Valdieron thought his eyes turned towards him more often than not.

The man came closer. His path would take him directly past them, so he awkwardly released the Princess, who seemed unaware of the stranger. She hung her head as she settled back, and secured the pendant to a chain around her neck rather than on her forehead.

The stranger's presence and closeness exacerbated the uneasy feeling and Valdieron knew it was not due to the princess. There was something about the stranger that was not right.

His boots. They were not the type usually worn by lords at a ceremony, being thick-soled for walking not dancing, and they still bore the stains of dust as if hastily wiped over.

The figure was passing then, and as Valdieron sensed something was wrong, the man spun and lunged at him. A dark blade appeared in his hand as if by magic. Caught in the crouch, Valdieron as barely able to bat the man's hand aside as he rolled, away from Kitara to draw the man's attention.

With dazzling speed the man spun again and thrust at him, repeatedly jabbing the blade to keep him at bay. Behind the figure, Valdieron saw Kitara still seated, and wondered why she had not moved.

"She is caught in my spell, Kay'taari. I will enjoy her when I am done with you."

The man's sibilant words made Valdieron shudder. What magic had the man used and why hadn't he used it on him? Surely that would have been far easier than trying to use the dagger he wielded.

Not that he was beyond ability with the weapon. Valdieron felt the blade pass within a hair of his face as he jerked back from a cut. The man thrust again, but Valdieron was ready and stepped to the side of it. Using one arm he hooked the man's wrist and with the other jabbed with the open palm into the man's elbow. There was a cracking as the elbow snapped, and the figure screamed as the blade dropped to the ground. The pain did not last, however, and he spun and struck Valdieron in the stomach. The force knocked him into the air and back, where he rolled to his feet gasping for breath. Looking up, the figure was gone, and guards were running from the hall, Kalamar leading them. Kitara was rising groggily to her feet, shaking her head as if to shake off fatigue, and she stumbled to Valdieron.

"What happened? What are you doing there? I feel like I fell asleep for a moment."

Valdieron looked around for signs of the man, but he was gone without trace. Kalamar was there then, and he grasped the man's dropped dagger like it was made of ice. The dark blade gave off no reflection in the moonlight.

"We were warned by Dhoric's magicians that there was dark magic being done in the palace." He glanced at Valdieron and shook his head. "I figured it would have something to do with you. Who was that guy?"

Valdieron shrugged, but another voice cut him off. "That was an Ashar'an Assassin, Kalamar, someone even you should be fearful of."

Kalamar spun, and his own rapier was in his hand in a flash as two figures stepped from the nearby bushes. Valdieron did not have to squint as he looked at them, and his eyes widened in surprise. He almost thought one of the figures, the one who had spoken, was Astan-Valar. The other man he could have mistaken for Thorgast, though if possible this Barbarian was taller but leaner. On his back rested a huge sword, and though he did not move at Kalamar's action, his dark eyes took in everything.

"No need for weapons, Kalamar. If I were an enemy, you would be dead by now. Advice is what I have, advice that shall be heard. Take me to your king."

Valdieron stepped aside with Kitara as the two passed, and he was surprised when the old man turned to him. "You will come too." His eyes, like pools of dark ash, seemed to evaluate Valdieron.

"Who are you?" Valdieron whispered, knowing there was some link between this man and Astan-Valar. They appeared as brothers by their likeness.

"A friend of your father's, Valdieron." The old man's smile was warm and assuring.

The words came as a blow greater than that which the strange Assassin had given him. Valdieron felt like falling. What did the old man mean? He had never seen him before in his life, and the man would have to be a very old friend of his father's if he were indeed his friend.

Kitara led him, though he hardly saw where they were headed as his thoughts wandered. He had so many unanswered questions, and with every one he did find answers for, they were usually bad and merely conjured twice as many questions. He would get to the bottom of this, however. The doubts he carried with him would be assayed once and for all.

Chapter 36

The large room was noticeably tense as the old man seated himself by the large burning hearth. His huge Barbarian friend stood at his shoulder, scanning everybody. Two of Dhoric's magicians flanked the closed door, one in gray robes and the other in brown, with a dozen guards set without. Valdieron was seated at one of two windows in the far wall, overlooking the garden below. Beside him sat Kitara, while Andrak and Thorgast stood beside her. The Prince's hand rested on his sister's shoulder as he stared across the room at his father.

Dhoric was pacing before the fire, dressed in his fine clothing, while off to the side his eldest son, Arakon, stood beside the seated form of his brother Khalad. Where the heir was dark haired, tall and muscular with green eyes and a smiling, carefree demeanor, Khalad was short and muscular with sandy hair like Andrak, and had pale blue eyes. He was also crippled from the waist down, the result of a horse-riding accident during his youth.

"Who are you and what are you doing here in my city, old man? By what right do you request this meeting?" Dhoric was obviously not amused with the impromptu get-together.

"My name is meaningless to you, but know that I am called Ka'Varel. My big friend here is Tyrun, formerly of the Urak'Hai." Saying this, the old man looked specifically at Thorgast, who stood beside Andrak. His face was dark as if he wrestled with some inner turmoil, though he remained silent.

"As to what I am doing in this city, that is a story in itself. Sit thee down, and I will tell all."

With a scowl the King was brought a chair, and he sat across from Ka'Varel with a sigh.

"Remember not so long ago, these men," he indicated to the two men standing guard at the door, but by his gesture meant all of the magicians, "were sent to you with news from the Astral City. Can you recall what that message entailed?"

The King nodded. "It concerned the amassing of my army. Why?" His tone demanded to know how this old man knew.

"The reason for this was not given to you, other than the

warning that there may soon come a threat to all the realms of Kil'Tar."

Off to the side, Valdieron was silent, knowing what the old man was referring to, as did Kitara beside him. Her soft hand clutched his and he gripped it thankfully.

"This threat has become a reality over the last few weeks."

"What threat is this, Ka'Varel? I have been given no such indication, and I think I have a right to know."

"I have no doubt you know your histories, Majesty, so for the benefit of the others here I shall relate to you a tale." The old man paused slightly and made a whispering gesture, and Valdieron felt the back of his neck tingle. The two magicians at the door shifted alertly. Ka'Varel had cast a spell. "Forgive me," he breathed a little tightly. "I just set up a ward to prevent others from listening in on us."

Kalamar shifted from the shadows of the corner. "There are no spies or others within fifty yards of this room." He frowned with a cold certainty, as if Ka'Varel's actions were an insult to him. The old man spread his hands in supplication.

"Of course, Master Kalamar. But I do not speak of normal means, and there are many other ways, believe me."

Kalamar nodded his head, appeased by the answer and returned to his corner, though he looked around warily still.

"In the childhood of our world, the gods created a race known as the Essence Lords. Like most newborn, they were naive and stubborn, but they held within themselves great power. Their numbers were not great, for they seldom bred, due to their aloof nature and long lifespan.

A time came when the essence lords became divided. A large section, called the Ashar'an, wanted power and access to the Essence that is magic, while others knew of the dangers and rejected the Ashar'an."

The mood around the room became dark, and even the light seemed to fade around them, lending its weight to Ka'Varel's story. Valdieron, who had heard the story in even greater depth, grew intent as he listened.

"Harnessing Essence has devastating consequences for the world. With each use of the Essence, there is a portion that is tainted and released. This is called the Unlife, which breeds evil in the world like a dead horse breeds maggots. From this Unlife there came many creatures, the most cruel and nefarious of which being the Demons.

Unfortunately, the Ashar'an became more powerful than ever as they dabbled in more arcane magic. The remaining essence lords banded together to form the Kay'taari. They knew they had neither the numbers nor the power to defeat the Ashar'an, thus, they scoured the world for help, and came upon the Dragons, who are creatures attuned to the Essence. Their very existence is the antithesis of the Demons. The Dragons gave their aid, knowing what would happen without it, and there was a battle such as had never been seen and never will be seen again."

Ka'Varel paused for breath, and Valdieron took the opportunity to glance across at Kitara, who was staring entranced at Ka'Varel. He could see the others were also, except for the Barbarian, Tyrun, who caught his eye and gave a reassuring wink.

"Suffice to say that the Dragons and the Kay'taari were victorious, wiping out the stronger faction and driving the Demons back into the voids from where they came. They created portals, which were magically sealed, and destroyed many of the greater artifacts so the power of people would not rise to such heights again.

Unfortunately," the word brought gasps of surprise from some of the others, and Ka'Varel revealed a small grin. "Unfortunately, the new races which came along; the Elves, Dwarves, Humans and Barbarians, were also able to tap into the Essence, though to a lesser degree. Some of the Kay'taari who remained showed them how to control their powers so they would not upset the balance. Their controls were not strict enough, however, and the Seals locking the portals were shattered, and the Demons returned. There was another battle as the Loremasters battled the Demons, and once again the Unlife was driven back into the voids and the Portals resealed."

The old man's face became grave, and Valdieron knew what was coming.

"The Seals were not as powerful as they originally were, and even now they break, though the Loremasters are as strict as possible with the control of the Essence. The Demons have returned to Kil'Tar. This is the threat which you were not warned of, King Dhoric, a threat which may see the destruction of the world."

Almost everybody gasped. Shocked whispering erupted, even from the magicians who denied involvement. Kitara clutched Valdieron's arm. He was glad for the contact, but knew what fear lay behind it.

"How can you be sure of this, Ka'Varel?" asked the King.

Ka'Varel held his hand out. In it rested the dark dagger the Assassin had wielded. "Because already their minions strike. Earlier this evening, an Ashar'an assassin made his way into the palace and attempted to take somebody's life. Know that the Ashar'an are an order of zealots who follow the Unlife. Their assassins are known for their ability to kill and leave no trace. Fortunately, the attack tonight failed. That they would strike is a true sign they know the Demons are returning."

"How do we combat this Unlife?" asked Arakon grimly. His eyes belied his calm as they scanned the room frantically, searching for answers.

Ka'Varel shrugged. "As we always have; with courage, with strength and with luck. Yet it will be for naught if we banish them again only to have the Seals break in another century, and the process repeated. The Demons breed faster than we can replenish our power. We must ensure they are locked in their hell for eternity. For that, we need to remake the seals as they were originally made. The Artifact, called the Disk of Akashel, was used to shape the first Seals. With its power, we can see the Seals remade in even greater power."

"Where is this Disk, Ka'Varel? Surely we would know of such an artifact of great power if it were still in existence." This was from Dhoric, who appeared somewhat shaken. His mind was working through many things as he assessed the information.

"It was split into pieces after being used to create the first seals. They are being recovered as we speak, but will not be found easily or soon. This need not concern us, however. We need to make sure there is strength enough throughout the lands to stand up to these Demons when they come, so that they may be recast back into the Voids."

Khalad's face darkened as he spoke. "Why can we not take control of the Portals and prevent the Demons from coming through?"

"If only that were possible. Not only is our strength limited now, but also there are Portals we do not know the location of.

We are aware of only one opened Portal, yet at any time eight or more Portals can open, through which hordes of the Demon host will rush."

"How much time do we have, Ka'Varel?" asked Dhoric. "This Disk must be found. The Demons will need time to build their numbers until all of the Portals are open."

"That I also cannot say, Majesty. The Portals, called Nexus Gates, work on a power which is drawn from the between, that which links the voids with Kil'Tar. This power is depleted with each crossing, and takes a certain amount of time to recharge. Some Portals may let through five Demons in one day, and another may let pass ten thousand. But we estimate we have at least two seasons before the first of the Demons Hosts will attack."

A deep silence filled the room as the weight of the revelation hit home. In half a year, they could be seeing a war of catastrophic proportions against creatures many of them had heard about only in myth.

"And these Ashar'an?" The King was indeed going over many details. "What can we expect from them?"

Ka'Varel frowned wistfully. "I cannot say. They were never great in number, but their power and deadliness is great. If their numbers have swelled, they too will be a threat. They will not openly strike, preferring deceit and espionage. They have the powers of Loremasters, and the martial abilities of a Blademaster. They appear as mortals but they can be slain as any person, albeit with more difficulty. Few face the Balefiends and survive."

"What other assistance can we expect?" Kalamar was deep in shadow that his voice sounded almost disembodied. "What of the other races? What of the Astral City?"

Ka'Varel winced as if ruing the question. "The Astral City is not what it once was. There are many Bladesmen, but less students of the Lore. Their magic will have some bearing on the war, but we cannot hope it will shift the tide in our favor."

"But I thought you said that it was magic which creates this Unlife!" said Khalad. "Why hasn't it been outlawed so that this did not happen? How can we justify using it in this war?"

Ka'Varel smiled. "A good point, Prince, but do you not bathe in the river knowing that further down you are creating pollution? No. You find a means to make sure the pollution can be kept at a minimum. That is what the Loremasters have done in the Astral City. They have learnt that which taints the essence the least."

Valdieron had so much to ask the old man, but did not know what he should reveal in the presence of the others. Ka'Varel's gaze met his. "You say the Ashar'an are magic-users also. No doubt their magic is attuned to creating the most taint in the Essence. Does that make their magic more powerful than the Loremasters?"

All eyes turned to Ka'Varel.

"Yes. They have knowledge and power far beyond that of most of the Loremasters."

A low groan swept through the room, and Dhoric rose. "This news is both surprising and burdensome, Ka'Varel, though be assured I will act on it immediately. Will you stay and help?"

Ka'Varel shook his head. "Alas, I cannot, though my old bones argue that I should. There are other places I must journey to so they also know of this coming evil. I came to you first, though, King of Ariakus, for your family will have a great role to play in the war to come."

If he was surprised, Dhoric did not show it. He took a deep breath and ran a hand through his thinning hair. "Then there is some weight to the prophecies?"

Ka'Varel nodded. "Yes. The Dak'marians are closely attuned to the Kay'taari in that they are descended from them, though they have none of the power of their forebears. Most of what is written is speculation, and will not come to pass, but some of it will."

The mention of prophecy sent a chill through Valdieron. He remembered the dying whisper of Nortas speaking of 'The Prophecy'.

"Ease yourself with food and rest, Ka'Varel, and you also Master Tyrun. I would meet with you before you leave."

Ka'Varel inclined his head in thanks as Tyrun helped him rise. The man did not look older than the King, but it was obvious he did not carry his age well, or maybe he was ill.

The others filed from the room, led by the two magicians who disappeared quickly.

Kitara was led away silently by Andrak, both thoughtful and worried. Valdieron watched the princess depart ruefully. A big hand clapped him on the shoulder, and he did not have to turn to know it was Thorgast. "Grim tidings, Val. If only my people were not already burdened by war, we could lend our aid, but alas we must fight one battle at a time. I for one would like to lead men into battle against this Unlife."

"Well, I would rather we did not have to fight at all, Thorgast, but when the time comes, I'm sure you will be there."

"You are still leaving tomorrow?" He had told Thorgast he was leaving in the morning for Dak'mar, in search of the mysterious ties his family had there.

He nodded. "I must go, but do not think I have forgotten my oath to you. Look out for me."

Thorgast smiled. "It will be good to have you both by my side."

Valdieron turned to him in confusion. "Both? Is Hafri joining you?"

Thorgast raised his brow. "Didn't you know that Kyle will travel with me also to Chul'Haka? We have a need there of smiths, and he wishes to fight for our cause."

Valdieron was stunned. What could Kyle have been thinking? War torn Chul'Haka was the last place he should be going, especially after the recent events of his life.

He was halted outside the door by Thorgast's hand clutching his shoulder tightly, and he looked up to find Ka'Varel standing there. Tyrun stood further down the corridor, leaning against the wall as if he was asleep, though Valdieron knew he was alert.

"Speak with me, Valdieron." Ka'Varel motioned for him to step aside. "Tyrun would speak with you also, Thorgast." There was a light smile on the old man's face as Thorgast stepped past Valdieron, his face as dark as a thundercloud. Val had the feeling Thorgast knew this man Tyrun, and had little desire to speak with him.

"See you later, Val." The big man strode purposefully down the corridor, and the older Barbarian turned to greet him.

"How goes your search, Valdieron?"

Valdieron was shocked by the question as he turned from the two barbarians. How had Ka'Varel known he was searching for the pieces of the Disk? Did he know of Astan-Valar?

"What search?"

Ka'Varel's face darkened slightly, but it was enough to make Valdieron shudder. "I know more than you think, Valdieron, and you must trust me as you trust Astan-Valar. Finding the pieces of the Disk of Akashel is of the utmost importance. Do not think that your search will be easy. You were destined to meet the Princess and find the first piece, but the others will require great skill, intelligence and luck to find."

"How did you...?" Had the old man been eavesdropping before in the garden and overheard his conversation with Kitara? If so, why hadn't he assisted with the Ashar'an?

"Where will you go next?"

"Dak'mar. If these people are the descendants of the Kay'taari, chances are they were closest when the pieces were dispersed. I will check there first, anyhow."

Ka'Varel nodded. "You have a long road ahead of you, Valdieron, but you must find the strength to travel it, whatever the cost. The Ashar'an will try to follow you and kill you, so you must be careful every step of the way. Trust only those you have to, and even then do not turn your back for a second."

"But how do I fight these Ashar'an, if they are as powerful as you say? I got lucky before, I know that, because I sensed he was bad and he only had a dagger, but what if several come at me with swords and magic?"

"Then you do what you must, Valdieron. You will grow stronger as you go. Though you do not know it yet, the Ashar'an fear you like a man fears death. They know who and what you are, and their hatred is matched by this fear."

Before Valdieron could question him further, the old man turned and shuffled down the corridor. He passed the two Barbarians and Tyrun fell in with him without word, leaving Thorgast standing in the middle of the corridor, as still as a statue. When Valdieron finally came to him, he saw tears running down the big man's face.

"Thorgast, what is the matter? Who is Tyrun?"

The big man wiped his face dry and composed himself with a deep breath, though his eyes drifted after the two disappeared figures.

"Tyrun is my grandfather, Val. I had thought him dead. He told me some very strange things." The big man's eyes became slightly haunted then, but he turned to Valdieron with a smile. "Come on. I need a drink."

Valdieron could only agree with him and the two returned to the hall. Few people were left there still, but there was ale and wine aplenty on the outer ring of tables. They sat and drank for a short time in silence before Kyle entered. He looked like he had enjoyed himself by the slightly unsteady step and the joyful expression on his face. He spotted them and came over. He noticed Valdieron regarding him questioningly as he picked up a glass.

"Natasha and Kolin will stay here, Val. The King has agreed to it. Besides, I don't think I could tear her away from here now. She was born Noble, just in the wrong place. The Princess Kitara will look after her."

Valdieron nodded. In truth he was thankful that Kyle was making this decision, wanting Thorgast to have somebody he could trust at his side. Kyle was as loyal as anybody he knew.

For a time they chatted idly, knowing that within a few hours they would be torn away from each other, possibly never to meet again. Valdieron finally rose and embraced the two. All but the servants had left the hall, as if waiting for the three to depart.

"Take care of each other and watch yourselves. If I hear that either of you has been killed, I would rather not have to take revenge on the whole of the Haruken by myself."

With a smile Thorgast assured him they would stay safe. "You be careful also, Val. The world is more complex than you or I could imagine, and the further you go, the more mysterious and dangerous it will get. Just remember that I will always look for you on the horizon."

With his head bowed, Valdieron left. His gear was back at the Inn where he would rest for what remained of the night. As he left the palace he looked back in the direction of Kitara's room. Though he could not see it, he wondered if the Princess was asleep or was too caught up with thought. She had captivated him with her beauty and charm, and he wondered when they would meet again. He hoped it would not be before too long, and that she did not quickly forget him.

Swallowed up by the night he made his way back to the Inn. When he got there, he found Kaz resting in his quarters. He wondered what he would do with the Cat. He had all but forgotten about him over the last few days, and did not wish to drag him off to the far reaches of Kil'Tar. Still, the Moorcat had bonded with him, and would likely try to follow him if he was left behind.

He shed his clothes and slipped under the covers, careful not to wake the Cat. He drifted to sleep, deciding not to enter the Dream Plane. His dreams were many and varied, an indication of the myriad of confusing thoughts running through his mind, but one that he did remember contained Kitara, and if he could blush while asleep, he would have.

END

Here ends Demon Gates, Book 1 of the Nexus Wars Saga. Continuing with Book 2: Ashar'an Rising, we follow Valdieron in his quest through distant lands to recover the lost pieces of the Disk of Akashel, and in his own personal struggle with powerful enemies and his own self-doubt.

Printed in Great Britain
by Amazon.co.uk, Ltd.,
Marston Gate.